Life After Death

S.C. MUIR

To my husband, Dan. For your unwavering support.

But also:

To all the folks who have battled mental illness.

To my fellow adoptees.

To anyone who has worked through trauma.

To all of us with PCOS and endometriosis.

I see you. We are in this together.

Pronunciation Guide

Mari: **Mar**-ee

Zahir: Za-**here**

Pryn: **Prin**

Markus: **Mar**-kus

Anya: **Ahn**-yuh

Taryn: **Tare**-in

Illan: Ee-**lahn**

Ryker: **Rye**-kur

Maura: **More**-uh

Kiernan: **Kere**-nin

Hanan: Huh-**naan**

Rodrick: **Rah**-drick

Reina: Ray-**ee**-nuh

Seraphina: Sair-uh-**fina**

Amí: Uh-**me**

Morana: More-**ahn**-uh

Yu'güe: You-**gway**

Brahn: Br**ahn**
Lovíth: Low-**veeth**
Orcian: **Or**-see-in

Trigger Warnings

Please be advised this book contains graphic descriptions of the following: mental illness, PTSD, parental death, adoption, violence against queer folks, parental abuse, self-injury (for the purpose of healing magic practice), infertility, endometriosis, chronic illness, giving up a child, drowning, fire, death, discussion of the afterlife.

There are also mentions of the following: homophobia, death of a child, and suicide.

If you would like to know if this book contains something specific, you can email authorscmuir@gmail.com.

AUTHOR'S NOTE

A few main themes of this book are adoption, endometriosis, and Polycystic Ovarian Syndrome ("PCOS").

Adoption

As I am an adoptee myself, I would like to first state that all opinions and feelings expressed within this novel are my own and do not represent how all adoptees feel. Adoption is extremely nuanced. The feelings had or experienced by adoptees may be traumatic.

In truth, I never wanted to write about the nuances of adoption. I tucked those into a neat little box in my brain, locked it, and threw away the key. But, in reality, I can't pretend that my adoption doesn't affect me. Someone once asked me, after I had published Death by Fire, if my adoption had ever made it into my writing. And I immediately answered no. But upon further reflection, I realized it did. Not directly, but some of Zahir's experiences, which you will see in Life After Death, reflect some of my own. Writing Life After Death was very healing for me and I am so excited to share this big part of myself with all of you.

PCOS & Endometriosis

I have never seen PCOS or endometriosis in a fantasy novel. So, I decided to write Mari – a badass FMC with these chronic illnesses. It made me realize that I, too, am a badass. Fighting through pain every day just to do normal things like go to work is awful. And sometimes I feel like I should be able to do so much more but I'm so exhausted that I just fall asleep on the couch after dinner. I am learning to give myself grace. I am learning to listen to my body. And I hope, if you also have PCOS, endometriosis, or any other medical condition that you take care of yourself and know from one badass to another we will continue to fight the good fight, too.

Both of these illnesses are extremely under-researched. While there are some good papers in medical journals about PCOS, I hope to see more in the coming years (Yes, I am a nerdy scientist and read research papers in my spare time). Mari's experiences described throughout my novel are based on my own. Not everyone experiences the effects of PCOS and endometriosis the same. Like I said above about adoption, writing about my chronic illnesses has been very healing and validating. It gives me comfort to know that I can pick up a book where characters have gone through similar experiences to me. It makes me feel seen and heard and acknowledged and I hope that for all those folks out there that it brings some sense of comfort to you.

PROLOGUE

When she raised her hands, she was greeted by the army of the damned.

Chapter One

Mari

The eerie chill of the titanium sucked the air from Mari's lungs. It felt like needles pricked the tips of her fingers as air whooshed past her ears and sent goosebumps down her arms. When Mari inhaled, the odor of blood and metal stung her nostrils. Her feet clapped against the metal floor as she walked toward the room's center, surrounded by titanium. There was no escaping it.

Wiggling her fingers, Mari tried to reach inside to retrieve a soul from her arsenal. But instead, a gaping black hole existed — a vast chasm of emptiness, threatening to swallow Mari whole. Her heartbeat pounded in her ears as, slowly, Mari peeled her cloak from her shoulders and folded it neatly into a pile on the ground. She pulled a rapier from her waistband, the metal clanging as she unsheathed it.

With one last breath, Mari curled her hand into a fist and whipped around, raising the sword at her brother, Hanan, who froze, wide-eyed. Beads of sweat collected on his temples. Hanan repeatedly clenched and unclenched his left hand, his chest rising and falling with rapid breaths. He raised his rapier to the same height, his left leg forward. A corner of his mouth quirked as he lurched, slicing his weapon through the air.

Mari parried his blow, stepped to the right, and jabbed towards him again. The sound of their weapons colliding rang out in the empty, hollow room as they continued to parry to and fro. With every few blows, she glanced at his hips. During her training with Illan, he had taught her that hips predicted the direction of movement. With Hanan's hips positioned to the right, he would always move in that direction. Mari needed to catch his feet and hips in a disconnect—just once.

When Hanan's hips tilted left, Mari struck. She swung in his intended direction, landing a light blow to his left shoulder. Hanan stopped, shaking his head.

"It was my hips again, wasn't it?" he asked, breathless. He lowered his hands, allowing his sword to dangle.

"Always. It's *always* your hips." Mari laughed, wiping her bangs that had stuck to her forehead despite the chill in the air.

"Gods damn it! How? How do I fix that?"

"You have to act instead of react." They looked to the other side of the room where Reina stood, arms crossed and leaning against the titanium wall. Pushing herself off, she strode to Mari and Hanan, swishing her long black hair behind her. Mari forced a smile and shuffled aside for Reina to join.

"I understand that. I just can't seem to master it," Hanan said, handing Reina his sword.

Reina took his place and held the blade up to Mari. "Ready, Majesty?"

Mari laughed and held up her own. "Don't go easy on me."

She didn't. Reina barreled down on Mari, nearly scraping her shoulder on several occasions. Mari's first lunge missed Reina, who bent backward to avoid the blow. When she righted herself, she had no struggle deflecting Mari's second attack. Reina moved with the fluidity of water, consistently bending in ways Mari could never dream of.

Their weapons rebounded as they danced around the gym, until Mari cornered Reina, hoping to finally catch her and land a blow. Mari had never seen Reina fight, but she was an incredible swordsman, which made Mari wonder why she wasn't a soldier. But after Rodrick had been outed as a traitor and killed at Zahir's hand, Mari understood why Reina did not wish to protect the crown. Who would wish to protect the system that killed the love of their life?

Mari swept low at Reina's legs, pushing her further into the corner of the gym. Reina leaped up and propelled her body off the wall, scratching Mari's shoulder as she landed behind her.

"You've lost," Reina said with a laugh.

Mari spun, eyes wide. "How in the world did you do that?"

"Reina, what the hell?" Hanan said, clapping his hands. "You're incredible."

She shrugged. "My father was a soldier; his father was a soldier, and so on and so forth. Swordsmanship is in my veins. I wanted to be a soldier as a child, but my father forbade it." Reina wiped a hand across the back of her neck, where her long hair slicked against her dark skin. "He didn't want me to get hurt."

"I don't think he had anything to worry about," Mari laughed.

Silence followed Mari's laughter, allowing unease to nestle in her stomach. Reina shifted her gaze away from Mari and wrapped her arms around her waist. This was the first time Reina had accepted Mari's invitation to train with her and Hanan. Mari suppressed a sigh as she realized she had brought up a painful topic. Since Rodrick's betrayal and subsequent death, Reina had kept away from the palace, and according to Hanan, she isolated herself at home. After six moon cycles, Mari tried to reach out and rebuild her relationship with Reina. But today was the first time Mari had seen her, nine moon cycles later.

"How do you feel being in here, Reina?" Hanan asked, his arms wrapped around his torso. "I still can't stand it."

"It's uncomfortable. It feels like I have an itch I can't scratch," said Reina.

"Does it get easier?" Hanan turned his gaze to Mari, who shrugged.

"No, but the memories fade every time I come in here."

Ever since Mari lost her magic and was kidnapped by the rebels nearly a year ago, she had been terrified of titanium. For months, she barely slept or ate, unable to bring herself to *consider* returning to the palace's titanium gym. Only after Zahir left nine moon cycles ago, and she realized she had no one to protect her, did Mari face her fear. Mari would become her own protector. She would no longer submit to panic.

The first time Mari had mustered enough courage to enter the gym was three weeks after Zahir left for Lovíth. Opening the door, she welcomed the ice-cold air into her lungs. Mari stepped inside as the gaping hole in her chest reopened and sucked the magic from her heart. She'd choked out a strangled breath and counted to three. Then, she shut the door, ran upstairs to her room, and lay under the covers until the empty feeling waned.

It took another moon cycle before she even wanted to try again, and on that occasion, she brought Illan. If he was there, nothing would happen to her. After all, he had lived without magic for years and could coach her through the feelings. And he did. Before anything else, Mari and Illan worked on breathing exercises until progressing to basic tasks, like reading a page in a book. Eventually, short exercises turned to sword fighting, and day after day, Illan and Mari trained down there until she no longer needed to curl under her blankets for hours afterward. Until she could breathe without crying. Until the memories of her trauma faded to a murky gray instead of blaring red.

Mari had recently invited Hanan and Reina to train with her in the gym. Hanan had initially been skeptical but agreed, while Reina had declined the invitation despite the consistent invitations Mari sent to her door. For the last two moon cycles, Hanan joined Mari and Illan in their training sessions, yet today was Reina's first time.

"I should leave," Reina said suddenly. "I have to stop at the fruit stand before returning home."

"I'm glad you came," Mari said, stepping forward with her arms outstretched. "You are always welcome here."

Reina stepped back with a shake of her head. Then, she left, the heavy titanium door slamming shut behind her.

"I hope she's coming around," Hanan said.

"Do you know how she's doing?" asked Mari.

Hanan shrugged. "Raf says her grief comes in waves. Her fiancé was killed at the hands of her best friend, so that can't be easy."

Mari nodded. "I just hope she has someone to talk to."

"I think she does. Raf sees her often, and I think Kiernan does as well," said Hanan. "I should head home; Raf is cooking dinner for us tonight."

"That's fine, I must meet with Illan anyway. We're expecting another letter from Zahir today. We like to open them together." Mari wiped her forehead before going to collect her cloak.

"How many more moon cycles will he be gone for?" asked Hanan.

Mari shrugged and shook her head. "He hasn't said. Originally, it was supposed to be six."

"But it's already been nine."

"I know."

Mari led Hanan upstairs to the main palace. After the rebel attacks and Zahir's departure, Mari wanted to keep those she loved close by, but civilians were forbidden inside the palace walls. However, Ren, frightened by Mari constantly leaving the palace to visit her brother, suggested she negotiate with the advisors. In the end, the advisors agreed it was much safer for

Mari to bring people into the palace rather than leave on her own.

A guard shut and bolted the doors behind Hanan. Two rebel breaches into the palace had forced Zahir to increase security; three guards stood at every entrance, and that was at a minimum. Frequent rounds occurred inside the palace, where guards would check behind every door and every crevice. The patterns changed weekly, so they could not be anticipated. Ren, their captain, decided on the patterns; only they—and those guards assigned to the rounds that day—knew how the checks would go.

Mari snagged an apple on the way to Illan's chambers. She bit into its crunchy surface, the sweetness exploding on her tongue. She hadn't realized how hungry she was; she nearly moaned as she ate the apple.

"Mari!" Anya's voice rang out down the hallway.

Mari turned with a smile, greeting Taryn, who strode alongside Anya, their hands interlocked. "Hi, Anya. Taryn. How are you?"

"Great," Anya said, smiling at her partner.

Taryn's eyes gleamed as she grinned back before refocusing on Mari. "We are taking Roan into the city tonight for dinner. Would you like to join us?"

"I wish I could, but Illan and I have a meeting tonight. Maybe another time, though. Just as long as we don't go back to the place that undercooked the steak."

"Gods no!" Taryn suppressed a gag. "I wanted to take Anya and Roan to my family's restaurant. They just reopened now that my brother finished the renovations. It looks beautiful, like it's brand new. And they updated their menu!"

"I can't wait to see it. You'll have to tell me everything."

As the couple retreated down the hallway, Mari thought, and not for the first time, how much her relationship with Anya had changed. Without Zahir in the palace, Anya was much more tolerable. Mari didn't trust her fully—not at all, really—but they tried to have a relationship. While Anya still expressed her desire to get the crown, the permanent scowl on her face was more of a guest now.

Illan had expressed he didn't fully trust Anya either, especially not with the rebels painting a large "A" in the city. When Zahir rescued Mari and burned the rebels to the ground, news soon spread throughout the city. Most celebrated Zahir's win; after all, their King had saved the queen and his people from certain death. Others, however, compared Zahir to his father, believing him to be just as violent. They preferred Anya to rule Brahn.

Once Zahir announced himself as a dual mage, the dissent only grew. People begged the palace to put Anya on the throne. At least once a week, Mari and Illan tended to villagers who cursed their reign. Through it all, Mari kept a straight face and calmly asked for them to be removed from the premises. Yet as the weeks dragged on, Mari's calm façade was beginning to falter. With Zahir in Lovíth training to use his life magic, Mari was alone. An outsider. The people had not been happy with a death mage becoming their queen, and now that their King had left, the people seemed emboldened. Mari worried Anya would get her way and rule the clan once and for all.

Mari rapped her knuckles on Illan's door, and his jubilant face soon welcomed her into his room. The heavy oak door slammed shut behind her. Mari's favorite thing about Illan's room was that his sitting room was as large as the apartment Raf and Hanan rented in the city. Mari sat on one of the plush green velvet couches, picking up the cup of tea Illan had already prepared. Illan sat across from her in a large forest green armchair, perching his feet on a matching footstool. He took a sip of his steaming tea.

"How did your training go today?"

"Reina beat me," said Mari.

"She has been training with swords her entire life. You have been here for only a year now," Illan said. "You'll get there."

"I hope. Have we received a letter?" Mari asked, hopeful. They hadn't heard from Zahir for nearly an entire moon cycle.

Illan handed her a folded piece of parchment with the royal seal on it. "He wrote us each a letter."

Mari tore into it, dying to know what Zahir had to say. The nine moon cycles apart had put a strain on their relationship. Before he left, they had just become comfortable with each other, and despite the arrangement of their marriage, their feelings had developed rapidly. When you spend all day with someone and sleep beside them every night, it isn't hard to fall in love.

My dearest Mari,

I am so sorry for not writing sooner. My training has kept me increasingly busy as I learn and master new things. I hadn't even realized it had been almost a full moon cycle. I miss you.

I am thrilled to hear that you and Roan have been enjoying time together. He must be so happy to read with you each week. I knew you would be great with him.

How have you been feeling? Are you sleeping any better? I am so proud of you for working in the titanium gym. I admire your bravery and wish I could be there to support you.

My training is going well. I am excited to show you all my new tricks when I come back to Brahn. I am sorry to admit that I do not yet have a return date, but I hope it's not too much longer. My trainer, Markus, says I have much to learn.

I miss you dearly. The past nine moon cycles without your embrace have been increasingly difficult. I can't wait to be home with you, and when I return, we are going to spend every possible second together, I promise. I'm going to take you on the most elaborate evening in the city and then we will return home and hold each other before the fire. All I want to do is wrap my arms around you and never let go. I think of you constantly, and I hope you think of me.

Yours,

Zahir

P.S. I know you say Anya is different... but remember, Mari: you know what she is capable of.

Mari's chest burned as she read Zahir's letter. There was nothing she wanted more in the world than for Zahir to come home. Just as they had begun exploring their relationship, he had left. And now all they had were letters. It brought Mari back to when she was first betrothed to Zahir, when she had been forced to write a yearly letter to him all those years ago as a child. In those letters, she told him about her life in Yu'güe and expressed how much she missed her brother—when she thought he was dead. She didn't know who Zahir was then. Not really. It felt strange to think of those letters, remembering a time when all she had were some words on a page from a stranger, talking of a far-away land she would one day be queen of.

But now, Mari missed his presence, missed being wrapped in his arms, and missed the smell of him after he stepped out of a bath. She longed for the day she could help him dye his hair again. Zahir had admitted that when Mari first dyed his hair before the palace attack, he realized he was falling for her. It was one of her favorite memories of them, too.

"Zahir's training is going well," said Mari, glancing up at Illan. She folded her letter and put it down on the table.

"It seems so," Illan said, though he sounded unconvinced. "Do you ever worry that he isn't being completely honest?"

Mari furrowed her brow. From Zahir's previous letters, Mari had never gotten the impression that Zahir was being deceitful, but nor had he offered any information that contradicted Illan's worry. "What gives you that impression?"

"Zahir only ever says his training is 'going well.' He never gives us details."

Mari nodded slowly. Zahir never explained anything about his training to Mari, either. "Maybe he doesn't find it easy to describe his training."

"Possibly." Illan scratched his head. "I don't know why, but I have a feeling that something is wrong."

Chapter Two

Zahir

Zahir scraped his hair back into a tail at the crown of his head and wiped the sweat from his brow. Pulling his shirt off, he exposed his muscular, tanned back to the sun as he bent down to retrieve his sword and slowly rose to face Markus.

Markus lunged before Zahir was ready. Zahir stepped back and tried to re-center himself, but when Markus's sword swung for Zahir's face, he was ready. Their swords met, the sound of metal clashing across the bright green field. Zahir slid his sword along Markus's and tried to attack his hip, but Markus deflected, stepping aside.

Zahir groaned as he struck again, landing a blow on Markus's knee, who staggered back—but not for long. Rushing forward, Markus knocked Zahir's sword to the ground and hit Zahir's shoulder with the hilt of his sword. Zahir fell onto his left knee, offering Markus enough time for the killing strike. Markus lifted his sword under Zahir's chin until Zahir stared into his bright blue eyes.

"And now you're dead," Markus said with a laugh. He removed the sword from under Zahir's jaw and offered his hand.

"Let's go again," Zahir said, accepting it. He wiped his dirt-caked hands onto his orange trousers, streaking them with mud.

"I think we've done enough for today." Markus sheathed his sword into the scabbard. "You're exhausted."

Zahir's hands shook at his sides, but he quickly shoved them into his pockets. Sweat beaded across his neck, his hair slick against it.

"I'm fine," he growled as Markus picked up Zahir's sword, sheathing it for him.

"The more you exhaust yourself, the harder it will be to get better. You're a good swordsman, Zahir, but you need to be more patient. You attack too quickly and stay on the offensive."

"Yes, I know. You've been telling me the same damn thing for five moon cycles."

"I have been telling you the 'same damn thing' because you're still not listening. Your training has barely improved since you arrived." Markus rested a hand on Zahir's shoulder. "You need to start internalizing your lessons."

Markus was right, although Zahir was reluctant to admit it. In nine moon cycles, he had made very little progress. He struggled in his classes with Lily and could barely heal a minor graze on his hand. At this rate, he would never master his life magic and die on his thirtieth birthday.

The lawn outside Markus's house tickled Zahir's ankles when the wind blew, the breeze offering a nice respite from the sun. While it wasn't nearly as warm as Brahn, Zahir wasn't used to training in the heat. It was one of the nicer days of the week; it had been raining the past three days, yet Markus insisted they train outside. No matter the weather, Zahir trained with Markus, the best swordsman in Lovíth, every day.

"I am *trying*, Markus. I am trying so hard to do this. But every time I get frustrated, I feel blocked and stuck for days on end."

"I've been telling you to get treatment from Pryn. They're really good, Zahir. They will be able to get rid of that block with alignment."

Zahir rolled his eyes. "I don't think that will work for me."

The entire time Zahir had been in Lovíth, Markus tried to convince him to work with Pryn, their energy healer. Zahir had learned much about how life mages lived, including how they healed internal issues like concussions and broken bones. As Zahir understood it, energy alignment involved Pryn putting their hands on several parts of his body to channel energy through him, helping his body properly function and embrace life magic. In other words, it was absolute shit. Zahir hoped to improve his life magic through practice, as he had with his fire magic. This week, he began healing minor scrapes after his training sessions with Markus, but once healed, he would need to lie down. Zahir hoped it would get easier the more he tried.

"You're never going to master your life magic if your energy isn't aligned," Markus said. "I know you think it's strange, but I'm telling you it is the reason you haven't made any progress. Can you please just try it once? If it doesn't help, I'll stop bugging you about it."

After Zahir learned he was a dual mage, he moved to Lovíth to master his life magic and was taken in by Markus, the strongest swordsman in Lovíth. Markus, despite being only five years Zahir's senior, was a leader in Lovíth. Life mages had extended lives—sometimes double the norm—yet Markus had risen to leadership so early in his life. At thirty, he was helping to make Lovíth a better place, like his mother had before passing. Markus honored her memory by continuing her work: training mages to fight for themselves and tap into the parts of their magic they had never known before.

Markus had also invented several rituals to enhance life magic and prolong its strength for several days, though Zahir was reluctant to participate. He didn't understand how a ritual unrelated to natural phenomena could enhance magic. In Brahn, the summer solstice was known to magnify fire magic, but how could cleaning your bedroom with the window open—as Markus suggested—enhance life magic?

Zahir sighed as Markus led him back into the house they shared: a small cottage wrapped in dark green vines and bright pink flowers. The cylindrical house stood only two stories high; the gray stones were three different colors, differing from the shade received over the years. Zahir had been immediately enamored with the home and its quaintness. Living in the palace was all he knew, but there was something comforting about a small house with only one other person. The little kitchen was always stocked with fresh food and vegetables that Markus cooked each night. Zahir was learning to cook, too, but had very little luck, his food either coming out burned or severely undercooked—sometimes both. Zahir missed the meals from the palace: the rich sauces and juicy seared meats. While he enjoyed his newfound independence in Lovíth, he missed his bed being made in the morning and the freshly brewed tea delivered to his door—the small things.

Two mismatched couches made up the living area with a long oak table between them, where Zahir and Markus would play cards after dinner. Upstairs were two bedrooms, and Zahir's bed was more comfortable than the palace's.

The only thing missing from his home in Lovíth was his wife. Zahir could barely withstand the pain in his chest whenever he thought about Mari. Every night, as he fell asleep, he wished she were there, wrapped in his arms and taking up more than her fair share of their bed. He missed the way she whispered nonsensical things in her sleep, how she bit her lip when he teased her under the covers at night, and her gasp whenever he grabbed her thigh. He couldn't wait to be back in Brahn with Mari, counting down the days until she was back in his embrace.

While they had been writing letters, it was hard to tell Mari everything he wished to do with her. He wanted to teach her all his new sword tricks and the ways of meditation to ease her dark thoughts. In the letters between them, Mari mentioned her nightmares waking her from sleep—thoughts of the lives she had taken. It killed Zahir to read those letters. He yearned for nothing more than to hold her while she recovered from her dreams.

He longed to show her the new creases in his body and discover the changes in her body since they'd been apart. The longer he was in Lovíth, the fainter her voice became. Zahir could barely hear the way Mari said his name or how foreign words rolled off her tongue. He missed running his hands through her hair while they lay in bed at night and the soft smile gracing her lips whenever he complimented her—the smile that made his heart hammer in his chest. But as much as he wanted to go home to Mari, he needed to stay in Lovíth to ensure they had a long life together.

Zahir washed quickly and scrubbed the dirt off his body before changing into dark green pants and a black long-sleeve shirt. He went downstairs to help Markus prepare their meal. Zahir loved Markus's cooking. Markus had marinated quail in a sweet, dark sauce for several days and revealed to Zahir a list of ingredients he had never known, like brown sugar and honey. In Brahn, meats were not mixed with sweet things; desserts were the only meals made with sugar.

Markus had changed into a tight white short-sleeved shirt that hugged his muscular brown arms and fell below the waistband of his loose blue pants; stark black hair fell in thick locs down his back, and hunched over the counter, Markus sliced bright green vegetables. Even hunched, he was taller than Zahir.

Zahir pointed at the flowery vegetables. "Broccoli?"

"Yes. At least you're learning about vegetables," said Markus, elbowing Zahir's side.

"How can I help?" Zahir walked to the sink to wash his hands, and Markus jutted his chin towards the sack of light brown potatoes beside the sink.

"You can wash those potatoes. Give them a good scrub. Maryna only picked them today, and they're covered in dirt."

"Yes, sir," Zahir said with a laugh.

"Oh, hush." Markus threw the sliced potatoes into a large pot of boiling water. "Tonight is a new moon. How do you feel about joining me in my abundance ritual?"

Zahir had been hesitant about Markus's rituals since the first new moon in Lovíth, which Markus said was all about new beginnings. A clean slate. The best time to try something new, apparently. Every new moon, without fail, Markus performed an abundance ritual, another of his inventions. First, he cleansed his bedroom by wiping the windows and mirror with salt water, leaving a window open so the negative energy could escape. Then, he ground up a small pinch of cinnamon and went outside before blowing the cinnamon into the house. Markus had told Zahir that cinnamon was symbolic of abundance, and by combining these two practices, he "cleansed the old to make way for the new."

Zahir had yet to join Markus despite his insistence on each new moon. Truthfully, Zahir thought it was a pile of shit, yet Markus did seem to find life magic easier for the several days that followed, healing injuries he otherwise might have needed a second mage for. Just a few weeks ago, Zahir watched Markus heal a young boy's broken leg where the bone had completely shattered. *Trying* the ritual wouldn't hurt. At the very least, he might understand Markus better.

"Sure. I will try it."

Markus paused and turned to face Zahir. "Really? I'm surprised."

"I can only say no so many times."

"Well... then we need to go to town to get more cinnamon," Markus said, wiping his hands on a towel. "Let's go. Our potatoes have a while before they'll be ready to mash."

As Markus locked up the house, Zahir was surprised to see the stars. Days were significantly shorter in Lovíth. The soft grass tickled Zahir's ankles as they walked through the village. Lovíth was much smaller than Zahir had pictured. Throughout his life, he had imagined a large city with tall brick and stone stores towering above the sidewalks and tradespeople and shoppers bustling in the streets. He pictured it like Brahn.

His imagination couldn't have been further from the truth. When Zahir had stepped off his ship into town, he was welcomed by the entire clan—all two hundred mages. The small town was a single strip of gravel road lined on either side with small, one-story gray stone shops covered in vines and flowers. There was one of every store, including some strange ones: a metaphysical shop, the crystal cove, and the store of a self-proclaimed psychic. The hand-painted signs were so worn that Zahir struggled to read what they said.

Markus had been the first to greet him and help part the crowd. So many people wanted to welcome him to the clan, though some were not so excited by his arrival. Whispers of "dictator" were spat as he passed. Lovíth had once had a council like Brahn's until their leader abused their power and executed life mages who dissented with their views. After many years of chaos, a revolution had unfolded and the people decided to vote for representatives to make decisions for the clan. Zahir had never learned of this uprising or Lovíth's past dictator. In fact, despite Brahn's expansive library, only one history book existed on Lovíth, which left out such a vital piece of the clan's history. Zahir wondered why.

When Zahir discovered how many people in Lovíth were, as they called it, 'queer,' he wished he were not a King, so he and Mari could move here. Lovíth had names for every type of person who identified under this queer term. A person who liked someone of the same gender was called "gay"; a person who liked the opposite sex was called "straight," and Zahir, who liked both men and women, would be called "bisexual." Ren and Pryn, who call themselves "they," would be "non-binary", which means they are neither male nor female, and he was still learning many other terms, too. Never in his life had he felt so accepted.

Zahir vaguely remembered meeting Pryn upon his arrival. Alongside Zahir, they had pushed people asides, yelling to let them pass; once they were through the crowd, Pryn had greeted Zahir before returning to the rest of the clan.

When Markus walked Zahir through town for the first time, he was impressed with how much Markus knew about every-one. He explained the different shops, telling Zahir stories about each of them. The person who owned the Crystal Cove was named River. River was nearly two hundred years old and loved when anyone brought freshly picked blueberries to the shop for a snack. The women who ran the butchers, Aileen and Hettie, had been married for sixty years and officiated all marriages for the rest of the clan. Royce, who ran the spice shop, grew all the spices himself; the shop and garden had been passed down through his family for generations. Zahir instantly fell in love with the close connections between all life mages. There was something so surreal about knowing every member of your clan.

It reminded Zahir so much of Mari and how she spoke about Yu'güe. She knew everything about everyone. As Zahir spent more time in Lovíth, he knew Mari would love it. He desperately wanted to invite her to visit, but he could never leave Brahn without a ruler, especially with Anya actively trying to steal his crown. Now he was away, he feared Anya would terrorize Mari or steal the crown if she convinced enough people Mari shouldn't be left on the throne without him.

The door to the spice shop jingled as Markus and Zahir entered. The pungent smell of herbs bombarded Zahir's senses, and while he loved the store and its different spices, it was sometimes overwhelming and left him with a headache for the rest of the day. Shelves from floor to ceiling covered every wall in the shop; the spices were organized alphabetically in large glass jars from anise to za'atar, with a metal scoop in each. It was warmer in the store than outside. Whispers flew around the shop as patrons searched for their different spices. Behind the counter, Royce stood, ringing up a customer. Royce was a squat old man whose grey hairline receded more with each visit. His tan skin and gold eyes reminded Zahir of his own; he often wondered if he would look like Royce when he was that age. The patron turned after paying, tucking the remaining coin in their pockets. It was Pryn, Zahir realized, as they smiled and came up to the pair.

"Are you boys getting cinnamon?" Pryn asked. Their dark brown eyes, which sparkled in the torchlight, lit up upon spotting Zahir and Markus. They'd recently shaved their hair, the fuzz atop their head undetectable, and wore a loose red top and tight black pants, accentuating their lean build. Pryn waved at Zahir with a hand clad in three gold rings.

"We are," Markus said. "Zahir is joining me in the abundance ritual. It's his first time."

"Congratulations," Pryn said to Zahir with a bright smile. "I am excited to hear about your experience."

"I'm honestly a little hesitant, but I'm trying to appreciate your culture a little more," said Zahir.

"Enjoy it. It's an eye-opening experience." With that, Pryn left the shop. Markus watched their retreating form, his lips parting into a soft smile. "That reminds me... I need to get my crystals cleansed soon."

"*Please*," said Zahir, side-eyeing Markus. "I know you're soft for them." Every other week, Markus brought rocks for Pryn to cleanse despite Pryn saying it was unnecessary. Markus talked about the healer all the time and constantly sang their praises.

Markus shoved Zahir lightly on the shoulder. "If you tell anyone, I will embarrass you in battle."

"How is that different than every other day? I have not won against you *once*," Zahir said, elbowing him. He wished he had known Markus his whole life, who challenged Zahir in ways he hadn't thought possible.

"Let's just get our damn spices," Markus grumbled.

Zahir slipped on a pair of disposable gloves and grabbed the jar of cinnamon, bringing it over to a small wooden table housing a few wax bags, a pen, and a scale. He scooped the powdered cinnamon into a bag and handed it to Royce to weigh.

"Just this?" asked Royce.

"That's all for today," Markus said, pulling a piece of coin from his pocket and handing it to him.

"Have a blessed evening!" Royce called as they left.

As the door jingled shut behind Zahir, he inhaled the chilly nighttime air. He forgot how stuffy it got inside the spice shop. Something in there tickled his nose. Zahir and Markus returned to their home, finally prepared to complete the new moon ritual.

CHAPTER THREE

MARI

Mari's shoulders relaxed at the scent of old books. The enormous library doors shut behind her with a bang, and she closed her eyes, inhaling deeply. Something was calming about the smell of old books and scrolls. Thousands of books lined the shelves, housing everything from fictional stories to the clans' histories and combat guides. Colorful rays of sun filtered through the stained-glass windows, lighting the room in a spectrum of colors. To the left was a stained glass window of the Ever-Burning Candle, the symbol of Brahn; the constellation was depicted as white and gold stars on a navy blue background, symbolizing Brahn's resilience for always rising from tragedy stronger than before. On the right wall was glasswork depicting the city from a bird's-eye view. Mari first noticed how beautiful the palace looked in rainbow colors. The city square was only recognizable because no houses surrounded the open blue and green sea of glass. The intricacy of each design had floored Mari when she first saw them, and it still amazed her, even now.

As Mari journeyed through the shelves, the crackling fire grew in volume. A stone fireplace nestled into the wall at the back of the library; orange and red flames burned inside it, crackling, popping, and spreading warmth into the room. Over the mantle was a large shield engraved with the same symbol of Brahn. Two longswords rested behind it, mounted in an X. Two worn couches faced each other perpendicular to the fire, and between them was a soft fur rug and a short rectangular table. Illan sat on the couch to the left, his brown eyes twinkling in the firelight. On the table before him sat two large books and one thin, faded scroll.

Every week, Mari and Illan met in the library so he could teach her Brahn's culture and history, while Mari shared information about Yu'güe in exchange. He had expressed his interest in Yu'güe due to its isolation from the rest of the clans. With Illan's acquaintances with tradesmen, he had learned scraps of history about Lovíth and Orcian yet knew nothing of Yu'güe. The pair would discuss the other clans, too, combing through books and scrolls together. They had contacted the other clans to see if they would be willing to send their history books. While Lovíth had sent three, Orcian had never responded; they had to make do with the texts in the library.

"Good morning, Mari," said Illan with a smile. "What do you want to look at today? I pulled an old scroll passed down through my family, one book on Brahn's trade history and another on Orcian's political regimes."

Mari pointed at the scroll. "Can we start with this? When was it written?"

"Long before Morana lived. It was back when the clans lived together when dual mages flourished, and triads lived only for a short time."

Through their history lessons, Mari had learned about the life expectancies of dual mages and triads. If dual mages didn't master their second magic by their thirtieth year, they would die. If they did master it, they lived as long as a normal mage. Dual mages with two opposing magics, like life and death, had tumultuous lives; melding two contrasting gifts was incredibly taxing on the body. It was reported that life/death mages would accidentally kill, as opposed to heal, while fire/water mages lost control, torching or drowning someone without any memory of it. Triads were volatile, too, and no record existed of any triad living past the age of twenty-five. Triads would always be a combination of two opposing magics, thus had trouble controlling it.

Mari knew that Zahir was capable. After all, he had healed her injuries after rescuing her from the rebels. But Mari couldn't shake the doubt gnawing in the back of her mind. If Zahir couldn't master his life magic, she would be destined to a life without him—a possibility she couldn't fathom, especially with what little time they had shared thus far.

Illan picked up the scroll and splayed it flat on the table. "This is the story of the original mages, just after the Gods had granted them magic."

He placed a paperweight on each corner and ignited his left hand in flame. He waved it over the scroll, allowing it to come to life. Illan was still a little clumsy with his fire magic after only recently being able to use it again. Throughout their time together in the library, Illan and Mari had discovered how Illan's magic had returned. After Illan and Ryker murdered a group of insurgents to save their family nearly thirty years ago, Illan had been wracked with guilt, yet only when he saw Zahir do the same thing to save Mari did Illan realize he'd had no choice. Mari had read that magic was tied very closely to the psyche; when your psyche was strained, it took a toll on your magic. Illan felt guilty for using his magic for harm; thus, losing his magic was the physical manifestation of his guilt. Yet after saving Mari's life and countless others by defeating the rebels, Illan had finally forgiven himself. After thirty years, he was finally able to access his magic again.

Mari loved reading the scrolls in Brahn as fire mages could make the stories play out like a performance. Mari watched as small flames formed into people and moved across the table. Two women and two men erected from the fire and glanced around the room like they could see it. While the people were always a fervent, fiery red, the surrounding scenery tended to be hues of blue and green. Mari loved watching the story unfold; it was her favorite part of fire magic.

The four people introduced themselves: Iowyn was a fire mage, Vala was a death mage, Arun was a water mage, and Jai was a life mage. Five hundred thousand years ago, they walked the world as friends, as close as friends could be. Mari's eyes lit as they landed on Vala.

The flames suddenly changed, showing the four people as children. Iowyn stepped outside her blue house to where Arun played with a ball in the grass. Arun threw it towards Iowyn, who caught it and giggled before throwing it back. Together, they played. Iowyn asked Arun many questions, like his favorite foods and where he lived. As it turned out, his family had moved into the house next door.

Iowyn narrowed her eyes. "How old are you?"

"Six," Arun answered.

"Yes! I am finally not the youngest one in town."

Jai and Vala approached the other two and asked to join their game; Arun threw the ball to Vala in answer, who dropped it. Jai kindly picked it up and tossed it to Arun; thus, they played, too. And that began their unbreakable bond: a simple ball game that slowly became more as they aged.

The scene changed again, and the flame people were now young adults. Vala sat in a living room before a roaring fire, bouncing the infant in her arms.

"I want you all to meet my daughter," she said.

Mari's heart pounded, and she closed her eyes. She had heard this story dozens of times, and it never got easier.

Iowyn reached over and brushed the strands of hair at the crown of her head. "She is beautiful. I am so happy for you. You deserve the world."

"Thank you, Iowyn," Vala said, peering down at the swell of Iowyn's stomach. "When are you expecting?"

Iowyn looked over at Arun with a smile. "Just a few weeks, now. I'm hoping for a baby girl like yours."

"Your child will be as beautiful and powerful as the two of you, born of opposite magic. The luckiest baby alive."

The scene changed one last time. Iowyn knelt in bright green grass, her head in her hands as she knelt in a graveyard before two headstones. She wept loudly and screamed at the Gods for taking her two loves away from her. Etched words appeared on the headstones. *Arun, beloved husband and father. Wade, my son, taken too soon.*

Iowyn stood and faced Mari, who recoiled at the heartbreak on Iowyn's face. "My son was born a fire and water mage and had one tantrum we could not control. He burned my husband alive and drowned himself in an accident. I couldn't save either of them. I wasn't even home. As a word to the wise... a dual mage might destroy everything and everyone you love."

With that, the flames dissipated, and the story ended. Mari glanced at Illan, tears streaming down her face. It felt like someone had plunged a sharpened dagger into her chest. Illan's stoic expression surprised her. Mari had heard the story many times before, but it left her heartbroken each time. Watching it unfold before her was gut-wrenching. Yet Illan remained calm like he hadn't paid any mind to the tragic tale.

"That story has been passed down through your family? Why?" Mari asked.

"Iowyn is an ancestor of my wife, who was a direct descendent. After Iowyn lost her husband and son, she was a wreck until, eventually, she met another fire mage, and they had a healthy baby boy. Their family has always been warned of dual mages after this tragedy." Illan sighed.

"That's so horrible. Certainly, other families experienced similar things."

"Of course, they did. My wife told me that there were two schools of thought before Morana. One thought was that falling in love with a different magic user was not worth the tragedy, while the other deemed it worth the risk; if that dual mage made it to adulthood, they would be more powerful than anyone else."

"Well, that certainly is true. Morana made it to adulthood and was the strongest mage to ever live. But she invoked unimaginable tragedy, too." Mari shook her head. "But the thought that a *child* could do such harm…"

"It's a good thing Zahir has life magic as his second. To my knowledge, they don't have an attack to their magic, and if Zahir were going to accidentally use his secondary magic, it would only do good," Illan said before frowning. "I know it's wrong to speak poorly of the dead, but I don't know what Ryker was thinking."

Mari's brow furrowed as she opened and closed her mouth. How could he speak so bluntly about his brother's actions? Mari had been floored upon learning Zahir was a dual mage, but she didn't think Ryker had acted intentionally. But… had he? "He and my father wanted us to unknowingly make a triad. It's horrifying."

"It was wrong of them to keep you two in the dark, especially Zahir."

The clock chimed, and Mari glanced at it.

"I apologize for my abruptness, but I must go," said Mari, standing.

Illan checked the time and smiled. "Ah, your time with Roan."

Mari nodded. "It means a lot to us both. Roan really misses Zahir."

"But I'm sure he is thrilled to spend time with you."

Mari rushed into the hall, walking as quickly as she could. When she returned to her bedroom, Roan was already inside, sprawled on her bed with a book open before him. Mari was starting to worry about Roan. Since Zahir left for Lovíth, a few servants had revealed that Roan was constantly up in the middle of the night, asking for snacks; the dark circles under his eyes only seemed to worsen the longer Zahir was gone. But Mari didn't know what to do besides spend time with him.

"Good afternoon, Roan. What are you doing in here?" Mari asked, rubbing her eyes with the palms of her hands.

"You were taking forever with Uncle Illan," Roan said quietly. "I was starting to get worried you were going to miss our time together."

"I would never miss our time. It's important to me." Mari sat and pulled Roan into her lap. He giggled as she snuggled into him. "I am so sorry I made you think I would. Let me freshen up, and I will meet you outside in a few minutes, okay? Can you find me a book that you think I'll like? I just finished reading the last one you gave me."

"Yes!" Roan leaped off the bed and ran out, hopefully to the library. Every afternoon before dinner, Mari and Roan would sit outside beneath one of the large trees and read together.

Mari had read so many books because of Roan, both historical and fictional. Although they only spent an hour together, it was special to Mari. In marrying Zahir, she gained a new family she loved dearly.

In the time she had been in Brahn, Mari had received three letters from her parents. One congratulated her on the marriage three weeks after they returned to Yu'güe; the second was after Ryker's death once her father had heard of the rebel attack, and the third was three weeks ago, asking if she was with child. Mari had not responded to a single one. The longer she was away from her father, the less she wanted a relationship with him. After discovering Hanan was alive and her father had lied to her for years, she wished never to speak to such a heinous person again.

Mari's knees and back cracked as she stood, the wooden floor warm beneath her toes. She ran a comb through her hair, untangling the knots that had formed throughout the day, and slipped out of her dress. She put on an oversized short-sleeved shirt, courtesy of Zahir's closet, and a pair of black training pants that clung to her muscular thighs. Since Zahir had left for Lovíth, Mari had attained even more muscle in her arms and legs and had to replace several items in her closet because they no longer fit.

Grabbing a light sweater in case of a cool breeze outside, Mari headed towards the gardens, where Roan sat beneath their usual spot beneath a large oak tree. One book sat open in his lap and another to the side. Mari sat beside him, resting her back against the trunk and stretching her legs. Roan handed the book to her.

He seemed much older, somehow; his golden brown skin had darkened since their time outdoors, and his hair had grown.

"It's a fiction story," Roan said when Mari cracked it open. "It's about two people who fall in love even though their families own rival restaurants in a city."

Mari laughed. "That sounds very interesting; thank you, Roan. I do love a good romance book. What are you reading?"

Roan smiled, never taking his eyes from the page. "It's a fiction book, too. It tells the story of a soldier who travels into the mountains to fight a dragon—a big lizard with wings that breathes fire."

"How interesting! I might just have to read that one after you," Mari said, ruffling Roan's hair. "I adore the time we spend together."

"Me too. It helps me not miss Zahir as much, though he would never sit and read with me."

Mari laughed. "No, I suppose he wouldn't."

Roan laid down, so his head rested on Mari's thigh; he held the book up to shield himself from the sun. Although it was late in the day and the sun was setting, it was still warm and sunny.

As Mari dove into the book, she realized how well Roan knew her. He had picked a book where the main love interest was kind and not suffocating. The main female character was a strong woman, completely comfortable in her body and mind. Mari hated romance books where the woman's only goal was to fall in love. She never related to those women; her goals were much bigger than that. While she had found romance with Zahir, she craved much more than to be a wife and mother.

In fact, she didn't know if she even wanted to be a mother. Mari had never been good with children.

"Are you joining us for dinner?" Maura's soft voice jolted Mari from her book as she looked up to where Zahir's mother stood, a warm smile on her face; her long black hair blew in the wind.

"Oh, yes," Mari said, helping Roan sit up. "We must have lost track of time."

"I didn't mean to interrupt you, but I can't have you two going hungry."

Mari had to refrain from rolling her eyes; she would not starve from missing one meal when the rest were so filling. Mari had known rationing food before, and this was nowhere near close to that. In Yu'güe, the winters were so harsh that trekking into the mountains to hunt was impossible for several months of the year, meaning if food stores ran low, the meals became smaller until they had no choice but to venture into the storms.

Maura's long red gown flowed in the breeze as she led Roan and Mari into the palace. The gown was larger on Maura than the last time she'd worn it. Zahir's mother was not taking well to Zahir's departure, either. Maura sequestered herself in her chambers the first few weeks after Zahir left. Perhaps she was embarrassed now the truth had finally come to light about her husband's affair and Zahir being the first dual mage in millennia. But Mari would never ask her. She only interacted with Zahir's mother occasionally and did not feel close enough to ask such a personal question.

Every night for the last four moon cycles, the family had eaten dinner together. Everyone showed up and tried their hardest to be pleasant. Anya had been much less snarky since she and Taryn had finally confessed their feelings for one another during one of their huge fights. Instead of their usual screams of anger, ones of pleasure could be heard through all hours of the night.

Taryn fixed the collar of Anya's shirt with a wistful smile as Mari, Roan, and Maura entered the dining room. Taryn had grown out her short brunette bob and kept her hair in long braids that swayed as she walked. Anya's face, while still sharp and angular, was less intimidating now she always smiled. Her black hair was tied in a knot at the crown of her head, decorated with a tiara. When Taryn kissed her cheek, Anya tried to hide her blush, but to no avail.

"Mari! Did you and Roan enjoy your reading session this evening?" Taryn asked as Mari took a seat.

"Very much so. Roan picked out a stellar book for me." Mari held up the book so Taryn could see the cover.

"That's great. I'm very glad."

Mari glanced at her plate: smoked fish seasoned with thyme, roasted potatoes, and asparagus tossed with spicy pepper. Mari could barely believe that just a year ago, these foods had been so foreign to her. Now, they were as normal as the food she ate back home.

A memory bubbled to the surface of Zahir and Mari's picnic on the roof, where she'd eaten a spicy hot pepper jam that burned her tongue and the roof of her mouth. The spices were novel flavors she had never heard of back then, but now it was her favorite.

"How is your training going, Anya?" Mari asked, taking a long sip of red wine.

"Well. Illan is helping me to control my temper through meditation," Anya said with a slight roll of her eyes. "It works... sometimes."

"As long as you don't melt my things, I don't care," Roan commented, eliciting a laugh from everyone at the table.

"I know. Taryn and I were quite... *volatile* when she first moved in with us," Anya said. "Do you plan on producing your triad heir when Zahir returns, Mari?"

Mari nearly choked on her food. "I haven't given it much thought."

"Well, that *is* why Zahir was chosen as heir over me," Anya said, rolling her eyes. Although she had gotten more pleasant, she was not any less bitter about being passed over as heir.

"Yes, that is true. But it is a decision we will make together; it is not simply my choice." Evading Anya's questions without sass was something Mari was still learning to master.

"Maura, how are you doing?" Taryn asked, changing the subject.

"It comes in waves. Thank you for asking, Taryn." Maura refused to meet Taryn's eyes as she responded. Of course, Taryn was referring to Ryker's sudden murder during a rebel attack on the palace, which occurred shortly after Mari and Zahir married, and although it had been almost a year, Maura still very much grieved for her husband. She rarely emerged from her chambers, which was why Taryn had suggested daily dinners. Maura had initially declined, but when Roan said he never saw her anymore, she quickly changed her mind. Maura could never say no to her youngest.

"When my grandmother died fifteen years ago, I had a really hard time with it. I know this is nothing like what you are going through, but she was a big part of my life as a child. She kept me company while my parents worked; she took me to the markets for clothing and dessert. She taught me how to control my magic. When she died, it felt like a part of me died, too. I didn't know what to do without her. I could barely eat; I never slept. I had no desire to leave my room because everything reminded me of her. I understand what you are going through, Maura. It gets easier, but it takes a long time." By the time Taryn finished speaking, tears streamed down Maura's cheeks.

"Excuse me," Maura said suddenly, shoving back her chair so quickly it screeched against the floor. Her footsteps echoed through the room, the slamming door breaking the room's silence.

"Why did you have to do that?" Anya asked Taryn, narrowing her eyes.

"I thought it would be helpful to let her know she isn't alone in her pain. I did not realize she would be so heartbroken." Taryn sighed. "I'm sorry."

"It's a little late for that. Good job." Anya slid back from the table and followed her mother from the room, leaving Mari, Taryn, and Roan to eat their meal alone.

"That was not your fault, Taryn," said Mari, reaching across the table to pat Taryn's hand.

"Oh, I know. Anya doesn't want to show it, but she hurts just as much as Maura. She talks in her sleep and regularly dreams about Ryker. It's refreshing."

"What, to know she has a heart?" Mari asked with a laugh. "That has been the best part of you two getting together. She isn't tormenting me anymore."

"And she doesn't burn things down either," said Roan.

They laughed, and conversations about this and that occupied the rest of their meal. Mari and Taryn tried to include Roan as much as possible, but he clearly didn't want to talk. He had not spoken about Ryker's death in many moon cycles, but he was obviously grieving, too. His smile never quite reached his eyes. Mari just hoped he was talking to someone about his feelings; bottling up emotions always leads to disaster, especially when the bottle breaks.

Chapter Four

Zahir

As soon as Markus and Zahir walked through the door, they began their abundance ritual. Markus removed a sealed bottle of water from a cabinet and added it to another jar of cleaning solution.

"This is moon water," Markus said. "Every full moon, we fill a jar with salt water and leave it beneath the moonlight. It's used for cleansing and helps us to be more in touch with ourselves so we can be more in touch with our magic."

Zahir nodded slowly. "What do we do with the magic water?"

"It's not magic, Zahir."

"Oh, of course not." Zahir couldn't withhold the sarcasm that dripped off his tongue. "It's not like magic *exists* or anything."

Markus rolled his eyes. "We are going to clean our rooms from top to bottom with this. Open your window when you clean; this ensures there's only one way for the bad energy to escape."

Zahir drenched a cloth in the moon water and trudged to his room. He was already regretting his decision to join Markus for this ritual. Zahir didn't know how the moon could impart specific facets on a jar of *water*, but Zahir knew a change in his routine was needed, and if this ritual enhanced his life magic, even for a few hours, maybe he could make progress and return to Mari. So, he took the cloth and cleaned his room. He washed his desk and nightstand, where most of his items lived, and even wiped the ceiling.

Once they finished, Markus brought him outside with their cinnamon and poured a small handful into Zahir's hand.

"Blow it across the doorway and think about the life magic flowing through your veins beneath the surface."

Zahir didn't understand how blowing a pile of cinnamon through an open door could invite good things. Wishes were for children, and he was never afforded such luxury. But he did as Markus instructed and breathed slowly, as if meditating and felt the magic pulsing in his veins. The cool, calming sensation of his life magic ebbed and flowed from his heart to his fingertips and down to the soles of his feet. Zahir's fire magic intertwined with his life magic, and red hot power flowed through him, wrapping around the subtle coolness of his life magic. Without thinking, Zahir blew the cinnamon through the doorway, which erupted in a spice-filled cloud that crossed the threshold and scattered along the floorboards. Markus clapped Zahir on the back before sweeping up the cinnamon and collecting it in another glass jar. Zahir wondered just how many jars Markus had filled over the years.

"Can you feel your life magic?" asked Markus, putting the jar on the counter once they returned inside.

Zahir buzzed as the helix of both magics flowed through him. "I have never felt like this before."

Markus smiled. "Good. You will feel the benefits tomorrow. I would recommend going to bed before you topple over. After I first did this, I collapsed right on the floor."

Zahir nodded, his eyelids feeling heavier by the second. And when Zahir trudged to his room, he didn't even remove his socks before falling into the deepest sleep he'd ever had.

When Zahir woke, he felt more rested than he had in years. And today, Zahir was going to train his magic. At first, Zahir had been embarrassed that he was in a class with children all Roan's age. But as he spent time with them, his embarrassment faded. After all, he was learning about his life magic like these kids were. Although his life experiences differed, it didn't mean he was worse than the younger people in his class. Zahir knew, deep down, that it wasn't his fault he was so behind.

Nevertheless, he felt like a failure. Part of him felt like he should have figured it out sooner. His broken bones always healed faster than Anya's; his bruises faded within hours sometimes, and his scrapes and abrasions were better within a day.

Aside from his instructor, Lily, Zahir was the first in the classroom. Lily was a tall waif of a woman who wore dresses that dripped off her body like honey. Her bright green eyes shone in the sunlight, and she often wrapped a scarf around her bald head.

"Good morning, Lily," Zahir said, sitting on the floor. A mat was splayed across the floor, where the students sat in a circle each day. Zahir preferred his spot by the windows so he could lean against the wall.

"Hello, Zahir. Have you been practicing?" asked Lily, sorting through a notebook as she paced the room.

"Actually, yes. I was able to heal a minor cut on my hand," Zahir said, intentionally leaving out just how taxing this was for him.

"That's wonderful! How did you feel afterward?"

"Exhausted but proud. I'm ready to learn today."

"That's great to hear. The only way to master life magic is to first master the basics."

"I don't know if I will ever fully master it, but I hope to be good enough to help my family if they're ever in need again."

Zahir had spoken at length with Lily about when he realized he was a dual mage, revealing all the details about what happened, while skimming over the gruesome parts. Despite Lily's initial horror, she said it was pretty normal. Children in Lovíth usually use their magic for the first time when they scrape their palms or knees while playing. When Zahir had told her that he had barely used it since that day, she had issued the same cautious warning.

If you don't master the craft, death will claim you.

Zahir knew what was at stake and would not let this gift take him from his life and family.

As the children filed into the room, Zahir handed out their daily high-fives and hair ruffles. The children reminded him so much of Roan. One kid, Bojana, loved to tell Zahir fun facts about Lovíth's history. Another, Charlie, enjoyed reading under a large oak tree outside the school. Melinda wore big round glasses, and Darius laughed wildly when someone told a joke. These kids almost felt like Zahir's siblings.

"Okay, now that we're all here, we are going to meditate. Why is meditation an important part of our magic?" asked Lily.

A young boy, Kurt, with his glasses askew, answered. "Because it keeps us in touch with our bodies. We need to know what our bodies are saying to us."

"Excellent! Being in touch with yourself is as important as knowing how to heal injuries," Lily said with a smile. "Everyone, get comfortable for today's guided meditation."

Zahir straightened with his back against the wall and crossed his legs. Resting his hands on his knees, he looked straight ahead and waited for Lily to continue. Sometimes, it took the younger ones time to calm down, but they all got into position quickly today.

"First, we are going to take three deep breaths," said Lily. "In... and out..."

Zahir breathed deep through his nose and exhaled slowly through his mouth. He inhaled a little deeper with each breath, envisioning the air flooding his whole body, flowing from his nose to his toes, and back out again. By the end of his three breaths, his eyes were beginning to flutter closed.

"Take note of how your body feels and notice what it's trying to tell you. Think about any areas where you might feel pain."

Zahir felt a twang in his lower back, which was constantly sore from all the training he was doing with Markus. Whenever they had a tough training session, Zahir would try to heal some of the soreness.

"Call to mind something that is stressful and think about it from an outside view. Why is it upsetting you?"

Zahir thought about the pressure to have a child with Mari. Growing up, he had always expected he would be a father; he didn't know he had a choice. But after learning he was a dual mage, Zahir realized he didn't want children and was terrified to tell Mari that. There was pressure on the pair to birth Brahn's next heir. But he didn't want to bring a child into this world if they were destined not to live a long life.

As Zahir felt his mind race, he returned his attention back to his breathing, like Lily had taught him to do. He focused on the rise and fall of his chest and the sound of the air whooshing in and out of his body. Zahir's thoughts tugged him back to the notion of an heir, but he fought its pull for as long as he could.

When Lily called their time, he was extremely thankful for it. "Today, we are going to attempt to heal some animals," said Lily.

She produced several small cages housing chirping birds and excited rabbits. Some looked worse than others, injuries ranging from broken wings to thorns in their sides.

Zahir chose his animal last, wanting the children to have first pick. He ended up with a blackbird with a broken left wing. The bird squawked in Zahir's hands, and his heart twisted. The bird looked hurt and frightened, reminding him of Mari and her fear of birds. She would have *hated* today's lesson.

Returning to his seat on the mat, Zahir stroked the bird's head, trying to calm it down. It was a blackbird, which Zahir had never seen before. In Brahn, eagles and vultures were common, but the little birds he always saw in Lovíth were a rarity. Zahir whispered to it, promising to help it if he could, but the blackbird didn't understand, screeching and squirming in his grasp.

Zahir put the bird down in front of him so it had free movement and rubbed his thumb along its head, hoping to earn its trust. He took a few long, deep breaths to try and soothe the creature, and soon enough, it calmed and glanced at Zahir with curiosity instead of fear.

The bird walked into the palm of his hand. Its wing was bent at an odd angle, almost like the bird had fallen straight out of a tree. With one hand under the bird and two fingers on its fragile wing, Zahir took deep breaths and pictured his magic flowing through his veins and into the bird. It usually took Zahir two or three tries to muster up any of his life magic. But when Zahir saw the bright green light emanating from his fingertips, he blinked rapidly at the ease with which he called upon his magic. Zahir promised himself he would never doubt the cinnamon again.

The bird visibly relaxed as its pain ebbed. The sinew of the wing restitched, returning the wing to its original shape. Within a minute, the bird launched into the air, flapping its wings and chirping excitedly. Zahir relaxed against the wall. Surprisingly, his energy was not entirely drained, and Zahir thought maybe—just maybe—he could heal a second injury right then. The abundance ritual seemed to have worked, and Zahir needed to use it to his advantage.

"Great job, Zahir!" Lily said, clapping him on the shoulder. "You have made progress since our last lesson. Keep up the good work."

The rest of the class flew by. After practical lessons, the younger kids laid down for their naps while Zahir and Lily worked on their magic together. It was always during the kids' nap time when it struck Zahir how far behind he was in his studies.

As they sat face to face with their legs crossed, Lily worked with Zahir on feeling his energy. She instructed Zahir to focus on his body, and slowly, they moved through his different body parts, only moving to the next once Zahir assured Lily he could feel the vibrations beneath his skin. The most interesting thing about life magic to Zahir was he could *feel* it. His fire magic always felt absent, but his life magic... it buzzed through his veins and bubbled in his blood—the most calming and uncomfortable feeling he'd ever experienced.

At the end of the day, Zahir made his way home, watching as the children were welcomed into their parent's arms. His heart pulled, and thoughts of Roan emerged to the surface. He hoped Roan was doing well, given Ryker's death and Zahir's departure. Roan had seen too many horrors at his age and Zahir wished he could have given him an easier childhood.

As Zahir approached his home, yells resounded from inside. Pryn and Markus tended to get carried away when they played cards, and after a few too many glasses of mead, they would scream at each other, accusing the other of cheating if they won a hand. Watching them avoid their feelings by raising their voices was infuriating and amusing all at once.

Zahir opened the door in time to see Pryn throw their cards down on the kitchen table in a huff as Markus scooped up the pile of copper coins in the center. A half-empty growler of mead sat on the counter. The overwhelming odor slammed into Zahir, whose eyes watered. It smelled almost as bad as the tavern he visited with his friends back in Brahn... *almost.*

"Clearly, I'm late to the party," Zahir said, pouring himself a glass of mead and sliding into a chair between Markus and Pryn. "Deal me in."

They played cards, and Markus and Pryn became increasingly intoxicated as the game went on. He'd miss this when he returned to Brahn. In Lovíth, Zahir was only responsible for himself, focusing on his classes and training. He didn't have to think about rebels or policy or trade or even if he was spending enough time with his loved ones. Zahir was allowed to be selfish for the first time in his life. Free. And it was that freedom that he loathed to lose.

"Your energy is all fucked up, Zahir," Pryn said suddenly, pushing a coin into the growing pile at the center of the table.

"Thank you, Pryn. I appreciate the insight," Zahir said, trying hard not to roll his eyes.

"No, really. You ought to let me fix you up. You'll never be a life mage with your energy like it is."

"I'm a dual mage, not a life mage."

Pryn dismissed him with a wave. "It's the same concept. Your soul and body are all mixed up. Just come and visit me for alignment."

"I think my soul is just fine."

"They're right," Markus said. "I'm not even a healer, and I can feel it. You're not balanced. Parts of you are knotted up."

Zahir sighed and leaned back in his seat. "I'm advancing in my training just fine. Today, I healed a bird's broken wing."

"Oh, great! It took you nine moon cycles to learn what would take a child just two," Pryn said, shaking their head. "You are behind, Zahir. You were only supposed to be here for six moon cycles, which was plenty of time to get your magic to a level so you wouldn't die."

Zahir ran a hand down his face. It was true. The children in his class were advancing much faster than he was; at this rate, he didn't know how he was ever going to leave Lovíth.

"And I will get there. I know I will. I'm getting closer."

"Zahir," Pryn put their cards down and looked him in the eye. "Do we need to remind you what you stand to lose?"

"I *know*, Pryn. If I can't master my magic, I will die. How could I forget?"

"If you don't get a handle on your life magic, you are sentencing Mari to a life without you; Roan will lose his older brother; Anya will take the crown, and Illan will lose the closest thing he has to a son. Your death isn't something that only affects you, Zahir, and for some Gods-damned reason, you can't get that through your thick fucking skull!" Pryn threw their cards down on the table and crossed their arms.

Zahir ran a hand down his face. "Fine. *Fine.* If it will get you to shut the fuck up, you can align me."

Pryn stood suddenly and offered her hand to Markus. "I told you I would get him to crack. Pay up!"

Chapter Five

Mari

Hanan and Mari sat on the balcony side by side with a half-empty bottle of wine resting on the table between them. The sun had sunk below the horizon, bright silver stars speckling the sky instead. The palace gardens were beautiful, even at night. Moonlight reflected in the pond where she had first told Zahir about her fear of birds, silver glinting off the trees and flowerbeds. Beyond the palace grounds, the radiant city of Brahn looked alive. The expansive city glowed, the lights of businesses and homes bright for miles. Mari didn't realize how big Brahn was until she saw it lit up at night. The cool breeze removed the sweat from Mari's exposed neck. Hanan tilted his head back to look at the sky, his breaths loud in the silent outdoors. Mari examined him, noting Hanan's jaw was shadowed in moonlight as he watched the stars. Even after all this time, Mari couldn't believe he was alive. While her anger towards her father had not subsided, she felt eternally blessed he had lied to her.

"I will never get tired of this view," Hanan said, glancing at Mari. "It's different than the stars in Yu'güe. It's brighter here."

"It's absolutely beautiful." Mari took a long drink of wine and turned back to her brother. "Do you need anything? A cloak, perhaps? Your arms have goosebumps."

"No. Well... actually, there is something." Hanan leaned forward, resting his elbows on the table. "You could help me plan my wedding."

Mari nearly jumped out of her seat, her heart pounding. "You and Raf are engaged?"

"We are. I asked him yesterday, and he said yes."

Mari raced around the table to pull Hanan into her embrace, tears of joy streaming down her cheeks as she held him to her chest. She could feel the vibrations of his laughter as she hugged him tighter. Hanan's moved his strong arms from her waist to wipe his face; tears slid down his sunburned cheeks.

"Congratulations! I am so happy for you two. I would be honored to help plan your wedding, but I don't want to get in your way." Mari sat back in her chair, lifting her glass towards Hanan. "To you and Raf!"

Hanan clinked his glass against hers with a laugh. "Raf has more opinions than I do; it will be a nice bonding experience for you two."

"That sounds lovely. I am so excited to get to know my soon-to-be brother-in-law. Tell me how you proposed!" Mari finished her glass and refilled it, as well as Hanan's.

"I brought him to our favorite restaurant for dinner, where the chef created dishes from each clan but with a twist. I was so nervous the whole time, and Raf was clueless. Afterward, I took him to the ocean, where we watched the sunset, and when the sky was lit, I pulled out the ring and asked Raf to be my husband. He tackled me into the sand as he said yes." Hanan laughed. "I'm *still* trying to get sand out of my hair."

Hanan's eyes were glassy, his smile the brightest Mari had ever seen. "That sounds magical—the proposal, not the sand. I'm so glad you found happiness here, Hanan."

"Me, too. I never thought that I could be this happy." Hanan paused, his smile slowly fading. "We haven't had a chance to talk about our father, Mari."

Mari took a deep breath and bent over, resting her elbows on her knees and her chin in her palms. "I think we've both avoided it to not ruin our reunion."

"It's time, I think." Hanan and Mari quickly swallowed the rest of their wine and emptied the bottle into their glasses.

"We need more wine for this conversation," Mari said, pushing her chair back and standing. She grabbed the neck of the wine bottle and went back into her bedroom. She kept a rack of wine bottles underneath the writing desk so she wouldn't have to go down to the kitchens whenever she wanted a drink.

Mari returned to her seat with the new bottle of wine, picked up her glass, and leaned back in her chair, waiting for Hanan to speak. He peered over the dark gardens as if he could see what lay within the shadows. Mari could barely make anything out besides the trees, so she wondered if Hanan was looking at something in particular or merely trying to formulate words.

"I want to say that I'm sorry for lying to you about who our father truly is. But... I'm not. You didn't need to know; you were way too young. I think it would have just made things worse if you knew."

Mari recoiled at Hanan's candor. She understood why Hanan hadn't told her—after all, she was only six years old when he left—but she resented the fact she'd spent fifteen years mourning her brother. What would Mari's life have been like had she known Hanan was alive? Would she have obeyed her father? Or would she have run away, like Hanan? She didn't know. But, while she was still overcoming her anger at Hanan's decision not to tell her, she knew his intentions were pure. He was trying to protect her like he had for the first six years of her life.

"Our father told me he killed you. I figured out what kind of man he was pretty quickly. He never hurt me, but I knew he was capable of it, and I knew why he hated you, which is absurd."

"Here, things are different. No one cares."

"That's not true, unfortunately. It doesn't matter if you're common folk, but if you're the heir to the throne, you have to be willing to marry someone you can produce biological children with," Mari said, rolling her eyes.

"So, King Ryker could have an affair with a life mage and have Zahir, a dual mage. But if Zahir liked men, he couldn't marry one? How does that make *any* sense?" Hanan asked, leaning back. He ran his hand through his hair, knocking wisps of hair over his eyebrows.

"It doesn't. I wonder if it's like this everywhere or just Yu'güe and Brahn."

"I'd like to think it isn't. We deserve happiness, too. We deserve full lives and the ability to marry whomever we choose."

"I hope Zahir comes back from Lovíth and tells us no one cares about who you love."

"I wonder if our father would have hated me still, even if I weren't betrothed to the Orcian girl. If we were just a normal, boring family with no power... would he have cared?" Mari had never considered that question before. She had never wondered what their life would have been like if their parents weren't the leaders of Yu'güe's government.

"I don't know. Father never made his feelings obvious unless it was anger. I couldn't guess. But *I* would have loved you the same, whether or not you left. I was mad for so long because I didn't understand how you could leave me like that. I didn't comprehend how our father could do something so heinous. Part of me blamed you for no reason, and for that, I am sorry."

"You were just a child; you had every right to be angry. The issues with our father started way before my betrothal, though. He never thought I was manly enough. I should have taken over the council as I got older, but he didn't think I could handle it. I think that's why he wanted to marry me to some princess; I'd be far enough away that he wouldn't have to deal with me being such a disappointment to him." Hanan's head lolled back as he stared at the sky. "I was never good enough for him. But once I left, I realized it didn't matter because I would make my life what I wanted. I'm just glad that he didn't do to you what he did to me."

Mari refrained from scoffing. While their father hadn't physically hurt her, he was still awful. Mari was never good enough. Her father nitpicked every single thing she did. When Mari got stuck in a blizzard while hunting and had to spend a night in a cave, her father berated her for being so stupid and irresponsible, screaming about how she would never make a good leader if she only thought about herself. Every time she made a mistake, Mari's father reminded her that *he* murdered Hanan and would not hesitate to kill her if she disobeyed him again. While he never lay a hand on her, Mari's mental scars cut deeper than any wound.

"He didn't hurt me physically like he did you, but his words were just as harsh. I was *terrified* of him. He'd convinced me that he'd murdered you, and I thought if he was willing to murder his son—his firstborn—what would stop him from doing that to me? I had to obey his every word. I couldn't say no to anything."

"Did you ever try to say no?" Hanan asked.

Mari nodded. "The last time I tried to dissent was when he told me we were leaving for Brahn. He only gave me two days' notice. I told him that wasn't nearly enough time for me to pack my things and leave, but he wouldn't hear it. He said that I would behave unless I 'wanted to end up like your brother.'" Mari imitated his voice.

Hanan reached a hand out to Mari. "I'm sorry you had to suffer."

"At least we both got to start over. Yes, I am living the life he wanted for me, but I am doing it on my terms. He probably expected me to have had at least one child by now, and knowing that I am disappointing him is a good feeling."

"It is, isn't it?" Hanan grinned. "I don't know what I would do if I saw him again. I don't know if I would beat him senseless or cower in fear. I won't know until I see him, but I hope I *never* have to again. But something doesn't sit right with me about his plan to send you here. Opening trade and talks between clans can't be his only motivation. I feel like there's more to it."

"I never thought about it like that," Mari said. "I always just assumed he wanted to end Yu'güe's isolation."

What was her father's goal? Was it to make alliances with the other clans and open Yu'güe's borders? Did he know Zahir was a dual mage and wanted her to birth a triad? Mari was unsure of her father's intentions but didn't want to know. Marrying her off to Zahir was the best thing he could have done for her. Otherwise, she would still be in Yu'güe, terrified of her father.

"I want to *kill* him," Mari said, balling her fists. "He deserves to die for what he did, not only to you but to me, too. To all of Yu'güe. Do you think our mother knows what kind of monster he is?"

"How could she not?" Hanan scoffed. "She watched him and I fight constantly and did nothing about it. She didn't stop me when I ran. When I told her I was thinking about running away, do you want to know what she said? She told me I would never go through with it."

"Our parents expected us to give up the life we were born into for something that *they* wanted. We never got a choice," Mari said. "All I wanted was for us to be happy and have a say over our lives, but we were born to be pawns in their game. We were never going to be happy."

"We are now," Hanan said. "We get to make our own lives."

Mari couldn't help the laugh that escaped her. "Maybe you do—and I am *so* happy you can be the person you were meant to be—but I don't. I'm here, locked up in this fucking palace, ruling a nation I wasn't born into. My people are talking about whether or not I am going to have a child; people I don't even know speak about me and my husband and what we do behind closed doors. Having a child should be a decision between Zahir and me. But it's something our entire clan is a part of."

"What if you didn't have an heir? What would happen?"

Mari opened her mouth to speak but closed it suddenly, realizing she didn't know the answer. What would happen if she and Zahir didn't have an heir? The people and the council would be outraged. The throne would either go to Anya or Roan, but Mari wasn't sure who would be next in line. Ideally, she and Zahir would choose the next heir. Mari thought Roan would make an incredible King, but she wouldn't want to force it on him. Zahir never had a choice, and Mari wondered if he would want the next heir to be able to choose whether they accepted the crown.

"I don't know. Whoever is next in line would take the throne, I assume. I don't know if that would be Anya or Roan."

"Gods, when did we get so depressing?" Hanan asked with a laugh and a hiccup. "I'm done talking about our awful father. Tell me about you and Zahir."

Mari suppressed her smile as she leaned back, filling her glass for the fourth time. Her heart dropped out of her stomach as she spoke. "I miss him incredibly. It's not the same here without him. The bed is too big and cold at night. Sometimes, I wake up and forget he's gone and wonder where he is. I have dreams of him dying. I know he needed to go, but I can't wait for him to come back."

"How much longer will he be gone for?"

Mari shrugged. "I'm not entirely certain. It was supposed to be six moon cycles, but we've long since surpassed that."

"Do you think everything is okay with Zahir?"

"Of course," Mari said, but he was the second person this week to ask her that. First, Illan, and now Hanan. Mari wondered if she was missing something.

Hanan shrugged. "Maybe I'm paranoid. It's just strange that he's been gone for so long."

Mari took a deep breath and finally told Hanan what she had been avoiding for months. "Hanan... I need to tell you something."

Hanan leaned forward, pressing his forearms onto the table. "You can tell me anything, Mari."

The words were on the tip of Mari's tongue. *I've stolen human souls.* Two souls lingered in her arsenal from the two attacks on the palace, and whenever Mari was overcome with grief, she called on them to apologize. But no matter how often or how loud she apologized, those souls could never understand her. They could fight and protect... but they couldn't hear her sobs or apologies in the middle of the night. Mari still woke to awful night terrors that coated her body in sweat and made her hands shake for days. She never practiced magic anymore, not unless it was to apologize to the men she'd murdered.

"Are you okay, Mari?" Hanan asked, reaching across the table for her hands.

Mari shook her head and withdrew her hands to her chest. Instead of trying to tell him, she decided to show him. Thrusting her hands toward her empty bedroom, Mari called upon their souls. The two men stood shoulder to shoulder, clad in a phantom of their titanium armor from when they were alive. They stared at Hanan and Mari.

"Look what I've done," Mari whispered, holding back a sob.

Hanan was silent for longer than Mari would have liked. He stared blankly at the souls, slowly nodding. He turned to Mari, eyes wide.

"Are you okay?"

Mari shook her head and put her face in her hands, letting the sobs take over as they had so many nights before. As Mari cried, Hanan wrapped two arms around her shoulders until she was done.

Hanan, too, had tears in his eyes. "I don't know what's happening to me." Mari pulled her hands away from her face and showed them to Hanan. The tips of her fingers were coated in what looked like black spiderwebs.

Hanan blinked rapidly. "It's a repercussion of our magic. You must know about this—the negative physical and psychological effects of murder. The more human souls in your arsenal, the more severe it gets. Mari, you can't do this again."

"I didn't want to, Hanan. It was either me and Zahir or them. I couldn't let him die, Hanan. I couldn't. But I don't know what to do now. I can't sleep."

"Have you tried writing to any of the elders back home? Someone has to know something about the effects and how to mitigate them," Hanan said, leaning back onto his heels.

"I'm too scared. Hanan, I was even scared to tell you. How can I tell the Elders back home, knowing Father will hear about it? I am going to be ostracized from Yu'güe," Mari said, closing her eyes. "I bet I'm the first death mage since Morana to kill another human."

"There is no way that you are the first one. It's been millennia... someone must have done this, even by accident. Our magic is sometimes unpredictable when we're young. Don't you remember when you were sick and sneezed out a bunny onto the kitchen floor?" Hanan broke into a smile and let out a little laugh.

"Mother was so mad. I scared her so bad she dropped everything she was cooking," Mari said.

"No one is perfect, and you acted in self-defense. You didn't go out into the streets and do this for fun."

"Does the intent matter?" Mari sobbed. She ripped her hands away from Hanan as if her very touch would infect him, too. "I have to carry them around with me for the rest of my life. It's a constant reminder that I took those lives."

"I don't know how you feel, and I hope I never do, but you did nothing wrong. If it were up to them, you and Zahir would be dead. Do you understand what your sacrifice did?"

Mari curled her legs up to her chest and rested her chin on her knees. Hanan was right. Her sacrifice saved Zahir's life and probably saved Roan's, too. Mari took a deep breath and watched the lined-up souls. For the first time, she understood that she had no choice. It was a life-or-death situation.

Suddenly, the souls dissipated without Mari using her magic. She rubbed her eyes with her palms, but they were gone.

"Hanan, they just disappeared," Mari said, staring at the open door to her bedroom.

Hanan turned around and then glanced back at Mari, his eyebrows furrowed. "That's strange. You didn't call them back?"

"No."

"Maybe because you're intoxicated, your magic is working without you knowing—the opposite of the bunny incident."

Mari laughed as she choked back another cry. This was the thing she'd missed the most about Hanan; he was good at making her laugh when all she wanted to do was sob.

Hanan said nothing before wrapping his arms around Mari and squeezing her to his chest. "Does Zahir know how much this pains you?" When Mari shook her head again, he continued. "Maybe you should tell him."

"Oh, yes. Let me just get the next boat to Lovíth."

"Did you know there's this thing called *paper*? You can write words on it and send it to someone. I think people call it 'letters.'"

Despite her sour mood, Mari couldn't help but snort. "You're such a wise ass."

"It's my role as 'older brother'. It's in the handbook."

"I love you."

"I love you too, sis."

Just as Hanan and Mari broke their hug, Mari's bedroom door burst open. Illan and Ren ran into Mari's chambers, a folded piece of parchment in their possession.

"Mari," Illan said, producing a small flame in his hand. "This just arrived."

Ren handed the parchment to Mari, and she read it aloud.

Kings and Queens have lived and died
All of which have only lied
I'll be here in the shade
The thing you are all most afraid
My reign of terror has just begun
Wherein your world will be undone

Mari's hands trembled as she met Illan's wide eyes. "Where did you find this?"

"It was delivered to Ren personally," Illan said, his voice barely a whisper.

"Did you see the person who gave it to you? Can we get a description out to the streets?" Mari turned to Ren, who looked greener than grass.

"They had a hood on; I could not see their face. Who is *M*?" Ren asked, glancing frantically between Mari and Illan. "Is it the rebels?"

"That's impossible. Zahir and I personally destroyed them all," Illan said, his eyes trained on Mari. "When we rescued you, we killed their whole crew."

"You thought that before, Illan, after Ryker died. We don't know how many there were. We don't know if they had several hideouts. We don't know if they are in other clans, too. We have no solid information." Mari re-read the letter, and suddenly, everything made sense. "We need to garner allies and support. I think it's time we write to Orcian and see if these rebels are attacking them, too. We do share a landmass, after all."

"Why write to Orcian when I can just go?" Hanan asked. Mari had nearly forgotten he was there.

"No," Mari said, whirling. "For all we know, Orcian might have something to do with these rebels. They could be harboring them."

"Mari, I have a connection with Orcian."

"What?" Mari asked, confused.

Hanan let out a little laugh. "You do remember I was engaged to Princess Seraphina, yes? We wrote yearly letters like you and Zahir did. I can talk to her. As long as she's not still mad at me..."

"Why would she be mad?"

"I mean... I did run away from our engagement, and instead of letting her believe I didn't want to marry her, I wrote her a letter explaining who I was and what I *liked*."

Mari slapped a hand to her forehead and let it run down her face. "You could have just let her believe you were dead."

"Yes, well... mistakes were made. And here we are. She *knows* me. I can go to Orcian and talk to her. A personal touch might help get us information. They're not going to write a letter saying, 'Oh, yes. These rebels have been quite pesky,'" Hanan said, putting on his poshest voice.

"I'm not letting you go to Orcian, Hanan. Not when tensions in Brahn are so high. We don't know the first thing about Orcian."

"But *I* do, Mari. I spent years learning about Orcian: who sits on their council, the royal family etiquette, which fork is the snail fork... I understand all of these things. You have to let me try. If you let me do anything to help, let it be this. I can get their support. I'll bring Raf so it's clear to Seraphina that I *do* like men and didn't break off our engagement for no reason."

Mari looked to Illan. "Do you think this is as absurd as I do?"

"Honestly, it's a good idea. Hanan's right—Orcian had a positive relationship with Ryker and Zahir, but no one knows you. We don't know how they feel about Zahir's status as a dual mage or even if they know at all. Hanan might be our best bet."

Mari turned back to Hanan. "You take Raf, Reina, and three soldiers of Ren's choosing. You come back within two days. We need a real plan for this; we can't let you just go in blind."

"So, is that a yes?" Hanan asked.

Mari groaned. "It's a begrudging yes."

Chapter Six

Zahir

The following night, bright stars littered the sky when Markus dragged Zahir from his room to meet with Pryn. The night air was chilly, reminding Zahir of the colder seasons in Brahn, where it got so cold that sometimes frost glinted on the grass in the morning. Zahir searched the sky for the constellation of the Ever-Burning Candle and spotted it far off in the distance.

"What are you looking for?" Markus asked.

"The Ever-Burning Candle."

"I've never been able to find it; can you point it out to me?"

Zahir stopped walking and pointed with his right arm toward the constellation. The fifteen stars making up the candle's body twinkled. The five stars forming the flame almost looked like they were moving, flickering like a candle in the breeze. The constellation burned bright against the sky. "Can you see it?"

Markus shook his head. "No."

Standing behind Markus, Zahir lifted his arm over Markus's shoulder so he could follow his finger closely, and just as Zahir found the constellation again, he noticed the stars in the flame dim for a second, almost like someone was blowing out a candle. Zahir blinked, but the constellation returned to normal.

"I still can't see it," Markus said, stepping forward.

"They say only fire mages can see it," Zahir said. "Mari can't even see the constellation, and she's the Queen of Brahn."

"That's weird."

"You say as you lead me to our friend's house who is going to fuck with my energy. Now *that's* weird."

Several people exited the Crystal Cove, little velvet bags cinched in their hands. Two young girls giggled as they chattered about their purchases. The crystal shop was one that Zahir had yet to enter; he wasn't entirely certain why he was afraid, though. Markus constantly used crystals to cleanse his own energy or enhance his intentions, like his self-love and nothing bad happened to him. But immersing himself completely in Lovíth's culture proved more difficult for Zahir than he had imagined.

"What is alignment like?" he asked.

"It sort of feels like meditation, but you go more into a trance, and you don't have to do anything. You just lie there."

"So, it's nothing like meditation?"

"No, it is. It's like when you wake up from a particularly restful sleep after a stressful day, and you can hardly remember why you felt so bad to begin with."

Zahir nodded. "That I understand."

"Sometimes weird things happen. Your soul can travel if you are particularly relaxed." Markus sighed. "I'm not doing a good job of explaining this, am I?"

Zahir laughed. "No, not particularly."

Pryn's house was through town, built into the crevice of a small hill, with only part of the house visible from the outside. Bright green moss covered the white stone building; spots of the dark brown roof popped through the cracks. A wooden door was the only access in or out of the house, while the small circular window let in what little light there was that night from the moon and stars. Tall oak and pine trees surrounded the house, providing shade during the heat of the day; Pryn had also planted bright purple and orange flowers along the walkway to the door—the only pop of color.

Without knocking, Markus led Zahir inside the house, lit with torches and candles. The house smelled like lavender and rose petals, the same scents Mari used in her bath. Zahir's heart felt heavy as he breathed in the sweet air. Mari would have loved this home.

The inside of Pryn's house looked like a strong wind had blown everything into place. Blankets and pillows littered the floor and boxes were scattered haphazardly around the room. Zahir nearly tripped over a bright pink blanket in a pile by the door.

"Welcome to my home," said Pryn, appearing from a doorway on the other side of the house. Their red-tinted face starkly contrasted their usually pale skin like they had spent too much time outside. Their blue flowing tunic and orange shorts looked extremely comfortable, and Zahir made a mental note to ask where they had got it. Zahir had been wearing Markus's old items to fit in. He'd forgotten just how short Pryn was, barely coming up to his chest. Countless metal piercings adorned their ears; at a glance, Zahir counted seven in the left ear and nine in the right. A ring pierced through their septum and another in their left eyebrow.

"I owe you this for convincing him to come here," Markus said, handing over a pouch of coins. "I also brought a couple of crystals."

"Do you need them cleansed... again?" Pryn walked over and winked at Zahir.

"Um, yes. Please. If you have time." Markus took a deep breath and retrieved a small red velvet bag from his pocket. He emptied the contents onto Pryn's outstretched hand—one oblong purple crystal and one shaped like a red cube.

"I always have time for you, Markus," they said with a smile. The height difference between hulking Markus and tiny Pryn almost made Zahir laugh. They would be the strangest couple.

"Would you be able to... align me?" Zahir asked uncomfortably, not sure how to phrase it.

"Let's get you set up while the moon is rising."

Zahir followed Pryn into the depths of their house. The back room of Pryn's house was extraordinarily dark, with a handful of lit candles at the end table. It smelled like the rest of their house like a lavender plant had moved in and exploded. In the center of the room was a padded mat. A fountain in the corner invited sounds of flowing water into the room.

Zahir lay down on the mat as Pryn collected white candles and put them around him in a circle, lighting them one by one. Pryn pulled several opalescent white stones from a bag and placed them on the floor beside their knees.

"How does this work?" Zahir asked. He searched Pryn's face for anything that might settle his thoughts; apprehension of the unknown was a feeling Zahir dreaded.

"There is nothing to fear, Zahir," Pryn said, their voice soft. "I'm going to place these moonstones on your chest if you are comfortable with that. Then, I will keep my hands above different parts of your body—your head, chest, stomach, and thighs—to feel the energy flowing through you. I will help guide your energies through your body to flow correctly. If I detect an energy block, I will try to break it up. If you want to stop at any point, just let me know, and I will immediately pause what I am doing. Does that sound okay?"

Though it still made no sense to Zahir, he nodded his consent. The weight of the moonstone on his chest both calmed and excited him. The small circular rock felt much heavier than it looked. He tried to stay still, but that somehow made him more anxious.

"Relax, Zahir. Close your eyes. Listen to the water and take slow breaths."

Zahir closed his eyes, listening to the flow of the fountain. The slow trickle of water and his relaxing breaths calmed his thrumming heart until he could barely feel it beating. The pads of his fingers grew warm as he waited for something to happen.

But the longer he lay there, the heavier his limbs felt until he couldn't move at all, even if he wanted to.

It didn't take long before Zahir opened his eyes and found himself lying in the middle of a bright green field. The cool breeze chilled his skin, and goosebumps lined his flesh as he sat up, glancing around. He was no longer in Pryn's home but in this seemingly never-ending field. The lush trees were the same color as Mari's eyes, and his heart ached at the thought of her. The soft grass brushed against his bare feet as he stood, spinning to survey his surroundings. The scent of the field reminded him of the flower beds in the palace gardens after it rained. A warming calm stretched over him as he took a deep breath of the flowery air and closed his eyes, homesickness burrowing deep in his chest.

"Zahir, it's good to see you." A deep male voice made Zahir nearly jump out of his skin.

Spinning around, Zahir recoiled as he came face to face with his father. Ryker's long white hair was tied back beneath his crown; his gold eyes glinted in the bright yellow sun. The bags under his eyes were no more, and the smile on his mouth was something Zahir had nearly forgotten.

"Father? What—where am I?" Zahir asked. He rested a hand on his chest to ensure he was, in fact, alive.

"The After." Ryker took a tentative step towards Zahir. "It's quite beautiful here."

"But you... you died. I don't understand."

"I may not know why we were brought together, but I'm glad." Ryker wrapped his arms around Zahir's shoulders and pulled him into a warm embrace.

The familiar feeling of Ryker's arms around his body made Zahir nearly break into tears. He couldn't remember the last time his father hugged him, but he recalled all the times he was in his father's arms as a child. If Mari's hugs were a home, Ryker's hugs were a haven.

"Gods," Zahir said, wiping a tear from his cheek. "I can't believe this. What is it like here? In the After?"

"I have never felt more at rest. Not once have I been able to exist without the demands of life and duty, but here, I can walk among the trees and dip my toes in the stream. No one expects anything of me. Here, I have recalled all my memories. Zahir, I am so sorry. I was horrible at the end." Ryker's voice dropped to a whisper, nearly swept away in the cool breeze.

"I forgive you for everything you did or said to me." It was true. Zahir had wanted to forgive his father, who had been very sick towards the end of his life. Zahir didn't know how much of Ryker's decisions were due to his illness or his innate cruelty. At times, Zahir would recall when he was a young boy, and Ryker would play with him. Ryker sang Zahir to sleep when he wasn't tired; Ryker taught Zahir how to ride a horse and wield a sword. But, as Zahir grew older, Ryker became more erratic. He ruled with a strong hand, and as murmurs of dissent emanated through the streets, Ryker instituted curfews and sent patrols into the city to round up and murder anyone associated with the rebels. Zahir had even watched his father's men try to kill a mother and child, and Zahir was forced to kill palace soldiers to save innocent people. And so, Zahir didn't know if he could ever fully forgive Ryker. But maybe it wasn't his apology to accept.

"I don't know how much time we have, but I want to tell you about your mother... your *birth* mother." Ryker walked towards the tree line, motioning for Zahir to follow.

"My birth mother," Zahir repeated, unable to grasp the full gravity of that.

Ryker glanced at his feet and wrung his hands together. "Her name was Zena. She was a tradeswoman from Lovíth. Before your birth, we traded openly with Lovíth; Zena met with me once a moon cycle to discuss goods and payments. She had the most beautiful eyes, Zahir. You have her eyes—that gold that glints so perfectly in the sun.

"Then, one cycle when we met, we decided to lay together—just once... I cannot regret what I did, Zahir. I didn't even know she was pregnant until she began to show four moon cycles later. Once she told me it was mine, I told your mother. We made arrangements for her to live with us until you were born. We all decided, together, not to tell a soul. We could not let the news of a dual mage out." How Ryker spoke about Zena and their decisions intrigued and infuriated Zahir. Three people made a life-or-death decision about him before he was even born.

"Why couldn't you tell just me? If you had never told me, I would have died."

"I didn't want to risk it," Ryker said, sitting at the edge of a stream Zahir hadn't realized was even there. "If you had accidentally told someone, the consequences would have been catastrophic."

"What happened to Zena?"

"After you were born, we allowed her to recover in the castle under the guise of your mother's wet nurse. She rested there and helped us care for you for several moon cycles. In the middle of the night, she left without so much as a note. Your mother and I scoured the city for her but never found her. We assume she traveled back to Lovíth to protect you, but we cannot be certain."

Zahir lurched. Zena was in Lovíth. His birth mother, this woman who gave him unimaginable power, was somewhere in the life mages clan. Where *he* was. Did she know he was there? Did she intend to see him? Perhaps she recognized him when he got off the boat from Brahn...

She ran away from him when he was a mere baby; what would she think of him as a grown man? Would she be curious? Did she ever lay awake at night, wondering what kind of person he had become? Ever since Zahir had discovered his true identity, he spent hours wondering who his biological mother was and what she was like. He wanted to know if he looked anything like her, what her eyes were like, and if she was tall like him. He wanted to know what ran in his blood and if she was a powerful mage or one who never truly mastered her abilities.

So many questions ran through his mind, and he desperately wanted answers to all of them, so when he rose with a start, nearly knocking Pryn off their knees, he wanted to rush out of the house as fast as he could. The moonstone dropped to his feet as he sat up, knocking Pryn on their back with a thump. The pounding thrummed in his ears, and his vision swam, black dots spotting the already dark room.

"Zahir, are you all right?" Pryn asked, their voice thick with concern.

Zahir wiped a hand along his neck, slick with cold sweat. Something had happened to him. Had he died? There was no other explanation, was there?

"I... I saw him." Zahir panted. "I saw my father. How is that possible, Pryn? My father is dead."

CHAPTER SEVEN

MARI

Mari hugged Hanan, Raf, Kiernan, and Reina at the door to the palace before they headed to Orcian. Reina had brought Kiernan along for the journey, too, and though Mari hadn't requested Kiernan join the trio, Reina had asked for him to join, and Mari wasn't going to say no.

Mari still wasn't entirely sure about the plan to send Hanan to Orcian, despite his former relationship with their princess. The rebels were still out there, and while Mari needed to know if the attacks were isolated to Brahn, she was scared of putting her brother in harm's way. The rebels had breached the palace twice, and Mari was *terrified* of them getting back in.

"Be safe," Mari said. "Remember, only give them enough information so that they trust you, and if anything feels wrong, get out of there."

"When in doubt, get out," Hanan said. "That's the saying we grew up with. You can trust me, Mari. It's going to be fine. When I get back, we will have so much more information than before."

"Be careful. I'll see you in a few days," Mari said before turning from Hanan to Reina. "I know I don't need to tell you to be safe, but I have to say it anyway."

"I'll make sure we all come back alive," Reina said.

"Thank you, Reina. For helping. I appreciate it."

Reina glanced over her shoulder at Hanan and Raf. "I'm doing this to protect *them*."

As Ren shut the palace doors behind the group of Mari's loved ones and the three accompanying guards, Mari loosed a shaky breath. It was time to meet with the council. Ren escorted Mari back to her room, where she walked towards her wardrobe and changed into her armor. Ren stood in the hall, waiting to escort her to the council whom Illan was dragging from their beds at an ungodly hour of the night.

The door to Mari's dressing room slammed behind her, and as soon as it did, she fell to her knees, grabbed fistfuls of her hair, and screamed. Mari screamed until her throat was raw, until her fingers dug so hard into her scalp that it brought tears to her eyes. She yelled into the ground, furious at the Gods for allowing the rebels to continually assault her home.

When Mari thought she had nothing left in her lungs, she stood and straightened. Slipping into her royal armor made her feel stronger immediately.

Mari's reflection made her want to throw up. The bags under her eyes showed her lack of sleep, while her trembling lips showed her fear; worst of all, the tears streaking her cheeks gave away how close her resolve was to breaking. Mari sat before her mirror, pulled out makeup she had not worn since her wedding night and began to paint.

By the time her eyelids were bronze and her lips dark red, she looked fierce. The dark kohl around her eyes made them seem narrowed in concentration, the light concealer hiding the circles of exhaustion beneath her bright green eyes.

Mari left her chambers and was greeted by four guards alongside Ren, armed to the teeth with swords and knives. Their armor glinted beneath the candlelight as they formed a box around her as she walked to the meeting chambers. The only sound was the simultaneous stomping of the guards' boots as they marched beside her. Mari was still not used to the increased security. Before Zahir left for Lovíth, he had made significant changes to their security measures, and even though it had been nine moon cycles, Mari was still unsettled by the amount of guards having to escort her to the council room. Mari knew she could take care of herself, but there was no shame in accepting help when the threat was bigger than the whole sky.

The advisors were already assembled in their chairs when they reached the meeting room. The two chairs at the front of the half-moon table were empty, though Illan stood behind one. After Zahir's departure to Lovíth, Mari had shifted into Zahir's usual chair and allowed Illan to take the other. Appearances were important, after all. Thirty guards lined the room's perimeter, and as soon as Mari was through the door, they barricaded it from the inside. Mari couldn't remember the last time there were this many guards in one place. During the palace attack, she and Zahir had been alone.

The second Mari sat beside Illan, the entire room erupted into chaos. Mari was too stunned to speak as the advisors lurched from their seats, blurting their ideas and opinions.

"We must get ahead of this immediately!" Keir said, pounding a fist on the table.

"We don't even know if these claims are true or if someone is playing a nasty game!" An older woman, Isla, yelled.

"How can we be sure it is the same rebels?" Fenris asked, pointing a finger at Keir.

"There is simply not enough information to make a decision," Grimes said; their bangs flopped into their eyes as they shook their head.

"Enough!" Mari stood and slammed her hands on the table, leaning forward. She shot a scathing look at Illan for having told the advisors before she arrived. She was the fucking queen, and it was time everyone started treating her like one. A brief smirk graced Illan's lips as he watched her assume control of the room. Slowly, the advisors sat one by one, eyeing Mari with intrigue. When they were all seated, Mari continued. "We will not react to this like we did the news of a dual mage. We will take this threat with full credibility. The best thing we can do is get ahead of these claims. Addressing the public before we have all the information is not the right course of action. First, we need to send out teams into the city to see if we can gather any further information because, at the moment, we're going off scraps. Is this something we can all agree on?" Mari slowly sat, keeping her eyes straight and chin elevated: a picture of royalty. Her armor clanged against the chair, and her heart hammered in her chest, but she refused to let her unease show.

"We need more information," Keir said, nodding furiously.

"We simply do not have the bandwidth to send reconnaissance into the city. We need the guards here, protecting our leaders," Isla said. She moved to stand but seemed to think better of it when she looked at Mari.

"Then we hire soldiers," Mari said. "Plenty would sign up to help the royal family."

"Do not forget it was a guard—a friend of the King, no less—who betrayed us," Isla countered.

Mari resisted the urge to flinch. Rodrick selling out Zahir was still a sore spot for everyone; even Reina was only beginning to come around to Mari. Zahir had been extremely traumatized from that incident, especially Rodrick's betrayal.

"I know who we can ask," Mari said. "High King Zahir has four extremely close allies who would be more than willing to assist."

"It was one of those allies—"

Mari cut off Grimes with a hand. "They *are* allies. I trust them with my life. However, we must wait a few days to ask for their help. My allies have gone to Orcian to gather intel—"

"How could you make such a decision without our input?" Grimes asked incredulously.

Mari slammed her fist on the table, finally having enough of the council's antics. "Because I am the *queen*. We need information and support from the other clans. We have been fighting a losing battle for too long. If Orcian is experiencing the same trouble with these rebel groups, we *need* to know. Therefore, they have gone to Orcian."

"Why send people who know nothing of politics and etiquette?" Keir asked.

"The former fiancé of the Princess of Orcian is leading the quest. He was trained for years on Orcian's politics and etiquette. There is no one better suited for the task," Mari said, hardly able to keep the smirk from her lips.

Just as Illan opened his mouth to speak, a loud boom shook the ground. White dust floated from the ceiling and littered the table. Screams echoed around the room as several advisors shot from their seats. Mari was up and out the door with Illan hot on her heels. By the time they reached the front of the palace, Mari could already hear screams. Rushing past the guards at the palace entrance, Mari stopped dead at the apex of the stairs, her heart dropping into her stomach.

Brahn was drowning.

Bright blue waves surged through the city at high speeds, snaking through the streets and flooding houses through blown-in windows. Screams lifted up the stairs to Mari's ears, and without thinking, she raced down the stairs of the palace. The water rushed violently through the city, faster than any river Mari had ever seen. She couldn't discern where the water was coming from, but it flowed towards the palace and snuck up the stairs, lapping at the eighth stair from the bottom. As she ran, Taryn and Anya sprinted down the stairs to join her.

"Mari, go back inside. It's too dangerous for you to be down in the city!" Taryn yelled over the commotion. Horses ran in the streets as people screamed, trying to clamor onto their roofs and rescue loved ones.

"These are my people, too, Taryn. I'm not going to hide away when I can help them." Mari reached the bottom of the stairs and broke into a run toward the heart of the city, clumsily dodging people and horses as she weaved through the streets. The water rode up to her ankles and soaked her feet as she ran as fast as she could. She began shedding her armor piece by piece as it was too heavy to run in, and soon, all she wore was a black tunic and tight black pants, completely soaked through.

Mari began to panic as she splashed through the water. She had just allowed her brother and two closest friends to travel to Orcian, and nearly an hour later, Brahn was flooded. The water mages had not responded to Mari's letters since Zahir had left, ignoring her introductions and proposals on bolstering trade with them. What did Orcian really think about the death mages?

Mari silently cursed. Orcian must be behind these attacks, and Mari sent her brother right into the hands of their enemies.

Cries of "help" could be heard in every direction as the water surged into buildings and shattered windows. Glass rained down on women, whose arms flew up to cover their heads. As the trio ran through the streets, water splashed in all directions, rising to Mari's knees.

"Where are we headed?" Anya yelled over the rushing water.

"The outer districts. They need more help out there," Mari answered, beginning to pant.

Taryn pushed Mari out of the way of a falling piece of wood that splashed into the water, as without it, Mari would have been hit right on the head. Mari slammed into the side of a carriage, which creaked under her weight. She groaned and grabbed her left arm; that was going to be one hell of a bruise. Anya screamed for Taryn as a wave knocked Anya off her feet.

Taryn dove under the blue water after Anya until the two emerged near Mari, panting and gasping for breath. Anya's hair was stuck to her forehead as she pulled Taryn into a brief hug.

Taryn moved closer to Mari, grabbing her arm and pulling her forward. "I have to get to my family's house."

"Lead the way."

Mari trailed behind Taryn and Anya, trying desperately to keep up. Taryn was in much better shape than Mari; she hadn't slowed in the slightest, even with the water up to their shins. Anya grasped Taryn's hand as they raced through the water, wave after wave hitting their stomachs. Mari's lungs burned almost as much as her thighs, and she tasted metal on her tongue as she pushed her body to its limits.

Anya and Taryn stopped short outside a small one-story home with a drenched roof. As soon as Mari pulled up beside them, Taryn had already raced towards the door where her mother stood, holding an infant in her right arm, and the door open with her left. Tears streamed down the woman's cheeks, and the baby wailed.

Mari and Anya rushed forward together, and Anya grabbed the door from the woman. "Go, we will get anyone still inside."

"I can't leave my children," the woman sobbed. "They are all I have."

"They can't lose their mother, either." Mari widened her eyes at the woman, hoping she would understand. "Protect your baby."

As Anya escorted the woman to safety, Mari rushed inside the house and was immediately smacked in the face as a wave slammed her against the wall. Mari coughed, wading through the waist-high water.

"Taryn?" Mari called. "Where are you?"

"I went right. Go left!" Taryn yelled back. She sounded far away.

Mari coughed and turned, going towards the left side of the house. Three doors were situated at the end of the hallway, and she opened each one. Inside, two rooms were blocked by floating furniture. Mari quickly shut the doors to keep the furniture from blocking anything else in the house. The third door was locked, so Mari threw her body against it, hoping it would open. By the fifth try, she shoved her way inside and found a young boy splashing helplessly as his head went underwater. Mari raced to him and lifted the boy into her arms before heading back to the front door. By the time Mari emerged, Taryn was standing with her mother and five other small children who cowered and sobbed together. Anya held Taryn by the waist, pulling her close. But when Mari emerged, Taryn ran towards her, tears streaming down her cheeks.

"Gods, Jamie!" Taryn took the boy into her arms and walked swiftly from the house.

"We must get you all out of here. Come back to the palace with us," Mari said, coughing violently at the end of her sentence. "Our medics will help you."

"We can't take them there; they've never been allowed," Taryn said, eyes wide and worried.

"I'm the fucking queen. I'll deal with any repercussions," Mari said. She looked down at the gaggle of children. "Who wants a lift?"

As the group waded through the water back to the palace, they were often stopped by people, asking for help or thanking them for coming into the city.

"My Queen, what are you doing in the city?" asked an elderly man, coming out of his home to greet Mari and the little girl on her back.

"I came to help," Mari said, a sympathetic smile ghosting her lips. "Do you know what happened? Do you know where this water came from?"

The man nodded. "The dam on the north side of the city." He raised a hand towards the woods, where Mari saw the remnants of a dam; smoke billowed from it up into the sky. "My neighbor saw the dam burst, and then the water came flooding in."

From the smoke clouds, Mari knew this was no accident. This was an attack on Brahn. "Thank you. I appreciate your insight. Do you need anything? Are you hurt?"

"No, Your Majesty."

"We will have a plan soon to ensure your safety. Try to stay dry."

As Mari stopped to talk to the man, Taryn and Anya had gone ahead with the rest of Taryn's family. Mari waded through the flood with Taryn's younger sister latched to her side; the little girl swung her legs around Mari's hips, splashing and giggling. This only made it harder for Mari to walk, but she wouldn't tell the girl to stop; if splashing helped her stay calm, Mari would let her do it the whole way to the palace.

When Mari finally got out of the water at the seventeenth step of the palace stairs, she found the palace in chaos. Guards made their way quickly through the halls, securing all entry points. Ren was screaming at the top of their lungs for people to move out of the way for Mari, Taryn, and their guests.

"Status report, Ren," Mari said, scooping another one of Taryn's brothers from the floor just as he was about to cry. She placed the little boy on her other hip as the group made their way towards the medical wing of the palace.

"Orcian flooded the city," Ren said, their chest heaving. Their wild eyes scanned the halls. "We're fucked, Mari. All we can do is keep people from drowning by getting them up to a higher elevation point."

"We sent Hanan and Raf and Reina to Orcian, Ren. They're going to *die*," Mari said, panic creeping up her throat. Mari closed her eyes as images of what might be happening to Hanan surfaced.

"There's nothing we can do. We can't get to them in time. Reina will keep them safe. And, if all else fails, Hanan is a death mage," Ren said, putting a shaking hand on Mari's shoulder.

Mari shook her head. "He can't kill anyone. It would destroy him."

"Mari, we need to focus on Brahn."

Mari shook her head, ridding her thoughts of her brother. There was nothing she could do about it, not now. "How many soldiers did you send down into the city to start an evacuation?"

"None."

Mari stopped dead in her tracks. "Where are they? Get them into the city now."

"We need authorization from Zahir to—"

"Zahir is in Lovíth. Illan and I are standing in his place. You have *my* authorization. Get Illan's immediately, and then send all our soldiers into the city to help Brahn. We are not leaving them out there to drown," Mari said sternly, refraining from yelling.

Once Mari and her party were safely in the medical wing of the palace, Ren left them and sprinted out the door. Immediately, nurses swarmed Mari. Before they could even assist her, she laid Jamie down on a bed and sternly told the nurses to treat him and all others who needed anything.

"Taryn, I'm going back into the city. Don't feel obligated to come; stay with your family," Mari said, resting a hand on Taryn's shoulder.

Taryn looked over her shoulder at her mother, and with a shaking breath, she spoke. "I'm coming with you. They are safe now. We have a duty to Brahn."

Taryn was hot on Mari's heels as they ran back through the labyrinth of the palace and down into the city. Anya was waiting at the top of the steps. Grabbing Taryn's outstretched hand, the three women plunged into the ocean of a city. The screaming hadn't ceased, and now there were even more people on their roofs, watching the water gush through the streets.

Mari helped young parents carry their children to safety on their rooftops while Taryn and Anya worked together to scoop up children without their families. Mari tried to console anyone she encountered, but there was only so much she could say as the water swept away their belongings.

As Mari rounded a corner to find the next people in need of help, she stopped dead in her tracks. Standing in the center of Brahn's square was a tall, ethereal woman. A dark, wispy cloak hung around her body, and black-stained hands protruded from her sleeves, her fingertips the color of soot. The rest of her hand was white like snow. Her dark green eyes were narrow slits, her black hair waving in the wind behind her head.

Mari's heart dropped onto the stone path beneath her when the woman sent an army of human souls running through the city.

Chapter Eight

Zahir

Zahir sat with his knees pulled up to his chest as he held a steaming cup of tea. The tea had been at a constant temperature for hours as Zahir released his stress in the one way he knew how—his magic. He couldn't very well burn down Pryn's house, so he'd slowly released fragments of energy by heating his tea instead.

Pryn and Markus sat on a plush brown couch in front of Zahir. Markus' left knee leaned on Pryn's right, and his arm draped across the back of the couch behind Pryn. Pryn slid closer to Markus as they picked up a cup of tea from the table before them while Zahir took up the entire loveseat and stared at Pryn's knees, not wishing to make eye contact with either of them; he knew they wanted to talk about what he had seen during his alignment.

Meeting his father had unsettled him. What could be creepier than having a conversation with your dead parent in The After?

Nothing. Zahir had never heard of The After. It felt like a very real hallucination. Was that truly the afterlife? Had Zahir's soul left his body? Zahir couldn't believe what had happened, and while he had reconciled with his father's death, he was now more confused than ever.

"Are we going to talk about what happened, Zahir?" Pryn asked, leaning forward with their hands in their lap.

Zahir shook his head slowly and blinked absentmindedly. His unbound silver hair stuck to the cold sweat on the back of his neck and fell into his eyes when he moved. He clenched his jaw, biting hard on nothing. He couldn't seem to stop.

"Zahir, you experienced something life-altering. We should discuss what you saw," Markus said quietly. His deep voice always penetrated Zahir's soul when he was gentle and supportive. "We have all experienced something like that during alignment."

"You've spoken to your dead parent and found out information about your birth mother?" Zahir asked the floor.

The silence that followed was a clear enough answer. No, they had not.

"What did you find out?" Pryn asked after the silence had stretched for several long seconds.

"Her name is Zena. She lives here in Lovíth."

"I don't know anyone by that name," said Markus.

"What do you mean?" Zahir asked. "My father said her name was Zena."

"I have never heard of anyone named Zena. Did he describe her at all?"

Zahir shook his head. "He just said I had her eyes."

Pryn stared hard at Zahir's face. "You know who you can ask? Her name is Lydia. She knows everyone, and she's a seer."

"A seer?"

"She reads cards and can see the future and things from your past. She might know who your birth mother is."

"Do you even want to meet your birth mother?" Markus asked.

Zahir opened his mouth to speak, but nothing came out. Did he want to meet her? Of course. Why wouldn't he? Meeting her would mean getting answers to the countless questions that had arisen over the past several moon cycles.

But... what if it went poorly? What if she wanted nothing to do with him? And what if she hated him for what he was: an abomination?

He was the first dual mage in millennia, and while that came with unimaginable power, it also came with the risk of people deeming him evil. His birth mother had left him in Brahn, knowing what he was and what he could do, abandoning him with two people she didn't truly know. She probably hated him, for if the truth was ever revealed about her, she would forever be known as the person who gave birth to another dual mage.

Zahir didn't know if he could take that rejection. If their reunion went badly... he didn't know what he would do.

"I don't know," Zahir said finally.

"You don't have to decide right now. Just know the option is open if you want to meet her."

"Was that a dream?" Zahir asked, mostly to himself. "It can't be, can it? I didn't think getting information I wouldn't have known from a dream would be possible."

"It's not a dream," Pryn said softly. "Your soul went into what we call the dreamscape. During alignment, a healer changes how the magic flows through your body. We work it through your chakras to make them align. If, at the right time when you are relaxed, your chakras align—even for a second—you can be launched into the dreamscape, where you can sometimes meet dead relatives."

"That doesn't even make sense... Wouldn't that make *me* dead?"

"In a way, but your soul isn't ready to fully leave your body. The best way to describe it is a nap versus a full night's rest. When you nap, you don't *need* a full night's rest, and you wake up when you don't need to rest anymore. When it goes to the dreamscape, your soul isn't ready to make its home outside your body," Pryn explained.

"This makes absolutely no sense," Zahir said.

"Your soul leaves, but only for a few seconds. It might feel like a long time, but it's not."

Zahir nodded. "Now *that* makes more sense."

"Can we do anything for you?" Pryn asked, exchanging an uncertain look with Markus.

"I think I need to be alone." Zahir stood and placed his tea on the table between the couch and chair.

Without looking at Pryn or Markus, Zahir wandered from Pryn's small home in the opposite direction of the town square towards the woods. The one thing Zahir hated about Lovíth was its flatness. While there were small hills, there were no mountains for him to hike when he was stressed or high rooftops for him to perch on when he needed to be alone or escape life's stressors. The woods provided some solace, but not enough.

Zahir wandered through the trees, trying to think of anything but Zena and his father. He tried to think of Mari, but that only made him homesick. He was desperate to return home and lay with her in his arms, snuggled up beneath the moonlight. At that moment, Zahir would do anything to be with her.

Before long, Zahir arrived at a clearing: an open field spanning several hundred feet in every direction. He walked to the center and took five slow, deep breaths before his arms burst open and bright orange flames roared across his skin. They flickered in the moonlight as Zahir threw his arms directly above his head, palms to the sky, and watched the fire spiral upward in a cylinder. As it rained back down, flames shot out from either side of him.

Zahir kicked his left leg up in an arc, and when he slammed his heel onto the ground, magic exploded out of him in a fast-spreading circle completely decimating the grass until the tree line.

"Why did you do this to me?" Zahir screamed at the sky.

He shot fists of fire up towards the moon as if trying to send them to his father. Zahir hovered as magic spewed from his feet, but as soon as he realized what he was doing, his magic faltered, and he dropped, managing to steady himself before falling face-first.

Zahir straightened and rolled his shoulders back with a deep breath, his eyes closed. After several long breaths, he opened his eyes, and a pang of guilt gnawed at him. The entire field had been scorched by his magic. He was so used to the fireproof rooms at the palace that it hadn't even occurred to him that everything in Lovíth was flammable. The life mages were very protective of their home, and Zahir had destroyed a part of it without a second thought. Would they be angry that an outsider had decimated their land? Zahir didn't know how to rectify the situation, either. There was nothing he could do but accept the consequences of his rash behavior, and if that meant casting him out of Lovíth, he would take the punishment. Because this wasn't his home, he was here to learn from the life mages.

Zahir slowly turned on his heel and walked back to town. He desperately needed a drink and knew the tavern would be open. When the dirtied paths transformed into gravel, Zahir's gaze flickered to the signs above the buildings. The Little Apothecary was closing its doors and locking up for the night. The black-smith, who preferred to work at night when it was cooler, was forging a new dagger inside the walls of his shop, the furnace a blazing red. Smoking Cloak had been closed all day, the whole store absent from an illness. A small sign in the window let patrons know they would reopen within a few days, given they all recovered.

Raucous laughter drifted out of The Quiet Berry into the street as a patron entered the building, yellow light spilling onto the street. The portico of this run-down building was lined with black columns and an oxidized cluster of berries above the entrance. The door hung open, greeting Zahir with the smell of freshly baked bread.

The Quiet Berry was a misnomer—there was nothing quiet about it. Loud voices, clinking glasses, and fists banged on tables as Zahir entered the hall. The interior showed a main hall with card tables, where people drank large pints of ale, and several private rooms off to the side. Crimson cloth draped across the circular card tables, decorated with a repeating pattern of assorted berries. There were no windows, only lit lanterns lighting the room in a dusty yellow. A bar lined the left wall, and a woman hidden under a black cloak served drinks to patrons. She had a mess of curly red hair pulled back to show her freckled face. She smiled at Zahir, who stood at the entrance, unsure where to sit.

A young man approached him, a slight sway in his step. He had two daggers strapped to his hips; his bright blue eyes glowed in the lantern light, and his bright red hair was cut short to his head.

"Welcome to The Quiet Berry. The name's Graeme. Are you here to drink or play?" Graeme said with a unique lilt Zahir had never heard.

"I'm not sure. What are you playing?" Zahir asked. Gambling was not his thing, but he didn't want to drink alone.

"Cards."

As if Zahir was supposed to know what that meant, he said, "Just a drink for me."

Graeme gestured for Zahir to follow him to the bar, where he grabbed Zahir a seat and flagged the bartender. "Take care of him, Blair."

"I know how to do my damn job, Graeme," she said, rolling her eyes. She had the same accent that Graeme did. Her 'r's' were rolled slightly when she said Graeme's name.

Blair placed a nearly overflowing glass of dark ale in front of Zahir, who picked it up by the thick handle and took a long sip. The drink tasted like bread and tickled his tongue as he drank. Zahir couldn't help but take another sip. Brahn's ale was much lighter than Lovíth's. In the months Zahir had been here, he hadn't drunk much. He had been so exhausted from training every day that he barely had the energy to carry himself to bed at night, let alone go out for a drink. Markus often invited him out, but Zahir had declined every time. Besides, it was good for Markus to go out alone with Pryn. If he were ever going to admit his feelings for them, they would need ample time alone.

Zahir scanned the bar, watching as a fight broke out on the card table. Clamoring voices erupted, and the word *'cheat'* was thrown every so often between blows. The large man, who had attacked the younger one, seemed to be losing the fight. The little one jumped up on the table and slammed the larger one to the ground, straddling him and landing blows to his face.

"Does this happen a lot?" Zahir asked, turning to Blair, who watched the fight with ambivalence.

"Aye, nearly every night." Blair rolled her bright green eyes and shook her head. "Men."

Zahir cocked his head at her as if she weren't speaking to him—a man. "I would never beat someone up for cheating in a game of cards. They probably have a reason."

"That reason, Young King, is because Gerald likes a fight. He doesn't need to win."

Zahir paused at the nickname *Young King*. Is that what people thought of him? "Young King?"

"You are the Brahn king, no? And you are young, yes?"

"Yes, but why does it matter if I am young?"

Blair put down the glass she was drying and tossed the dish towel over her shoulder. She leaned forward over the edge of the bar and folded her arms. "It only matters if *you* think it does. So, tell me, Young King, does it matter?"

Zahir recoiled at her forwardness. *It only matters if you think it does.* Did it matter? Did it matter that shortly after his rise to power, he left to gallivant in the fields of Lovíth? That he left Mari to rule in his place while he trained? That he was truly the youngest king in Brahn's history?

"Maybe it does," Zahir said, downing the rest of his ale in several long gulps. "Do you have a pen and paper?"

Blair gave Zahir a funny look before ducking down behind the bar to pass him a pen and a piece of crumpled parchment. He thanked her and began writing.

My darling, Mari,

There is no time for pleasantries. I spoke with my father. With Ryker. We were in The After. I don't have time to go into specifics... but it's this weird life mage thing.

He told me the story of my birth mother. He said her name is Zena, which he'd already told me, but Markus and Pryn don't know of anyone by that name.

I don't know if I should try to find her. On one hand, I will never have this opportunity again, but on the other... what if she thinks I am an abomination? She abandoned me in Brahn. Why would she want me now after all these years? What if she rejects me again? I don't know if I am ready to meet her.

Mari... what would you do? I need you. I wish you were here. I am overwhelmed, and I have no idea what to do. Please... what would you do? Should I try to find her?

What do I even say if I were to meet her? "Hello, I'm Zahir, the son you left in Brahn. Can I come in for a cup of tea?" That's absurd.

She isn't going to want me. She abandoned me. She left me in Brahn so I could become king, while she chose to return here and live her life the way she wanted. I know you will understand this—the absence of choices in your life.

I don't know that I'm ready to meet her, but what if I never have this chance again?

Please, help me. I miss you. I would give anything *to be with* you tonight.

Yours,

Zahir

When Zahir put down his pen, he wanted to crumple the letter and throw it in the fire. Instead, he folded it and tucked it in his shirt pocket before paying for his drink and leaving The Quiet Berry. Sounds from the bar flitted out into the street as Zahir trudged back home. He barely noticed the noise quieted as he distanced himself from the bar.

Zahir kicked a rock along his path as his mind raced. If he met Zena and she wanted nothing to do with him, he would be devastated as it would mean she truly never wanted him, forcing him to live the rest of his life not knowing where he came from. Or, if she welcomed him with open arms, he would learn about the life he may have had. If she had never told Ryker she was pregnant, he could have lived in Lovíth, free to be himself without the restraint of the crown. Zahir truly wasn't sure which was worse.

CHAPTER NINE

MARI

"Who are you?" Mari yelled towards the ethereal woman.

"You already know who I am, darling." Her voice was low and raspy as if she hadn't spoken for thousands of years. She stood with her left leg crossed in front of her right, like she was preparing to step forward; her arms were bent as she raised her hands towards the sky, her fingers curled inward. Vines of black marred her snow-white skin, crawling down her palms and forearms until disappearing beneath the sleeves of her tattered black cloak. Her long, wispy black hair blew in the wind around her hips. The woman's gaze leveled with Mari's, a slow, feral smile spreading across her lips.

"Morana," Mari whispered. "It can't be. You're supposed to be dead."

Morana cackled. "No one can kill me."

After thousands of years, it was impossible. Mari had to be hallucinating. Morana could not be alive.

"What are you doing here?"

"Taking back what should have been mine," Morana said, raising a hand towards the sky. Out of the ground, dozens of human souls emerged. Besides their translucent shimmer, Mari had never seen a human soul look so real. The clothing style varied from soul to soul, with some wearing outfits Mari had only seen in paintings from centuries before. Without even a command, they were sent into the city to do Morana's bidding, a trail of ice beneath their feet. Thunderous footfall and screams echoed through the street as the souls terrorized Brahn.

"You must leave this place. You are not welcome here," Mari said.

"This is my world. I am welcome everywhere."

Mari raised a hand toward Morana. "Don't make me do this." Mari's arm trembled, and she hoped Morana could not tell. She needed to protect Brahn, and if that meant trying to kill the most powerful mage in history, she would do it.

"Do you think *you*, of all the people who have tried and failed before, could kill me? I have evaded death for thousands of years; your magic is no match for mine."

Mari tightened her hand into a fist and yanked her arm towards her with the intent of lifting Morana's soul from her body. When Mari didn't feel the familiar sensation of a soul flying towards her, she realized Morana still stood there, smiling and unaffected.

"How?" Mari whispered.

When Morana raised her hand, Mari leaped behind the corner of a building, shielding herself from the magic. An icy sensation filled her veins, and Mari felt her heart slow and extremities grow cold. As Mari stood behind the building, the icy feeling dissipated.

Morana cackled louder as thunder boomed overhead. Mari scanned the street, hoping to find a way out of this impossible situation. Taryn and Anya raced towards her.

Anya's furious eyes met Mari's terrified stare, and she pulled Taryn off to the side, out of sight. They hid behind a building nearly forty feet from Mari. Taryn poked her head around the corner, meeting Mari's gaze. Taryn motioned for Mari to come towards them. There were no obstacles in the road, but if Mari wasn't fast enough, Morana could take her soul. With a glance at Morana, Mari ran for it.

Pushing off the wall, she bolted toward Taryn and Anya. Her vision swarmed, and her legs started to give way as she ran across the road. Without a second thought, Mari sent an elk toward Morana, screaming at it to attack. Mari's field of vision lessened until she could barely see Taryn's outstretched hand. Mari tried to reach for it but could barely lift her hand.

"What's wrong?" Anya asked as Mari landed limply on the ground beside Taryn.

"Morana was taking my soul," Mari said, panting. Her vision slowly materialized, though her hands still shook. Anya cursed, and Taryn reached forward, grabbing Mari's hands. "She is alive."

"What?" Taryn and Anya said simultaneously, their eyes wide and mouths open.

"Morana. After all this time," Anya said, shaking her head. "Do you think she was behind the rebel attacks on the palace?"

"I don't know."

Anya paled as she placed a hand over her mouth. She looked like she was going to be sick. Taryn stared at the ground, rocking back and forth on her heels.

"Morana," Taryn whispered. "How is she alive?"

Anya shook her head and swallowed. "Gods, I can't believe this. Are you sure?" Anya turned to Mari.

Mari could barely hear herself think over the screaming in the streets, but she was paralyzed. She couldn't move to help her people. Souls of animals and humans attacked the people of Brahn, and the three strongest women sat on the cobblestone street behind a building, horrified and unable to move.

"Yes," Mari said, starting to emerge from her trance. "It's her. My magic is useless against her. I tried to take her soul, but nothing happened."

Mari peeked around the corner and saw the elk pin Morana against the wall with its antlers. Morana pulled a dagger from her waist and slashed it through the elk's head. It dissipated. Mari cursed; Morana must have a titanium dagger—the only weapon to stop a soul from attacking. Mari reached her hands out and sent a mountain lion and three bucks running toward Morana.

"Well, that's... unsettling," Anya said, peeking around the corner of the building.

"Don't look!" Taryn wrenched Anya backwards. "She could see you. I swear to the Gods, if you die because you did something stupid, I will resurrect you only to kill you again."

"That's a little dramatic." Anya winked.

Mari blanched. This was *not* the time for Anya and Taryn to flirt. "What are we going to do?"

"Is there anything we *can* do? Your magic is useless against hers; plus, she's a life mage. She can heal if we burn her," Taryn said, running a hand through her hair. "Our options are to drive her out of Brahn or run away."

"We can't just leave her to run amuck in the city!" Mari said, indignant.

Mari groaned as Morana fended off the souls with ease. How could she evade four animals like they were mere nuisances? Mari noticed the soul of a boar slam into Morana as she sliced through the last buck, but Mari hadn't sent it. She had never even killed one. Had Hanan returned from Orcian already? Mari glanced around wildly for him but saw nothing except the wraith herself, her cloak billowing in the wind.

"Well, we can't kill her," Anya said. "The Gods are fucking with us. How in the world is she alive? It's been *thousands* of years."

"Is resurrection possible in death magic?" Taryn asked Mari.

"Not to my knowledge." Mari had never heard of such a thing. If resurrection was possible, it was not talked about.

But Mari realized many weren't talked about in her clan. For one, her brother's "murder," and two, no one spoke of Morana. Warnings of the negative effects of killing another with death magic were never spoken about, either. So, if resurrection were possible, anyone who knew about it was keeping it hidden.

Mari stole another glance around the corner to find Morana had disappeared. But had she traveled further into the city or left, returning to where she came?

"She's gone. We must see if she's moved somewhere else in the city. Let's go."

Mari ran beside Taryn and Anya through Brahn's streets, water splashing against their backs. While the waves no longer rushed into homes, the inches of water that flooded the street continued destroying the houses. People were beginning to climb down from their roofs to pull waterlogged items from inside their houses. Some stopped their tasks to yell their thanks to the women, while others barely noticed who raced past them. Mari's heart sank as she watched people empty their homes of their destroyed possessions. She had no idea how long it would take to rebuild the city, but it wouldn't be easy.

But Mari still needed to determine if Morana and Orcian were working together. She didn't know if water mages could do so much damage with their magic, but after facing off with Morana, anything was possible.

A loud cackle reverberated through the streets to the east, and the trio dashed to the sound. Three streets away from the noise, a pile of bodies lay in the street. Fifteen men, women, and children—murdered. Morana was nowhere in sight. Even though Anya held them back, Mari saw the tears pricking the corners of her eyes. It was the first time she had seen Anya show emotion about her clan that wasn't rooted in anger.

A part of Mari wondered if Anya was working with the rebels. Rodrick knew a lot about the palace because of his time as a guard, but there were some things he would not have known that the rebels did, an example being the entry key to the safe room, which only a handful of people had the key to. The only way Rodrick would have gotten his hands on that would be if one of them had given it to him.

Mari reached out and held Anya's shoulder. "We can help those who are still here."

Anya took a deep breath and looked up to the sky. "They didn't deserve this."

"No, they didn't."

The ladies headed back towards the palace, helping to empty houses along the way and to join the prayers for those in mourning. Several small children wanted to play with the legs of Taryn's flowy pants, and she let them if only to bring a smile to their faces for a moment. Mari hugged several crying people who nearly fell into her arms, all asking for her help rebuilding the city. Illan and the council would hate for Mari to make promises she didn't know she could keep, but promised to do everything she could to find a way to help.

Upon returning to the palace, Taryn and Anya made a beeline for the medical wing to be with Taryn's family. Wanting to give them space, Mari went on a quest to find food and Illan. In the kitchens, she found both. Illan stood against the edge of the counter, sipping a bowl of steaming stew.

"How bad is the damage in the city?" asked Illan. "I could see only some of it. Ren instructed me to stay at the palace in case anyone tried to attack. Now that I have my magic back, I am needed again."

"The damage is immense, Illan," Mari said, sighing. "So many homes have been destroyed, and people have nowhere to go."

"Oh, that's—"

"Morana is alive," Mari blurted. "I spoke with her. I tried to kill her. My magic was *useless*."

"What?" Illan nearly dropped his bowl of stew.

"She's *alive*, Illan. She is supposed to be dead. Can life mages live that long?"

"They have extended lives, but I've *never* heard of anyone living that long."

"I don't understand. This should be impossible!"

"We didn't think Zahir was a dual mage, Mari. Anything is possible now."

"How are we supposed to fight her? If she has been alive this long, we'll be useless. She's had *millennia* to train. There is no way we can win against her, and we still don't know if the city flooding was Morana or Orcian or both."

"We have to take this one step at a time."

"How can we? The city is flooded, and my brother is in Orcian, probably *dead*. We don't know if the flooding and Morana's attack are connected or if it was just a coincidence. How can we? We have possibly two *huge* threats knocking at our door. We can't pick and choose which threats we respond to."

"You're right. But first, tell me about Morana."

Mari recounted the entire exchange and every detail she could remember about Morana. Shivers trickled down her spine as she told Illan about how her magic had done nothing to slow Morana's attacks. Morana's smirk as she sliced through the animals with her titanium blade sent chills up Mari's arms; she felt like she was breathing underwater, her breathing quickening.

"She vanished. Taryn, Anya, and I scoured the city but found no trace of her. It was almost as if she vanished out of thin air." Mari leaned against the countertop, her hip barely supporting her as she finished the story.

"We must meet with the council immediately."

"Can I bathe first? I can't face the council looking like this." Mari glanced at her clothes, which were completely soaked through.

"Don't bother," Illan said as he marched towards the door. "They'll know for sure you were down in the battle if you look like that."

Chapter Ten

Zahir

Markus and Zahir sat in The Quiet Berry, drinking in silence despite the rowdy bar clamoring on behind them. Zahir took a few sips of his ale, his stomach in knots. He'd barely been able to eat or sleep since finding out about his birth mother. Nothing could calm him—not writing to Mari, fighting with Markus, or meditating with Pryn. His mind spiraled into the abyss with no bottom in sight.

The musty smell of body odor and ale permeated every space in the bar. Sweaty bodies crammed in beside him and Markus as they ordered drinks between rounds of cards. Blair worked at the bar again tonight, her curly red hair bouncing atop her head as she filled glasses of ale on repeat.

Once Zahir had successfully drunk half of his ale and forced himself to eat a bowl of soup, he was ready to tell Markus... something. At first, he stared at Markus's waiting expression, wondering what to say. If he spoke about his birth mother, someone in the tavern might overhear.

"How can I become a better life mage?" Zahir asked, finishing his ale in one long sip.

Markus shrugged. "You could take your training a little more seriously."

Zahir was taken aback. He'd been training effortlessly to master his magic, working every day for nine damn moon cycles so he could get back to his wife and people. Markus's accusation stung. Zahir thought he'd been working harder at this than anything else in his life.

"I'm trying," Zahir said, signaling for another round of ale.

"No, you're not. You don't pay attention in lessons; your instructors tell me you always look like you're lost in thought, and if you fail on your first attempt, you are reluctant to try again."

Zahir was stunned into silence. No one had ever been so blunt with him. But as he sat and absorbed Markus' words, Zahir realized he was right. He didn't take his lessons as seriously as he should, and when he did fail, he only anticipated he would again. Zahir was reluctant to try after failing.

"You aren't wrong."

"I'm usually not." Markus winked.

"Okay. How can I be more present during lessons?"

As Zahir and Markus discussed his lack of attention, Zahir realized he could never pay close attention to anything. In all his lessons throughout his life, it had been hard for him to grasp when inundated with information. He sometimes had trouble focusing on tasks unless he was extremely invested in them.

When he was absorbed in something, he'd work a whole day on it, forgetting to take breaks or eat.

"You should also probably meet your birth mother," Markus said.

"What? Why?"

"Life magic is strongest when your connection to your soul is at its peak. For example, during your alignment sessions, you were able to speak with your father. It happens when your physical and spiritual self are aligned."

"What does any of that have to do with meeting her?"

"You have trauma surrounding your birth mother and the nature of your life magic. You found out about your magic in your adult life, which couldn't have been easy, but you also discovered that you had another parent who abandoned you in Brahn."

"She *did* abandon me," Zahir said shortly.

Markus lifted his eyebrows as if to say *this is what I mean.* "Coping with trauma is a huge part of life magic. Your spiritual and physical self must be in tandem. Without that, you'll never be able to master it."

"So, you have no trauma then? It feels like I'll never be able to work through all the trauma I have."

Markus shifted in his seat and peered down at the bar. "We all have it, Zahir. I found my mother's dead body in our house when I was seven. She killed herself."

"Fuck, I'm sorry, Markus."

"Thank you." Markus downed the rest of his ale. "It took a *long* time for me to resolve that."

"How did you? Eventually?"

"Through meditation, forgiveness, and alignment sessions. The more you try *not* to think about it, the harder it will be to get through it."

"I don't know if I'm ready to meet my birth mother."

"You might never be ready, and if you don't want to, that's okay. But you have a lot of thinking to do about the dynamic of your family," said Markus, signaling to the bartender for another drink. "I don't mean to be blunt, but you're returning to a mother who kept this secret from you your whole life."

"I know. I need time—and space." Zahir took a long, slow breath. "Aside from working through my trauma, what else can I do to become a better life mage?"

Markus clapped Zahir on the shoulder with one of his large hands. "You can also practice magic with me. I'm not opposed to some minor injuries if it helps you learn."

"I'm not going to injure you just to heal you," Zahir said, shaking his head. "That is ludicrous."

Markus quickly whipped out a knife from his pocket and slid it lightly across his hand until small dots of bright red blood bubbled to the surface. "Heal me."

Zahir stared at Markus's hand, stunned. He couldn't believe that Markus would injure himself so Zahir could practice his magic. Gods, Zahir could barely heal himself in lessons. Zahir looked around the bar to see who noticed Markus' action, but in the rowdy bar full of gambling patrons, people paid Zahir and Markus no mind.

Zahir grabbed Markus's hand between his and focused on the injury. He took long, measured breaths and imagined the cut healing until the skin appeared as it had before the injury. He pictured the green life magic flowing through his veins, away from his heart, into his hands, and into Markus' flesh to heal the wound.

"I can't do this," Zahir said, shaking his head.

"You can. Just keep picturing what healing it would look like," Markus said.

As Zahir refocused on Markus's hand, he slowly closed his eyes. His heart pounded in his chest like a heavy drum; the rushing of his blood was loud in his ears and sweat prickled along the back of his neck. The noise of the tavern quietened until he pictured only Markus's hand sealing without a trace of any injury.

A bright green light filled Zahir's vision, and he strained to keep his eyes closed, but as fast as it appeared, it was gone. And suddenly, Zahir felt exhausted. It took every ounce of energy for him to open his eyes again. Peering down at Markus's hand, Zahir saw the cut was completely healed. If he didn't know better, he would have never known there had been a cut to begin with.

"I did it," Zahir said, breathless.

"How do you feel?" Markus asked, removing his hand from Zahir's.

"Like I'm about to pass out," Zahir said with a breathy laugh.

Zahir swayed when he stood, bracing himself against the bar. Markus rushed forward and grabbed Zahir's arm to keep him from toppling. Wrapping one arm around Zahir's waist, Markus half-dragged, half-carried Zahir back to their home. Along the way, Zahir mumbled about when he first used his magic to heal Mari and how he'd never felt *this* exhausted, but the stakes were much higher, and he didn't have to focus as much. He hoped that the magic wouldn't always exhaust this much of his energy.

Markus plopped Zahir in his bed, which had never felt more comfortable. Before he could even readjust, he was asleep.

That night, Zahir had wild, incoherent dreams, where he was trying to save someone but couldn't reach them. He watched an entire city drown. He sat with an animal in his lap, petting its soft fur. He held Mari in his arms back in their bed in Brahn; she felt so real that he almost thought she was there.

Zahir awoke with a start at a loud bang from inside the house. He dragged himself out of bed despite the pounding headache and ran as fast as he could. Zahir readied a ball of fire in his hand as he rounded the corner into the kitchen, but instead of an intruder, Markus and Pryn stood, cooking a meal together.

"Welcome back to the land of the living," Markus said, turning. Eyes wide, he looked at the fire in Zahir's hand. "And I thought we made progress on our friendship the other night."

Zahir quickly extinguished the flame and rubbed his eyes. "What time is it?"

"Nearly dusk," Pryn said, picking up a knife from the countertop.

"Oh, I wasn't asleep that long then," Zahir said.

Pryn and Markus exchanged a look before Markus spoke again. "You've been asleep for over a day, Zahir."

Zahir blanched. "What?"

"You completely depleted yourself," said Pryn. "I came here to give you some energy healing. Markus said you were completely wiped out after you healed that minor scrape on his hand."

"I... Thank you, Pryn. Is it normal to be that exhausted?"

"Normal? No. But, you must remember nothing is normal about you. You're a dual mage. None of us know what is normal for you to feel. Children tend to be tired after using their magic when they're young, but they will sleep for eight hours or so, not a day and a half. We aren't sure what your recovery time looks like," Pryn explained.

Zahir ran a hand down his face. "When I healed Mari from substantial injuries, I didn't feel this level of exhaustion."

"Had you ever used your magic before then?" Markus asked, stirring a pot on the fire.

Zahir was about to say no but stopped himself. He hadn't *intentionally* used his life magic before coming to Lovíth, but that didn't mean he'd never used it. Zahir thought back to his injuries, specifically his broken nose after the rebels invaded the palace the night his father died. Mari had been healing for nearly a fortnight before the pain had gone from her throat injury, while Zahir's bruising and swelling were significantly better after a day. As a kid, he never seemed to have scrapes despite constantly falling out of trees.

"Not intentionally, but yes." He relayed to Markus and Pryn what he had realized. "Even when I healed Mari, it wasn't intentional."

Pryn nodded and put down the knife. "Your magic will work by itself if you sustain any injuries, especially minor ones. It sounds like that's what was happening. With Mari... it sounds like your love for her triggered your magic. Love and fear are strong emotions. It's much easier to harness your abilities when you have a surge of emotions and adrenaline, which could also be why you were not as exhausted."

"So, how do I get to the point where I can use my magic without exhaustion?" Zahir asked, nodding slowly to absorb all the new information.

"You must practice. It gets easier," Markus said before tasting the food. He spluttered, spitting it out in the sink. "That's disgusting. Let's go out for dinner tonight."

Zahir let Markus and Pryn go to dinner without him, still drowsy from sleeping all day. He snacked on some almonds as he paced the kitchen, his mind racing with thoughts of his birth mother. His shuffling footsteps were the only sound as he spiraled down a dangerous path.

Zahir needed to meet his birth mother, but the thought didn't sit right with him. *Maura* was his mother, and meeting Zena introduced a new layer to his family dynamic that made his skin crawl. This woman had given birth to the first dual mage in millennia—the future king of Brahn—and then returned home without so much as a note. She forced him into a life of royalty, where he had no choice in his future. He was destined to be the king.

While positive things had come from his destiny, like marrying Mari, he was furious with Zena for leaving him like that.

Zahir had a rocky relationship with his father on a good day; on bad days... they could barely be in the same room without screaming at each other, so knowing his birth mother hadn't even left a note was perplexing. Wouldn't she want him to know where he came from? Did she know that his parents would keep the true story of his heritage from him for most of his life? If she didn't know... would she have left?

Zahir had so many burning questions. Did she have a partner here in Lovíth? Did she leave because she thought he would have a better quality of life in Brahn? Or was it because she didn't want to raise someone who could destroy the world?

"Why did you leave?" Zahir asked into the void.

Zahir knew he was never going to be able to process this trauma on his own. And since his father was dead, and his mother was back in Brahn, it left him one option. Zahir needed to meet with Lydia and find out who his birth mother was.

Chapter Eleven

Mari

"Morana is alive, and—" Mari couldn't finish her sentence as the council room exploded with voices.

"We need to build a fortress!" Grimes slammed their hand on the table.

Isla shook her head. "We can't just build a stronghold."

"Our focus should be on rebuilding," Mari said, but no one seemed to hear her. The city was decimated. Businesses and homes were destroyed; their citizens had lost their livelihoods and safety. Building a stronghold would be a misguided call; people needed to rebuild their homes.

"We need to protect the people," Grimes said, shaking a hand at Isla.

"Do you know how long it would take to build a wall around the city? And what do we do until then?" Isla asked. "Do we just let people go on living like they are now?"

"How do we protect the citizens?" asked Grimes.

Mari took a deep breath and listened to the advisors, trying to devise a plan. Aside from the time required to secure the city with a fortress, the money could be better utilized to help rebuild destroyed homes and businesses. If the goal was to protect Brahn, they needed to start in the streets, as the people wouldn't feel safe until they had somewhere dry to sleep. Nearly every home was flooded and damaged beyond repair, so giving the people a place to live in the interim while the city was rebuilt was the first step. If something like this had happened in Yu'güe, the whole clan would have banded together to first resolve the damage and *then* hunt the threat. But, as Mari realized time and time again, Brahn was *not* Yu'güe.

Having finally had enough, Mari stood and slammed her palms on the table. Silence fell across the room immediately. "What are we going to do to rebuild the city?"

"But Morana—" said Grimes.

Mari cut Grimes off. "Our people are more important. Their *livelihoods* are more important. Yes, we must protect them, but helping provide their basic needs *is* protecting them."

"There is a threat on their lives with Morana out there," said Isla.

"Is there not a threat to their lives if they have no roof to sleep under? If they have no food or income because their business was destroyed, and their city is underwater?"

For the first time, no one responded. Illan offered Mari a small smile, and she knew he was proud. Lips pursed, Grimes leaned back in their chair, folding their arms over their chest. Isla winked subtly at Mari.

"So, I ask again, will we rebuild Brahn?"

"Building shelters is an option, although I'm not sure where we can set those up, considering the entire city is underwater," Isla said, scratching her head.

"Is there any option of setting them up closer to the mountains?"

"That's quite far from the city. Asking our people to trek out there when there's a real threat to their homes... I don't know if that would work," said Grimes.

"I have to, unfortunately, agree with Grimes," said Illan. "It's a hike, especially for people with small children."

"Where could we set up shelters then? The only high elevation in Brahn is the palace, and we can't invite the whole clan past our doors," Mari said. As much as she would love to offer everyone a place near the palace, she knew it wasn't safe. After the rebels had penetrated the walls twice, there was no way she could bring hundreds into the palace, even for a few nights.

"Our only option is the mountains or outside the city limits. We can offer transportation or a closer location for people with mobility issues or small children." Illan pointed out. A few of the advisors muttered at his suggestion, with Isla nodding her agreement, and Grimes chewing their bottom lip.

Mari appreciated that Illan was always looking for ways to support her ideas. "That's a great idea, Illan," she said. "We will set up shelters near the mountains until we can rebuild. We need to figure out a way to dry the city."

"Do we know if Orcian had a hand in flooding us?" Isla asked.

Mari shook her head. "I heard two things—one person believed it was intentionally done by Orcian, and the other being that a dam broke, and water rushed in."

"The dam to the north is guarded by Orcian. It is their responsibility to maintain it," Illan said. "If that's the one, they could have had a hand in breaking it."

Mari took a calming breath to keep her mind from worrying about Hanan. "We will know more when our allies return from Orcian."

"If Orcian wasn't behind the attack, we might be able to ask them to help us dry the city," Isla said with a shrug.

"Above all else, I hope Orcian played no part in these attacks."

It was like Mari manifested it because the second the words were out of her mouth, Hanan, Raf, Reina, Kiernan, and a woman Mari had never seen before were ushered into the council room. Mari jumped from her seat. Giving no thought to appearances, she rushed to her brother and hugged him. The tension evaporated from Mari as she embraced Hanan, thankful she hadn't sent him to die. Hanan melted into Mari's embrace, who was sure he was just as relieved to be reunited.

"Why is the city wet?" Hanan asked as he released Mari.

"It was flooded. We heard that a dam broke," Mari explained, eyes glancing at the stranger. "Hello, I'm Queen Mari. I don't believe we've met."

The woman's bright blue eyes brightened as she smiled. "Pleasure. I am Princess Seraphina of Orcian. I was *almost* your sister."

Mari choked out a strangled laugh, and from the corner of her eye, she spotted a few advisors exchanging concerned glances.

"The pleasure is all mine," Mari said. "Welcome to Brahn!"

"We brought Seraphina back because Orcian has been having trouble with rebels, too," Hanan said. "Can we sit?"

Mari motioned for five more chairs to be brought around the table. As her friends and allies sat, Mari asked about their journey.

"When we got there, King Edward nearly had us killed as he thought we were rebels, and then when I told him who I was..." Hanan trailed off.

"I am fairly certain that only made things worse," Seraphina said, rolling her eyes. "He was *furious* with your father. Perán had told my father Hanan had died, so this was quite a shock to him. I had kept the truth to myself all these years."

"We drank wine and broke bread once the swords were lowered," Hanan explained. "Orcian is *beautiful*, Mari. You must go under a waterfall in a boat to get into their city. It's made of all these canals, and they just walk on water."

Mari's heart throbbed as Hanan spoke of Orcian's beauty. An early memory with Zahir flooded her mind, where they sat under one of the trees in the garden, peering out upon the lake. There, Zahir had told her about Orcian and its waterfalls and how the water mages stopped the water from falling to get in and out of the city. Zahir spoke of the city's beauty, about how every building was the blue-green hue of sea glass. Listening to Hanan's descriptions and remembering Zahir's, Mari hoped she could visit Orcian one day.

"I can't wait to hear all about it, Hanan. But, please, tell me more about the rebels in Orcian first."

"Men," Seraphina said. "We spoke of rebels as we, too, have had attacks on our palace. Violent insurgents who want to overthrow us. We were nearly about to write to King Zahir when Hanan knocked on our door."

"I have to ask," Mari said tentatively. "Do you know about Zahir's status?"

"As a dual mage?" Seraphina said, lifting an eyebrow. "Of course. News travels fast between our clans, but his birth is no matter. If he is fit to rule, then we will continue doing business with Brahn."

Mari gave a sigh of relief. "Do you know what happened with this dam?"

Seraphina nodded gravely. "There was an attack on it this morning. We sent guards to protect it once the frequency of the rebel attacks increased. We didn't want something like this to happen. But the guards were slaughtered, and the rebels destroyed the dam. I'm sorry that Brahn felt the effects of it."

Fear washed over Mari as she realized how widespread the attacks were. Brahn wasn't the only clan being targeted, and she worried that Lovíth would soon be in danger, too. Knowing that Morana was alive, Mari wondered if it was all part of one big orchestrated scheme. But Mari didn't know how forthcoming Seraphina was, so she decided to keep Morana's resurgence close to her chest for the time being.

"It's not your fault. I'm sorry to hear that you are facing similar struggles."

"I brought a dozen soldiers with me to help repair Brahn. If you would like our assistance drying out and rebuilding, we are happy to offer it."

"We would greatly appreciate the help." Mari motioned to the guards toward the back of the room. "Please find Princess Anya and Taryn so they can show Princess Seraphina and her allies the damage in the city."

"You are not coming?" asked Seraphina.

"I will be there shortly. There are a few things I need to discuss with my council, but I will come down to the city afterward. Thank you again for your help."

"Of course," Seraphina said as she stood and followed the guards out of the room.

"Thank you," Mari said to Hanan. "You did an incredible job."

Hanan leaned back in his chair. "I know."

Mari stood to address the council as the doors closed behind Seraphina. "These are the allies I was telling you about. They allied with Orcian and brought us assistance. If anyone thinks we cannot trust them, speak now." The resounding silence was the confirmation Mari needed. "I need to discuss extremely sensitive information. Can I count on your discretion?"

"Of course," Raf, Hanan, and Reina agreed. Kiernan nodded, too.

"It is clear the rebels have not been thwarted, but we now have an even bigger threat in Brahn. Morana is alive."

Reina lurched forward, her jaw dropping open. Raf reached for Hanan's hand, who pulled his lover's arm into his chest. Kiernan's face drained of all color as his eyes widened.

"That's impossible," Reina whispered.

"I assure you it is very possible," Mari said. "I faced her in the very streets of Brahn. She lives, and she has murderous intent. I would like to ask for assistance from the four of you. I need a task force to assist me in tracking and defeating Morana before she destroys Brahn."

"What would be required of us?" Hanan asked, folding his hands along the table's edge.

"Join us on a hunt, where we will explore the surrounding areas and attempt to track her down. Should we encounter rebels, we will deal with them accordingly. If we see Morana, we will retreat as fast as possible. We will not take her on without a plan of action," said Illan plainly.

Reina folded her arms across her chest. "Do we have a choice?"

"You always have a choice, Reina." Mari nodded at her. Reina would have reservations, especially because of how the palace treated her after Rodrick's death—holding Reina in the palace and questioning her for hours until she could go home. "I would not blame any of you if you refuse."

"I need time to think." Reina pushed her chair back to stand. "I will let you know in a few days."

As the door shut behind Reina, Hanan stood and nodded. "I will help."

"Illan will take care of all my duties here, and I will go as well," said Mari, looking at her friends sitting across the table from her. "What say you to this mission?"

"I will assist the crown," Raf stood and gave Mari a terse nod. Hanan grabbed Raf's hand, peering at him with glowing pride.

"You can count on me, too," said Kiernan, standing slowly and looking at his friends.

"You cannot go," Grimes said to Mari. "It is far too dangerous for you to go on this mission."

"Grimes," Mari said, as level as she could. "I am one of the only people who has seen Morana. She used death magic against me; I can resist her attacks."

"It isn't safe for you to be outside the palace walls with Morana running amuck."

"We will bring Ren and several other soldiers. We will have shifts during the night to ensure we are not ambushed," Mari said, trying to convince the council. "We could send Princess Anya and Taryn in place of me, but they need to be here with Taryn's family, who've experienced great loss. They will not be focused on the mission but will worry about their loved ones."

"If we allow you to go, we have no way of knowing if something has happened to you," said Isla.

"We can put a time on the mission. If we are not back within a certain number of days, we can assume I have been killed."

"We can't allow this," Isla said.

"I refuse to let my allies go on this mission without me. I am the *queen*. I will make decisions regarding my safety. I will be safe with several guards. If you want to stop me, you're going to have to kill me," Mari said with finality.

Mari glanced at Hanan and Raf and tried to convey her thanks with a satisfied nod. Now that it was decided, planning their mission would be a lengthy task. Mari requested Ren be brought to the room to help her lead the mission.

"Now, the next order of business is whether or not we should tell Orcian about Morana," said Mari.

"We obviously should," said Hanan. "If we know who is knocking at their door, we should tell them."

Grimes glared at Hanan for speaking in a meeting he shouldn't even be attending. Hanan opened his mouth to speak, but Mari stopped him with a raised hand and turned to Grimes.

"You will *not* disrespect my brother. He secured an alliance with Orcian; he brought back others to help rebuild the city. What have *you* done today other than contradict me?"

Grimes lowered his gaze and mumbled an apology while Hanan bit his lip, hiding a smile.

"How can we be sure Orcian isn't working with Morana, and they destroyed the dam together?" Isla asked.

Mari hadn't thought of that. Zahir had told Mari that trade between Orcian and Brahn had never halted. They had traded for the last several millennia, but there was no conflict between clans since Morana, so their alliance wasn't political. Mari didn't know anything about Orcian, but Seraphina had seemed genuine. Then again, she didn't know her.

"That is something we should consider," said Mari.

"Seraphina isn't working with Morana," Hanan said. "She is too kind to do something like that."

"Hanan," Mari said, raising her hand. "You don't really know her."

"We should wait to tell them of Morana until we have more information about the dam," said Grimes. "If it's true they had nothing to do with it, then we can revisit the idea of telling them."

"Then it's settled," said Mari. "We will not tell Orcian about Morana, but we will work with them to dry the city."

Mari ended the council meeting before any more opinions about her role in the search party could be voiced. She needed to go. Morana had bested her once, and Mari was determined not to let it happen again.

As Ren led Mari into the city, she watched in amazement as Seraphina and several other water mages pushed waves of water through the city and into the river. Waves higher than the tallest buildings journeyed through the city, and as Mari followed behind the water mages, the road beneath her became visible once again. Once the inches of water covering the ground were back in the river, the water mages began to pull water from the drenched buildings instead.

Seraphina's outstretched hands moved in graceful clockwise circles as water drained from the soaked furniture and walls; as she worked, her body became consumed by a helix of water as she passed it to another mage who would direct it out of the city. The way that water mages could push and pull the water between each other was unlike anything Mari had ever seen. She had never seen any fire mages pass flames between them. However, the water mages passed water between them like it was nothing.

Taryn and Anya led three water mages to the other side of Brahn, which had been hit the hardest compared to the other neighborhoods. Mari marked the houses that had been dried by Seraphina and her crew with a painted white X on each door. Drying the city would be a monumental task and would need to take place over several days. While Mari couldn't help with that, she could work on setting up the shelters. The people in the streets thanked her and Seraphina for their help with tear-filled eyes as Mari informed them that shelters would be set up within the next few hours so they would have somewhere warm to sleep.

While their Orcian allies worked, Mari and several of Ren's soldiers collected tents, bedrolls, pillows, and blankets to set up a makeshift camp. They rode out to the base of the mountains and began pitching tents. Mari hoped a more permanent structure could be built within the next few days or weeks, but for now, giving the people somewhere dry to sleep was better than nothing. Two soldiers set up campfires and began boiling warm batches of soups.

As the group began to finish up, Mari and Ren rode back into the city to bring as many people as possible to the camp. Those who didn't want to wait were escorted on foot by guards, but transportation was provided for those who couldn't. Wagons and carriages full of people drove out towards it, and even as the sun set, people still waited for their rides to the mountains.

When the moon rose high in the sky, Brahn was emptied of people. It was strange to see the city devoid of any activity, the only sounds being that of crickets and water moving through the streets. Mari found Seraphina and her soldiers still hard at work.

"Thank you for everything," Mari said to Seraphina, who passed another collection of water to the mage beside her.

"We're glad to be assisting," she said.

"It's getting late; you all must be tired. Our cook has made a meal, and we have set up rooms in our palace for you all."

Seraphina wiped the sweat from her brow. "Thank you. That sounds lovely."

By the time Mari brought Seraphina back to the palace, they had dried a quarter of the houses in the city. Without their help, Brahn would have been in a much worse state. It would have taken months to rebuild. Seraphina had made a huge difference by offering her help, and Mari was glad to have made alliances with the Orcian Princess.

Once Seraphina was comfortable in one of the many lavish spare bedrooms, Mari allowed herself a moment of respite. Sitting on the balcony, Mari leaned back in her chair and tilted her head to the starry sky. As Mari breathed in the fresh outdoor air, she could have sworn she saw the outline of the Ever-Burning Candle, if only for a moment.

CHAPTER TWELVE

MARI

Mari twirled the pen as she thought about what to write to Zahir. Crumpled pieces of parchment littered the floor, the failed beginnings of letters. There appeared to be no good way to tell Zahir to meet Zena.

My love,
Darling,
Zahir,
Fuck
My dearest Zahir
Just knock on the door and tell her that you are Zahir, her son.

Finally, after what must have been her fifteenth attempt, Mari had an idea of what to say.

My love,

You should meet your birth mother. In the worst scenario, she will turn you away, but at best, she may wish to have a relationship with you. You're very charming; I'm sure you can come up with something that won't scare her off. Knock on the door, ask if she is Zena, and then tell her the truth. There is nothing better than honesty. It will be terrifying, and I wish I could be there with you. I promise you that you can do this.

I know that you must be struggling. I hope that meeting your birth mother will close that stressful chapter in your life. Even if she turns you away, there won't be this big unknown weighing on your chest every day. You'll have an answer, even if it's not the one you want.

What do you want out of this meeting? Do you want to have a relationship with her? Or do you just want to see if she is alive? What if she invites you in and wants to spend quality time with you? Would you be okay with that?

I think you need to decide if you want to have a relationship with her or not, so you don't go into this meeting blind. Having a plan is always better.

Zahir, before you read this next bit of information, you must promise me that you will stay in Lovíth. We are okay. We are all safe. Morana is alive. After thousands of years, she walks this world again. I faced her in the streets.

Brahn flooded. The rebels destroyed a dam, and it decimated Brahn and plunged the city underwater. But Orcian came to help us after Hanan traveled to Orcian to see if they had the same rebel problem. He brought Princess Seraphina back with him, and she and her allies are drying out the city with their magic. It's incredible. They offered their aid without a second thought.

We have set up a camp for our people at the base of the mountains. It's nothing special, but we have given them a dry place to sleep for the time being until we can rebuild. Our family is safe. No one has been harmed.

I wish we were together. I wish you were here, or I there. I would give anything to be with you tonight.

Come home soon,

Mari

When Mari put the pen down, she felt a sudden stabbing pain in her abdomen. Nausea rolled in her stomach as she rushed into the bathroom, but she got there just in time. Her bleeding had started. Mari cleaned herself up and folded a cotton rag to catch the blood rushing from her. As she clutched her abdomen, white-hot pain shot through her core while she stood before the mirror, tears streaming down her face. Mari ducked and rushed to her dressing rooms, changing into loose black pants and a tunic before crawling into bed and pulling the covers over her head.

Mari hadn't bled since arriving in Brahn, which wasn't abnormal for her. She never understood why people called it a *cycle*. It never came at the same time. She was lucky if it came every three moon cycles. How could anyone stand to have it more often than that? The pain in her abdomen was so excruciating that she usually spent three days sick in bed, where it felt like she was being stabbed in the stomach by the dullest of swords.

Growing up, Mari had been told to stop being lazy during her bleeding. No one else was in as much pain as she. Mari's mother never told her it would hurt. So, she thought she just had a low pain tolerance. She would vomit over her floor and be forced to clean it up, with no one seeming to care about her agony.

A sharp knock came at the door, and Mari meekly ushered the person in. She sat up in bed and leaned against the wall despite the waves of nausea in her stomach. Ren appeared in the doorway, shutting the door too loudly for Mari's liking.

"Mari, we need to get started on—" Ren stopped. "Are you all right?"

"Fine," Mari panted.

"You don't look fine. Are you ill? Should I get Amí?"

"I don't think Amí can do anything for me," Mari said. Her breaths were shallow, and she could feel her heart slamming in her chest.

"I'm going to get her." Ren exited the room, leaving Mari alone once more.

Mari lay back in bed and closed her eyes, allowing the tears to come. Back in Yu'güe, she would wet a rag with near-boiling water and lay it across her stomach to help her fall asleep, but once it cooled off, she was again rocked by the murderous pain in her abdomen. On a few occasions, she had fainted on her way to the bathroom, where her mother had found her unconscious in the hallway of their home.

Amí and Ren rushed back into the room, closing the door lightly behind them. Their footsteps grew louder as they approached, but Mari had long since closed her eyes to stop herself from vomiting.

"You said she was sitting up. She is lying down," Amí said, her tone disapproving.

"She was sitting up when I got here," Ren protested. "Mari, are you okay?"

"I just need a nap," Mari mumbled.

Amí put her hand on Mari's forehead. "You aren't warm. What's wrong with you?"

"It's my bleeding," Mari said. "I get like this."

The silence that followed was deafening. "You are in this state every month with your bleeding?"

"No. I haven't gotten it since I came to Brahn."

"Could you have been with child?" Amí asked with a hint of sadness.

"Definitely not. This is not abnormal for me." Mari proceeded to tell Amí and Ren how she regularly skipped bleeding. Then she told them about the vomiting and fainting, about how she wanted to die every time it came.

"This... this is not normal, Mari. You shouldn't be in this kind of pain," Ren said, concern laced in their words. "Whenever my wife gets her bleeding, she has a little pain for a couple of hours, but usually a cup of ginger tea helps."

"Well, this is how I always feel. I must have a low pain tolerance."

"A low threshold for pain wouldn't reduce you to a pile of mush, Mari," Amí chided. "Why did you never tell me about this?"

"Like I said, I haven't gotten it since coming here," Mari groaned. "Can you let me sleep, please?"

Amí clucked her tongue. "This will not do. I will return."

Mari could hear Amí's heels click on the wooden floorboards as she left the room. Mari still hadn't opened her eyes, but she felt the bed shift beside her, where Zahir would have laid. Ren put a hand on Mari's shoulder.

"I'm going to stay with you until you feel better. I'll have my second-in-command take the lead today. She is more than capable. I'll send word to her once Amí returns," said Ren, rubbing circles on Mari's back.

"Please don't do that," Mari said. She curled into a ball and drew her knees to her chest. "The rubbing, I mean. It's making me sick."

Ren took their hand off Mari. "Sorry. Can I do anything for you?"

"Not unless you can rip my abdomen out and keep me from ever bleeding again," Mari said.

"If only I could. I'd do it for my wife, too. It's torturous not being able to touch and comfort her for a week; it makes her nauseous just like it makes you," Ren said with a laugh. "Don't get me wrong, I love to snuggle, and the sex is *great* after, but it sucks to not be able to touch her."

Mari couldn't help but laugh. "I am so glad we are friends, Ren."

When Amí entered the room again, she rolled in a cart. The wheels squeaked like a knife forcing into Mari's skull. Mari opened her eyes briefly to see Amí stop beside her with a cart of bottles.

"Sit up," Amí commanded. Ren helped Mari sit up, piling pillows behind her back to make it comfortable. "Drink this."

Mari was handed a cup of tea. "I don't know if I can. I feel like I'm going to throw up any second." As if to prove it, Mari gagged.

"Drink. If you can't keep it down, we will figure something else out."

Mari sipped the piping-hot liquid as ginger tea flooded her mouth and ignited her taste buds. At first, the sharpness of the ginger heightened her nausea so much so Mari didn't wish to finish it, but Amí's wrath was undoubtedly worse, and she proved Amí right as she sipped the tea, and her nausea lessened. Mari's head spun with the caffeine, but her stomach no longer rolled in waves. Once she finished it, Amí handed Mari a tincture of a light pink color. She told her it was for the pain.

Mari drank the mixture in one sip and coughed violently. "What is that? It tastes *disgusting*."

"It may taste horrible, but it works miracles."

Amí was right yet again; it worked wonders on the pain. While the pain was still unbearable, it didn't make Mari want to beg for death. Mari stood to go to the bathroom and nearly fainted if not for Ren catching her.

Ren talked about everything to distract Mari. They spoke of their wife, Alex, and how they met. Ren had bumped into Alex and scolded her to 'watch where she was going' before realizing that Alex was the most beautiful woman they had ever seen. They offered to buy Alex dinner as an apology, and the rest was history. While the pain didn't go away, Mari could at least hold a conversation; she laughed, imagining the look on Ren's face upon falling in love with their wife's beauty.

As the friends talked, the pain increased in severity. Ren passed her another tincture Amí had left, who had instructed Mari take them every few hours. Mari gulped down the mixture before the pain grew to be excruciating.

"Are you feeling up to talking about Morana?" asked Ren once the second painkiller had kicked in.

"Not really, but now is as good a time as any. I'm going to feel like this for a few days. There is no point in putting it off that long," said Mari, adjusting her position so she was lying down and peering up at Ren. Mari had never noticed how blue Ren's eyes were until now; they looked like the sea Mari had crossed from Yu'güe to Brahn. Up close, Mari noticed details she had never seen before, like a couple of freckles dotting their cheeks.

"I know we discussed a preliminary plan for tracking her down with the council, but I feel uneasy about it. I think we need to do something differently," Ren said.

"Okay, what do you think we should do instead?" Mari asked. Their plan was simple. They would scope out potential hiding spots based on the latest intel about the rebels.

"We are trying to find a pin in the forest. If we don't have a plan, it will be impossible to track Morana down. What if we brought in a tracker?" Ren said. "Illan and I spoke earlier, and he said he knows somebody."

"You talked to Illan already?" Mari was a little hurt. It seemed like everyone seemed to rely on Illan more than their queen. While Illan was knowledgeable, she was the governing body while Zahir was gone. He had no real standing. He was only invited into the council room while Zahir learned to take over for his father. Illan provided a mentorship Zahir and now Mari needed. But since Zahir had left for Lovíth, Illan had undermined Mari's authority several times, and it was beginning to get on her nerves.

"He stopped by my office when I was working and told me he didn't like the council's plan. We have very little information, and using what we knew about them from nine moon cycles ago seems like a waste of time."

Mari nodded. "Okay, we can explore the idea of using a tracker."

"It does mean involving someone outside the palace in our operations."

"Ren, we already have Hanan, Kiernan, and Raf. One more person won't make a difference," said Mari. Reina had not yet given Mari an answer, though she didn't blame her. If Mari were in Reina's position, she probably would have refused to help. "Tell me more about this tracker."

Ren launched into details about Kane, a tracker Illan had known from a young age and had been one of Illan's guards. After he retired from being a soldier, he became a tracker, hunting people who owed the crown a debt. He found every single person he was asked to, sometimes within a day or two of receiving his assignment.

He wanted to pull Kane into the mission because there was no one with more experience, and after the methods discussed in the meeting, Illan thought it would be a waste of time. Now she'd heard Ren's rendition of Illan's concerns, Mari couldn't help but agree. Truthfully, she knew nothing about tracking the most infamous person to exist.

"Has Illan reached out to Kane yet?" Mari asked.

"No, he wanted me to talk to you first and ensure we are all in agreement," said Ren.

Mari thought about it for a minute. "I think it's a good idea. Hanan and I are skilled in tracking, but I'm sure there are nuances to tracking people as opposed to animals. Which of your soldiers are you bringing with us for protection?"

"I have a few in mind. Do you have any preferences?"

Mari shook her head. "It is completely up to you. I trust you."

Ren nodded. "I plan to bring my three strongest fighters. All are fire mages and can disembowel a man in two slashes of a dagger."

"Sounds great. I need a few days to recover, but as soon as I can ride, we set off at the tracker's discretion. We must acquire supplies for our journey—food, water, weapons. Can your people take care of that? I wish I could help more," Mari said, feeling useless. "How are Seraphina and the water mages doing with the city?"

"Don't feel guilty about resting, Mari. Seraphina is a delight. She and her people have been working all day. As soon as the sun rose, they went into the city and have gone through nearly half of it."

Mari felt guilty for doubting Seraphina. Usually, she only saw the best in people but had doubted Seraphina's intentions. Orcian was going to be a great political ally.

"They are incredible allies to have," Mari said. "I hope one day we can thank them properly for everything they do for us."

"They are true allies," Ren said. "Rest up, Mari. We need you better before we go. We can't have you passing out in the middle of a fight," Ren said, resting a hand on Mari's shoulder.

"Thank you, Ren," Mari said with a yawn. "I think it's time for a nap now."

Mari pulled the covers over her head and closed her eyes, and for the first time during a bleeding, she fell into a doze without begging the Gods to kill her in her sleep.

Chapter Thirteen

Zahir

As Zahir lifted his hand to knock on the small wooden door of the moss-covered cottage, his breathing became shallow. Vines of ivy and clumps of moss coated the rounded roof of the cottage. Circular windows on the first and second stories showed a small candle sitting on a ledge. Zahir shoved his hands into the pockets of his blue pants and counted the passing seconds as time droned on. How long had he been waiting? A minute? Two? Five? He couldn't be certain. But it didn't seem like Lydia was home. The longer he stood there, waiting, Zahir wondered if he had made a wrong decision in coming here and if he was ready to question a seer about his birth mother. He had spent the last nine moon cycles focused on his training, and then seeing his father in the dreamscape... it had been too much. It messed with his mind and made him unfocused.

Just when Zahir turned around to walk away, the door creaked open. "Can I help you?"

Zahir spun to face an older woman standing in the door frame, a cane in her left hand. A black dress hung off her frail frame and swayed when she stepped towards him, her gold eyes sparkling in the sun. She'd swept her gray hair into a bun, showing off her wrinkled face.

"I'm Zahir," he said, clearing his throat. "Are you Lydia?"

Something flitted across Lydia's gaze, but it was gone before Zahir could recognize it. "I am. Did you come for a reading?"

"I did," Zahir said. Gods' knows why. *What did I just agree to?*

"Come on in." Lydia turned back into the house and led Zahir inside.

Zahir immediately relaxed inside of Lydia's home. The familiar scent of lavender greeted him as sunlight streamed in through the large windows lining the walls; there was a small living room featuring a well-loved couch and a wood-burning fireplace. A pot sat on the stove and bubbled occasionally with the scent of tomatoes and garlic—scents foreign to Zahir until he came to Lovíth. The warmth from the fire filled Zahir with energy, and he felt the fire magic rumble in his veins, calling to him. He had never experienced his magic moving inside of him and wondered if this was part of his life magic bleeding into his Fire.

Lydia led Zahir to a wooden table where she sat across from him and began shuffling a deck of purple cards with gold-painted edges. She passed the cards between her hands, and only the rustling of cards broke the silence, along with the occasional crackle of the fire.

"Before we get started, have you ever had a reading before?" asked Lydia.

"No, I have not," said Zahir. "Markus told me I should come here."

"He's a good kid." Lydia handed the deck of cards to Zahir. "Shuffle these until you feel like they are ready. Then, separate them into three piles with your dominant hand."

Zahir moved the cards between his hands. "Do the piles have to be even?"

"No, cut the deck as you see fit."

As Zahir shuffled, a tingling sensation trickled up his forearms, but he held onto the cards. He stared at his hands as he shuffled, too scared to look at Lydia, who watched him with an intensity that made him shift in his seat.

When Zahir felt he was done shuffling, he cut the deck into three piles with his right hand. The one in the middle was slightly larger than those on the ends. The back of each card was adorned with a drawing of an eye, and vines creeping up the cards' borders.

"Which pile do you feel most connected to?" asked Lydia, resting her elbows on the table.

Zahir stared at the piles for a minute before answering. He couldn't take his eyes off the pile on the left, and he didn't realize he was pointing at it until he spoke. "This one." Zahir didn't know how to explain it, but his breath hitched whenever he looked at it. The other two piles made his skin crawl.

Lydia reached forward and flipped the two piles Zahir hadn't chosen. Two cards stared back at him. One was a skeletal hand holding a rose, and the other a castle struck by lightning. She inhaled sharply.

"There is a major change coming to your life. The end of a cycle is nearing, and you are getting ready to begin the next phase of your journey. But,"—She pointed to the card with the castle— "You are stuck in your ways. You think you are unstoppable and that you are always right. This is going to stop you from accepting change. You must open your mind to the idea that others may know more than you do."

Zahir was taken aback. Thinking he knew better than others had been a big point of contention between him and Mari, and he'd regretted ignoring her advice when he asked. Maybe things would have turned out differently if he had listened. As for the major change... of course, a change was coming to his life. He was about to ask a stranger about his birth mother, who he had only just learned existed.

Lydia picked up the pile of cards Zahir felt most connected to and laid three cards out before her from left to right. Nodding, she looked between them, as if connecting the puzzle pieces. "You are working through childhood trauma, and it's tough for you. But if you keep pushing, you'll come out on top and be better off than you were before."

Lydia pulled another three cards, and Zahir's heart raced. How could she tell he was working through trauma? It must be general; everyone has trauma. The following cards were a woman with a scepter and a crown sitting on a throne, a man who was a king, and what looked like two lovers dancing in the rain.

"Are you in a relationship?" asked Lydia.

"Yes, I am married," Zahir said. He lifted his left hand to show Lydia the band around his finger.

She nodded. "You and your partner are very well balanced. One of you is more emotional, and the other is more level-headed. You bring out the best in each other. You work in tandem; the other is strong when the other is weaker. This relationship was meant to be as you are so perfectly in balance. It must have been true love."

"Actually, it was arranged," Zahir said, but as soon as the words left his mouth, he wished they hadn't. Lydia didn't even know who he was. She didn't need to know everything about him.

"Then it was a match made by the Gods," she said.

The next three cards appeared on the table faster than Zahir wanted. He pressed his feet firmly into the ground. Were he and Mari meant to be together? They did work well together, especially when they listened to one another. Zahir couldn't keep the smile that spread across his face and the warmth growing in his chest. His heart panged hard as he remembered how much he missed Mari. Though every so often he forgot the pain of missing her, when he remembered, it struck him so hard he couldn't breathe.

"You have experienced great loss, and it has affected you more than you realize, twisting your emotions without you even recognizing it. There is life after death. This person isn't truly gone, but you must accept that their physical body is no longer here so you can move on and remember them with joy rather than heartache."

"How do you know all of these things?" Zahir asked, breath-less.

Lydia gestured to the cards. "They are telling me."

"But they're just cards?"

"They are so much more than that. I use them as a tool for divination. Sometimes, they tell me stories that are spot on. Other times," Lydia shrugged, "I am wrong. It's not a science, more of an art. If someone is open to it, the reading is usually clearer. When someone is closed off, it's like wading through murky water."

Zahir took a deep breath. "I'm looking for someone. Can those cards tell me how it will go when I find them?"

Lydia nodded and handed the cards back to Zahir, who reshuf-fled them before handing them back. She spread them out in a semi-circle between their bodies. Lydia instructed Zahir to pick one card from the deck and hand it to her. After a long exhale, Zahir waved a hand over the cards. A shock ran up his arm as he hovered over one card. He plucked it from the spread and passed it to Lydia. He stared at the imagery of the final card as she flipped it over. A hand held a dagger towards the top of the card, a never-ending spiral positioned behind it.

"This card is about fairness and equality. It might show up when you're dealing with imbalance. You must be open to *both* sides of a situation. Maybe you're thinking about how it will affect you and not the other person."

"But how will that reunion go when I find them?" asked Zahir.

Lydia shrugged. "I can't tell you the answer to that. I am sorry."

Zahir took a deep breath and perched his elbows on the table. His gold eyes met Lydia's, and it took everything in him to speak. "Do you know anyone named Zena? I am looking for someone here with that name, but no one seems to have heard of her."

Something flashed behind Lydia's eyes, gone before Zahir could place it. "I don't know anyone who lives here by that name."

"Are you sure?" Zahir asked, leaning forward. When Lydia hesitated, Zahir cut in. "You *do* know something about a Zena, though."

"I really can't help you. I'm sorry," said Lydia, sliding her chair back from the table. "I think it's best if you go."

Zahir stood abruptly from his chair. "I think you know something and are hiding it. This Zena woman is supposed to be my birth mother."

Lydia gripped the back of her chair, her knuckles white. "There is no one here who goes by that name."

Zahir focused her words. *There is no one here who goes by that name.* Zahir stared into Lydia's gold eyes, and it clicked. "It's *you*. I think I'm the son you had with Ryker."

Lydia froze, her eyes widening. "We can't speak of this."

The truth settled on Zahir then. His birth mother had been in Lovíth the entire time he'd been here, and now, he had finally found her.

"Lydia, I only just learned about you recently. I had no idea who I was," said Zahir. "If you don't want to speak of it, I'll leave. You're right; I wasn't thinking about how this would affect you, but I needed to meet you. I needed to know where I came from."

"Your father never told you what we did?" Lydia asked, moving a hand to her chest.

Zahir shook his head. "I only learned about my life magic after I saved my wife from death's door. I got a letter from Ryker after that which told me everything."

"A letter?" Lydia's brows furrowed.

Zahir closed his eyes; he hated being the bearer of bad news. "My father is dead. He died during an attack on the palace."

Tears welled in Lydia's eyes. "He's really gone?"

"Yes," Zahir said, his voice shaking. For the first time in a long time, he shed tears for his father, caught off guard by his grief. He hadn't cried since he came to Lovíth; there had simply been no time for crying. Zahir wiped hastily at his cheeks.

"I wish I had gotten to say goodbye," said Lydia, sitting back in her chair. "I cared very deeply for your father."

Zahir sat before speaking. "Then why didn't you say goodbye when you left Brahn? Why did you just leave in the middle of the night?"

Zahir was unsure why he felt so emotional about this when he barely knew she existed in the first place. How could he mourn something he never had?

"You are the son of a king, Zahir. I had no choice. You were never going to be *my* son," Lydia said, dejected. "Your father had more claim on you than I ever would, simply because he was king, and I was in his country. If we were in Lovíth, maybe it would have been different. You were going to be a prince, and there was nothing I could do. Even if I wanted to, I couldn't tell anyone in Brahn that their king had an affair and I birthed a dual mage. These were secrets that were never meant to be discovered. I had no choice but to leave you."

"Why didn't you stay in Brahn then?"

"Because I live here in Lovíth. As life mages, we are spiritually connected to our homes. I am sure you've noticed that all you can think about is going back."

Zahir let out a long breath. "You're right."

"I have not let myself think about you for twenty-five years, Zahir. Because if I let those thoughts come, I would have rushed back to Brahn to bring you here. I encouraged Maura and Ryker to tell you, but they were adamant that they would wait until you were older. Children have a nasty habit of saying whatever they please."

Zahir laughed, thinking of Roan. While most of the things he said were helpful or in line with the conversation, he had asked Taryn and Anya if they had feelings for each other in front of other people, which was definitely not his brightest moment.

"Do you regret what you did?"

Lydia shook her head. "I missed you for twenty-five years, but now you're sitting in my home in Lovíth. I will not lie; I was *terrified* of a disastrous dual mage, even though there are so few instances of that ever happening. Morana gave us a bad name," Lydia winked, and Zahir's heart skipped. Suddenly, his palms were sweaty, and his body felt weak. He leaned forward. "Us?"

"Yes. I, too, am a dual mage."

Chapter Fourteen

Mari

Nearly a week had passed since Mari's bleeding began, and she couldn't be happier now it was finally over. The pain tincture Amí had concocted helped immensely, and each day, the pain subsided bit by bit. Eventually, Amí replaced Ren by distracting Mari from her pain and taking care of her. Although Amí didn't speak much, she read books to Mari to distract her mind from the cramping in her stomach and legs.

As soon as Mari could walk on her own, she persuaded a few guards to take her out to the camps erected for the citizens who lost their homes in the flood. Semi-permanent structures had been built within the last week, and there were more sheds than tents now. Hundreds of people resided there, families clinging to each other in small cots.

The people of Brahn swarmed Mari when she arrived, all wishing to ask questions about the rebuilding. Mari assured them it was going well and asked how she could make them more comfortable. The people of Brahn seemed in good enough spirits, all things considered. Some asked her to pray with them, seeking the Gods' forgiveness for whatever they did to anger them. They prayed for help, guidance, and patience as they waited here instead of in their homes; they asked to be provided for and thanked the Gods that their lives had been spared. It broke Mari's heart to think that her people thought the Gods flooded their city. Even though Mari explained that a dam had burst, the people still asked why the Gods had allowed it to happen. Mari felt a pang in her chest each time she was forced to lie to her people and keep the truth about Morana from them. Morana may not have been a God, but she acted like one. But this world was not hers to destroy, despite what she might desire.

After going through the city and removing water from every building, Seraphina and the other water mages asked for a few more days before allowing people back into their homes. They wanted to go through again to ensure there wasn't obscene damage to any house they might have missed. Mari admired Seraphina's willingness to help and do the work herself instead of asking others to do it. She had a good ally in Seraphina and hoped to one day repay the Orcian Princess for all her help.

Mari changed sheets on cots, doled out bowls of stews, and handed out new pillows to the people who received her with gracious thanks and hugs. Though some insisted she didn't need to help them, they appreciated her insistence nonetheless, even if she merely occupied someone's child for a few minutes so the parent could eat their meal in peace. Many of the children in the shelter were too young to understand what was happening. Occasionally, a child would approach Mari, tug on her skirts, and ask her to play dolls. Many parents were appalled their child would be so bold, but Mari immediately appeased them, ruffling the child's hair and asking to see their dolls. Once, a little girl grasped her leg and followed Mari around the shelter, her short pigtails smacking Mari's leg every time she moved, but Mari didn't mind. If she could distract one child from the sadness of the truth, she would.

Mari didn't want to leave the camp. Her presence had lightened the spirits of the occupants; if she were in their position, a visit from the ruler would make her feel better, as it showed they cared—and Mari *did*. Brahn was her home now, and the people were hers to protect.

Whenever tragedy struck Yu'güe, the people banded together. If someone was injured and couldn't hunt, the entire clan would hunt extra to ensure they had something to eat. Mari remembered when her friend Fahran's mother, Gil, was pregnant with Fahran's sister but was having a hard time, constantly in pain and barely able to move. After her husband died shortly after she fell pregnant, she was the sole caregiver for her three children. As soon as word got out about her struggle, the clan joined together to help her through the last few months of her pregnancy. Mari distinctly remembered her mother taking her to Fahran's house every day after lessons and cooking a meal. Fahran was the oldest of his siblings. Mari and Fahran would then do the dishes while her mother helped Gil eat and bathe. While Gil was bathing, Mari would change diapers and occupy the younger siblings if they woke up from their naps. In Yu'güe, no one was left to their own devices when struggling. It was times like this when Mari missed her home—the closeness—but not the secrecy and lies.

Though Brahn's people grouped together after the city flooded, people seemed more concerned about their own homes before others and rarely did anyone hug or comfort each other. Protecting the people meant providing their basic needs—food, water, shelter. However, the advisors' thought protection was only about their physical safety.

Illan waited for Mari as she was escorted back to the palace. He stood with a tall man with intense brown eyes and a thin, white scar tracing the left side of his face from temple to chin. He wore a long, buttoned-up cloak that concealed most of his body, and Mari glimpsed the tips of daggers at his waist when he moved. Kane looked lethal—deadly—and Mari immediately straightened in his presence.

"Mari," said Illan as she approached. "This is Kane, the tracker I was telling you about."

Mari extended a hand to Kane. "Pleasure to meet you. Thank you for helping us in our endeavor. I assume Illan has filled you in?"

Kane shook Mari's hand firmly. "Of course, Your Majesty. I am honored to be a part of your efforts. I did a preliminary search outside Brahn's borders, and I found a trail leading to the west. I believe she was heading towards the mountains. We should start there."

Mari frowned. "The mountains don't offer a good vantage point. Is that the most likely place she would be?"

"I think she is more likely to be somewhere with cover. Her entire plan would be ruined if anyone spotted her."

"She must have people working with her. There's no way she could have been hiding in secret for this long without help."

"Morana may have help from the rebel forces that attacked you recently," Kane said, averting his eyes. "But another option is that she could be alone, killing anyone she comes in contact with."

Mari shook her head. "If she has been killing people for thousands of years, why haven't there been piles of bodies? People looking for their missing loved ones? She couldn't have survived this long without help."

"Can you beat her in a fight? Or does death magic cancel each other out?" asked Kane.

Mari shook her head; panic immediately rose in her throat as she remembered the sensations of Morana trying to steal her soul, how her vision swam, her legs felt heavy, and how when she finally jumped to safety, it still took her time to recover. Morana, on the other hand, had seamlessly fought Mari's souls. She couldn't win a fight by herself.

"My magic is useless against her. I tried. We are going to need to use the titanium."

"We can give Ren's soldiers the weapons. We will only use them if necessary," Illan said, and Mari nodded in agreement.

"So," Kane began, "When do we leave?"

***

My dearest Zahir,

I wish I had better things to write, but before you read this, you must promise me that you will stay in Lovíth. Please do not rush home. There is nothing you can do.

We have assembled a combat team consisting of Hanan, Raf, and Kiernan. They will join me, Ren, and three other soldiers on a mission to track Morana. Illan has introduced us to a tracker who will help us find Morana, too. We're leaving as soon as we are ready. Even if you come back to Brahn, we will be long gone. So, please, I beg of you—stay in Lovíth.

This isn't the kind of thing I wanted to put in a letter, but I fear I have no other choice.

I have been struggling mentally with the guilt of taking those human souls when the rebels raided the palace. The nightmares still plague me, and I can't seem to forgive myself for what I did. Hanan convinced me to tell you, and though I was going to wait until you came home, things are getting worse. With every human soul I take, my psyche is damaged. I know that Morana took thousands of lives, but what if I become as insane as she? Sometimes, I think I see shadows in our room, although I know they are just phantoms of the mind.

If you, or anyone in Lovíth, have recommendations for how I can heal my psyche, I am all ears. Please let me know if you hear anything.

I miss you dearly.

All my love,
Mari

Mari sighed and leaned back in her chair, rereading her words. How could she put those things in a letter? How could she tell Zahir that the thing they were most afraid of was actually walking in this world? Mari nearly crumpled the letter up, but what would that accomplish? Zahir needed to know. Regardless of how the letter was received, he needed to know.

Mari pressed a seal onto the folded letter and tucked it flush against the side of her desk before a knock came at the door. Mari stood and stretched, her posture stiff from hunching. As she opened the door, Mari looked into the smiling eyes of Roan, who carried two books in his arms.

"Do you want to read?" Roan asked, passing a book to Mari.

Mari took it and smiled. She didn't have time to read; she needed to begin preparations for her trek into the mountains, but she couldn't say no to Roan, especially since she would be gone for a while.

"Of course."

Mari followed Roan into the gardens to their usual tree and leaned against it, stretching her legs before her. Roan lay on his back, resting his head on Mari's thighs. He pulled the book up to his face and cracked it about halfway open to begin reading. Mari glanced at the book in her hands and realized Roan had picked out a history of death magic; she had never seen it in the library before. The dark black leather-clad tome titled "Yu'güe and Its People" had a beautiful gold etching of the mountain range that surrounded Mari's village on the cover. Mari stroked her fingers over the summits. She had read every tome on death magic from Brahn's library, but she had never found this one.

"Roan, where did you find this book?" asked Mari.

"It was in the library, but not with the rest of the history books; it was with the fiction stories. I thought you might want it."

"Thank you. I *do* want it."

Mari cracked open the book, and the binding creaked as she flipped through it. The yellow and worn pages held faded black ink Mari struggled to read. She skimmed through the first few pages until she found something of interest.

Death mages use their magic to hunt. When they steal the soul of an animal, the soul becomes part of their arsenal which they can use to protect themselves at a later time. Death mages respect the lives of all animals, and after killing one, the death mages will lean their foreheads on the soul of the animal and thank it for giving its life to them.

As the death mages believe all life is sacred, taking a human life is the worst crime a death mage can commit. Taking the lives of animals is a means of survival, but stealing a human soul is not only wrong but dangerous.

Death mages who steal the souls of humans experience side effects of their magic. Paranoia, insanity, depression, and mania are some of the most commonly reported consequences. As death mages take human souls, their lifespan increases; for every soul stolen, the death mage is said to gain another year of life.

With every soul, death mages live another year. If it were true, it meant Morana could have hundreds or thousands of years added to her lifetime. So, that was how she lived so long. Mari needed to tell Illan this information but couldn't end her time with Roan, especially as they had just sat down.

"You aren't reading," said Roan, not taking his eyes off his book.

"Of course I am," Mari responded. She turned the page in pretense. Roan didn't need to know everything that was going on.

"I have read ten pages, and you haven't flipped your page once."

"I must have gotten distracted."

Roan made a noise of acknowledgment, and Mari tried again to read the book. It was exceedingly hard to focus when she got distracted by even the chirping of a damn bird. They were everywhere today. The leaves rustled above Mari's head, and she nearly jumped up to run inside, but she didn't want to disrupt Roan or their time together, so she stayed where she was despite her heart hammering in her chest. As Mari turned the page, her fingers trembled. Mari glanced around quickly but didn't spot any birds nearby, thank the Gods.

Drifting back to her thoughts, she flipped through the book; her mind was stuck on the spirits she had seen disappear when she spoke with Hanan. How could they just *disappear*? Mari had yet to call them again since that day yet... she had slept through nearly every night since. Though she woke up every morning drenched in sweat, she was no longer emptying her guts every night.

Morana caused the isolation of the clans. Her actions had isolated Yu'güe from medicine and trade for millennia. Mari couldn't even begin to count how many times she had trekked miles to the sea to collect moss from the rocks when her mother had a fever, mixing the moss with tea to help break it. Yet in Brahn, Mari could access something so simple as a pain medication for her bleeding. No pain medicine like that existed in Yu'güe.

Yu'güe's isolation was even clearer when Mari came to Brahn and learned the other three clans had been trading. She'd been furious, unable to believe the rest of the world had cut her clan off completely. Did Yu'güe's leaders know they were the only ones in isolation? She wondered if it was punishment for Morana's actions. If so, then Lovíth should have been punished, too. But why would they punish the clan known for healing? It's much easier to cut off the clan representing death and destruction. Leaning her head back against the tree, Mari closed her eyes.

At dawn tomorrow, the party would set out to track Morana. And there was so much for Mari to do.

Chapter Fifteen

Zahir

"Yes. I, too, am a dual mage."

"What?" Zahir asked. He could barely speak. Another dual mage existed? And of all people… After all this time, not only was he meeting his birth mother, who cursed him with a deadline, but he was also meeting another dual mage. What was her second magic? Zahir's heart thrummed. Zahir may not have inherited life magic from Lydia; what if she was a water or death mage? It couldn't be… "Am I a triad?"

"I am a fire and life Mage. Our entire lineage goes back to the four mages; do you know their story?" asked Lydia.

"Of course, I know the story," Zahir said. He had heard the story of the four mages as a child. Four friends, one from each clan, grew up together, and one pair birthed a dual mage born of fire and water, who burned his father to death and drowned himself. It was the cautionary tale of dual mages, and it was that story, and Morana's reign of terror, which divided the world into four clans, isolated from one other. Death mages moved halfway across the world out of guilt and shame after Morana used death magic to kill people.

As a child, Zahir was constantly reminded about the four mages and had been terrified of them, hence why he feared his people's thoughts about his marriage to a death mage. Now, his concern seemed almost comical to know *he* was the thing he had always feared.

"Jai, the life mage, is our ancestor. We have traced our lineage back. Somewhere down the line, we added a fire mage into the mix."

"But if it was just once... how do we still have fire and life magic?" asked Zahir. From his understanding, the second magic would slowly dissipate through the generations.

"Because it wasn't just one time, Zahir," Lydia said, leveling her eyes at him. "After that instance, it became our family's duty to continue the dual mages. We kept it a secret and pretended we were solely fire mages; some of our family even moved to Brahn to fall in love, and the whole time, we never told a soul. After Morana... it got trickier."

Zahir slid his chair back from the table. "So, our ancestors... and *you* continued to breed dual mages? Why?"

"Because dual mages aren't harbingers of destruction, not once has someone in our ancestry done something terrible. Morana is the exception, not the rule."

Zahir couldn't believe what he was hearing. Dual mages had always existed; they had never been eradicated. He'd spent so long trying to find one in Brahn yet it had been him all along. And... there was another one in Lovíth.

"Do you think there are more than just us?" Zahir asked.

A slow smile spread across Lydia's face. "I *know* there are."

Zahir was taken aback. "What, is there a club?"

Lydia let out a low laugh. "We meet in secret every few moon cycles. Whenever someone finds a new dual mage, they bring them to our meeting place. We keep tabs on each other to ensure no one finds out the truth."

"But why? If you are found out, it will cause too many issues," Zahir said.

"Because we aren't staying silent forever," Lydia said with a defiant raise of her chin. Power glinted in her gaze. "Once there are enough of us, we're going to normalize it again. No one should have to hide what they are."

Zahir reeled in his seat. Dual mages existed, waiting for their time to tell the world. Zahir had been so concerned about having a child with Mari and creating the first dual mage, yet it seemed a ridiculous fear now, knowing how many lived in hiding. Lydia seemed proud of her status as a dual mage, but Zahir felt terrified and ashamed, like an outsider in a community he knew nothing about.

"No one should be a dual mage. Brahn resented my marriage to Mari because we would have a dual mage child. Rebels ran amuck in my city looking for *me*—to kill *me*. They kidnapped and tortured my wife because of it," Zahir growled.

"That is not our fault," Lydia said, shaking her head. "I never told a soul what Ryker and I did. So, unless someone inside the palace found out—or knew all along—there was no way it should have gotten out."

"Are there other dual mages in Lovíth?"

"Yes, there are," Lydia said. "There are four of us here—five if we include you."

"Are there any who have opposite magic?"

"No," Lydia said. "Yu'güe is extraordinarily isolated. We couldn't get to them even if we wanted to."

"So, there are no fire and water mages then?" Zahir asked. Lydia's silence was an answer. "There are?"

"Yes, there are."

Zahir's thoughts immediately returned to the story of the four mages. Dual mages of opposing magics had more difficulty controlling it and finding the balance. Zahir had struggled with his life magic for nine moon cycles; he couldn't even imagine how much he would have struggled to learn water magic.

Morana was a dual mage of opposing magic and had murdered thousands of people. How much of her insanity came from her magic, he wondered. Could the opposing magic be what drove her to insanity?

"How has this not gotten out in *thousands* of years?" Zahir asked.

"The reaction from your clan regarding your wife should give you the answer you need. People live in fear of the name Morana and the idea of a dual mage."

"What is the point of coming out and confessing dual mages never ceased to exist? Do you not realize that the whole world hates us?"

"Like I said, Morana is the exception, not the rule. If we can show we haven't seen a single dual mage like her in thousands of years, then maybe the isolation will end."

"I thought the isolation only extended to Yu'güe."

"Zahir, we can't leave our homes. We are trapped in Lovíth. Even if we wanted to move to another clan... we would never be allowed to," Lydia said, exasperated.

Slowly, Zahir was beginning to understand what Lydia was saying. While they didn't feel isolated, they remained trapped in their clan, something Zahir understood well. He would always be in Brahn; there was no question about it. He was always going to be king, marry, and produce an heir. His life had been laid out for him.

For his whole life, Zahir understood having a child was an obligation, thus never allowed himself to consider what *he* truly wanted out of life. He didn't want a child. Not only would it be a child he was *forced* to have, but the child would be a triad. And if the history books were accurate, triads were volatile with short life spans. How could he bring a child into this world who was doomed to fail? Zahir had been trapped his whole life yet never grasped the extent of it until recently.

Zahir thought about Hanan, who disappeared to escape his father's abuse, moving to Brahn and laying low for years. He was able to escape a horrible situation, but what about people without such means? Hanan was lucky to have found peace and happiness in Brahn, yet not everyone has that luxury.

Zahir was terrified of telling Mari his feelings about children. She was a very motherly person and was fantastic with Roan. He didn't know where she stood on the idea of children, especially now they knew he was a dual mage. Were children even on her mind, or did other pressing matters take priority? Now discovering dual mages with opposing magics were viable, where did triads play into that? A conversation of such significance couldn't be had over letters that took days—or even weeks—to deliver, yet he had to have this conversation with her soon. When he returned to Brahn, everyone would expect them to have an heir.

"I understand what you mean," said Zahir. "Why did you lie to my father about your name?"

Lydia was quiet for a moment. "I didn't. My birth name is Zena. My mother's name was Lydia. Part of me wanted to stay in Brahn and help raise you—Ryker and Maura offered me that option, but I knew I would always feel like something was missing. Lovíth is my home. I didn't want to be found when I came back to Lovíth; I wanted you to grow up thinking nothing was amiss. So, I left. And when I returned to Lovíth, I changed my name. Very few people know my birth name."

Zahir shook his head. "Did they ever come looking for you?"

"No, but I'm sure having three children and being the monarch of a clan had something to do with that," said Lydia.

Zahir had one more burning question that burst out of him. "Did you know I was here, in Lovíth?"

Lydia took a deep breath before answering. "I did. I thought about going to Markus's home but wanted to wait for you to be ready. When I saw you get off that boat, I wanted to yell out that

I was your birth mother, but my wife dragged me away before I could."

Zahir raised his eyebrows and leaned back in his chair. He was unsure how he would have reacted if Lydia had shown up on his doorstep confessing to be his birth mother. Truthfully, he probably would have slammed the door in her face, though a small part of him wondered if he would have acted differently.

"Thank you for giving me the space," Zahir said after a minute of silence.

"So, now that you know about my family, can I ask about yours?" Lydia asked.

Zahir was quiet for a long moment. He didn't know how much he wanted to tell Lydia; after all, he didn't know her or how to feel about her yet. On the one hand, she had been nothing but kind and honest with him, but on the other... how did he know she was telling the truth?

Lydia leaned forward on the table, waiting for Zahir to speak, her gaze never straying from his face. Her soft smile reminded him so much of his own. Watching her now, Zahir was surprised he hadn't recognized her straight away, and the more time he spent in Lydia's home, the more he enjoyed her presence.

Zahir began talking about his family. He told Lydia about Roan, Anya, Mari, and Illan. He spoke of his favorite things to do with Roan and how much his little brother meant to him; how he sang Roan to sleep for years, and how Roan still came to him when nightmares plagued him.

When Lydia asked about Anya, Zahir explained it was hard to get along with her growing up, but he hoped they could repair their relationship now they were adults. He explained Taryn's role in his family—how she became Anya's confidant and partner while leaving out the part where he slept with Taryn. After all, Lydia didn't need to know everything.

"Did you have trouble learning any of your magic when you were younger?" Zahir asked after he finished recounting a story about the first time he beat Anya in a fight only a few years ago.

Lydia nodded. "I did have trouble with my fire magic. Unlike you, life magic was the first gift I learned, though I never really excelled in it. I was unable to heal major injuries for the longest time, and I had a tough time when it came to fire. I couldn't do anything."

Zahir nodded at the familiar feeling Lydia was describing. "I am having so much trouble with my life magic."

Lydia nodded slowly, pursing her lips. "To be fair, you aren't connected to your soul. As I said, life magic is connected to your home. Lovíth is not your home, Zahir. Brahn is. Your life magic is connected there; it will be harder for you to learn here."

"How can you tell I am not connected to my soul?" asked Zahir, furrowing his brow.

"It's the fate of us dual mages. You didn't know your birth mother. I didn't know my birth father. So on and so forth. Unfortunately, it is hard to grow and heal when you are missing a huge part of your history."

"It doesn't feel like there's 'trauma' around it like Markus describes."

"It is traumatic," Lydia said with a light laugh. "Regardless of whether you realize it or not. You've just learned about a whole part of you that you never knew existed. Your entire world has been turned upside down. Everything you've ever been told is a lie. Maura isn't your mother—"

"She *is* my mother," Zahir said firmly. Lydia's lips parted at Zahir's shift in tone. Whether or not Maura gave birth to him, she was his mother, no matter what anyone else said.

"She is your mother in every way that counts. She raised you and made you into who you are today," Lydia corrected. "Regardless, you learned a horrifying truth and discovered that *you* are the thing you most feared."

Zahir felt suddenly overwhelmed as Lydia put his feelings into words. Lydia was right: he was the thing he'd learned to fear.

"I should get going; Markus is expecting me," Zahir said, sliding his chair back from the table and standing. He could no longer stand the overwhelming confusion flooding his chest.

Lydia broke eye contact with Zahir and took a slow breath. "It was great to meet you. Thank you for stopping in. You are welcome here anytime. We are family, after all."

Lydia gave Zahir an awkward hug before he left the house, and on the walk back home, his mind wandered. He had just met his birth mother—the woman his father had an affair with—another dual mage, who only pursued his father to continue her lineage. Zahir wished he asked if Ryker knew she was a dual mage... something wasn't sitting right with him.

When Zahir arrived home, he nearly knocked Markus over, lost in his thoughts. Markus grasped Zahir by the shoulders to keep them from colliding; his face and hands streaked in dirt.

Zahir spotted the pile of weeds in front of the house and the new flowers planted around the door and—

"Are you all right?" asked Markus, concern lacing his features.

Zahir opened his mouth to respond, then promptly closed it. How could he answer a question like that, given all he had learned?

"Lydia is Zena. She's my birth mother."

Markus inhaled sharply and glanced back toward the house. "Let's go inside. I'll make us some tea. You must be so confused."

"I have so many thoughts, and I'm unsure how to begin filtering through them."

"Chamomile it is, then."

Chapter Sixteen

Mari

Mari sucked in a breath and flattened herself against a tree. She glanced at Hanan, who hid behind the next tree over. He raised a single finger to his lips, his bangs splayed across his forehead from the sheen of sweat above his brow. Hanan peeked out from behind the tree.

Mari waited for the signal, and when Hanan made eye contact with her, they leaped from their hiding spot and raised their arms towards the two elk drinking from the river. In tandem, they clenched their fists and yanked their arms back toward their torsos. The bodies of the elk collapsed as their souls flew toward Mari and Hanan.

"Thank you for giving us your life," the pair said simultaneously. They rested their foreheads on the elk souls before they dissipated, the familiar electricity running up Mari's spine as the elk's soul joined her arsenal.

"I don't think we thought this through very well," Hanan said, wiping the sweat off his forehead.

"Why's that?" asked Mari, taking a knife from her waistband to clean the animal.

"How are we getting two elk back to the palace, several miles away?"

Mari peered over her shoulder and realized, for the first time, how far they had trekked. She had convinced Hanan to sneak out with her to hunt for their journey and had helped him onto the roof, much like Zahir did for her when they were getting to know each other. Mari had shown Hanan the way out of the palace, leaping onto another rooftop and scaling the wall. Hanan had gaped as she landed on the other side. Mari's fear of heights was nothing compared to Hanan's. She had forgotten how bad it was until he'd screamed and threw himself off the palace roof. Hanan smacked Mari's arm when he reached her, scolding her for doing something so dangerous.

Mari laughed. "I think we made a mistake."

The deep rumble of Hanan's laughter made Mari dissolve into giggles. She watched Hanan laughing and couldn't remember when she saw him so happy. When they were children, Mari would never have described her brother as 'happy'; he'd been shy, sad, and quiet. Now, that description couldn't be further from the truth. Hanan's sadness was a symptom of their father's abuse and hiding a huge part of himself from his family and people. Mari couldn't imagine what that was like, locking a part of yourself away for so long, but she was so happy he could be himself with Raf in Brahn. Mari had offered to host Raf and

Hanan's wedding, and the pair had agreed. But between the flooding and Morana's return, they had set the wedding planning aside for now to focus on the situation at hand.

As Mari glanced at the two elk, a memory resurfaced from when she was a child. Mari and Hanan had trekked in the mountains; it was custom in Yu'güe for an older sibling to take a younger one on their first hunt. Hanan led Mari through the snow, explaining how to track animals. Yet, at six years old, Mari was more interested in catching falling snowflakes than trying to kill an animal. At the time, she hadn't understood she was killing an animal to eat it.

Hanan chided Mari every few minutes for not listening. Holding her little left hand in his right, he dragged her down the paths while she asked about the different trees, where snow came from, and when they were returning home. Hanan gave her dried meat any time she complained about her hunger, but it did nothing to keep her stomach from grumbling. The smell of fresh snowfall was familiar to Mari, reminding her of playing in the snow with her friends. Every five minutes, she would ball up some snow and toss it at Hanan, dissolving into giggles every time he shook the snow from his hair and shoulders. He'd told her to stop bothering him; otherwise, they would never catch anything.

Hanan finally got Mari to quiet down with the last of his dried meat and pulled her behind a boulder. He pointed to a family of deer drinking from a stream that had yet to freeze over. If it weren't for Hanan's hand over her mouth, she would have scared them away, and after a few minutes of watching, he removed his hand. Mari stood on her tiptoes, peering over the boulder and lifting the hood from her eyes. She gasped when one of the deer turned to look at them.

"Use your magic and get the deer, Mari," Hanan had whispered.

Mari nodded at her brother, and with perfect precision, she captured the soul of the deer nearest to them. The other three immediately scurried away as the deer's soul flew towards her. When it stopped before her, Hanan showed her how to accept the soul into her arsenal. The electric shock that ran down her spine brought tears of surprise to her eyes. After that, Hanan taught her how to strap the animal to a sled and get it down the mountain. Mari couldn't stop staring at the dead deer as they trekked home. She had killed that animal, and while she knew it was necessary for her survival, she couldn't escape the guilt pounding in her chest.

Mari's parents were *so* proud of her successful first hunt. Mari's mother taught her how to skin and bleed the animal until they could butcher and cook it for meat. It was Mari's first time working on a stew. To her, nothing could have ruined her success.

But she was wrong. As her family ate at a small wooden table, Hanan and Mari's father, Perán, got into an argument. Mari couldn't remember what it was about, but it quickly escalated. Hanan stormed out of the house, his stew half-eaten. Perán went after Hanan, slamming the front door behind him while Mari's mother shook her head and followed, leaving Mari alone with three half-eaten bowls of stew. She finished her stew, cleaned her dish, and went up to her bedroom to bundle beneath her comforter. Perán and her brother fought constantly about things Mari didn't know or understand; she was too young. Looking back, Mari realized it must have been about his arranged marriage.

So now, as tears sprung to Hanan's eyes from laughing, a sense of calm washed over her. For the first time in her life, her brother could be himself. And most importantly, he'd found a partner who would stand by him through it all.

Mari reached out to Hanan and wrapped her arms around his waist. He stopped laughing suddenly and hugged her back, crushing her in his arms.

"Is everything okay?" he asked.

"You're happy, and that's all I have ever wanted for you," Mari said. When she pulled back from Hanan, tears brimmed in his eyes. "It's all I've wanted for both of us."

"Me too, Mari," Hanan said. "Now, let's try getting these animals back to the palace."

Hanan tied the back legs of the elk together with rope, while Mari tied the front legs. "This isn't going to work," Mari said, panting.

"Maybe not, but we have to try."

Mari and Hanan both grabbed a length of rope and pulled with all their strength. Mari dug her heels into the grass, ripping out clumps of dirt, but with one hard tug, she lost her footing. The rope burned her hands as she slipped and fell onto the grass. A shock shot up her spine as she landed.

"We need to go back to the palace and get help," Mari said, standing. She dusted the dirt off her pants as Hanan nodded his agreement.

The siblings walked the long distance back to the palace in silence as Mari worried about what Illan or Ren would say. After all, she and Hanan had snuck out of the palace, which neither would take lightly. Mari would have to tell them; she couldn't request for guards to assist her without telling Ren why. While Mari had known it wasn't the best idea to leave without protection, she was tired of feeling weak. The constant presence of the guards made her feel like a child.

She couldn't do anything by herself. It had taken several conversations to convince Ren that she didn't *need* a guard in her room while she slept. If something did happen, her screams would alert the guard posted outside her door. Mari would never have slept if there was a stranger inside her room at all hours of the night.

Mari's fear of Illan's wrath was well justified. He stood atop the palace stairs, his arms crossed over his chest. His red face popped, contrasting his snowy white hair and beard. Mari couldn't tell if his coloring was from the sun or his anger. Illan stared at Mari and Hanan with narrowed eyes as they walked up the staircase. A pang of guilt hit Mari. Ren stood beside Illan, too, anger burning brightly in their gaze.

"Where were you?" Ren demanded, stepping forward to Mari as she finished ascending the stairs.

"Hanan and I were hunting for our journey into the caves," Mari said. She tried to emit a façade of confidence to avoid the chastising.

"Unprotected?" Ren said. "Do you understand how *unsafe* things are right now? Morana is out there. She could have killed you."

Mari shook her head. "Hanan and I are both death mages. We aren't unprotected."

"You could have been surrounded by dozens of rebels! They could have captured you both," Illan finally said with a shake of his head. "I can't believe you snuck out of the palace at a time like this."

"You told me Ren and Illan knew you were leaving," said Hanan, shooting an accusatory look at Mari.

"I lied. Why did you think we had to jump off the roof?" Mari asked her brother. Hanan ran a hand down his face, muttering something about his ignorance under his breath.

"You need to take guards with you and let me know if you want to leave the palace," Ren said. "But in a time like this, I would not have let you go."

"I don't need constant protection," said Mari, throwing her hands up in exasperation. "I am a *death* mage. Hanan is, too."

"And yet, you're the only one who has taken a human life," Illan said, narrowing his eyes. Mari froze.

"For now," Hanan said under his breath.

Illan glared at him. "Now is not the time for bravado, Hanan. Go home. I will have a guard escort you."

Hanan moved forward, but Mari rested a hand on his arm to stop him, narrowing her eyes at Illan. "*I* am the queen. *I* get to decide who comes into the palace."

"Your judgment is compromised, Mari," Illan said, his nostrils flaring.

Mari balked. How *dare* Illan question her judgment? Since Zahir had left for Lovíth, Illan had been given more power as he helped Mari assume her role as queen. But over the last few weeks, he had been overstepping. He had interfered with the council by giving them information before Mari could; he was making decisions without her input, and now, he was trying to undermine her authority as queen.

Mari turned to Ren. "We require assistance bringing two elk back to the palace. Hanan and I will need a team of soldiers to help bring them back."

"Tell me where they are, and I will send guards. You will stay here," Ren said.

"I did not *ask*," Mari commanded, rolling her shoulders back.

Ren blinked several times at Mari, their lips parting. "Yes, *Your Majesty*," they said through gritted teeth.

The familiar pang of guilt tugged at Mari's heart as she watched Ren stalk through the palace door and slam it behind them. She regretted issuing a command to Ren; they were only doing their job. But Mari had let her frustration get the better of her.

"You shouldn't talk to them like that. They are your friend," said Illan.

A short laugh escaped her lips. "They would never think to speak to Zahir like that."

"Zahir wouldn't sneak out of the palace," Illan retorted.

Mari bit her tongue. Zahir was the one who had shown Mari how to get out of the palace in the first place, sneaking out with his friends on every full moon and regularly patrolling the streets of Brahn. He'd taken Mari up the mountains the night before he left for Lovíth, too—all instances that Illan knew nothing about, and Mari was not about to tell him.

Thankfully, Mari didn't need to respond. Just then, Ren emerged with a large group of guards to help Mari and Hanan bring the elk back. Mari and Hanan led the slew of guards to the elk, but when they arrived, they would not allow Mari to assist in moving the elk onto the sleds, much to her dismay. They let Hanan help, though, but not without berating comments that he never should have agreed to this.

"I am fully capable of making my own decisions, thank you," said Mari. "Need I remind you that I am your queen and Hanan is my brother? You *will* show him the same respect you show me."

"Your Majesty, we just worry for your safety," said one of the guards.

"And I worry about my mental safety while trapped in the palace."

"There are people who want to kill you. You were kidnapped."

"And our former king, rest his soul, was murdered *inside* the palace. Do I need to remind you about that?"

"Good one," Hanan whispered as he passed Mari.

The walk back to the palace was silent. Mari tried to control her breathing as she silently seethed. Her hands clenched and unclenched at her sides to keep her from punching every tree she passed. Barely blinking, she stared at the back of the carriage, stewing at the soldiers who told her she needed to be more careful. She was the fucking queen, and it was time they treated her like one. Mari was tired of everyone telling her she "needed to be more careful" or "couldn't go outside without a guard." Yes, she had been kidnapped. Yes, there was now a murderous dual mage on the loose. But she wanted to move forward, not backward. If she stayed at a standstill, she would never be able to escape the dark pit in her mind.

Mari would be lying if she said the kidnapping and the invasions didn't still plague her nightmares. She still kept her hair short and regularly woke from sleep drenched in sweat. On more than one occasion, the guard outside her door had rushed inside, fearing someone had broken in to murder her. Yet Mari barricaded her balcony door every night ensuring no one ever could; an intruder would have to get through several layers of guards before they even reached the bedroom wing of the palace.

Mari couldn't stand feeling weak, so she pretended she was strong. Every day, she woke up, put on her armor—never a gown—and told people she was fine. But when she couldn't sleep, she went down to the titanium gym with Ren, and they fought. They fought until Mari could barely lift her arms, until her legs gave out beneath her, until the pain in her chest from the titanium was worse than the pain in her mind. Never again would Mari be weak.

When Mari and Hanan returned to the palace, the anger on all sides appeared to have subsided, and Mari met with Illan and Kane. She donned her armor and crown and called for her team to meet in the library. The palace didn't have an actual war room for strategizing. The last conflict had been when Morana was alive, thus eventually, the war room was turned into a second ballroom. Mari had decided the library would be their meeting space, the large tables providing enough room to lay out maps and plans.

Raf and Hanan stood beside each other, leaning over the map with their hands flat on the table. Raf had to keep pushing his glasses up his nose as he glanced down at it. Kiernan reclined in a chair, arms crossed as he listened to the various areas Morana could be hiding and occasionally interjected with a suggestion. Ren stood beside Mari, their hand never leaving the hilt of the sword. They hadn't said anything to Mari since their spat, and while Mari knew she needed to apologize, she was waiting to get Ren alone. Illan and Kane were at opposite heads of the table, leading the conversation by pointing out areas of interest and marking them on the map with large circles. Ren's three recruits for the team were beside Mari and Ren, listening with rapt attention. None of them said anything during the meeting, not unless a question was directed to them. Mari glanced around the table at her friends and sent a plea to the Gods to let them all come back alive.

Kane circled an area at the base of the mountains. "I think our best bet is starting with this cave under the mountains. It provides a fair amount of coverage while still being close enough to Brahn to attack."

"Why stay there if she can stay here?" asked Raf, pointing to a dense forest separating part of Brahn and Orcian. "That would be a better vantage point to keep an eye on Orcian, too."

"We have not received any reports of Morana terrorizing Orcian," Illan said, running a hand through his beard.

"They have had rebel attacks. Can we assume they were Morana's rebels?" Mari said. "If I were her, I would want to keep an eye on both Brahn and Orcian."

"I don't think we should assume anything. Besides, there's significantly less coverage there," Ren said. "It *would* make sense for her to be in the mountains; plus, she could have other people hiding in the forest. But if I were her, I would want to be hidden."

Kane nodded at Ren's words. "Morana has evaded humanity for thousands of years. She wouldn't have been able to do that without hiding."

Mari took a deep breath and shivered at the memory of facing Morana. "If she were out in the open, it would be too obvious. I saw her; she isn't inconspicuous."

Her magic had done nothing against Morana, and Mari had never been more terrified in her life. She was completely defenseless and had no idea how to kill an immortal mage.

"We should set out for the caves tonight. It would be best to move at nightfall in case she has watchmen. Once inside the caves, we can set up camp."

"We are going to need a watch schedule then," said Ren. "We can have four people rotate throughout the night every two hours."

"So, one pair will have a break each night?" asked Mari.

"No," Ren said, shaking their head. "You will not be sitting watch."

"What?"

"You are part of the royal family. We can't have you out in the open. I know you want to help, Mari, but we can't let you be on display."

"It's true, Mari," Illan agreed. "We can't advertise that you are part of this group. It would be a liability."

Mari cursed Illan's uncanny ability to say the right thing to convince her.

"Fine," she grumbled.

"There will be plenty for you to do, Mari," Ren said.

Once the team planned their course for the night, everyone set off to pack their gear. Mari was given a large rucksack that she filled with several pairs of training clothes, soap, dried meat, matches, and a water skin. She stuck a few knives in her pockets and a length of rope, just in case. She didn't know what else to bring or how long they would be gone. The plan was simple. They would hike into the cave, explore it as best they could, and return to the palace to make a new plan if they didn't find anything. But Kane was convinced they wouldn't come back empty-handed.

Mari stepped out onto the balcony of her chambers and clamored up onto the railing. Grabbing the roof's edge, she hoisted herself up and walked until she sat to look at the setting sun, casting an orange glow on the mountaintops. Mari sat where she and Zahir had once shared a picnic, where she'd tried a jam that was too spicy for her. She couldn't believe how much had changed in such a short amount of time. When she first came to Brahn, she thought things were too much, yet the only pressure was falling in love.

But now... Zahir was a dual mage. Morana was alive. Mari had stolen human souls. Brahn had flooded. Things were more backward than they were a year ago. She could hardly believe what her life had become. She wished Zahir were here; he always kept her from spiraling out of control. But for the past nine moon cycles, she had to be her own anchor within this sea of panic.

As Mari stared at the mountains, she caught another glimpse of the Ever-Burning Candle sitting above the mountain peak—but only for a second. She swore she could see the flame's outline, and it was the confirmation she needed to know she had saw it the other night. Maura had said only fire mages could fully see the constellation. While Mari was no fire mage, she was the Queen of Brahn. So maybe, just maybe, the Gods would allow her to see the constellation of her people.

Before Mari was ready, Ren's face popped up over the edge of the roof. "I would remind you that you shouldn't be up here, but what's the point? You're going to keep doing it anyway."

"You know me so well," Mari said with a laugh.

Ren lowered themselves down onto the balcony. "We have to leave now."

Mari sighed, taking one last look up at the stars. "Please bring us home safe," she pleaded to the Gods.

All she could hope was that the Gods would listen to her plea, but they didn't always have time for their children.

CHAPTER SEVENTEEN

ZAHIR

Markus and Pryn had been flirting all night, and Zahir was one pint away from forcing their heads together to kiss. Pryn had their hand on Markus's forearm every time he made them laugh, and with every touch from Pryn, Markus inched closer, hanging off their every word like it was their last. Every so often, he would slide his hand closer to Pryn's, as if working up the courage to reach out.

The three friends spent their evening at a very noisy Quiet Berry after Zahir tried to cook dinner but smoked out the house. He stopped all the flames immediately with his magic and managed to quell the smoke; a beautiful thing about Zahir's fire magic was his ability to save the house from burning down, which proved particularly useful given Markus regularly knocked his candles off his bedside table while sleeping, waking Zahir with the smell of burning wood. Zahir extinguished the fire without

Markus even stirring from his slumber; how Markus hadn't died yet, Zahir was unsure.

Alas, dinner had been ruined, and now the group was out. The longer Zahir stayed in Lovíth, the more he dreaded returning to Brahn. In a perfect world, he would move Mari and the rest of his family here, but unfortunately, he had to return to a clan where he was king—a prisoner in his home. That was the best part about Lovíth: the freedom. He was no one but a dual mage learning his life magic here. No one cared that he was Brahn's king, or at least not in the ways that mattered. Every so often, someone would ask him what Brahn was like or if Brahn was planning to open themselves up to travelers and immigrants, but those were all questions he didn't have answers for, and he said as much. Other than that, Zahir was just another person who came and went as he pleased. His only responsibilities were caring for himself and training his magic and swordsmanship.

That morning, he and Markus spent an hour practicing knife combat after Zahir's class. Why anyone would bring a knife to a sword fight was beyond Zahir's imagination. A knife required getting closer to your opponent, whereas a sword was long reaching. But, as Markus showed Zahir, knives were useful in battle. Zahir and Markus walked through drills using two-handed fighting. Zahir had a hard time keeping track of both of Markus' knives and regularly, Markus would feign an attack on Zahir's stomach. Whenever Zahir blocked it, a second knife would tickle his throat. Something wasn't clicking in Zahir's brain about tracking both knives. Markus had no problem, constantly blocking all of Zahir's attacks. Markus had accidentally nicked Zahir's cheek at one point, and Zahir mended the cut with little effort.

Since Zahir had met Lydia, he found his life magic was coming to him easier. He could heal minor cuts on his body with little effort and didn't feel exhausted after small uses of his magic anymore. He was *finally* progressing toward mastering life magic. He had been practicing before bed every night by soothing his sore back after training. By the time he lay down to sleep, the soreness was gone.

When Zahir spoke with Lily about how he was able to call his magic easier, she said it was likely because he was working through his adoption trauma. If he continued to work through his pain, he would probably see a significant increase in his abilities.

Zahir was still uneasy about his meeting with Lydia. Zahir had told Markus everything, revealing that he and Lydia were not the only dual mages but that many existed. Markus had nearly fallen from his chair at the news as Zahir recounted his visit with Lydia, fidgeting and shifting in his seat. Whenever he wasn't talking, Zahir sat perfectly still, listening intently to whatever Markus had to say.

Markus and Zahir had talked until the sun came up, discussing whether it was beneficial for Zahir to keep spending time with Lydia. Markus had been torn. On the one hand, it would help tremendously with his life magic, but on the other... Lydia's plan to expose the dual mages was a dangerous feat that could backfire terribly. Zahir weighed the pros and cons of such a revelation, understanding his entire clan could turn against him if news got out. They'd believe he always knew of their existence.

Pryn's voice pulled Zahir from his thoughts. "Zahir, are you okay?"

"Sorry." Zahir shook his head as Pryn smiled at him.

"Blair wants to know what you want to eat."

Blair stood before Zahir, arms crossed and scowling.

"I'll have whatever Markus is having," said Zahir. He had no idea what Markus had ordered, but food was the furthest thing from his mind. "What were you two talking about?"

"We were just talking about the lunar eclipse next week," Pryn said.

"Is that next week already?" Zahir asked. He couldn't believe that the eclipse was already upon them; he had anticipated being back home in Brahn for it.

The winter equinox and summer solstice were interesting phenomena for the fire and water mages. Fire mages drew their power from the sun, and water mages from the moon. Full moons and the winter equinox were powerful days for the water mages as their magic was at its peak, meaning they could perform impossible feats of magic, like raising the oceans with minimal effort. On the other hand, the summer solstice was when water mages were at their weakest and could barely access their magic. Fire mages were the opposite; Zahir recalled the itching in his veins when he couldn't reach his power during the winter equinox. However, it was a different feeling to that of titanium. When cut with titanium, Zahir felt a gaping hole in his chest when he couldn't reach his magic yet during the equinox, he felt the fire in his veins; it was like there was a dam, where only a trickle of power could reach him. If he had to choose, he would take one thousand cuts of a titanium blade rather than sit through the equinox. Solar and lunar eclipses had a similar effect on fire and water mages, but it wasn't as significant as an eclipse. It lasted only a few minutes.

In Brahn, a festival was held every summer solstice as this was when fire mages were strongest. Vendor booths would fill the city square; restaurants offered samples of their most popular dishes, and clothiers had special wares for purchase, like dresses made from the finest fabrics. Armorers held demonstrations of how they forged their weapons and offered instructions to curious adults; jewelers crafted the most stunning jewelry to sell and sometimes would hold classes for small children, teaching them to make bracelets with clay beads. But Zahir's favorite part of the celebration was always the street performers. There was one person who did sleight-of-hand tricks, riling up the crowd during their performances, making items disappear and reappear before your eyes. They'd involve the crowd, too, bringing audience members onto their makeshift stage to pick a card. After they shuffled that card back into the deck, the performer would pull the participant's card out of the deck without fail.

Before Zahir fully understood that he could only be a king, he had wanted to be a performer and tried to learn the tricks he saw, though never quite mastered them. Zahir once asked the performer to teach him, but it never happened. Ryker had gotten word of Zahir's ambitions and sat Zahir down, explaining that he was destined to sit on the throne, not perform tricks in the street.

And now, Zahir was missing his family's eclipse celebrations for the first time in his life. It was the first time he wouldn't eat a gooey slice of date cake from Jolie's Sweets on the palace steps while they all watched the eclipse. The second the moon was concealed, Zahir's veins *burned* with energy, and he'd breathe puffs of fire into the air.

"Do you have any celebrations for the eclipse?" Zahir asked Pryn and Markus.

"Nothing special, but Markus and I tend to climb onto the roof of my house and watch it together," said Pryn. "Will we do that again this year?"

"Of course," Markus said, touching Pryn's shoulder. "I wouldn't miss it for the world."

Zahir rolled his eyes as he finished his ale, waiting for Pryn and Markus to finally admit their feelings. Lately, it appeared like they were getting closer to confessing it. Zahir had overheard Markus telling Pryn that their eyes shimmered in the sunlight.

"I wouldn't miss it, either," Pryn said, a blush creeping onto their cheeks.

"Do you want to join us, Zahir?" Markus asked, breaking eye contact with Pryn.

Pryn visibly deflated at Markus's words. "No, thank you. The last thing I want to do is ruin your date."

The words were out of Zahir's mouth before he could stop them. Both Pryn and Markus glared daggers at him, and though

Zahir opened his mouth to amend his statement, he couldn't find the words.

"It's not a date," said Markus.

"What do you mean it's not a date?" Pryn asked. "I always thought it was."

Markus gaped and turned to Pryn. "You did?"

Pryn laughed. "Yes, Markus. We split bottles of wine and snuggle on the roof. What is your idea of a date then, if not that?"

"I *always* wanted it to be a date, but I didn't know if *you* wanted that."

"I do. Want you, that is."

Markus leaned in towards Pryn, and Zahir took that as his cue to leave. Sliding his chair back from the bar, Zahir left, the ruckus from the other patrons filtering through the door as he shut it behind him.

Goosebumps prickled on Zahir's arms as he walked home. He hoped that Markus and Pryn wouldn't decide to come back and make noise... he desperately needed a good night's rest. Zahir had nearly passed out that morning when one of the little girls, Riley, broke her wrist when she tripped. Lily was busy with another student, so Zahir tried to mend the bone himself. With a lot of focus and a couple of tries, he could fix Riley's wrist, but after that, he could barely use his magic. Lily confirmed Zahir had healed Riley's arm and then sent him home to rest. Zahir had taken a long nap but woke up groggy, which probably explained his terrible cooking.

As Zahir approached the door of his home, two pieces of parchment stuck out from the small metal box nailed to the house. Zahir's heart raced. *Mari.* The familiar emblem of Brahn's official notary sealed the letter shut, and Zahir took it, rushing upstairs. Although no one was around, Zahir had learned to always read Mari's notes alone after she had written a particularly *private* letter, which Markus had read over his shoulder. Zahir ripped the first note open as he crossed the doorway into his bedroom.

Skimming the first few words, Zahir's heart plummeted into his stomach, and as he read on, it became increasingly harder to breathe. Bile rose in the back of his throat, and he thought he was going to be sick. Morana was alive. She had decimated the city. And she was going after his family. The letter was dated eight days ago.

Zahir tore into the second letter, but it was no better, dated three days ago. He re-read the same line over and over again: *I found out that with every human soul I take, my psyche is damaged. I know that Morana took thousands of lives, but what if I become as insane as she?* Mari was in pain. And in danger. She was going after Morana.

By the time Zahir finished the letters, he already had his back-pack. He flung the letter to the ground and haphazardly packed his clothing and personal items. This couldn't be happening. Morana couldn't be alive. She had walked the world thousands of years ago and had been stabbed with a titanium blade. Yet, Mari had faced her: the most evil mage to ever exist. He would be damned if he was going to stay in Lovíth when Morana was threatening his family. He'd sworn to himself that he would always protect them, especially after the rebel attacks. But now,

Morana was a threat, and he was days away from Brahn with no real way of getting back. All he knew was that his family needed him, which was good enough for him.

Zahir slung his backpack over his shoulder and scribbled a short note to Markus: *I had to go back to Brahn. I'm sorry.* Without a plan, he headed to the docks to see if there was a merchant ship that would be willing to take him back to Brahn. He needed to get home *immediately*.

He didn't know how to process that Morana was alive. If Mari's magic was useless against her, what was he going to do? Could fire hurt a mage who could heal themselves instantaneously? The only way Zahir could think to harm Morana was with titanium, but that had proved to be ineffective, considering she still lived. If titanium and death magic didn't work... what would? Zahir desperately needed answers, and he wouldn't find them in Lovíth.

At the docks, Zahir spotted a small sloop that deckhands were filling with small wooden crates. One of the men stopped what they were doing as he approached.

"Can I help you?" he asked.

"Are you sailing to Brahn? I need passage," Zahir said, breathless.

"We can't bring passengers; it's against our trade agreement."

"I'm the High King of Brahn. I'll allow a breach of contract."

The man gave Zahir a once-over. "I don't know..."

Zahir lifted his hands, igniting them in bright orange flames. The man's eyebrows shot upwards. "Is that proof enough?"

"Zahir, what are you doing?" The familiar sound of Markus's voice resounded through the crisp night air.

Zahir whipped around, his hair flying and hands still blazing. "I'm going back to Brahn."

"You can't leave," Pryn said, coming up behind Markus. "You're not ready."

"I don't fucking care if I'm ready or not. My family is in danger, and I am going home. *Now*."

"Zahir," Markus started, taking a tentative step towards Zahir. "Let's talk about this before you burn someone's ship down."

"I am so tired of talking," Zahir said. "My wife is in danger, Markus. My people are being threatened."

Pryn walked right up to Zahir and reached towards his hands. He immediately snuffed his flame so as not to hurt them.

"Zahir," Pryn said, grabbing hold of Zahir's wrists. "What happened?"

Zahir glanced around; the deckhands watched with rapt attention. "We can't speak here."

"Let's go to my house. We can talk, and then if it's that important, you can go, okay?" Pryn said. "Just tell us what happened first."

"I can't delay—"

"Humor me," Pryn said.

As Pryn clung to Zahir's wrists, his anxiety and terror slowly melted. He didn't realize it at first, but Pryn calmed him with their magic. He didn't know why, but slowly, he nodded, allowing Pryn to lead him from the docks. Markus took the pack from Zahir's back while Pryn kept one hand wrapped tightly around

Zahir's wrist. As they took the twenty-minute walk to Pryn's house through Lovíth, it became harder and harder for Zahir to remember why he was so upset. After all, it was just a letter. Mari hadn't actually said she was in danger.

When Pryn led Zahir to the couch and let go of his wrist, his anxiety levels spiked. Terror seeped into his mind, even after Pryn forced a cup of tea down his throat. Zahir's hands trembled as he set the cup down, and Markus had wrapped a blanket around his shoulders. Zahir was not cold; he had never been so damn scared in his entire life.

"What the hell happened, Zahir?" Markus whispered after minutes of silence passed.

Zahir looked at both of his friends in turn before taking a deep breath. "Morana is alive. And she's terrorizing Brahn."

Pryn dropped their cup of tea on the floor, and the mug shattered into dozens of ceramic pieces. Markus sat frozen in place, staring in horror at Zahir as though he had murdered someone. The silence lasted longer than Zahir would have liked as his friends processed the news.

Pryn pulled their knees up onto the couch. "How is that possible?"

"I have no idea," said Zahir. "She should be dead."

"It has been *thousands* of years. Life mages don't live that long," Markus said, his voice shaking as much as Zahir's hands.

"We don't know much about life and death dual mages, though," said Pryn.

"But she was killed with a titanium blade," Zahir said. The man who stabbed her—the creator of the titanium blade—brought everyone to her body to see she had been killed. Hundreds of people paraded by her body to confirm her demise. Then, the man who stabbed her wrapped her in a cloth and burned her to ashes, like they had done to Ryker.

"Or so they said," Markus said, running a hand down his face. "Is it possible that she could be alive? Truly?"

"Could she have faked her death?" asked Pryn.

Zahir opened his mouth to respond. The only person who wrapped her body was the one who stabbed her. What if she hadn't been in the cloth?

Instead of that, Zahir said, "My birth mother is a dual mage."

And as Zahir unraveled the truth about his biological family and the other dual mages roaming the world, there were even more questions than answers. Zahir told Pryn what he had already told Markus: dual mages had never ceased to exist but went into hiding. Pryn asked many questions, most of which Zahir answered with a simple "I don't know."

"This is why I need to return to Brahn immediately," Zahir said.

"Zahir, you can't leave," Markus countered.

"My family is in danger, Markus. Do you not understand that?"

"Your family will *always* be in danger. You're the king; people will always want to kill you. If you leave now, you're going to die, Zahir."

"I will continue practicing on my own."

"You need to be here in Lovíth. Our magic is connected to our roots, and part of yours is here. You have tutors, trainers, and energy healers here. In Brahn, you're alone. You will never master your life magic if you leave now."

"If I stay here, I'm leaving Mari by herself." Zahir took a shaky breath as he pictured Mari's sleepless nights after returning from the rebel's capture. "Brahn is my home. I can't let it be destroyed."

"If you leave, you're sentencing Mari to a life without you. You'll be leaving her alone forever," Pryn said, their voice barely a whisper.

"You don't know that," Zahir choked.

"Zahir, if we know anything about dual mages, it's that you need to master both of your magics."

Leaning back onto the couch, Zahir pressed the back of his head into the cushion and squeezed his eyes shut, jamming his fists into his temples. Pryn was right. As much as he hated to leave Mari alone, he couldn't leave her forever. If he didn't master his magic, she would be alone for the rest of her life. He needed to stay, even if that meant leaving her unprotected.

Zahir's magic had improved, especially in the last several days. If he continued to work on his magic while he was on an upward path, it might not take him much longer before he could return home. And then not only would he have survived the curse of being a dual mage, but he could also return to his wife. If he stayed in Lovíth, he could spend more time working on his magic to ensure he stayed with Mari for years.

Images flashed through Zahir's mind of Mari's fear and stress after her kidnapping, but he forced himself to remember her bravery. Mari was not a damsel in distress. She was a strong woman who could take care of herself. She knew how to use a sword—mostly—and Zahir was certain she had improved while he'd been away. She was capable and strong; she was motivated, but his love for her shielded him from always seeing her capabilities. All he wanted was for her to be safe, but she could protect herself.

If she was with Illan, nothing would happen to her, not to mention that five guards, including Ren, always protected her. Hanan would also be there to help her, too, and her magic was more powerful than even Zahir's fire. Mari could take care of herself. Nothing would happen.

Roan was a good mage, but he hadn't quite mastered his swordsmanship, yet Anya and Taryn—the strongest fire mages in all of Brahn—would protect him with their lives. They would teach him whatever he needed to know. Roan was smart; he could pick anything up quickly.

"Okay," Zahir said, straightening. "I'll stay. But we need to speed up my training."

Chapter Eighteen

Mari

Mari's sword wavered with every step she took. She hadn't secured it well enough while getting ready, and they wouldn't make it to the cave's entrance in time if she stopped to fix it. Mari was uneasy about leaving the palace. While she didn't worry about Illan's capabilities of standing in her place, she worried it might look like she was abandoning her post, especially with Zahir gone.

Kane led the group away from the palace and towards the mountains. He'd explained the cave's entrance was at the summit, which entered the bowels of the mountain. Hanan hadn't left Mari's side the entire time. He carried a large backpack filled with wrapped and sealed elk meat to cook for dinner once they set up camp. The chefs at the palace were thrilled when they were presented with the elk; they rarely got to work with elk as the creatures were so hard to kill.

A familiar voice called out to them when they were barely half a mile from the palace.

"Wait!"

Mari turned to find Reina running towards the group with a sword strapped to her back and her dark brown hair tied into a bun. She'd strapped a bag haphazardly over her left shoulder and held it with one hand as she approached.

"You came," Mari said with a smile, stopping so Reina could catch up.

"We need to take her down."

Reina joined the group and walked beside Mari, gesturing to the back of the group with her head. The pair fell back, taking up the rear. Ren tried to approach the pair but retreated when Mari shook her head. Though she had apologized earlier to Ren for their spat, Mari still felt guilty for how she behaved.

Once they were a few yards back from Ren, Reina spoke.

"I have to tell you something," Reina said, wringing her hands together.

"Something as a friend or as an ally?" asked Mari.

"An ally," Reina said. When she didn't continue, Mari gestured for her to finish. "I found a journal of Rodrick's. I read it..."

Reina took a shaking, deep breath, and Mari placed a hand on her arm. "Take your time."

"I don't know how much you know about Rodrick and Zahir's friendship. They became friends after Rodrick became a guard. I met Rodrick a few weeks after that, but Rodrick was working with the rebels long before he became a guard; it was part of some elaborate plan to infiltrate the palace." Reina shook her head.

Mari cursed. "Did the journal mention if there are others in the palace working with the rebels?"

"There are." Reina nodded. "Rodrick mentioned others but didn't specify or give any indicators as to who, but that's not the worst part of the journal. Rodrick asked me to marry him after Zahir's betrothal to you was announced. Rodrick wrote..." Reina paused, dabbing at a tear in the corner of her eye. "That he never loved me and I was merely a pawn in his game. He wanted to gain Zahir's trust so they could 'share their experiences as husbands.'"

"Gods, Reina," Mari said, shaking her head. "I am so sorry."

"I don't know if Rodrick was working with Morana. I can only assume so, but that's why I'm here. I want to help. We need to destroy these rebels and Morana, and we can't fail."

"Well, I am glad to have you. You are an incredible fighter. We need your skills."

Reina nodded, staring at the ground. "Thank you for understanding."

"I don't think I will ever understand what you went through, Reina, but if you want to talk about any of it, I will spend hours listening to try and understand."

Mari and Reina caught back up to the group; Reina joined Kiernan, and Mari returned to Hanan's side. She couldn't stop thinking about what Reina had told her. Rodrick had always been a spy and manipulated Zahir into being his best friend without him realizing it. Rodrick hadn't turned evil; he always had been. He'd been working against the royal family the entire time and mentioned other spies in the palace, too. Mari dreaded imagining how many rebels were walking around her halls, pretending to be on her side. The thought chilled her to her bones.

As the sun fell below the horizon, Mari's anxiety heightened. The sun had just set before the group left, and all Mari could think of was the rebels remaining in the palace. The rebels had help from someone on the inside; how else would they have found the safe room? As Mari started to spiral, Hanan put a hand on her arm and furrowed his brow. She shook her head, as if that would knock the thoughts from her mind, and focused on the ground as they walked, refusing to think any more about the rebels.

As the path up the mountain narrowed and became more treacherous, Kane didn't allow them to use torches to light their paths in case Morana had a lookout. They were doing everything they could to avoid notice, dodging sticks and downed leaves to keep quiet. Kiernan had accidentally stepped on one, and the group halted, waiting for something to happen. But nothing did. The only sounds were those of their beating hearts and ragged breaths. After a few minutes, they continued their path up the mountain.

The party stopped at the mountain's peak for a few minutes before heading into the cave. The bright lights of Brahn glowed in the south—the city of a thousand flames. It was not as bright as it should have been. The last time she was on a mountain peak, Brahn seemed to go on forever, but now, it was at least half the size. She thought of all the people who'd lost their homes and vowed to punish the person responsible. After Seraphina confirmed that the dam was destroyed, Mari knew Orcian wasn't behind the attack. It must have been the rebels or Morana, or both. Lastly, to the north, the shimmery glare of the moonlight reflected off the ocean. Mari wished she could spend forever up here if only to stare at the world's beauty.

The last time Mari was on top of a mountain was with Zahir, the night before he left for Lovíth. They had snuck out of the palace to hike it. She could still feel his arms wrapped around her waist as they stared across the city. He pulled her into his warm chest and rested his chin on her shoulder, peppering her cheek and neck with feather-light kisses. When she thought the night couldn't get any more romantic, he'd tugged her into a dance, humming the song they danced to at their wedding. While she wasn't in love with him when they married, she couldn't deny the burning love in her heart now. After they'd laid together, Zahir pulled Mari to his chest and pointed out the constellations beneath the stars as the pair dreamed of a life without pain.

Too soon, Mari was dragged from the beautiful view and into the mouth of the cave. As they ventured further in, with one of the guards, Sal, at the front lighting the way with his magic and Kane at the rear, sword readied, the natural light dimmed until only Sal's flaming hands were visible. He held one before him to light the way ahead and the other at his side so no one tripped over anything sticking up off the floor. Mari kept her eyes on the ground and followed behind Hanan, who kept one hand on the hilt of his sword, just in case. Mari's hand flew to her sword at every noise until realizing it had been an echo from someone in her group or a drop of water falling from the cave's ceiling.

Eventually, a fork formed in the path, branching into two tunnels. Ren went through each one before returning. Neither path produced anything of note, they said, so after some deliberation, the group decided to split in two. Mari, Ren, Hanan, Raf, and Sal headed left. The rest of the group went right. If thirty minutes of walking produced no results, they would turn around and rejoin. Ren was hesitant to split the party but ultimately agreed it was the best thing to do.

Sal led the group and continued lighting up the path. Mari's hand remained locked on the hilt of her sword. Water dripped off stalactites and echoed as it hit the cave floor. The formations on the ceiling looked like claws and reminded Mari of Morana. While she didn't have claws, her bony fingers looked longer than they should have been.

Were they doing the right thing, going after her? Morana was extraordinarily powerful. If she couldn't be killed by a titanium blade, then what could kill her? Part of Mari wondered how much truth the old stories held and what parts had been lost in translation over the years. Someone back then would have known she was alive; someone must have helped her. Morana could not have escaped death without help. Perhaps the titanium blade hadn't pierced her heart but simply missed and badly wounded her instead.

The group stopped at a dead-end: a circular room with a high vaulted ceiling. It looked like the perfect place to set up a camp. As they searched the area, Mari found nothing except bugs crawling along the stalagmites and cave walls.

"If I were them, I would set up camp here," Sal said. He peered up at the stars, visible through a crack in the cave.

"Maybe *we* should," Hanan suggested, peeling himself away from one of the walls.

"It's a dead end; there is less ground to cover during watches," Ren said.

"I think it's as good a spot as any."

"So, should we wait for the other group?" asked Mari.

"There was the fatal flaw in our plan," Raf said, his expression grim. "What if both groups find something and we can't find each other?"

Everyone was silent for a minute until Ren spoke up. "There's no way..."

"Should one of us go back and wait? It's been nearly a half hour," suggested Sal.

"If someone's going, it should be two of us," Ren said. "Sal, take Hanan or Raf. I will stay with Mari."

"I will go with you, Sal," Raf offered, giving Hanan a quick kiss. "I'll be back soon."

"Be safe," Hanan said. He squeezed Raf's hand before Raf and Sal began their trek back towards the fork in the road.

"We shouldn't have split the party," Mari said. "That was a bad decision."

Ren shrugged. "It will be fine, but while we're here, should we get camp set up?"

Mari, Ren, and Hanan began setting up their tents and bed rolls. It was difficult to see what they were doing, but they could finally set up their tents. Mari rolled out her bedroll and lay down briefly, closing her eyes. She could almost feel the cold air of Yu'güe, reminding her of the time she got lost during a hunt and camped in a cave overnight.

"Does this remind you of Yu'güe, too?" Mari asked Hanan as she crawled out of the tent.

Hanan smiled. "A little bit. It is *significantly* warmer here, though. It feels almost refreshing to be up in the mountains, don't you think?"

"That's the one thing I miss about Yu'güe," said Mari. "I wasn't trapped in the house. I went to school, the neighbors, and up in the mountains to hunt. But now... I must ask permission to go into the city."

"No, you don't," Ren said with a laugh. "You sneak out into the city *constantly*."

Mari laughed. "It isn't constant, and besides, you always know when I'm going out there."

"Yes, and I hate it. If something happens to you, and someone finds out that I knew about your idiotic plan, I would be charged with treason."

"Wait, you sneak out every time we get together?" Hanan asked. "You told me the palace knew."

"Technically, *I* know, and Ren knows. That's two-thirds of the people who matter," said Mari.

"Illan would kill you if he found out how often you sneak out," Ren said.

Illan's disappointed gaze flashed in Mari's mind, remembering his reaction when he learned she and Hanan had snuck out to hunt. "I know."

"You shouldn't be sneaking out so often. It's going to get you into trouble one day."

Mari was about to speak but paused at the sound of footsteps. Immediately, she brandished her sword, holding it before her. Ren and Hanan followed suit and stepped in front of Mari, shielding her. Hanan extended a hand, ready to rip souls if needed to. Mari's heart dropped at the thought of using her magic again in battle. While it was a huge asset, she couldn't live with herself if she was forced to kill another person.

"I thought we were friends," Reina said with a laugh as she led the group into the room.

Mari breathed a sigh of relief. "Oh, thank the Gods."

Sal explained that he and Raf found the other half of their group already heading down the path. Kane said that the other side kept going, but they found nothing of note. After seeing the dead end here, Kane said they would all venture down the other path in the morning. Until then, it was time to set up camp for the night.

Once the rest of the tents were pitched and sleeping mats unfurled, Sal lit a fire in the center of camp, tendrils of smoke curling around the elk meat. Mari sat with her knees pressed against Hanan's. There was enough room for the tents, but the remaining space in the tunnel was lacking. Their fire was nested near one of the stone walls where Kane was leaning, and the heat was so intense it seared Mari's cheeks, warming her more than she would have liked.

"So, what is the plan?" Mari asked Kane as she ate her meal.

"We rest for a few hours and have a watch rotation. Ren and I will take the first watch," Kane said before explaining the order of shifts. After he and Ren had their turn, Raf and Hanan would go for another two hours before waking the next pair of soldiers, and lastly, Reina and Kiernan would take their shift. Mari felt guilty that she couldn't take a turn but understood it could dismantle the whole mission. The rest of the group was unknown; she threatened their safety.

"We get up early with the sun tomorrow. If anyone is hiding in this cave, they will be up around then, too. Hopefully, we will find something," said Kane.

While Kane and Ren settled into their positions for the first watch, the rest of the group padded into their tents to get all the rest they could. Once Mari had closed the flaps, she opened her backpack and peeled off her sweaty clothing for a fresh set. She refused to bring a nightgown; if they were attacked in the middle of the night, she didn't want to wield a sword in a silk dress. Instead, she slipped into a pair of long stretchy pants and a loose black shirt after raiding Zahir's closet for his training shirts that still smelled like him.

Mari lay on her back and closed her eyes, pulling the small blanket up to her chest. She allowed her hands to drop to her sides and focused on relaxing her body, practicing the meditation techniques her mother had taught her. Mari brought her focus to her breath, extending her inhales and exhales while intentionally loosening the muscles in each part of her body one by one. Soon enough, her body tingled, and it felt like weights held her to the ground. Even with the anxiety of what was to come, Mari was relaxed enough to fall into the deepest sleep she'd had in a long time.

Chapter Nineteen

Zahir

When Zahir opened his eyes within a lush forest, he realized he was in the dreamscape again. He and Pryn were working on his alignment. After he had told Markus and Pryn about Morana, Pryn had suggested alignment. First, Pryn meditated to cleanse their energy before working with Zahir and Markus. Zahir had immediately slipped into the trance, his subconscious needing a break from the chaos of the evening.

The chilly breeze tickled Zahir's neck as he walked around the green meadow. He made his way towards the trees, the scent of pine filling his nose as he walked. Before long, he found the stream where he had met with Ryker the first time he was here. He wondered if his father would return or if he would simply be alone this time. Zahir sat upon a large boulder and rested, staring at the river before him, where the water parted over the rocks.

"Zahir?"

Zahir whipped around at the sound of a voice he would recognize anywhere. He stood up, his lips parting in surprise. Tears pricked his eyes as he realized what this could mean. Zahir rushed forward and wrapped Mari in his arms, and just like Ryker, Mari felt real, like she was actually *there*. Mari's arms wrapped around his waist, and together, they stood in each other's embrace for what felt like forever. Zahir's tears fell into her hair as his heart felt fit to burst. Having her wrapped in his arms felt like home.

When Zahir pulled back to look at Mari's face, she was crying, too. He wiped the tears from her cheeks and pulled her in for a kiss. She melted into him as their mouths collided. Zahir's stomach filled with butterflies, reminding him of the first time he kissed her.

Mari pulled away too soon, and Zahir's heart nearly shattered. "Where are we?"

"Please, Mari. Tell me you are not dead," Zahir's voice broke on the last word.

"Dead? No, I'm not dead. At least, I don't think so," Mari peered down at herself. She wore one of his shirts and a pair of tight black pants. Her hair had grown slightly from when he'd last seen her, falling over her forehead; her normally pale skin had a golden hue from spending time outside, and her arms filled the shirt well. It was clear she'd been training. When Zahir's eyes trailed over her body, he was reminded of *just* how much he missed her.

"How are you here?" Zahir asked, breathless.

"I must be dreaming. That's the only explanation."

Zahir shook his head and smoothed Mari's hair. "No, you're not dreaming." He then launched into a lengthy explanation about the last time he entered this realm. The last time he was here, he was with Ryker and had referred to this place as The After. Zahir shared how Pryn told him it was called astral traveling, where your soul leaves your physical body.

Mari smiled. "I know about astral traveling, Zahir. I didn't know other mages could do it, too." She then proceeded to tell him a story, one Zahir could almost picture for himself.

Mari was sixteen. She and Fahran, the boy she once loved from Yu'güe, were in his home alone while their parents attended a council meeting. Fahran was one of the strongest death mages in Yu'güe and simultaneously the most revered and feared in the village. Mari learned quickly why he was so strong; he practiced all types of death magic, even the forbidden parts. She'd kept this a well-guarded secret, never letting it far from her chest.

Fahran and Mari sat knee to knee in his small bedroom, her back pressed against his bed frame, the plush pelt beneath them keeping her legs from getting cold. Bright white candles flickered around them like half-moon shapes. Fahran rested his hands on his knees, his palms upturned as he spoke in low murmurs. Mari could barely hear him. His eyes were closed, and his fluffy black hair fell below his eyebrows, occasionally shifting with each strong exhale. He had a blanket wrapped around his shoulders. They were practicing what others called "darkness."

Darkness in Yu'güe had not been discussed since Morana was killed, as it was part of the magic she practiced, or so the legends said. Young children were told it would kill them, though that wasn't true. While Mari knew it had to have a negative effect, she never dared to ask. Asking was just as bad as doing. There were things that death mages could do that no one spoke of or Gods-forbid practiced, except Fahran. Fahran desired to know all he could about the darkness existing in his blood; Mari, nervous about the implications, couldn't stop exploring it with him.

As Mari watched Fahran put himself into a near-catatonic state, the chilly air caused bumps across her forearms despite the thick shirt she wore. The flames on the candles dimmed until it was as dark as night.

Mari's eyelids drooped with her breathing, and she let them fall close. Before long, she was so relaxed she could barely control her limbs, and it was snowing when she opened her eyes. Her boots crunched on the snow beneath her, and she whipped her head around, confused how she had traveled so far from Fahran's house without moving. Fahran had told her what darkness was like, but it was extremely disorienting to experience it for herself.

Mari found Fahran and ran over to him, tightly grasping his hand. She asked where they were, but he seemed to ignore her, his eyes trained ahead. Mari looked to where a woman stood in a thick coat, staring up at the snow as droplets fell on her face. She couldn't have been more than twenty or thirty; her long black hair fell to her waist, starkly contrasting her white coat.

Fahran led Mari over to the woman with tentative steps. When they approached, the woman made eye contact with them.

"Who are you?" asked Fahran, squeezing Mari's hand twice. That had been their signal that everything would be all right.

"I have not been hosted in quite some time, my dear." The high-pitched, crackling voice that emerged from her mouth was ear-splitting. "I am Vala."

"Vala, what a pleasure it is to speak with you. When do you come from?" asked Mari. As much as she loved learning about dead souls, there was something creepy about speaking with one.

"I was one of Yu'güe's first chosen people," Vala said.

"Wow. What was that like, if you can remember?" asked Fahran, taking a tentative step forward.

"I remember it all, my dear. In those days, it was a curse. We didn't know how it worked, and I could barely control it. Do you know how many I inadvertently killed? It still haunts me, even though I no longer walk in the world. I killed my mother, you know. I was so angry at her, and I could not contain my magic. One minute, I was arguing with her, and the next, I was weeping over her corpse."

"I am sorry for your loss." As Mari was about to ask her next question, the light in the sky flickered. From Fahran's explanations, she knew it was time to wrap things up before they were thrown back into their bodies. "I have one final question. What is it normally like here, in the After?"

"It is more beautiful than you could imagine. It is so colorful. Nothing can harm you here. You cannot harm anything, either. It is your own personal paradise."

With her final words, Mari and Fahran were thrown back into their bodies and fell forward, smacking their foreheads together. They groaned as they lay down on the pelt. Mari pulled a blanket over them as she curled into his side; her body felt weak like she was going to vomit. When Fahran did, she wrapped him in a blanket, kissed his cheek, and stumbled home.

"I didn't realize life mages could do this, too," said Mari.

"It makes sense that death mages can," Zahir said. "You work with souls; it makes sense you can talk to them."

"Zahir..." Mari paused. "Did you receive my letter?"

His eyes darkened as he nodded, recalling the dread of the past two days as he distracted himself and focused all his attention on training. He allowed himself to think about the letters for the first time since reading them. "How could you put that in a letter?"

"What did you expect me to do?" Mari asked. "You needed to know. Please tell me you are still in Lovíth."

"Markus and Pryn stopped me from leaving. Mari, I was about to burn a ship if they didn't take me home to you."

Mari put her hands over her eyes. "Gods, Zahir. You *need* to master your life magic."

Zahir pulled away from Mari, even though it ripped his heart in half. "I know I do, Mari. I know I will die. I *know* all of this.

But I also know that if I stay here, and something happens to you... life won't be worth living."

"I want a life with you, Zahir. But we can't have that if you die. I don't know what I would do without you."

Zahir stepped back towards Mari until he towered over her once more. Reaching up, he grabbed her chin and tilted it towards him. "I will come home to you, my Queen."

Zahir kissed her then—slowly. Kissing her was as easy as breathing. After nine long moon cycles, he was finally with her, even for a moment, and it finally sunk in what he was fighting for. He was fighting every night and day to be with Mari, training to grow old with her and cuddle on the roof beneath the stars. He was fighting to love her for the many years to come.

When they broke their kiss, Zahir searched her eyes. "Please be safe, Mari. I love you."

Mari's eyes shimmered with tears. "I love you, too."

Too soon, Zahir was thrown back into his body. His eyes fluttered open, and even though he knew it was impossible, he felt Mari's lips on his. Zahir sat up slowly, running a hand down his face. He choked back tears as Pryn handed him a glass of water. It didn't help. All he could think about was being apart from Mari.

He stood up slowly, answering Pryn's questions to the best of his ability.

"Did you see your father again?" asked Pryn, sitting back on their heels.

"No," Zahir ran a hand through his hair, brushing the sweat at the base of his neck. "Mari."

Pryn lurched back. "Mari? Gods Zahir, I don't even know what to say."

Zahir looked at Pryn's terrified expression and the blood draining from their face. "She's not dead."

Pryn put a hand to their chest, then furrowed their brows. "How did you meet with her then?"

"Death mages can access the After, too."

"Does she know how she did it?" asked Pryn, standing.

Zahir shrugged as he paced the room. "They call it astral traveling."

"Can she do it on command?"

"I don't know."

"Did she know she could do it?"

Zahir was desperate for a minute alone to process. "Yes."

"Is she okay?" Pryn asked, blowing out the candles on the floor.

"Yes," Zahir said.

He couldn't take the questions anymore. Before Pryn could ask another, Zahir left Pryn's house for a minute alone. Markus asked if he was okay, but Zahir waved him off.

Zahir leaned against the ivy-covered wall of Pryn's house, allowing the door to close behind him. The night sky was peppered with bright stars, and Zahir stared at them, searching for anything that would ground him. He whirled, desperately trying to find Brahn's constellation, and when he found the Ever-Burning Candle twinkling in the night sky, he finally unclenched his fists.

Zahir had told Mari he loved her for the first time. Best of all, she loved him, too, but then she was gone. While Zahir wasn't certain the next time he would see her, he did know he would never let her go. He would tell her he loved her every morning when they woke and every night before they slept. Zahir could barely believe he told Mari this after meeting for the first time in nine moon cycles. Before he left, he was worried the distance would make them grow cold and distant. Zahir was relieved that hadn't come true and was beyond thankful that Mari returned his feelings. Mari felt like home, and her embrace was the only thing he needed. All he wanted was to return to her in Brahn, but he needed to master his magic first.

Before Zahir even processed the thought, he walked towards Lydia's house. Markus and Pryn were convinced he needed to heal that part of his history before he could master his magic, and he would do just that. He would do whatever it took to get home to his family, even if it meant ripping his heart open and slowly restitching the wound.

When Zahir knocked on the door, he didn't even think about how late it was. All he knew was he didn't need sleep—he needed answers. Lydia answered the door in a satin robe, her hair tied in a knot atop her head. She rubbed her eyes and yawned.

"Zahir? What are you doing here?" she asked.

Zahir stared at her, dumbfounded. "Gods, I am so sorry. I don't know why I thought it was okay to just show up here at night. I will come back at a different time."

As Zahir spun to walk away, he felt Lydia's hand on his shoulder. "You are welcome here any time of day or night. Come in. I'm already awake; we may as well talk."

Lydia led Zahir into her dark home and lit candles with her fingertips as she passed. Watching his birth mother perform fire magic in Lovíth was almost unsettling; it was one thing to hear she was a dual mage, but another to see her use her secondary magic... Zahir didn't quite know how to feel.

Lydia sat Zahir on the couch with a cup of chamomile tea and sat in an armchair beside the couch. She silently sipped her tea, waiting for Zahir to start, but the problem was... Zahir didn't know where to begin.

"I need to master my life magic, but I'm struggling with it," he said.

Lydia nodded. "I understand. When I learned my fire magic, I had the hardest time."

"How did you get through the struggle?"

Lydia shrugged. "I had a fantastic tutor. I listened to everything she said. We practiced all hours of the day and night. I barely slept for weeks. When I was eating, I read books. Every night, I wouldn't sleep until I did something, even something small like lighting or extinguishing a candle beside my bed. Slowly, it became easier until it was second nature."

Zahir nodded, absorbing every word. Lydia had worked hard, day and night, and it finally sunk in that Markus and Pryn were right. He hadn't been working hard enough, as much as he believed he had been. He hadn't been listening to everything he was told; he hadn't read books; instead, he would frequently go to bed frustrated.

"I find myself struggling with my energy when I practice life magic," Zahir said after a moment of silence.

"Yes, well, it does take a toll on the body. You must fight through that exhaustion a lot of the time. Even the most seasoned life mages will feel that fatigue. My wife is upstairs, completely spent after her alignment session. You can't berate yourself for being tired; your body needs to heal after you heal someone else."

"But why? This isn't a part of fire magic."

"It's taxing on the body to use your magic to heal someone. When we heal, we are creating something from nothing. In fire magic, you are using things that already exist to aid your magic. It's like when you ignite a candle, the wick is flammable, but when you heal a cut, for example, you're stitching together skin with fibers that don't exist. You're creating something from nothing."

Zahir nodded as Lydia spoke, finally understanding how life magic worked. He hadn't understood the difference between how fire and life magic operated until then and could now forgive himself when he was exhausted.

Lydia picked up a letter opener sitting on the coffee table and sliced her palm, letting blood droplets pool on the surface. "Heal me."

Zahir put his tea down and leaned forward to grab Lydia's hand. He wrapped his hands around hers and pictured the magic flowing through him. Within seconds, bright green light encased his hands and magic poured from his fingertips. When he pulled away, the last bit of skin had stitched together, leaving nothing but a thin white line.

"Are you tired?" asked Lydia. When Zahir shook his head, Lydia sliced through her hand once more. "Do it again."

And they did this over and over until Zahir could do it without even focusing his magic into his hands. By the end, Zahir felt better about his ability to perform life magic. If processing his mother-related trauma would help enhance his magic, then he would spend every minute with Lydia until he could return to Brahn.

Chapter Twenty

Mari

Breaking down camp was significantly harder than setting it up, as they tried not to leave a trace. Mari and Raf took the lead in preparing breakfast, dividing up helpings of dried venison, berries, and slices of baked bread.

Mari had slept through the night and hadn't woken up once. It wasn't until Ren shook Mari's foot that she shot up, the memory of meeting with Zahir fresh in her mind. Tears pricked the corners of Mari's eyes as she changed into her day clothes. It was incredible to see Zahir, even if it was by using her darkness. Yet it broke her heart to know she wouldn't get to see him again for several moon cycles. She could hardly believe he had confessed his love for her, and while deep down she knew he loved her, hearing it from his lips felt different.

Part of Mari wondered if she had really been using her darkness or if she'd been dreaming. It felt so real being with him, like it had felt when she and Fahran did it.

The group began their trek through the cave, with Sal again at the front. He lit the path for them again, but today, the group took quieter steps. They turned left down a path halfway down; they could have continued straight and taken a right at the end, but Kane wanted to explore each pathway. Morana was somewhere in this labyrinth, so it made sense to check all routes. However, as time passed, the search felt tiresome—risky, even. By going down every route, they were exposed, their paths becoming predictable.

The next area led to a dead end, so they went the other way and took the right turn. About fifty feet later, they made two lefts in a row and were met with yet another fork.

This time, Sal went ahead to scope out where each path went. When he returned, he said the path straight ahead turned left and then immediately right, whereas the path to the right took an immediate left. Kane opted for straight, and after a series of several turns, the party faced a wide river.

"We can hop across the boulders," Kane said.

"Those look really mossy," said Ren. "We can't risk falling and being swept away by the current when we don't know where the river ends."

"We will be fine," said Kane, stepping onto the closest boulder.

Mari was uneasy about hopping across a river, especially as they couldn't see its end and had no idea where it might lead. If someone fell in and got swept by the tide, they could die. Mari was unwilling to risk anyone for something they could avoid.

Just as Sal was about to step onto a rock, Mari stopped him. "Kane, go tell us what you find. Sal will stay and light up the room while the rest of us wait here."

Kane nearly slipped off a boulder as he responded. "Okay, I will report back soon. I only have one torch on me, though. I was hoping to save it if we split up again."

"We have extra torches. Be careful, and yell for us if you need help," said Mari.

As Kane disappeared from view, Hanan whispered. "Was that unsettling for you, too?"

"A little. There was another path we could have gone down. I am not confident in his decision-making."

Mari was a little uneasy about Kane's choices. Illan had vouched for him, and though Mari trusted his opinion, Zahir had been friends with Rodrick, who ended up being a traitor. Despite how well you might know someone, you will never know *everything* about them. Mari trusted Kane only because of Illan's word, but she wouldn't risk crossing a river for him. She knew there was a chance of death if they found Morana or the rebels, but *that* was a risk she was willing to take.

"It looks like the path circles around." Kane's voice made Mari jump as he approached from the side.

"Thank you for scoping it out; I'm glad we did not all cross the river."

The group began to travel down the path with the double right turn. Mari slowly approached Ren and Hanan and lowered her voice. "Something isn't feeling right with Kane."

"The thing with the river put me on edge," Ren whispered. "Why would he make that choice when there was another way? In fact, *two* other ways."

"Well, one of them just lead to the other side of the river," Hanan pointed out.

Mari rolled her eyes. "Yes, thank you. That was very helpful."

"Okay, now is not the time to be siblings," Ren said, their tone sharp.

Mari bit her lip to keep from laughing. "We are in too deep to change our plan, but we need to keep an eye on Kane."

Kane lifted his head. "I smell smoke. They must be close."

Kane slinked around to lead and overtook Sal. Within minutes, the group stumbled upon what looked like the remnants of a camp in a chamber, exactly like the one they were in last night. The area was clear of debris, save for a pile of burning embers in the center of the room. Mari glanced up and saw small tunnels about twenty feet above where they were. As Mari shifted her gaze, something metal glinted in the sunlight and streamed through the open-air ceiling.

"Get down!" screamed Mari as the first arrow sailed through the air, landing a few inches from where she stood.

Ren rushed to Mari and pulled her from the chamber. One of Ren's soldiers immediately followed, walking backward; she raised her bow, ready to shoot. Mari heard a handful of arrows fly as the three of them made their way back. As soon as Ren got Mari out of the open room, three men clad in silver chainmail brandished their swords before them.

Mari and Ren immediately withdrew their swords, swinging at their assailants. Mari took on one man while Ren took on two. Ren's swordsmanship was unmatchable, even against two opponents. On the other hand, Mari was below the skill level of her opponent—but only just. When she struck, her opponent dodged it and immediately swung at Mari's legs, who jumped and stepped back before launching forward, nicking the man's armor as he narrowly dodged her blow. Before Mari could get another hit in, Ren swooped in and sliced the man's head clean off. Blood sprayed Mari in the face while Ren stood over the man's corpse.

Ren looked back at Mari, their face splattered with blood. "Are you okay?"

"Fine," Mari said, staring wide-eyed at the now-dead man. Even though he was trying to kill her, it hurt her soul to watch him die. Mari hadn't used her offensive magic in so long as it had been too much the last time she used it, even though it had been for her own protection. Even when faced with her own demise, she couldn't stomach the thought of using it again. She held her sword tighter and took a deep breath.

Wiping blood from her mouth and eyes, she turned to look at the battle behind her. Now, their small group faced more assailants than she could count. They were clad in silver armor that left little flesh exposed, their expressions animated as they fought—a mix of gritted teeth and narrowed eyes. They didn't fight with ease like Morana had, and as the fight raged on, a few appeared tired—drained. These were not trained soldiers.

Sal tore through the crowd, fighting titanium swords with his blade engulfed in flames. It was remarkable to watch; whenever he hit an opponent, they were slowly set alight. Mari watched as he burned opponents to the ground and made his way through the room. Hanan and Reina faced a couple of opponents each. Mari watched Hanan's hips and silently begged him not to mis-step. They had been practicing in the titanium gym, but he had yet to be cut by it. The sensation of the gym would never compare to being cut by a blade.

Before Ren could stop her, Mari raced onto the battlefield and raised her sword. As she ran, she released the soul of an elk and yelled for it to attack. She made contact with an assailant's sword, the reverberation of the impact shooting up her arm. Pushing against the other blade, the opponent stepped back, allowing Mari to swing again. Surprising herself, Mari sliced clean through her opponent's hand, and their sword clattered to the ground. As they screamed, Ren came up from behind and shoved their sword through the opponent's chest. The scream-ing turned to gurgling before it stopped altogether.

"Are you okay?" Ren asked. "Stop trying to do everything."

"I'm not helpless," Mari growled, swinging at someone who headed straight for her. She and Ren had the man down in seconds.

"I know, but you are still the queen."

"Then have my back," Mari said as she raced further into the fighting. Together, Mari and Ren took down man after man, sending them to their deaths. But as they took down one person, it seemed like ten more appeared in their place. Mari had no idea where they came from as their numbers grew. Ten against one hundred were not good odds.

"Mari, behind you!" Hanan yelled from across the room; he released the soul of a large buck, commanding it to attack.

Ren whipped around before Mari could, stabbing a man through the stomach. She clapped Ren on the shoulder before the two of them moved on, and after a few minutes, they found their way to Kane, who made quick work of the assailants.

"Where are they coming from?" asked Mari, assisting Kane in taking someone down.

"The tunnels above us. They keep rappelling down," Kane responded. He slammed the hilt of his sword onto the head of his last opponent. "Morana must be near."

"If she were here, why wouldn't she show herself?"

"She likes to make an entrance."

Mari stopped fighting for a second and looked at Kane. "You speak like you know her."

Kane's sidelong gaze confirmed her concerns. Kane wasn't working for them.

They spun to face each other, and their swords clashed. Mari was no match for Kane's strength. Kane pressed against Mari's sword, forcing her to step back. He whipped his sword at her again, their blows connecting. Mari narrowly escaped his titanium blade, wisps of her hair falling into her eyes as she dodged.

"Ren!" Mari yelled.

"They're occupied," snarled Kane.

Mari risked a sidelong glance to where Ren fended off three assailants. They couldn't get over to her fast enough. The soul of her elk evaporated as an assailant slashed it with a titanium blade. Mari returned her gaze to Kane and narrowed her eyes; she would *not* let him beat her.

Mari was able to get one solid hit in, destabilizing him long enough to get away. Spinning, she sprinted in the opposite direction toward Hanan and sent the soul of a large buck over her shoulder towards Kane. Before she reached him, someone screamed.

Mari stopped short and spun. The buck was nowhere to be seen. Kane locked eyes with Mari, the smirk on his lips making her blood boil. Kane fought through each of her friends, forcing them to their knees one by one. Kane knocked Ren's sword from their hand and stomped on their fingers, shattering through bones. Ren picked up the sword with their other hand and swung, but Kane knocked them back once again, sending them skidding across the floor toward a group of five assailants.

Kane was too quick for Sal to get his hands on him. Sal ignited himself in flames and shot fire at him, but as the titanium blade pierced Sal's left shoulder, it was over. As Sal grabbed his wound, Kane knocked his temple with the hilt of his sword and knocked him unconscious. Mari and Hanan shot four animals from their arsenal toward Kane, but it was like he anticipated it. Two other assailants came to his aid, and the three fought the souls with little difficulty.

Mari sent a mountain lion towards him, her voice shaking as she commanded it to kill. It pounced on Kane and knocked him to the floor, and Mari's heart pounded as the animal moved to rip out his throat. The soul disappeared—a sword protruding from its back as it dissolved. Mari cursed.

Once Kane was back on his feet, he went for two of Ren's soldiers, but they were expert fighters. Only when two of Kane's allies joined him were they overpowered.

Raf rushed toward Hanan, and Mari watched in horror as Hanan joined his fiancé. She reached for her sword and stepped forward, following her brother. Within three steps, Kane slashed his sword through Raf's side, who wavered on his feet, blood spurting from the cut. Kane threw Raf aside, and he slid across the smooth rock floor, his sword flung twenty feet in the opposite direction. Hanan forced his gaze from Raf and brandished his sword.

Mari stopped, frozen, as Hanan fended off Kane, deflecting his blows. Kane sidestepped Hanan, who landed a single cut to Kane's bicep as he moved. Stepping back, Hanan raised his open palm, but Kane dug his sword into Hanan's dominant arm before his soul was taken. Blood spurted from the wound, and Hanan dropped his weapon, pressing the gash to stop the bleeding.

He was not anticipating that Kane would strike again. Eyes locked with Mari, Kane shoved his blade through Hanan's stomach, its tip jutting out of Hanan's back. He pulled the sword from her brother's body and tossed the weapon to the side like it was nothing. Hanan rolled onto his back, his arms limp beside him, eyes open but unseeing.

And then Mari began screaming.

"HANAN!"

Grief burrowed into the depths of her heart as she reached out toward the battlefield, and when she pulled her hands back to her chest, every enemy in the room collapsed.

Chapter Twenty-One

Zahir

Zahir's class was exhausting. Lily had Zahir observing a higher-level class with kids only ten or so years younger than him. They were conducting an exercise their teacher called 'clinic,' where the students practiced their magic on volunteers who came in to be healed by the novices. In Lovíth, not everyone was a mage, so they sought out life mages for healing. Zahir was impressed because the kids couldn't always heal their patients, but the volunteers were always understanding before letting an observing adult healer help.

Zahir was shadowing the oldest boy in the class, Jay, who had healed three broken bones, six kitchen accidents, and two burns in just a few hours. The only case he couldn't heal was someone with a concussion. The difficulty of healing internal sickness came from the inability to visualize the problem. With a scrape, Zahir could see the body part that needed healing, but with a concussion, there was swelling in the brain, and Zahir couldn't see that.

The patient complained of a headache after falling. Jay shone a light in their eyes, but their pupils didn't react as fast as they should have. Zahir knew this was a concussion; he had read a lot on internal injuries but struggled to visualize where his magic should go to treat it. Eventually, one of the adults overseeing the clinic came over, rested their hands on either side of the patient's head, and engulfed their entire head in green light.

"If someone has chronic pain from something like a broken bone that didn't heal correctly, can you help them with that?" asked Zahir. In all his time in Lovíth, he had never seen someone heal anything chronic.

"No," Jay said. "That's the limitation of life magic. We can only heal acute ailments. Chronic illnesses or injuries can only be managed, sometimes, with herbs and medicines. Mental illnesses, too, are like that."

"Why?"

"Life magic stitches together broken and torn things. Something that doesn't have a physical element cannot be healed. My mother has horrible headaches, yet her magic does nothing for the pain because there wasn't anything that *caused* the pain. She was born with it."

"That's awful. What does she do for them, then?"

"She puts a cold cloth on her forehead and lays in a dark room until it goes away. Once in a while, she'll try taking a pain tonic, but she says it doesn't do all that much. So no, life magic cannot heal chronic things," Jay said. "Let's have you try to heal our next patient."

Jay waved a man over who looked about Zahir's age with short brown hair. He held his left wrist and grimaced as he moved.

"Oh, I don't know if I'm ready for that," said Zahir.

"You will be fine."

The man sat down in the chair, and Zahir began the treatment like he'd watched Jay do. "Hello, my name is Zahir. What's your name, and what brings you here today?"

"Pleasure," said the man, his face pale. The wrinkles in his face revealed his age, and his paper-thin skin highlighted his veins. He grimaced with every inch he moved. "My name is Mace. I think I broke my wrist."

"What happened? Do you mind if I take a look?"

Mace shook his head and allowed Zahir to hold his wrist. "I fell off a ladder, and when I landed, it felt like my wrist was bent in a direction it was never meant to."

Zahir gently poked Mace's wrist. He apologized when Mace winced. This was the first time that Zahir was healing an injury he could not physically see. He could see what he was doing with the cuts and scrapes he'd healed before, yet he couldn't even tell if Mace's wrist was broken.

Zahir wrapped his hands around Mace's wrist and searched for the injury—something he had only done once before. Breathing deeply, he called to his life magic. The familiar feeling of the magic weaving through his body sent hums up Zahir's spine. It came alive as he searched for the injury, and as the magic worked towards his hands, he began to picture the injury in his mind's eye. He could see the fracture down the length of the bone, about an inch in diameter. He had done it. Zahir had been able to visualize the break.

Zahir smiled. "I'm going to try to heal the injury now."

Zahir held Mace's wrist gently and focused on the fracture. He pictured the magic approaching the surface of his palms and transferring to Mace's wrist. He envisioned Mace using his wrist and rotating it fully. When nothing happened, Zahir took a cleansing deep breath. He could do this—he just had to focus. Zahir closed his eyes and tried again, and after several long seconds, Zahir opened them. Bright green light engulfed his hands.

Once his magic dissipated, Zahir gently lowered Mace's wrist. "How does it feel?"

Mace gingerly raised his hand and smiled as he moved his wrist. "It's a little sore but significantly better. Thank you very much."

"I am glad I was able to help. I hope you feel better soon," Zahir said as Mace rose to leave.

"That was great, Zahir," Jay said, smiling.

"Thank you. I had never healed a break before."

"You should feel proud. You did very well. How do you feel?"

Zahir hadn't realized that his eyelids were heavy until Jay asked. "Honestly? Pretty tired." Zahir blinked as the words left his mouth, immediately wishing to close his eyes and sleep. Black spots danced across his vision.

"That's normal," said Jay. "Take some time to rest before you try anything else."

"I don't have time for rest," said Zahir, though mostly to himself.

Zahir was desperate to return to Brahn. All he could think about was practicing magic so Markus and Pryn would let him return home. He thought about what he would do if he saw Morana. Though Zahir *wanted* to say he would attack her with a ferocity he wasn't sure he possessed, he knew the truth. He would be frozen in place—terrified. What if she was too strong and he couldn't win? Would Mari pay for his inaction? Would Roan?

Clinic ended shortly after Zahir healed Mace. All the students returned to their homes to rest and prepare for the following day. Zahir was invited to join clinics as often as he wanted, and upon speaking with Lily, she suggested that Zahir moves to the clinic full-time. When Zahir asked why she wanted him to advance so quickly, her response was simple: the best way to learn life magic was to *do* it, and since he was still a beginner, he would benefit from more rigorous practice.

When Zahir told Markus the news, he was thrilled. Zahir was still exhausted from the clinic, but he and Markus had scheduled time to train in combat. The two men sparred for a few hours under the bright sun of Lovíth. Zahir still couldn't beat Markus, but he was getting closer with each round. It was hard to anticipate Markus's moves because his fighting was unique. Zahir always tried to watch his opponents to gain a sense of their fighting style, but Markus adopted an eclectic fighting style after training with multiple people. Because of this, Zahir was *never* able to anticipate his attacks.

After several long hours in the sun, Zahir was close to collapsing. But Zahir was not done. Lydia had asked Zahir to accompany her to the dual mages meeting that evening. Zahir had given a non-committal answer at the time, hesitant to put himself in a situation exposing him to so many more people. Part of him wanted to meet others like him—to know he wasn't an abomination like he had first thought—while the other part deemed it too risky. After pondering it all day, Zahir decided it was in his best interest to attend the meeting, at the very least, to gain some insider information to report back to Mari and Illan. He had learned a lot in Lovíth, and he was desperate to return to Brahn and share everything with them.

After washing off the dirt and grime, Zahir headed to Lydia's house. All she had said was if he wanted to come, he should join her before dusk. It was well before dusk, but he wished to spend time with Lydia before the meeting. The more time he spent with his birth mother, the more he slowly brought down his walls, accepting her as part of his life. While he would *never* view her as a mother, she was still a guiding figure who taught him about their bloodline. Zahir still had a thousand questions for her and hoped he would get to ask them.

Lydia was outside when Zahir arrived, tending to the hydrangea bushes outside her front door. She smiled when Zahir approached, offering him a hug, which he tentatively accepted.

"Have you decided to come to the meeting then?" asked Lydia, peeling off her dirty gloves.

Zahir nodded. "Yes, I want to meet others like us. I think it would be a good experience."

"Well, I'm thrilled. Do you want to come in? We have some time before we need to leave; we could have a cup of tea."

Lydia led him into the house and prepared a cup of steaming jasmine tea. The familiar smell reminded him of his first face-to-face conversation with Mari. It was right after they were wed, and the first thing she had asked him was if he liked jasmine tea. Even now, he recalled the look of pure embarrassment on her face, which he'd found oddly endearing. Thinking of Mari made his stomach hurt, remembering the danger she was in. When he returned to Brahn, he wanted Mari to be alive and happy and safe, so he could spend the rest of his life beside her. He wanted to wake up with her in bed every morning for the rest of their lives and take her to restaurants in the city to show her the beauty of the other clans. But most of all, he wanted them to be happy.

Lydia and Zahir talked over their cups of tea. Zahir asked a few of his burning questions, like who the first dual mage in their family was—their name was Jul, and they were a life and water mage—and if anyone in their family had been around when Morana was slain; in fact, there was someone, but they didn't witness it for they had run in fear. Zahir had not told Lydia about Morana's resurrection, mostly because he didn't know how much he could trust her.

After getting lost in conversation, Lydia sprung out of her seat and told Zahir it was time to head to the meeting place. Zahir was surprised when Lydia led him through a back door in the Quiet Berry, which, as usual, was anything but. Blair led them into a back room with six different locks. Once opened, a set of stairs greeted them, traveling below ground. Zahir and Lydia lit a small flame in their hands, lighting the path as they descended.

The stairwell led to a large, plain cement room full of thirty people of varying ages. The oldest person in the room seemed to be one hundred while the youngest was around twelve. People chatted and laughed loudly in conversation. Though Zahir deemed it unlikely, he scanned the room to see if there was anyone he recognized. His eyes halted on a familiar brown face framed by a short bob. He would have known her anywhere.

"Taryn?" Zahir said, mostly to himself. He left Lydia and made a beeline for Taryn, who talked animatedly to an elderly woman.

Her eyes met his in surprise, but she smiled and rushed forward, throwing her arms around him. He froze, unable to hug her back.

"Gods, I am *so* happy I can finally tell you. You have no idea how many times I've come to talk to you only to find you with someone else. Zahir, you are very hard to find alone," Taryn gushed.

"Taryn, what in the world are you doing here?" he asked, still in shock. His thoughts *immediately* went to the upheaval in Brahn. As a twin flame, Taryn was one of the strongest fire mages. If Taryn was here, was Anya the only one left defending Roan? As much as Anya loved Roan, he didn't trust her to take care of their brother.

"I am a dual mage. Fire and death," she said, pulling out a small bird from her arsenal. As the bird soared around the room, a smile lit up Taryn's face.

"What?"

"I know it's a lot to take in. I am sure you are overwhelmed by how many of us there are. My mother is a death mage, you know; she just tells everyone she's mortal. It's a very good cover for her. After the four clans split, her family never went to Yu'güe; they've been hiding in Brahn for the last millennia. All my siblings are dual mages, too, but we alternate who comes to these meetings as it would be too difficult to get all of us here. I convinced them to let me come to this one, even though it wasn't my turn; Lydia wrote and said you might be attending."

"You knew about Lydia?"

"Zahir, I knew about Lydia before you did, but I couldn't tell you. I wanted to," Taryn said, a wet sheen glimmering in her gaze. "I didn't think it was right they had not told you about your gift. One night, I overheard your parents talking about it, and I'd already met Lydia, so I pieced it together pretty easily. I'm sorry I didn't say anything. If I could go back in time, I would have," Taryn apologized. Zahir had forgotten how fast she spoke, but it felt refreshing to talk with her again.

"I understand, Taryn. I do. I'm just a little confused. Does Anya know?"

Taryn shook her head. "I want to tell her one day, and I hope she doesn't hate me for keeping it from her for so long."

"How can you have a twin flame if you're a dual mage?"

"Honestly, Zahir, there is so little information on dual mages—and even less on twin flames—that I have no idea. None of the other fire mages have one. I'm the only dual mage with a twin flame, and I know it will break Anya's heart when I tell her,"

Taryn said, wringing her hands. "Especially since she's been my girlfriend for a while now."

"Right! Congratulations, I'm very happy for you. I was under the impression that Anya's feelings were unrequited."

"They weren't," Taryn said with a shy smile. "I was worried about what might happen if it didn't work out. We're twin flames; we're bound to each other. If we didn't work as a couple, I don't know if I could have been around her. But she got mad at me for going easy on her in training, and we got into a whole screaming match that ended in—"

"Please don't finish that sentence," Zahir said, raising his hand.

Taryn laughed, throwing her arms around Zahir's neck again and hugging him tightly. "I am so happy to see you."

Zahir wanted to ask how Mari was, but Lydia called the group to attention before he could. He glanced around the room, taking in the diverse group of dual mages. The youngest person was even younger than Roan, filling and emptying a cup of water from the table. Beside her, an elderly woman leaned on a cane and watched the child play. Two people stood in a heated conversation, their coats thrown over their forearms. Zahir wondered if they were from Yu'güe; he had never seen a coat like that.

Zahir leaned over to Taryn. "Can you stay for a while after the meeting?"

Frowning, Taryn shook her head. "My returning ship leaves as soon as this is over."

"Good evening everyone, and thank you for being here. I know some of you have traveled very far," Lydia began, gesturing to the two people with coats. "We have new members here tonight, so let's welcome them!"

The room erupted into applause. Zahir glanced around at the three other people who appeared as overwhelmed as he felt. Two of them were the people with coats, and the last was an older man who leaned back in his chair, his eyes halfway closed.

"We have been waiting for thousands of years for the right time to reveal ourselves, and I think that time is sooner than we think. Morana gave dual mages a bad name. We are not evil; we are not harbingers of destruction. So, we will announce ourselves to our home clans in three moon cycles."

As Lydia detailed the plan, Zahir and Taryn exchanged a concerned glance. They were the only two in the room who knew Morana was alive and terrorizing Brahn. With a raise of his eyebrow, Zahir hoped to convey to Taryn it was the wrong time for such a revelation. With Taryn's slight nod, she agreed.

"We will no longer be silenced. We will be able to walk this world without fear of someone discovering our secret. If we do this in solidarity, it will be harder to silence us. Know that we will not be taken to lightly. People will call us liars; they may try to cause us harm, but we cannot give up. We must *not* be afraid."

Cheers erupted around the room. The applause was deafening, but Zahir was unconvinced. He remembered how his clan had reacted to his marriage with Mari; they wished her dead simply because she could bring life to a dual mage.

But the one thing that sat uncomfortably in Zahir's mind was that he was not the only dual mage living in Brahn's palace, and if *that* was the case, how many others lived in the walls of his city? And how many knew that the oldest dual mage had been resurrected?

Chapter Twenty-Two

Mari

Mari rocked back and forth on her heels and pressed her hands into her chest while Raf stood beside her, clenching and unclenching his fists. It had been six hours, and Hanan's condition had not improved. The absolute panic rebounding off the walls of the hospital wing did little for Mari's nerves as she trained her eyes on Hanan's body on the cot, his blood soaking the sheets and dripping onto the floor. The weak rise and fall of his chest was the only indicator he was alive and breathing. Mari needed Hanan to live. She would not survive grieving him a second time.

When Kane stabbed Hanan, Mari was convinced he was dead, and without a second thought, her grief consumed her. She annihilated over fifty people in one hit. It felt like electricity had burst through Mari as all those souls traveled to her at once. She'd blacked out, but when she came around, Raf stood screaming over Hanan's body. The base of her skull *burned* as she crawled to her brother, tears streaming down her face. It was only when she reached him that she realized he was breathing. His breaths were extremely shallow but he was alive.

Ren hadn't tried to hide the disbelief on their face as they surveyed the battlefield. Bodies littered the ground, and blood poured from injuries, painting the cave crimson. Blood trickled from Kane's skull, inching closer to Mari with every passing second. Reina stared at Mari, eyes wide and lips parted, while Kiernan had refused to come within five feet of her. He couldn't even look in her direction. Raf wouldn't look anywhere but at Hanan while Mari surveyed the cave, bile rising in the back of her throat. When the guilt became too much, she walked to the corner of the room and emptied her stomach. She wiped her mouth with the back of her hand, and the group was on the move when she turned back.

Wounded, bloody, and exhausted, the party had made a makeshift stretcher and moved as fast as they could back to the palace. Sal had broken his wrist during his fall, so he couldn't do much except light the pathway. Ren and their soldiers carried the stretcher despite their injuries. Blood gushed from a wound on Raf's head, and Reina had dislocated one of her shoulders. Mari took up the group's rear and walked backward, ready to kill anyone who neared.

She couldn't believe what she had done. She had killed *fifty* people, and their souls were a part of her. Kane was a part of her, too. She would carry his soul with her for the rest of her life. Mari couldn't escape the image of the battlefield as they journeyed back to the palace. This couldn't be happening. She couldn't have done this.

As they neared the palace, Mari ran ahead of the group to ensure the medics were ready to take care of Hanan. She sprinted as fast as her legs would carry her, her chest burning as she ran. The group moved slowly, carrying Hanan while dealing with their own injuries, but Mari ignored the searing pain in her limbs. She would do anything to save Hanan.

When she arrived at the palace, Mari rushed towards the hospital wing, bloodied and wild-eyed. She ignored the concerned glances from the servants and guards; she refused to stop, even after the guards yelled her name. Mari needed Amí.

Mari burst through the doors of the hospital wing, and Amí jumped from her seat.

"Your Highness, sit. Let me tend to your injuries," she said, rushing forward.

Mari shook her head. "Hanan is hurt," she managed between gulps of air. "He's nearly dead. Help him first. I am fine."

Amí nodded. "Where?"

Mari led Amí and three other medics through the palace, where they intercepted the group at the door. Somehow, Hanan looked even paler inside the palace walls. Amí had clutched her chest but quickly composed herself, leading the group back towards the hospital wing, where medics rushed around him, tending to his wounds, and checking the damage caused. The wound in his stomach was still wide open; it looked worse the longer she stared at it. Hanan's guts spilled from his body while

Mari sat helplessly beside him. If they didn't get a handle on the stomach wound, the medics said he could die.

Mari reached for Raf's hand and squeezed. She peered at her soon-to-be brother-in-law; the blood drained from his face. He was so pale Mari almost got him a chair in case he fainted. But she didn't want to call attention to his state in case it made him feel worse. For now, Raf was steady on his feet, but Mari didn't know how long that would last.

After several long hours of watching the medics work with Hanan, Illan, and Maura had to drag the pair away, forcibly removing them from the hospital. Amí had tried to treat Raf and Mari's wounds, but Mari refused, demanding that she go help Hanan. If anyone knew how to heal him, it was Amí. She was the best medic Mari had ever known.

Now, sitting outside the door to the hospital, Mari and Raf held cups of tea to their chests, untouched. Blankets had been draped around their shoulders, and food sat forgotten beside them. Numbness had worked its way into Mari's legs and up her back. She couldn't move. The base of her skull burned but had faded to an irritating buzz. Mari wondered how hard she'd hit her head when she fainted as she was barely cognizant of anything except the door, willing for someone to come out and tell them Hanan was recovering and would live a normal life. After all the pain Hanan faced growing up, this was the *last* thing he deserved. Hanan deserved peace and happiness to live the life he never thought he'd get.

Slowly, Mari stood and wrapped the blanket tighter around her torso as a chill set into her bones. Her legs nearly buckled beneath her, but she took a few steps, enough to rid some of the numbness. Raf watched her pace the hallway.

"What?" Mari asked after ignoring his stare.

Raf stared at her, unblinking. "Your hands."

Mari glanced down at her fingers that peeked out from under the blanket. Her fingertips were black as night. Tossing the blanket off her shoulders, she peered at her arms, where tendrils of the deepest black crept up her body; her veins, normally a pale blue, were replaced by dark black lines. Worst of all, Mari felt invigorated; even after the exertion of battle and racing back to the palace, Mari felt no exhaustion.

"What's happening to me?" whispered Mari. She immediately picked the blanket back up and hid her hands beneath it. "No one can see this."

"How are you going to hide that? Is that from your magic?"

Mari winced at Raf's words.

She had still not processed the gravity of what she'd done—murdering fifty people with her magic. She didn't even know she was capable of that. But as Mari stared at her hands, it hit her right in the chest. She had used her magic again. Mari leaned against the wall, bracing herself with her palms splayed across it. Bile rose in the back of her throat.

"What did I do?" she whispered.

And that was when the door to the hospital opened. Raf immediately stood as Amí emerged. "He is stable but not well."

Mari breathed a sigh of relief. "He is going to live?"

"I cannot be certain, but his healing process has started."

Mari and Raf collapsed against one other. Even the slightest chance he would live was good enough for Mari.

"Can we see him?"

Ami shook her head. "Not yet. Everything is very clean in there; we can't risk having anyone come in. We are going to bar off this area and set up a temporary medical center in the ballroom. Hanan will have constant care. We will give him pain tonics as well as something to keep him sedated. Hopefully, the sedation will help his body heal, but... we may need to call for our King to come home and help us."

Mari's breath hitched. As much as she wanted Zahir to return, he needed to stay in Lovíth to master his life magic to ensure his survival. He couldn't come home for this. But if Zahir had mastered some of his magic, he could help Hanan, and Mari would give anything to save her brother. Choosing between the life of her brother or husband was an impossible choice to make.

"I don't know if Zahir can come home."

Ami cocked an eyebrow. "If I know anything about him, his family always comes first. If you ask, he will come." When Mari didn't respond, Ami continued. "Can I *please* tend to your wounds now, my Queen?"

Mari gave a solemn nod, allowing Ami to lead her and Raf to the ballroom, where a team had already set up a few cots and carts with various supplies and tonics. Sitting on the edge of a cot, Ami cleaned and bandaged Mari's scrapes, none were serious and would have healed on their own. Nevertheless, she allowed Ami to tend to them, if only to appease the medic.

"What is this?" Amí asked, lifting Mari's hands into hers. Mari breathed a sigh of relief at Amí's tone—it was curious but lacked all judgment.

Mari stared down at her lap. "My magic. I murdered a host of people."

Amí nodded, almost in understanding. "I cannot fix this."

"I know."

Ideas danced in Mari's mind about how she would ask Zahir to help. She knew it was the right thing to do, but she didn't want to beg him to come home if his tutors didn't think he was ready. Mari couldn't let Zahir come back to save Hanan if it meant he would die instead. But she couldn't let Hanan die either.

Exhaustion settled into Mari's veins as she journeyed to her chambers; all she wanted was to take a batch and sleep for several days. Anya nearly collided with her, neither woman watching where they were walking.

"Watch where you're going," Anya spat, glaring.

Mari shook her head and moved aside, but Anya blocked her path, shifting her weight. "What do you want?"

"How is your brother?"

"Alive, thank the Gods. I am so overwhelmed. All I want is a nap."

"Do you really have time to sleep when rebels and a vicious dual mage are running amuck? Especially after being back-stabbed by one of Illan's allies."

Mari blanched at Anya's words. "How do you know?"

She shrugged. "Illan shouldn't speak so loud to the advisors."

"Illan hasn't spoken to the advisors since I returned."

"Hasn't he?"

Mari gritted her teeth. Of all the days Anya could taunt her, today was the one where Mari had no patience. Between Anya's taunts and Illan's overstepping, Mari's anger boiled over.

"I would love to discuss the rudeness of your eavesdropping, Anya, but I cannot deal with this right now."

"You don't care?" Anya asked, cocking her head to the side.

"I *do* care; however, I have much bigger things to deal with than worrying about you fucking spying on us. So, you can either move out of my way, and we can talk about this another time. Or," Mari pulled the titanium knife from her waistband and raised an open palm to Anya as if to use her magic, "I am going to stab you with this titanium knife."

Anya narrowed her eyes. "You would *never* cut me with that."

Mari brandished the knife, slicing a thin line in Anya's loose shirt. "The next one breaks skin. Move."

She barged into Anya's shoulder, who gasped, whirling to watch Mari storm into her room. Mari smiled; it felt good to finally be taken seriously. Mari tucked the knife back into her waistband and locked the door behind her. She leaned her back against it, staring blankly at the bed. She desperately wanted to slide under the warm covers and sleep, but she couldn't while covered in more than one person's blood.

So, Mari slipped into the bath and cleaned herself. She scrubbed her hair several times, but nothing could rid the feeling of Hanan's blood from it. Once Mari had washed her body, she sank under the water and let the pressure build in her chest. She wondered what would happen if she never went up for air. The burning in her lungs kept her grounded—she was really there, and everything was real. This was no dream, despite how much she wished it were.

Mari came out of the hot bath as red as flame. Wrapped in a plush towel, she wiped the steam off the mirror and stared at herself. Her eyes were half closed, and the minor scrapes on her face made her appear even more exhausted than she felt. Mari touched her face but recoiled at the sight of her fingers. Her nails were coated in black. She stared back at her reflection. She was a monster. Mari murdered fifty people because one of them had tried to kill her brother—a man she would now be stuck with for the rest of her life. Kane was a part of Mari now, and she *hated* being tied to a traitor.

Ever since she killed all those people, a faint buzzing re-sounded at the base of her skull. She would feel a shock down her spine whenever she stole a soul, but this was different. It was the same shock but focused on one spot, and it hadn't gone away. She hadn't felt anything like this after killing an animal or even those two rebels last year, but now she couldn't escape the sensation.

Mari pressed her fingers into her temples and squeezed her eyes shut, somehow making it worse. When Mari finally had enough, she screamed, releasing the souls into the bathroom. Fifteen of them, including Kane, lined up before her. Kane looked exactly as she remembered, and Mari had to refrain from lurching back. He was dead; he couldn't hurt her.

"She likes to make an entrance," Kane said.

Mari's heart turned to stone. "No."

"Morana must be near."

Mari clutched her chest with one hand and balled her other into a fist. This couldn't be happening. Kane was speaking to her, repeating the last things he had said. Mari leaned against the bathroom sink and rested a hand on her forehead. She must be feverish. But as Mari touched her head, the buzzing hushed.

And that's when she heard it. The low murmurings of the souls lined up in front of her. They spoke, their words indistinguishable. Their mouths moved, almost in sync. It hadn't been a buzzing in her head—it was the culmination of fifty voices.

Mari slipped under the covers and pulled Zahir's pillow into her arms, wrapping her body around it and closing her eyes like the pillow was him. It no longer smelled like him, and the realization broke her heart. She stood and grabbed one of his shirts, where his smell still lingered—the familiar aroma of smoke and leather filling her nose as she inhaled. Gripping the shirt in her fist, she held it close to her face, and with every inhale, she got a comforting smell of Zahir.

Mari tossed and turned all night, overcome by wild dreams where Hanan really did die, or it was Zahir instead. Over and over, the dreams plagued her until she couldn't think of anything else. And when the sun rose, Mari was thankful because until the sun set, she would not relive her nightmares. The bad dreams were soon replaced with the buzzing.

For the first time in a long time, Mari dressed in a gown. She couldn't remember the last time she had worn one, preferring her royal armor whenever she attended council meetings and training clothes during her day-to-day. Mari dug through her closet until she pulled out a pair of cream gloves. The gloves, coupled with the gown's long sleeves, would hide the tendrils creeping up her arms. She could hardly stand to look at them, a constant reminder of what she did. Mari had only seen these marks once before—on Morana's hands. Were these markings permanent? Would this forever be a reminder of what she'd done? Mari gripped the sides of her head and pulled at her hair. This couldn't be happening. She had killed without remorse.

As much as Mari told herself that she was saving the lives of her loved ones, it didn't penetrate through the chasm of guilt in her chest. Mari's initial shock and grief controlled her actions, and she would never have killed so many people otherwise. Yet the thing that made Mari's skin crawl the most was the sheer destruction she had caused in seconds. In all her life, she had never killed more than one thing at a time—to kill fifty people at once wasn't something Mari deemed possible. Guilt wracked her as she remembered the surge of power she felt in the fleeting seconds before she passed out. She'd felt invincible. But as soon as she awoke, shame replaced the feeling of invulnerability.

Mari nestled her crown atop her head and rolled her shoulders back, her eyes narrowing and lips pressing into a straight line. With a slight lift of her chin, her expression went from murderous to confident. It was a face she had perfected during Zahir's time away. Even if she didn't feel confident, she looked it.

Mari made her way to the hospital wing and knocked on the door. A medic greeted her and said Hanan was resting and stable, but she was still not allowed in. Amí promised to find Mari as soon as Hanan was allowed visitors. Mari then continued her path toward the council room. As she neared the door, she remembered what Anya had said about listening to Illan and the advisors. The doors to the council room were so thick that it was impossible to hear Illan through them. Mari wondered if Anya had a hideout above the council room where she listened in. So, Mari hiked upstairs and began her search. After much trial and error, she found a small closet where Anya had cut a hole into the floor. Anya had already set up camp inside the room; blankets were piled high on the floor, and a pen and several pieces of paper lay beside it. Mari frowned. Anya had been paying close attention to the council. How much did Anya know? Did she know everything? Mari knew she had to prevent Anya from spying on today's meeting.

Back in Yu'güe, Mari had become an expert at keeping her father out of her room when Fahran snuck in at night. One thing she'd learned was how to take the spindle out of a doorknob. While she wasn't allowed to lock the door, her father couldn't get mad if the door simply broke. She had never been caught; her father rarely tried to enter her room, so it had been more of a precaution.

Retrieving the knife from her waistband, Mari peered over her shoulder before getting to work. She made quick work of unscrewing the door handle and detaching the spindle. Within seconds, she was able to screw the doorknob back on, and with a quick test, the door to the closet wouldn't open. She slipped the spindle into her glove, deciding to dispose of it on the way to her meeting.

As Mari turned, Anya rushed down the hall toward her. "What are you doing here?" she spat.

"I was trying to see if you were spying on us today. I thought you were already inside, considering the door is locked," Mari said with a shrug. "Clearly, you aren't inside yet. Are you trying to keep me from seeing your lair?"

The color drained from Anya's face. "What do you mean it's locked?"

And as Anya jiggled the door handle, Mari could barely keep the smile off her lips. "Well, it looks like you're going to miss a council meeting. I'll be seeing you, Anya."

Mari walked quickly down the hallway, smiling as Anya's curses and banging filtered through the door. Halfway back to the council room, Mari dropped the spindle into the dirt of a potted plant and obscured it with one of the plant's green leaves.

The council room was deadly silent when Mari entered. Her advisors watched intently as Mari's heels clicked against the tiles on the way to her seat. Illan sat in his chair beside her, having vacated Zahir's spot upon her return. Illan's eyes followed Mari's every move; he pursed his lips as she approached and sat at the head of the round table. Folding her hands in front of her, she took a long breath before speaking.

"There is much to discuss today. First," Mari glanced to Illan, the humming increasing in her mind. "I would like you to explain how the tracker *you* recommended was secretly working against us the whole time."

Illan shook his head as the room erupted with low murmurs that buzzed through Mari's brain.

"I am as confused as you are, my Queen." Illan sighed. "I honestly did not know that Kane was a traitor."

Mari narrowed her eyes at him. She wanted to believe him, but she couldn't forget how her brother now clung to his life because of the man Illan had trusted. "My brother nearly died. I could have died because of Kane. You vouched for him. So, I ask again, how did he deceive *even* you?"

Illan's eyes widened with Mari's words, but what flashed across Illan's face was more anger than unease, nostrils flared and eyebrows furrowed. "Kane assured me that he would do anything necessary for his queen; he was proud to help find Morana and promised to keep our people safe. Little did I know that Kane was a master of deception," Illan said, shaking his head sadly. "I don't know how I missed it. And for that, I am sorry."

"Do you think we defeated the rebels?" Grimes asked, leaning forward on their elbows.

Mari couldn't help the laugh that escaped her lips. "I do not even wish to remind you how many times we foolishly answered that question with a yes. From now on, we must assume that we have *never* defeated anyone who harms us.

"We have met two groups of rebels, whom I would like to assume work for the same cause. However, I do not know. There are the ones who work with Morana. Then, there are the others who dissent against King Zahir. I do not know if Zahir told you of this previously, but we saw a rebel mark throughout the city one night. It was an A surrounded by a circle. In speaking with our friends, we learned it was a symbol to show the people wanted Anya on the throne instead of Zahir," Mari explained.

"People are openly calling for a different ruler?" asked Grimes.

Mari nodded solemnly. "I hope that these people have since been convinced that Zahir and I only want good things for Brahn, but I cannot be certain. We have been so focused on the external threats to Brahn, but I am optimistic that these people have found peace, especially given our efforts to rebuild the city and help those who lost their homes."

"And if they aren't happy?"

"Then we need to listen to them and learn what they want to see from us."

Fenris leaned forward. "King Zahir is the first ruler in a long time who is not the firstborn child. Obviously, we know why Zahir was chosen to be king, as do the people. But people do not like change, and this is a big one."

"I am sympathetic, but Zahir had no choice in what he is. He did not choose to be a dual mage. That decision lay with King Ryker and Zahir's birth mother. Zahir is a rightful heir to the throne."

"We must learn if these people are still calling for Anya or not," said Illan. "If so, we need to put a stop to it immediately. We cannot have Zahir return home to dissent."

"When is King Zahir supposed to return to Brahn?" Keir asked. "Originally, he was intended to be gone for six moon cycles."

Mari and Illan shared a glance before Mari said, "Yes, Zahir has been away for a little longer than anticipated. However, at the discretion of his trainers, he was requested to stay. He does not yet have a return date, but we anticipate it to be soon."

"King Zahir being gone this long raises questions of his loyalties."

Mari clenched her jaw and leaned forward, pressing her elbows into the oak table. "Is it not clear that if King Zahir does not master his life magic he will die? If he is to die without an appointed heir, how do *you* think Brahn will take to that?"

The silence was deafening. Mari leaned back in her chair, the left corner of her mouth quirking. She knew what made the council tick. The fact that she had not fallen pregnant before Zahir's departure boiled their blood. Ryker and Maura conceived Anya almost immediately after Ryker's coronation, and Zahir was born just a year after. Mari and Zahir had been married for over a year and had yet to produce a child.

Becoming a mother was something that Mari had always been expected to do. In truth, she dreaded the day she would have to bear children, and so she prayed to the Gods that it wasn't possible. Because it would be much easier to say she couldn't have children instead of admitting she didn't want them.

Personal feelings aside, Mari knew manipulating the council by speaking of children was the only way to shut them up about Zahir's departure. They had become increasingly angsty the longer he was gone, and while Mari was beginning to worry about when Zahir would return, she didn't see it as the big problem her advisors did. Zahir staying there meant he had a greater chance of mastering his life magic or risk Mari having to say goodbye to him before they grew old together which simply was not an option.

Chapter Twenty-Three

Zahir

The days after meeting with the dual mages were busy for Zahir. After meeting so many dual mages who had mastered both their magics, Zahir was more determined than ever to master his. He was able to catch Taryn for a minute before she returned to Brahn, though he didn't get the answers he'd been hoping for. When he asked about the status of the city, Taryn told him that his people lived in shelters outside of it while the city was being rebuilt. It would take a long time before it returned to how it was. Zahir wanted to ask about Morana but didn't want anyone to overhear. If the other dual mages knew she was alive, wouldn't they be talking about it too?

Zahir woke up each morning and went to the clinic to study with Jay. He observed as Jay cured wounds, and sometimes Zahir would try a few himself. Jay was very patient, letting Zahir work through the healing before jumping in with suggestions or advice. Zahir enjoyed clinic work; he could see a direct result of his actions on people rather than animals. Jumping headfirst into his training as opposed to learning it bit by bit benefitted him more. Unfortunately, he didn't have the time to learn it the right way—slow and progressive—but had to learn it all at once.

After his clinic sessions, Zahir and Markus would train for a few hours. While he still couldn't beat Markus, Zahir was noticing a significant improvement in his skills. He had learned new attacks with a blade and had nearly perfected healing his sore muscles after their workout. After training, Zahir would bathe, make himself a plate of food, and meditate. Meditation helped him feel more connected with himself and the intricacies of his body. What he liked the most was how he could feel *exactly* which muscle hurt and describe the pain better when asked. After meditating, Zahir would feel more connected with himself and work through some life magic exercises Markus had shown him. The one he hated the most was harming himself to then heal it, and he struggled to overcome the mental block he'd first had when practicing. But once he got over that, it became easier to do the exercise. It was easier for life mages to heal themselves than others because it didn't involve giving away parts of their energy.

Before dinner, Zahir would head to Lydia's to practice magic or talk; sometimes, she would teach Zahir about divination. While he didn't want to learn how to read the cards like she did, he wanted to know how it worked. She explained that the cards were called tarot. Tarot was not a science, but it was an art that had real-world meaning. Individually, the cards tell you something, but together they form a story.

Today, Lydia handed Zahir the deck of purple cards, and he did as she instructed. Zahir shuffled the cards between his hands and then passed the deck back to her. She refused to take it.

"You read today," she said.

"I don't think I'm ready for that," he said. "I only know what a few cards mean."

"We will dissect it together, but you should play them."

Taking a deep breath, Zahir put the deck on the table before him. The eye on the back of the cards stared up at him, calling to Zahir to flip them over. He inhaled as he turned over the first three cards.

The first card was a woman holding a sword up to a ginormous swan. "This card is telling you that your day will be focused, and you will act with logic and reason. Stay objective and think carefully about your decisions," Lydia said.

Zahir flipped over the next card, which was a familiar one: a horned demon sitting upright on a throne. "I remember this one. It's about feeling stuck, right?"

Lydia nodded. "This is the card about what to look out for in your day. You are feeling stuck, but you hold the keys to your freedom; just remember to put them in the lock."

The third card was unfamiliar to Zahir. He had never seen it in any of Lydia's readings. It was the opposite of the former card. A woman in regal attire sat with a large crown on her head, emanating power and confidence.

"What does this one mean?"

"It means that you need to attend to your inner voice. Your intuition is telling you something, but you're ignoring it. When you have a gut feeling, don't let it go. Your initial reaction is always right, but our minds try to convince us otherwise. Do not let that happen."

Zahir nodded, trying to absorb the information. The last time his gut reacted to something big, he nearly left Lovíth to return to Brahn before Pryn and Markus had stopped him. Had that been the right decision? Obviously he needed to master his magic, but Mari was in trouble. Despite the several letters he'd sent, he hadn't heard from her since. The longer he went without hearing from her, the more nervous he became.

When Lydia's wife came home, Zahir took that as his cue to leave. Tonight, it was his turn to cook dinner. Zahir had asked to take the lead on the meal two nights a week to help enhance his skills. Tonight, he planned to make a traditional meal from Brahn—salmon slathered in a ginger honey sauce with roast green beans tossed in garlic and spicy peppers. If he felt up to it, he would make mashed potatoes, too. But as he walked home, Zahir realized just how tired he was. Over the past few days, he'd stayed up late into the night to practice his magic, and though he was progressing quickly, it became harder to recover as the days went on.

Zahir stood at the counter with an apron tied around his neck and his hair pulled back into a tail at the crown of his head. He noticed, and not for the first time, how bad his roots had become. Zahir had dyed his hair several times since being in Lovíth, but he couldn't remember the last time he did it. At least an inch of his dark brown roots was on display, and he cringed at his reflection, vowing to dye it soon. It was easy to forget about in Lovíth—he didn't have an image to uphold.

The salmon was already in the oven, slathered in light brown sauce. The smells were overwhelming. Zahir cut the potatoes into quarters and slipped, slicing his middle finger and nearly severing it. Instead of healing it right away, Zahir wrapped it in a cloth and tied it together; since he'd learned to heal his injuries passively, he hoped the wound would mend while he worked. Zahir drained the water from the potatoes and piled them in a bowl with a heaping pile of butter. As Zahir mashed, the cut on his hand still bothered him.

Zahir put the potatoes aside and unwrapped his finger, wincing. He was shocked when he saw that the cut had barely healed. While it was no longer bleeding, a massive scab had formed instead of a thin white scar. By now, it should have completely healed. Zahir focused on the injury and instructed his magic to heal it. His finger lit up green, but only momentarily. It sputtered out, but the cut did not change. Cursing, Zahir walked to Markus's room.

Zahir was about to open the door without knocking, as Markus often did to him, but the soft moans from inside made him pause. He couldn't help but snicker as he returned to the kitchen; his cut wasn't so bad.

Zahir wrapped his finger back up and continued preparing dinner. Once everything was done, Zahir set the table, served himself, Pryn, and Markus equally for the meal and poured everyone an oversized glass of red wine. Zahir took a few sips, hoping it would quell the throbbing in his finger as he walked to the bottom of the stairs.

"If you two are done, dinner is on the table," Zahir yelled, stifling a laugh. Since Pryn and Markus had admitted their feelings for one other, they were inseparable. Zahir had begun putting a pillow over his head in the middle of the night to quell the sounds of their amorous activities. Zahir was thrilled for them, but he wished they kept it quiet; it certainly wasn't curbing his exhaustion.

Pryn was first downstairs, their shirt wrinkled and a huge smile on their face. Markus came down a few minutes later, his buttoned shirt askew, one button sitting without a hole at the bottom.

"Dinner smells amazing, Zahir," said Markus, squeezing Zahir's shoulder before sitting beside Pryn at the table.

"Thank you," Zahir said. "I hope you enjoy it. This is one of my favorite recipes from Brahn."

Pryn moaned in delight, and it took everything in Zahir's power to refrain from joking that his food wasn't as good as sex. The three ate in silence, enjoying their dinner. Zahir was impressed with his cooking as he ate it. While his salmon was nowhere near as good as the palace chef's, it was still damn good.

"What happened to your finger?" Pryn asked Zahir, nodding to his wrapped hand.

"I cut it while cooking. I am a little tired, so I wasn't able to heal it right away," Zahir said, taking a long drink of wine.

Markus and Pryn exchanged a look before Markus spoke. "You might want to rest, Zahir. You have been training a lot lately."

"I am fine," Zahir said, shaking his head. "I have it under control."

"Do you?" Pryn asked. "How bad is your finger?"

"It is fine."

"I can heal it for you, Zahir," Markus said.

"No, I can manage it."

"Can I see it?" Markus asked, narrowing his eyes.

Zahir sighed and unwrapped his finger. The bandage clung to the dried blood, and he winced as he took it off, some of the scab sticking to the white bandage. The cut looked like it did before, red and swollen.

"See, it's not that bad," Zahir said.

Pryn rolled their eyes. "It doesn't look *great*. Just let Markus heal it."

"I will take care of it," Zahir said, wrapping it back up. "I am capable of healing a minor injury."

"Not when you're this exhausted," said Markus. "When was the last time you took a break?"

"I had a nap this afternoon," Zahir said.

"Your fifteen-minute span with your eyes closed on the couch hardly counts as a nap. You need real rest."

"Markus, I am progressing in my studies. Last week, I could barely heal a bad cut. Today, I healed two broken bones. I am doing well. I need to continue to do well so I can return to Brahn. I have been gone for too long."

"If you don't rest, you are going to burn out. If that happens, it will take days to get back to where you were at," said Markus with a disapproving shake of his head.

"I can align you before you rest if you would like," Pryn offered, finishing their wine.

"No, that's okay. I could use the alone time."

The rest of their dinner was filled with tense silence and terse conversation. Zahir was frustrated. While he knew his friends were only looking out for him, he couldn't help but feel they didn't believe in him. He was exhausted, but the cut would soon heal. One night of rest would be enough for him to feel better. He had the day off tomorrow from clinic, which meant he would get to practice magic himself. He would wait until his usual afternoon studies with Lydia if that would appease Pryn and Markus.

Zahir's eyes were half closed by the time he collapsed into bed. Within minutes, he was curled up under the covers, thinking of home and promising Mari he would return soon.

***

Zahir woke with a start, drenched in a cold sweat. The dream that had ripped through Zahir felt so real—so vivid. He'd knelt on the ground, holding Mari in his arms while a battle raged around them. The smell of blood flooded his nose as he pressed on Mari's stomach. Her breaths were labored as she reached up to caress Zahir's face, her bloodied hand staining his cheek.

With her last breath, she told Zahir she loved him, and Zahir watched as the light drained from her eyes. Mari stared at the sky, unseeing.

Zahir leaped from his bed and changed into training clothes without a second thought. He threw the rest of his items into a bag and raced down the stairs, taking them two at a time. His heart pounded in his ears, and tears pricked the corners of his eyes. If this wasn't a sign for him to return to Brahn, he didn't know what was.

Markus met Zahir at the bottom of the stairs and stopped him from running out the door with two firm hands on his shoulders. "Where are you going?"

"Brahn," Zahir said. "You need to get out of my way."

"Zahir, you can't leave," Markus said.

"Markus, get the fuck out of my way, or I swear to the Gods I will burn you where you stand!"

"What the hell happened?" Pryn stood, walking behind Markus.

"I had a dream that Mari died. I am returning to Brahn at once. I should have gone back days ago."

"You can't leave," Markus repeated. "You need to finish your training."

"Markus, I am leaving whether you think it is a good idea or not. My wife is in danger. My family could be on death's door. I am taking the risk, and I am leaving." Zahir pushed Markus away and ran out the door before they could stop him.

When Zahir reached the docks, he noticed a merchant ship pulling up their anchors. "Are you headed to Brahn?" Zahir asked, panting.

"Yes. Why?" A burly man asked from the deck.

"Please allow me passage. I need to return at once. I am their king."

"Zahir, wait!" Pryn yelled. Zahir turned to where Markus and Pryn raced towards him.

"I need to get on your ship; I will give you whatever gold you need as soon as we make land. Please," Zahir begged.

The man threw down a rope ladder for Zahir to climb, and just as he was halfway up, Markus reached the bottom, hoisting Pryn up the ladder, too. This only made Zahir climb faster; he would not be stopped again.

Zahir flung himself onto the deck and thanked the man who allowed him passage. Pryn and Markus landed on the deck seconds after Zahir did, panting.

"I *am* leaving. You can't make me stay," Zahir said, crossing his arms.

"We know," Markus said. He stood up and slid the backpack off his shoulder. "That's why we're coming with you."

Chapter Twenty-Four

Mari

Mari grasped Hanan's hand in hers as soon as she sat beside him. His face was pale. His light brown hair fell limply over his forehead; while it was no longer grimy, his natural oils had built along his scalp, adding a shiny tone to his hair. His ripped shirt lay on the floor, exposing his chest and abdomen, which were covered in several large bandages. On his right bicep, another bandage concealed the large gash beneath it.

Hanan and Ren took the hardest hits of all the people who went to the cave. Kane targeted Hanan as he was important to Mari, and Ren because they continuously threw themselves in the line of fire to protect everyone else. Ren had returned home to their wife, their left arm supported by a sling; they'd dislocated their elbow during a fall. Mari had told Ren to take a few weeks away from the palace to rest and recover, but they refused. And after one short week, they were back, commanding the guard with even more vigor.

Mari rubbed the back of Hanan's hand with her thumb as she stared at him. She had cast her gloves aside. If Hanan woke, she would not hide the truth from him. She talked to him while he was unconscious about the voices in her head and how Kane's soul spoke to her when she called upon him. Hanan would never judge her for what she did. Hanan would offer the right advice or a comforting remark; Mari was sure of it. Only three people knew about the dark tendrils creeping up Mari's arms: Amí, Raf, and Illan. The three of them constantly stared at Mari's hands, even when covered. Raf had yet to leave the palace. He stayed in a guest bedroom near Mari's chambers and would remain there until Hanan was ready to go home. Being home alone and away from your injured partner was a fate Mari never wished for Raf to face.

"You can't die, Hanan," Mari said tearfully. "I grieved you once, and I refuse to do it again. You *must* live."

For the first time, Mari let the tears come. She sobbed uncontrollably into Hanan's hand, bringing it to her face and holding it there while she cried. Her body shook with sobs, her shoulders heaving with every breath. Hanan was at death's door, and there was nothing she could do to help him. While she had full faith in Amí and the palace healers, she wanted Hanan to be better *now*. Mari wished Zahir was here to help; after all, he'd healed her after the rebels had taken her. He could definitely heal Hanan now he was trained.

Mari cried not only for her brother but herself. She had taken lives without a second thought and would forever carry that burden. They followed her around, whispering. If she focused for too long, she could hear Kane's voice, the loudest among them all: *Morana is near*.

Mari wiped her tears and took several deep breaths. She needed a distraction. "After you left, and I thought you had died, I always visited your grave. Father marked a boulder halfway down the Yanhua Mountains, the one you used to take me up to for our hunts. He told me that was where your body lay. Every time I went hunting, I would stop at that boulder and make sure to tell you that you weren't a disgrace, that our father was wrong, and that I would always love you. Because he was wrong about you, Hanan. He will *always* be wrong about you."

The memory that flashed in Mari's mind was one she couldn't recall until now. It occurred a few weeks before Hanan left. They were in the shed behind the house, cleaning up their latest conquest—two large deer. Hanan told Mari about someone he had a crush on in their village.

"He is the sweetest person I have ever met," Hanan said as he hung one of the deer.

"I like a boy, too!" Mari chirped, trying and failing to lift the stiff creature.

"You can't tell father that I like a boy, okay?" The first spots of facial hair poked up in spikes on Hanan's chin, though his baby fat remained. Mari wondered if he would have a thick beard like their father when he grew up.

Mari gasped. "Am *I* not allowed to like boys either? Oh, no. I already told Mother about Fahran."

Hanan laughed and patted Mari on the shoulder. "No, it's fine, Mari."

"Then why can't I say anything?"

"Well, I'm supposed to go to Orcian and like a *girl*," Hanan said, hefting the other deer to hang it.

"Do you think you will like that girl?" Mari asked, wiping her hands on a towel.

Hanan shook his head. "No, I don't think so."

"Then tell father you like this boy. Maybe you can marry him instead."

Mari laughed at her childhood self, so naive. She wished it had been that simple for Hanan to have simply been himself in Yu'güe without needing to run away and hide. Mari's anger towards her father was insurmountable; she didn't know if she could ever face him again. After years of his lies, she wanted nothing more than to tell their whole village what he did and cast him out of Yu'güe. While she didn't wish death upon him, she didn't wish good things for him, either. Had her mother known what kind of person Mari's father was?

It was then that Hanan stirred, and his eyes fluttered open. With a low groan, he went to reach for his stomach until Mari grabbed his wrists, stopping him. When their eyes met, Mari's tears started again.

"Amí!" Mari yelled. "Hanan is awake."

"Now I understand how people feel during their bleedings," Hanan said, panting.

Mari released Hanan's wrists and rested a hand over her mouth to refrain from sobbing. Hanan was alive. He was okay.

"Like you have had a sword shoved through your stomach and out your back?" Mari laughed, sniffling.

"Exactly like that."

"How are you feeling... other than that?" Mari asked, resting Hanan's hands on either side of him.

"Exhausted," Hanan said, moving his neck. "How are my wounds?"

"Healing," Mari answered. "You have been asleep for nearly a week."

"Where is Raf?"

"He's here in the palace. He just went to get some rest. He's been sitting outside your door every day with a book, waiting to see you," Mari said. "He loves you very deeply."

"Well, I should hope so, I am marrying him," Hanan said.

"How are you feeling, Hanan?" Amí asked as she approached. "My Queen, with all respect, please move."

Mari chuckled as she slid away from Hanan's bed and stood, leaning against the wall. Amí checked on Hanan's wounds and said they were healing nicely. The one on his arm was not at its best. It had been caked in dirt when he'd arrived, and though it wasn't infected, it was still swollen.

"Would you like another sedative, Hanan?" Amí asked.

Hanan slowly shook his head. "No, just something for the pain if you have it."

Amí made him drink a pain tonic, and within a few minutes, Hanan looked and sounded much better. He still wasn't allowed to sit so as not to disturb his abdomen. Raf was summoned, and soon, Hanan, Raf, and Mari were together, tearfully laughing in relief. After spending a few more minutes with her brother, Mari left them alone.

She headed up to the library to see if she could find anything in the books about the use of death magic on such a large scale. Taking human lives took a toll on the death mage; she wondered if the tendrils on her arms were a physical manifestation of her attacks. She shivered when she pictured Morana's hands, just as charred as hers.

The torches in the library were already lit, and Mari heard footsteps deep inside the library. "Illan, is that you?" Mari called.

"Mari, what a surprise," Illan yelled. "I am about halfway down the shelves."

Mari followed the direction of Illan's voice, eventually finding him crouched on the ground, holding a small dusty book in his right hand and thumbing through it with his left. He snapped the book closed as she approached and stood, his knees and back cracking.

"What are you looking for, Illan?" asked Mari.

"A book that might explain what is going on," Illan said, gesturing to Mari's covered hands.

"That is why I came here, too," Mari said. "Have you found anything?"

Illan shook his head. "Nothing. I am certain there is something here, but I have yet to find it."

"It must be from my magic, but I don't know how to get rid of it."

"I wish I had answers for you."

Mari ran a hand down her face. "I am so exhausted, Illan. I'm tired of searching for answers or fighting people who want our family dead. I'm so tired of being strong when all I want to do is weep because my brother nearly died, and my husband is halfway across the world. I can't be strong all the time. I just want a normal life with Zahir and the people I love. But we will *never* get that."

"The Gods chose you for this life because you are strong enough to handle it," Illan said, placing a comforting hand on Mari's shoulders.

Mari shrugged off Illan's hand and stepped back. "I don't give a fuck what the Gods think I am strong enough to handle. I don't *want* it. We will always be King Zahir and Queen Mari. Our lives will be scrutinized by everyone in Brahn. My ability to bear children is a topic of conversation among *strangers*," Mari said, balling her hands into fists. "I wish my choice to bear children was between only Zahir and me, but instead, it is between us and the whole clan. How is that fair?"

"It's not fair, Mari," Illan said. "My wife and I didn't want children."

Mari balked. "Illan—"

Illan put a hand up to stop Mari from talking. "It's all right. I can talk about my wife and daughter. When we were married, it was because my father thought we would make strong children, despite Daria and I never wishing to have any. Honestly, we didn't talk about it at first. I assumed she wanted them, and she assumed I did. So," Illan laughed, "we were both taking contraceptive tonics without the other knowing. After a while, I came clean to her, and she laughed and told me she was doing the same thing.

"This only made our relationship stronger. It was our secret, and we never told anyone—until now. When Daria's sister was seventeen, she ended up pregnant, and her partner left her. Daria's mother was *furious*. Priya didn't want to be alone with a baby, so Daria and I decided to raise her in the palace with Priya. We invited Priya to live with us and conjured a rouse; we would tell the clan it was our child so we could stop answering their endless questions. Priya died during childbirth, and Daria and I were left with Meg. We would never do Priya a disservice and give away her child. After all, she gave her life for this baby. So, we raised Meg. While we still didn't *want* to be parents, we had a child."

"Wow, Illan. It was so selfless of you to raise that baby," Mari said, resting a comforting hand on his forearm.

"Daria and I were not good at raising a child, which was where Amí came in. We spent time with Meg, played with her, and helped her learn, but we never tried to be parents. We didn't enforce rules and we let Meg make mistakes."

"Whether or not you tried to be a parent, it sounds like you raised her well. I wish I would have gotten the chance to meet her—and Daria."

"Me too. What I am trying to say is that it isn't fair to be forced into something you don't want to do. Don't hide your fears and feelings from Zahir. Although it worked out for Daria and me, that will not always be the case."

"I know you never wanted to be a parent, but Zahir looks up to you like a father," Mari said. "You don't have to have your own children to have an impact."

"Thank you, Mari." Illan coughed, and they broke eye contact. "Now, let's find some answers."

Mari and Illan skimmed through tome after tome, searching for anything about the widespread use of death magic. Yu'güe tried to hide the truth about their powers, Mari was realizing. In all her life, she thought she had learned everything about death magic: how to kill animals, how to use their souls if members of Yu'güe were ever in danger, and the risk of using the darkness. While it was obvious that killing people was wrong, there was nothing that said what would happen if she did it. She never learned that she would be traumatized for moon cycles or that it could cause psychological and physical effects. The further that Mari removed herself from Yu'güe, the more she realized that they weren't as pious as they made themselves seem. Hiding the ramifications of death magic infuriated Mari.

"I think I found something," Illan said, holding a scroll.

Mari put down the book and walked beside Illan, reading it over his shoulder. About halfway down, there was a paragraph that stuck out to Mari.

While it should be noted that killing people is morally corrupt, in extreme circumstances, it may be necessary. If you find are in that situation, do not be afraid to use your magic. Do not feel guilt; your life would have been at stake without it. It has been shown that death mages who feel immense guilt about their magic have physical symptoms that arise after a killing. If used on a large scale, death magic will manifest on the skin as tendrils as black as night. Several treatments have proved effective in dispelling the physical manifestation of guilt. First, alignment by a life mage will usually solve the problem. Second, speaking with each taken soul, thanking them for their life, and apologizing individually. Lastly, meditation and self-reflection help you to understand that if there was another way, you would have taken it. No sane person enjoys taking lives, but in desperate times, you cannot be blamed. For without you, who knows who could have died...

Mari took a step back and leaned against one of the shelves. "This is just my magic?"

Illan nodded slowly. "It would seem that way."

"I don't particularly want to sit with each soul one-by-one. I don't think that would help me."

"Would you wait for Zahir to come home and align you?" Illan asked. "If he knows how, that is."

"That is a big 'if,' Illan. Right now, meditation might be my safest option."

"Mari, whatever you need to do, I will support you. There are no council meetings today; if you need the afternoon to yourself, I will ensure you are not disturbed."

Mari laughed. "I think the two guards outside my door are more than capable of that, but thank you, Illan."

Illan offered to walk Mari back to her chambers so she could meditate. She feared that it wouldn't work, unable to escape the extreme anxiety about the whole situation. Nevertheless, she had to try. As they rounded the corner near the front doors of the palace, they overheard a commotion and many people yelling and talking over one another. Exchanging a glance, Mari and Illan quickened their pace.

Fifteen guards surrounded a group of people who rushed through the palace doors. As they slammed shut, Mari made out two unfamiliar faces: a bald person with piercing green eyes, a sunburnt face, and a backpack slung over their shoulders. They peered around the palace entryway in awe and held hands with a tall, dark-skinned man with deep brown eyes and long locs to match. His head swiveled back and forth as he talked over the guards, his deep voice echoing around the room. Over the commotion, Mari could barely make out his words.

It was then that she realized what the true commotion was about. Charging forward, her heart hammering in her chest, Mari trained her eyes on the silvery hair amid the group. Mari elbowed her way past the guards and flung herself into Zahir's chest.

Zahir stumbled back a step as Mari latched onto him. "Mari."

"You're home," she said, staring into his eyes.

Zahir wrapped his arms around Mari's waist and pulled her closer. Without a second's hesitation, he kissed her fiercely, the commotion in the entryway fading to nothing as their lips interlocked. Mari could've sworn they were the only two people in the room.

A cough forced Mari to pull away from Zahir, her cheeks warming. They stared at each other, smiles dusting their faces now they were reunited.

Zahir cupped Mari's cheek and searched her eyes. "I promised I would come home to you."

Chapter Twenty-Five

Mari

Zahir kept Mari's waist frozen in place on his lap, absent-mindedly brushing his fingers along her hip bone as he spoke. The warm bath water enveloped them, bubbles bursting against their skin. Mari caught the smoky scent of Zahir among the lavender bath oil while the occasional pop of bath foam broke the silence. Mari toyed with the ends of his hair as her eyes scanned his face, noting the curve of his lips and the square of his jaw. His roots had grown out, his natural brown hair now covering a few inches on the top of his head. Mari wondered if he would ask her to dye it again. As they sat together, Mari memorized every inch of Zahir's face, never wanting to forget a single thing about him. Her eyes trailed to his collarbone and the square of his shoulders, the toned muscle of his biceps and bare chest. Zahir had trained; that much was clear. And Mari was *not* about to complain.

Zahir pinched Mari's hip lightly. "You're not listening to me, are you?"

A burning heat rose on Mari's cheeks. "Yes, I am," she lied.

"What did I just say?" Zahir raised an eyebrow.

Mari waved a hand in front of her face. "Something about cinnamon."

"That was several minutes ago," Zahir said, laughing. He put a hand to his chest, feigning hurt. "You were ignoring me. Did you pay this little attention in council meetings?"

Mari rolled her eyes. "It *is* a little hard to focus when I'm in the bath with my naked husband, who I haven't seen in *nine* moon cycles."

Zahir placed a kiss on her bare shoulder. "You are forgiven... this time."

Mari and Zahir had gone to their room to spend quality time together for the first time in what felt like forever. But as they snuggled in bed, catching up on the past nine moons, they realized it was simply not enough. They needed to be closer. So, they drew a bath and now sat surrounded by a dozen candles and a half-empty bottle of wine.

"Please never leave me again," Mari said. "I don't think I could go through it."

Zahir tucked a strand of hair behind Mari's ear and stared into her eyes. "I would never dream of it, my love."

"Tell me more of Lovíth. What is the culture like?"

Then, Zahir launched into a long story about the amazing people he'd met—the child who taught him how to heal bones, Lily the teacher, Lydia, and her wife. Zahir recited many stories of Pryn and Markus, the things they'd taught him, and the drunken nights they'd shared. Mari had been excited to meet them. After she and Zahir had finished reuniting, Zahir immediately introduced her to his newest confidants. How Zahir spoke about the little town reminded Mari of Yu'güe and its close-knit community. Lovíth sounded like a utopia where everyone could be true to themselves.

"In Lovíth, they have names for people like me and people like Ren or Hanan." Zahir told her of the different words they used. "I am bisexual because I like men and women."

"That's lovely, Zahir," Mari said, holding back tears. Listening to him speak of a place where he could truly be himself without judgment made her heart soar.

"I would love to introduce these terms to Brahn, but I don't ever want it to be used as a way to divide."

Mari nodded. "If Lovíth can do it, what is stopping you?"

Zahir chuckled. "If only it were that simple. I am so happy that somewhere in this world, there is no judgment. People can love who they love, no matter who they are."

Mari wrapped her arms around Zahir's neck and pulled him into her. "I love you. And I am happy that you trusted me with who you are, even when you couldn't tell anyone else."

"You loved me despite anything I've ever told you. You have no idea what that meant—and means—to me."

The pair stayed like that for a long while, holding each other in the candlelight. Their hearts beat in sync as the rest of the world faded away, if only for a moment. When Zahir reached for his wine, Mari pulled herself away and picked up her glass, too.

Raising the glass towards Zahir, she said, "Welcome home."

Zahir clinked his glass against Mari's and took a sip. "Tell me about your time in Brahn. The good things."

Mari nearly laughed. In truth, thinking of the good things was hard. "Hanan and Raf are engaged."

Zahir's smile could light up the palace. "Oh, wow! That's amazing. When is the wedding?"

Mari shook her head. "I don't know. Hanan is currently re-covering; he was severely injured during our battle. The healers say he's doing well but isn't out of the woods yet. Once he is healed, I assume we will start planning their wedding. I told them we would host it... is that all right?" Mari realized she hadn't actually *asked* anyone if she could host their wedding, and Brahn was not open-minded to weddings between the same sex. Zahir hadn't been able to tell people he was bisexual, too fearful of the repercussions. But Mari still wished to host her brother's wedding, even if that meant unsettling the people. If the king and queen showed they were open-minded, would that help people open their minds? Or would it only make it worse?

"Of course," Zahir said without a second's hesitation. "We absolutely should host our brother's wedding. We might have to face backlash, but I would do anything for Hanan and Raf."

Mari wasn't oblivious to Zahir's wording of the phrase *our* brother. Mari thought of Roan and Anya as her siblings, too, and knowing Zahir felt the same for Hanan was more than she ever could have asked for. Hanan deserved to be loved and accepted after what their father had put him through.

"Did you still meet at the tavern?" Zahir asked.

Mari nodded. "We did. Not every full moon, but most. We trained here at the palace, too."

Mari told Zahir of her training sessions with Hanan and eventually Reina and how their friendship had started to re-form over time as Reina overcame what happened. Mari told Zahir about the journal that Reina found and how Rodrick had been working with the rebels for so long.

"How did you get Reina to come around?" Zahir asked.

"I kept inviting her to the palace to train with Hanan and me so she knew that she was welcome and we didn't hold anything against her. I knew she was hurting and angry with you, but I wanted her to know we could move past it if she wanted to," Mari said. "And eventually, after many moons of asking, she came to train."

"I am in awe of you, Mari," Zahir said, kissing her cheek.

Mari gave him a confused smile. "What do you mean?"

"You have changed this fortress of a home and made it yours. I was never allowed visitors as it was home only for the royal family, but you brought in friends and loved ones. You broke the high walls."

Mari shrugged. "I just didn't want to be alone. Everyone kept asking if I missed you, and of course I did, but the more they asked, the more alone I felt. So, I filled our home with the people I loved the most. I had routines, times, and days I would see everyone. If I knew when I would next see someone, I wouldn't have to miss them."

Zahir put his glass of wine down and pulled Mari closer, resting his chin in her neck. "I will never *ever* leave you again."

Mari kissed Zahir's forehead. "I love you."

"And I, you."

Mari and Zahir sat in silence for what felt like an eternity, enjoying the comfort of each other's embrace. She nearly lost herself in his arms if not for the words resting on the tip of her tongue. But she couldn't do it. She didn't dare risk ruining the moment. Yet now might be the only time she could speak. Taking a deep breath, Mari blurted the thoughts that had been sitting with her for a long time. "I don't know that I want children."

Zahir pulled back to look at her. "I know."

"What?" Mari shook her head and furrowed her brow. "How could you possibly know that?"

"Do you not remember what you said to me after my father died? When we were recovering, I was so focused on the fact that we needed an heir. It was all I could think about now I was king."

"I don't remember," Mari said.

"You told me that you weren't ready and had no choice. As time went on and I thought about it, I realized two things. One, you felt being a mother was an obligation you had to fulfill after being thrust into this life. That was never fair to you, Mari. To either of us."

Mari nodded, holding back the tears pricking the corners of her eyes. "And what is the second thing?"

"That I felt the same way."

Mari reeled back, searching Zahir's face for any flicker of deception. "You do?"

"I do. Being king, a father, a leader... none of it was my choice. I would be 'a great king' with 'strong sons.' My 'heirs would be the best rulers.' But none of those things were my choice, and the more I think about it, the more I realize I don't even want to have children. Aside from the fact they would be a triad, I just don't want them. I want to have a life with *you*. I want *you* to be my priority."

"You took the words from my lips, Zahir," Mari whispered. "Gods. Never in twenty lifetimes would I have guessed you felt the same way. We were married to have a child... and now we won't."

"We may change our minds, still."

Mari laughed. "Of course, we could. Though I don't think we will."

"No, neither do I."

"Although, if we both desperately wanted children, neither of us would suggest the possibility of changing our minds. Why is the reverse never said?"

Zahir shrugged. "Because the natural order is to have children and a legacy. To leave a part of yourself in this world."

"We are the king and queen. We already are doing that," Mari said with a laugh. "Who will take the throne then after you?"

Zahir shrugged. "We have time to think of that."

Mari leaned in and kissed Zahir softly. "I feel so lucky to have you."

He swept Mari into his arms and lifted them out of the bath. They were dripping wet, and Mari giggled loudly as Zahir put her down. She wrapped her arms around herself, the cool air pricking at her skin as he wrapped her in a plush white towel and dried her off. He started at her shoulders, working down her chest, torso, and finally, her legs. He peered up at her from his squatting position on the floor, a mischievous grin spreading slowly across his lips.

"Zahir, what are you—" Mari's words were replaced by a deep moan as Zahir attached his mouth to her core, his hands gripping her bottom and pulling her closer.

Mari snaked her fingers through Zahir's hair and tugged, eliciting a moan from him that vibrated throughout her whole body, sending a new wave of pleasure through her. Mari ground her hips against Zahir's mouth, and he moaned harder, swirling his tongue and plunging two fingers inside her. She had to bite her lip to keep from screaming his name as he pumped into her, hitting her sweet spot.

"Fuck, Zahir," Mari moaned.

The growl that ripped through Zahir sent Mari soaring over the edge of pleasure. She pulled roughly at the roots of his hair as she rode out her high on his face, and just as she came down from her high, Zahir stood and picked her up with two hands. Mari wrapped her legs around his waist and kissed him roughly as he pressed Mari against the wall of the bathroom, positioning himself before her.

"Are you taking a contraceptive tonic?" Zahir asked, eyes desperate with need.

Mari nodded. "Yes. Please, Zahir; don't make me wait any longer."

Zahir groaned as he plunged into her, spreading her legs apart. Mari gasped. It had been so long, but nothing could make Mari forget how good Zahir felt inside her. Zahir kissed Mari's neck as he rocked slowly. The rhythmic rolling of his hips elicited moans from each of them. Mari's eyes nearly rolled back as Zahir's lips closed around a particularly sensitive spot on her collarbone.

"Zahir!" Mari gasped.

"You are so beautiful," he whispered gruffly, biting lightly on her earlobe. "I thought of you all the time. You are magnificent. You always have been and always will be."

Words escaped Mari as Zahir picked up speed, pounding into her. Zahir's grunts were loud and low. He said her name, told her how stunning she was, and expressed how much he missed her.

And when Mari soared high into another wave of pleasure, Zahir went with her as she tightened around him. When they both floated down from their highs, hearts pounding and chests heaving, Zahir rested his forehead on Mari's, who closed her eyes and smiled.

"Welcome home, my love," Mari said with a laugh.

Zahir lightly pushed his hips once more inside her, making her gasp. Mari scowled at his laughter.

"Shall we retire to our bed?" Zahir rubbed his nose lightly against Mari's.

Mari giggled. "Absolutely."

Chapter Twenty-Six

Zahir

Zahir lay in bed with Mari, his arm wrapped around her while her head rested on his chest. He traced small circles on the usual spot on her bare hip. With Mari in his arms, he'd never felt so at home. Whenever he was with her, no matter where Zahir was home. Mari's hand rested on Zahir's chest; he tried not to stare at the death magic creeping up her arm. But it was not hard to after she told him what happened and what was wrong with her hands. She had killed fifty people in mere seconds, and it was taking a serious toll on her mind and body. Every time Zahir glimpsed her hands, his heart dropped into his stomach. It broke his heart to see the guilt she carried. When Mari told him of the voices in her head, it took everything in him to hide his concern. She heard the voices of the dead, and there was no cure.

If Zahir had never left for Lovíth, could he have stopped this from happening? Could he have assisted in the battle and given

Mari another option? She had killed so many people... Zahir couldn't even imagine how she must feel. He wondered if she wrongly compared herself to Morana, but Zahir knew Mari and how her mind worked. The guilt would be all-consuming, and he was helpless to save her.

As he relaxed, Zahir's thoughts returned to his reunion with his family. After Zahir and Mari reunited, he immediately hugged Illan. Tears pricked both their eyes as they broke the embrace; Zahir had missed his uncle greatly in the time he'd been gone. Shortly thereafter, word had reached the rest of the family, and before Zahir could even put down his backpack, Roan latched onto him and refused to let go. Laughing, Zahir scooped Roan into his arms, swinging him in circles, and accidentally knocking his square glasses off his face. Mari picked them up for him. His brother had changed much in just a short amount of time.

Maura enveloped Zahir in a warm embrace and kissed his cheek, welcoming him home. Zahir and Maura hadn't left on good terms as Zahir processed the news of his magic.

He introduced everyone to Pryn and Markus, who were welcomed with warm regards and shown to a bedroom in the palace. Watching them interact with his family was interesting, given their preconceived notions. While his friends hugged Illan tightly, they hesitated to shake Anya's hand.

While Anya didn't hug him, she didn't dismiss him either. She punched his shoulder in greeting and asked when he was returning to Lovíth. Taryn greeted him like they hadn't seen each other, acting ecstatic with her endless questions about what Lovíth was like. Zahir answered to keep up the appearance but knew no one would have ever suspected the truth—that there was more than just *one* dual mage in the room.

After the dual mage gathering, Zahir wondered why he'd grown up thinking no dual mages existed since Morana. The answer was simple: that's what everyone was told. But while Orcian, Lovíth, and Brahn traded goods and isolated Yu'güe, no one had expected more dual mages were being born. The clans had separated themselves to prevent another dual mage like Morana, yet they were naïve to think dual mages had ceased to exist. And now, Zahir knew they never had. Instead of being the first dual mage in millennia, Zahir was merely the first *public* dual mage.

And now, as Zahir lay in bed with Mari, he contemplated what to tell her. He was going to tell her about Lydia and his biological family's lineage, but he didn't know whether to reveal anything about Taryn or the others. It had been so difficult not to give away too many details in their letters in case they were ever intercepted. But now that they were back together, Zahir didn't want to keep any secrets from her.

Mari shifted on Zahir's chest. "Are you comfortable?" he asked, kissing the top of her head.

"Just fidgeting," Mari said, her voice akin to the one she uses right upon waking.

"Did you fall asleep?" Zahir asked, chuckling.

"I may have drifted off for a minute," Mari said. She looked up at Zahir through her eyelashes. "I'm so happy you are home."

"Me too. I missed you. When I first went to Lovíth, it was hard to fall asleep without you next to me."

"I had trouble, too. It wasn't the same having this big bed all to myself."

Zahir chuckled. "Well, you normally take three-quarters of it, even when I *am* here."

Mari lightly swatted Zahir's bare chest. "I do not!"

"Oh, you do," Zahir wrapped Mari in his arms and rolled them over so she was flat on her back with Zahir towering over her with his arms on either side of her head. Zahir's unbound hair cascaded around his face, resting on Mari's collarbone.

"Is this how much bed I normally give you?" Mari asked, chuckling as she toyed with the ends of his hair.

Mari's arm was resting right on the edge of the mattress. "This is a generous amount," he said, leaning down and kissing Mari, pulling a smile from both their lips. He could kiss her for an eternity and never tire. Kissing her was as easy as breathing, as simple as living.

"I love you," Mari said, giggling.

"I love you, too." Zahir smiled and slowly kissed down Mari's neck.

The knock at the door made Zahir jump and pull away from his wife. "Every fucking time," he grumbled, nipping one last time at Mari's neck. "We *will* finish this later."

As the door opened slightly, Mari yelled out, "Don't enter!" as she pulled the covers up to her chin. Zahir burst out laughing.

A muffled "sorry" came through the closed door as Zahir slipped back into his clothing and pulled it open. Amí stood there, a worried expression on her face.

"Amí, is everything all right?" he asked.

She shook her head. "Hanan has worsened. The queen must come immediately."

Mari sat up quickly, the blanket dipping to reveal her bare chest. Her face flushed a deep crimson before she scrambled to pull it back up. "Is he going to live? I will be there in just a second."

Amí couldn't contain the smirk on her lips. "We are not certain. Please, come down as soon as you can."

As soon as the door was shut, Mari leaped out of bed and threw on the first pair of clothes she could find. Not bothering with gloves, Mari raced from the room and through the palace as Zahir followed. He grasped Mari's hand and gave it a tight squeeze. He had no words of comfort but hoped the small gesture would help. Mari had already mourned Hanan once; he didn't know what would happen if she had to again.

Hanan lay in bed with Raf by his side, who dabbed a cool cloth on his partner's forehead. Hanan's eyes were closed, his face pale, and his chest moving with rapid, short breaths. The bandages were off his stomach and arm, the wounds swollen and bright red. Red lines stretched out from the wounds, indicating what Zahir knew was an infection.

Zahir dropped Mari's hand as she rushed to Hanan's side, grabbing his instead. "Gods Hanan, I told you that you couldn't die! What happened?" she asked Raf.

He shook his head, tears staining his cheeks. "They said his wounds are infected. Badly. The usual anti-infection medications aren't strong enough for him, and they don't have any stronger vials."

Mari cursed. "What are they going to do?"

"They don't know what they *can* do," said Raf. "They don't know if he's even going to live."

Zahir rushed forward and moved Mari slightly further to her left so she was up by Hanan's face. He placed his hands on Hanan's stomach wound, the area hot to the touch. Zahir had never cleansed an infected wound, but he had to try. Focusing on his hands, Zahir's heart hammered loudly in his ears. Without even thinking about calling his magic, his hands lit a bright green. Hanan's entire stomach was engulfed by bright light, his strained expression turning into one of comfort as Zahir worked.

Once the redness around the wound dissolved and became nothing more than a large scar, Zahir swapped places with Mari. He placed his hands over the gash on Hanan's arm and watched as the messy wound faded into nothing more than a scrape. When Zahir pulled away from Hanan, he stumbled over his feet, clutching the wall for support.

Amí brought over something to clean his hands off, and once he had, Mari pulled him into her, tears dripping onto his shirt. "Thank you, Zahir. I couldn't lose him again."

"I know." Zahir hugged Mari tightly.

"I guess your training was a success," Amí said, smiling. "What of those friends you brought home? Are they here to stay?"

Zahir shrugged. "I don't think so. Lovíth is their home, and even though I would love for them to stay here, our magic is tied to our home." And that's when it clicked. Zahir's life magic was tied to Brahn. His two incredible feats of life magic had both been done on Brahn's soil.

"Why did they come with you?" Mari asked.

Zahir felt his cheeks flush. "I had previously tried to leave Lovíth to come home, and they stopped me. The second time, they decided it was safer to join me instead. I'm not done with my training, but nothing was going to keep me away from you any longer, my love."

Mari gave his waist another tight squeeze before sitting down beside Hanan. Raf stared wide-eyed at Zahir.

"Thank you, Zahir. I don't know how I could ever repay you," Raf said. He stood and walked to Zahir, extending his hand.

Zahir took it before pulling him into a quick embrace. "No repayment will ever be necessary, not for you." He released Raf and put a hand on his shoulder. "You are one of my closest friends; you must know I would die for you."

"Not if I die for you first," Raf said, laughing.

The pair had been friends for over a decade. Zahir would do anything for Raf, especially after what happened with Rodrick.

"Mari told me you and Hanan are engaged. Congratulations. You deserve happiness," Zahir said.

"Thank you, brother." Raf returned to Hanan's side as Zahir smiled at the term. Once Raf and Hanan married, they really would be brothers.

Zahir moved to stand behind Mari, gently massaging her shoulders to relieve some of her tension. Massive knots sat at the base of her neck, and he channeled a small amount of his magic to relieve them.

"Will you marry us?" Hanan asked weakly, staring up at his sister.

"We already talked about this, Hanan. I'm going to help plan the wedding," Mari said.

"No," Hanan shook his head, shifting his gaze to Raf. "I want to marry you right now."

Raf laughed. "Hanan, you're high. Let's wait until you're better."

"I don't want to wait. I love you. If this near-death experience has taught me anything, it's that I don't want to spend another minute without you as my husband."

Raf lifted Hanan's hand to his lips and kissed it while Zahir and Mari shared a glance, soft smiles dusting their lips. "Okay."

"Can you marry us?" Hanan asked again.

Zahir looked at Mari. "We do have the power to marry anyone at any time."

Though Hanan and Raf didn't have rings, it mattered little. In the low light of the hospital wing, Zahir and Mari blessed Hanan and Raf in marriage. They vowed to love each other through it all, protect one another, and care for each other in times of stress and illness. And when they kissed to seal their marriage, Zahir grasped Mari's hand tightly in his.

It was right then that Illan burst into the room with Ren and a host of soldiers behind him. "Zahir, thank the Gods you are here."

Zahir whipped around and saw the panic on his uncle's face. His heart dropped. "What is it?"

"Morana. She is in the city once again," Illan said, panting. "We must go to the safe room at once."

"No," Zahir said. "I am not hiding from her. This means war." Zahir leaned down to kiss Mari, but she stood too.

"This means war," Mari repeated, narrowing her eyes at Zahir. "She will not best us any longer."

Ren escorted Mari and Zahir to their room with six additional guards. Despite Ren's arm in a sling, they held a rapier in their non-dominant hand.

Zahir rushed to don his armor; the solid armor was almost too tight on his chest and thighs, he noted as he tied his hair back away from his face.

When Zahir emerged, he noticed Mari wore a new set of armor. Instead of the feminine armor previously commissioned for her, Mari donned an identical set to his. She looked like a warrior with her sword hanging from her hip and two daggers strapped on her forearms.

"How are you going to fight without your left arm?" Mari asked Ren, who smirked.

"I can wield a sword with both hands. Please, Mari, don't assume I am captain of the guard simply because of my charming smile."

Mari cackled. "I would never dream of it."

"Let's go," Zahir said, closing his dressing room door behind him. Zahir was unsteady on his feet, exhausted from healing Hanan, but even though his body felt like lead, he willed himself forward. He couldn't rest, not while his family was in danger. He would do anything to protect them.

The trio raced towards the front doors of the palace, and the sight that greeted them was beyond anything Zahir could have feared. Smoke billowed from various parts of the city; screams lifted to the palace steps. At the bottom stood the wraith herself—Morana. She was cloaked in a billowing black cape flowing in the wind around her. From her hands, she shot souls in all directions as animals and humans alike ran from her and into the city, wreaking havoc.

Zahir willed his feet to walk but couldn't move an inch. Frozen in place, he stared at Morana, terrified and shocked by the sight of her. He hadn't truly believed she was alive before this very moment. There had been a part of him that wanted it to be untrue, that she hadn't truly lived.

Only when Mari and Ren raced past Zahir that he reacted and followed. He unsheathed his sword and ignited the blade in roaring flames. Halfway down the steps, two men met him, wildly swinging their swords. Zahir parried their blows and sliced at his opponents. Within seconds, they were both down, flesh ignited as they screamed in pain.

Zahir rushed towards Mari and Ren, who faced off with another pair. Just as Zahir approached, the two had their opponents down, groaning.

"You've improved," Zahir said, approaching Mari.

"Glad you noticed." She winked.

"We don't have time for this," Ren said, rolling their eyes. "Let's go."

Just as the trio reached the bottom of the stairs, they saw Taryn, Anya, and Illan running up beside them. Taryn and Anya already had flames coiled up their arms, unleashing an inferno in their wake. Markus and Pryn appeared behind them, blades in hand, trying to avoid the fire that spewed from the Twin Flames.

Zahir watched in wondrous horror as Taryn and Anya launched themselves at Morana, completely alight. Morana screamed as she dodged their attack, but not before her cloak was lit ablaze. She smacked at the flames to try and snuff them before raising her hands towards the pair. Zahir yelled for them to watch out, but they didn't need the guidance. Taryn and Anya rolled out of the way of Morana's attack just as she clenched her hands into fists.

Noting her distraction, Zahir unsheathed a titanium dagger from his forearms and launched it while Morana was momentarily distracted. It sunk deep into the flesh of her bicep. Zahir smirked. She was defenseless without her magic. Morana ripped the blade from her arm and flung it back toward him. He dodged it, watching with wide eyes as the cut on Morana's arm stitched back together.

"How is that possible?" Zahir whispered. Even after being cut with titanium, Morana still utilized her magic.

Morana raised her hands toward Zahir, who inhaled sharply. It all happened in slow motion, then. One second, her fingers were closing, and the next, he was lying on the ground with Mari half on top of him. Blood exploded from Mari's temple where her head hit the concrete.

"Mari," Zahir cried out, cradling her face.

Mari blinked. "Move faster," she grunted as she stood up to face Morana.

Raising her hands towards their opponent, Mari pulled her fists back towards her body, trying to steal her soul. Morana stood there, a feline grin slowly spreading across her lips.

"You must know I'm harder to kill than *that*." Morana laughed wickedly.

Morana danced around swords and evaded onslaughts of fire and souls. She moved like a phantom, gliding over the pavement faster than humanly possible. Markus and Pryn sliced at her arms each time she tried to take a soul. Anya lit the ground around Morana ablaze, trapping her in enough time for Pryn to land a blow to her hip. But again, Morana's cut healed within seconds, like she was immune to titanium. Taryn distracted Morana long enough for Illan to kick at her knees, sending her down to the pavement. Mari called upon three souls that rushed forward with Zahir. Two elk flanked him while a mountain lion prowled to where Morana stood. Ice spread across the pavement where the souls moved. Now, their allies trapped the wraith on all sides, encased in a wall of flame.

But Morana was quicker than anyone else. Reaching a hand to Taryn and one to Pryn, Markus and Anya jumped into action, lowering the defense long enough that Morana switched her attack, raising her hands to Zahir instead.

Illan leaped to Morana and tackled her to the ground, disrupting her attack. But when Zahir glanced back, Illan was caught in her grasp. One arm held him in a chokehold, while the other hovered beside his head in a claw, poised to steal his soul.

Zahir stopped breathing altogether. A flashback to when his father was killed flooded his vision, but instead of Ryker's throat being slit, Zahir pictured Illan falling to the ground, dead.

"Halt," Morana commanded. "You move, and he dies."

Zahir and Anya exchanged a glance, both igniting their arms in flames. Mari held her hands out as if to steal Morana's soul. Taryn's flames licked up her entire torso, covering her in an armor of fire. Pryn and Markus brandished their swords, ready to attack at the first sign.

"Let him go, Morana," Zahir said. "He has nothing to do with the crown."

"Oh, but he has *everything* to do with it." Morana's voice gave him chills, like the scraping of metal on rock.

"Release him and take me," Taryn said, stepping forward and snuffing her flames. "I am who you are looking for."

"*You* are not Brahn's dual mage."

With a mournful glance at Anya, Taryn turned and threw the soul of a deer to the ground before her, ice spreading around it in a web. Anya's lips parted as she slowly moved a hand over her mouth. "I may not be the king, but I am *a* dual mage. You want to be the only one. So, take me and release Illan."

"Taryn, no!" Anya screeched. Zahir grabbed her arm when Anya stepped forward, pulling her to his chest. She squirmed against his grasp, screaming for Taryn.

"This is impossible," Morana said, never taking her eyes off Zahir. "He is the first dual mage in millennia."

Taryn shook her head and laughed. "You really should get your facts straight before you make demands."

Only silence followed before Morana began to cackle. She released Illan, so he stood beside her, clasping his shoulder with a smirk. "Now, Illan, who will it be?"

Illan stared at the ground and shook his head.

"Come now, Illan. Where is that bravado that I love? The drive you had to get your hands on the crown?"

Zahir's breath hitched. Morana spoke like she knew Illan. But how could she? Mari's hands shook as her lips parted. Anya cocked her head to the side, her gaze shifting between Illan and Morana. Taryn bit her lip and shook her head.

There was no way this was happening. Illan stared at the ground, refusing to meet Zahir's eyes.

"Illan, what is she talking about?" Zahir asked.

"Oh, you don't know?" Morana crooned, a slow smile breaking across her lips. "Your *darling* uncle is a traitor. He let my people into your safe room to kill your father; he helped them kidnap your wife. And best of all, he helped me hide for decades."

Illan stared at his feet.

"Tell me this isn't true," Zahir rasped.

When Illan lifted his gaze, the truth was clear. The guilt in Illan's gaze brought tears to Zahir's eyes. The one person he trusted most in this world was never who he thought.

"I trusted you," Zahir spat. "I thought of you like a father. How could you do this?"

"I never meant for it to go this far," Illan said, barely audible above the commotion of the surrounding battle.

"Pick a side, Illan. It's as simple as life and death," Morana said, tightening her grip on his shoulder.

Illan said nothing but simply turned to Morana and nodded. Morana took a step backward, pulling Illan with her.

"Leave this place and never return," Zahir commanded Morana. "You will *never* have the power you seek."

"Darling, I already do."

A bright light engulfed them that had Zahir shielding his eyes. When it cleared, Morana and Illan were gone. Zahir released Anya and stepped forward, searching frantically for them—but they were truly out of sight. Shock gave way to rage as Zahir shot flames to the sky, hot enough to put the sun to shame. His pained scream was harsh enough to shatter even his own heart. Mari rushed forward into his line of vision, and he immediately snuffed his flames for fear of hurting her. And when Mari pulled him to her, he let himself hurt.

CHAPTER TWENTY-SEVEN

ZAHIR

Zahir paced back and forth, his hands clasped behind his back. The gaping hole in his chest from the titanium walls did everything he wanted it to—it numbed the pain. Instead of focusing on Illan's actions, Zahir thought only of the uncomfortable feeling in his body, where he could feel neither of his magics. While the feeling made Zahir want to scratch off his skin layer by layer, it was exactly what he needed to distract him.

Zahir had barely begun to process Illan's betrayal. If Morana's words were true, Illan had worked with her for years. But why? Why in the world would Illan betray his own family? Betray someone who was like a son to him? Illan had been playing the part of a supportive mentor for Zahir's entire life, and now... Zahir wondered how much of it was a façade. He needed to know how much information Illan had passed on to Morana and what he'd known and kept from Zahir or Ryker.

Illan had helped orchestrate the palace attacks. His father's assassination. Mari's kidnapping. He knew about Rodrick; he knew about every fucking detail and let it happen. Any ounce of love Zahir had left for Illan turned to ash; Zahir would never forgive him for this.

Zahir put his hair up into a tail at the crown of his head but immediately took it down. His head pounded. All he wanted was a tall glass of whiskey and a nap. But he had information to process, a council to brief, and a traitor to find. He didn't know what he would do if he saw Illan again, but it wouldn't be anything good.

Zahir barely heard the door open as Pryn and Markus entered. They both shivered as they walked into the titanium gym. After just two steps, they both stopped and exchanged a glance.

"Actually, no," Markus said. He scratched at his wrists and scrunched his nose. "I can't do this. Can you come to the door?" Markus turned around and seemed to relax the second he was outside.

Pryn shook their head but followed Markus out. "How are you doing, Zahir?"

Zahir trudged to the door. "I don't even know how to answer that question."

"Is there anything we can do?" asked Markus.

Zahir shook his head. "I don't know."

"Do you want to talk about it?" Pryn asked. "I can make us tea and biscuits."

"I don't think I will be able to keep anything down, even if I wanted to," Zahir said. He had been nauseous for hours as he processed the news. "I also don't want to talk about it."

"Well, if you do…"

"Do you know what makes the least sense?" Zahir cut Markus off. "Why did Illan treat us like his own children if he was going to sell us out in the end? That's what hurts the most."

"Maybe he was threatened. Zahir, there could be a thousand reasons," Pryn said.

"He could have told us. There are a thousand things he could have done, but instead, he killed my father and kidnapped my wife. He never loved me."

"I don't think that's true," said Markus.

"If Illan loved me, he *never* would have hurt me like this." Zahir shook his head.

"Have you spoken to Anya? I saw her crying," Pryn said. "Maybe you should go speak with her."

Zahir hadn't spoken to Anya since Illan had revealed himself to be a traitor. Taryn held Anya back after Morana and Illan disappeared, keeping her from running off to find them. Anya had screamed curses the whole way back to the palace, igniting anything in her path.

Anya was as devastated and as shocked as Zahir. And while Zahir hadn't shared a sentimental moment with her in years, he didn't want her to be alone with her pain, especially after learning that Taryn was a dual mage. She was still his sister, despite how much she angered him.

Zahir nodded. He needed to talk to her. "She might actually be helpful in this situation."

Markus and Pryn walked beside Zahir in silence towards Anya's room. All the while, Zahir stared at his feet, counting his steps and breaths. Pryn put their hand on his back, but Zahir shook them off; he didn't want to feel better. He needed to get through the pain himself.

Once his friends dropped him at the room, Zahir took a deep breath before knocking on Anya's door three times. A part of him wondered what he was doing while he waited. He and Anya didn't talk about feelings as he didn't trust her. But when Anya opened the door, red-eyed, Zahir—for the first time in nearly twenty years—pulled his sister in for a hug. And much to his surprise, she didn't hesitate to return it, a choked sob escaping her lips. It was strange to embrace Anya—the person who had spent years trying to make his life miserable. But now, as they both cried, it felt like they were children again. The last time Zahir had hugged Anya was when he was seven, and Ryker had made him feel like an idiot for not knowing battle strategy. Anya had hugged Zahir and told him he didn't need to know everything as he would learn it all one day. Now, as Zahir hugged Anya, he hoped he offered the same comfort she had given him all those years ago.

The siblings stood like that for a long time before either spoke or dared to move. Anya made the first move, motioning for Zahir to follow her. Zahir hadn't seen the inside of her bedroom in some time, and he was surprised at its beauty. The walls were cream, except for the velvet black wallpaper behind her bed.

To the left was a desk adorned with knife marks, like Anya had stabbed it repeatedly. Where two beds had once been, a large one existed in its place. The hardwood floor was littered with feathers from her pillows, and the feathers tickled his ankles as he followed Anya to a small sitting area by a fireplace. A small table sat in the center before a couch and two plush chairs. Zahir sat in the nearest chair while Anya splayed on the couch, hoisting one leg up.

They sat in silence for a while, watching the flames in the fireplace lick the grate. The wood burned a heady odor, the heat offering comfort. The flame grew and shrunk in time with his breathing the longer he focused on it.

"So, Illan's a traitor," Anya said, picking up an open bottle of wine. "I never saw that coming." She tilted the bottle to her lips and took a long gulp.

Zahir accepted the bottle when she passed it to him, and he drank for a long time before giving it back. "Me, neither. I... have no words."

Anya laughed. "If anyone was going to betray us, I thought it would be me."

Zahir couldn't help the snort that escaped him. "Honestly, me too."

Her eyes softened as she wiped a tear from her cheek. "I never worked with the rebels, by the way. I'm not sure where they got the idea of having me on the throne. I wouldn't complain, of course, but I didn't plant the idea."

Zahir pondered her statement. How could he believe her? After all these years of promising to take the crown. While her tears and hurt seemed genuine, Zahir didn't know if her words were true. She had lied and tricked him for years.

"You *swore* to me for years it would be yours. I am sure a servant overheard you on more than one occasion," Zahir said, rolling his eyes.

"Yes, well... that is a fair point. Do you think our father knew?" Anya asked, taking another drink.

"If that was the case, Illan would have been dead long ago."

"He wasn't the nicest, was he?"

"I thought you revered him?" Zahir leaned forward in his chair and took the bottle back from his sister.

"I wanted his power, the title. I revered his control of people and how he could persuade anyone to do anything, but he was a terrible father."

"Now that, I can agree with."

"He wasn't exactly... warm."

"No. He was not. I am better with Roan than Father ever was with me." Zahir passed the wine to Anya. "I saw him when I was in Lovíth."

"Father is dead, Zahir. You must have been drunk." Anya quickly drank the wine until she started coughing. "I wish *I* was drunk."

Zahir shook his head and told Anya about The After, his meeting with Ryker, and what they discussed. He explained how Ryker was kind in The After, the warm father Zahir had always wanted him to be. And when Zahir had hugged him, it felt so real that he'd forgotten what happened.

Anya wasn't crying when he finished, but she stared intently into the fire, unblinking. Her shoulders shook every few breaths. Zahir couldn't remember the last time he saw his sister cry. All his life, Anya had always been someone Zahir would describe as strong, proud—and cold. Despite her hatred for him, he admired her strength. Nothing shook her. Above all else, Zahir wished he could have that, too.

"Did he say anything about me?" Anya whispered in a voice so quiet Zahir barely heard her speak.

Zahir took a breath, deciding whether to lie to her or tell the truth. "No, he didn't."

Anya shook her head and drank several long sips from the bottle. "I hope the Gods damn him."

She drained the bottle and threw it across the room, where it shattered against the wall. Zahir jumped at the sound and moved beside his sister, who sat up and rested her face in her hands.

"He doesn't deserve your anger," Zahir said, putting a tentative hand on Anya's shoulder. "Save it for those still alive to feel your wrath."

Anya sat up with a sharp inhale and wiped her eyes. Her face morphed into white-hot anger as she stared ahead, eyes locked on the wall. She took deep, evenly spaced breaths.

"Did you know Taryn was a dual mage?" Anya asked.

"Not until recently. I only found out a few days ago."

Anya leaned back on the couch. "This is all so fucked up."

"Did you two talk about it?" Zahir wasn't entirely sure why he asked.

"We did. It went about as well as you could expect. She apologized, and I yelled. She cried, and I yelled some more. I told her I felt betrayed, and she explained how she couldn't tell me."

"Are you still together?"

Anya nodded, her lips twitching upward for a second. "My love for her is greater than my anger."

Zahir smiled. "Good."

"Illan will curse the day he sold us out. Morana will wish she stayed dead." Anya's topic change was a clear distraction from tackling her feelings. "What do you need me to do?"

Zahir stood and stretched. "For now, stay mad. We need a plan. We can't blindly go after Morana; it's too risky. Prepare for war because that is where we are headed. I'll fetch a servant to clean the glass and bring you another bottle."

"Thank you, Zahir," Anya said. As Zahir went to walk away, Anya caught his wrist in her hand. "I am not sorry for trying to take the throne. I still think it should be mine, but you are a better king than our father was."

"Thank you, Anya. That is all I wanted to achieve."

When the door slammed shut behind Zahir, he took a deep breath. He knew where he needed to go next. And as Zahir strode the halls, he found himself standing before the door to his mother's chambers. Part of Zahir didn't want to have this conversation with her, but he knew he needed to.

When his mother answered, eyes rimmed in red, tears rose in his eyes, too. She enveloped Zahir in her arms and stroked his hair, much like she did when he was upset as a child. And for the first time since he was named heir, he allowed his mother to comfort him.

"I'm so sorry we didn't tell you about Zena," Maura said as she released her son. "I regret every decision we made surrounding how we handled that."

Zahir shook his head. "You thought you were doing the right thing... Can we talk?"

He surveyed his mother's room as she led him inside. The curtains were ripped off the walls and glass shards littered the floor beside the fireplace. A vase that normally housed daisies was tipped over, the flowers crushed on the ground as water dripped off the end table. The filling from pillows was scattered on his mother's bed while a knife rested on her bedside table.

But Zahir ignored the damage to the room as they sat sideways, face-to-face. He wasn't entirely sure what to say. Should he tell her he met with Lydia but that she would never replace Maura? He wanted to tell Maura what she wanted to hear, but Zahir had to tell her what *he* needed.

"She changed her name to Lydia upon returning to Lovíth. I met with her several times while I was there," Zahir said. Maura tried to hide her surprise, but Zahir noticed her eyes widening. "She lied about her name to protect herself. She is married, and she's a Fire and Life dual mage. Lydia practices divination with cards and can see parts of the future, and she helped train me."

Maura wiped tears from her cheeks. "How did that go?"

"Well. We got along, and I learned a lot from her. But—" Zahir reached out to grab his mother's hand. "No one could ever replace you as my mother. She may have given birth to me, but you gave me everything. I love you. My relationship with Lydia will not impact ours, that I can promise."

"Thank you. I wish we had told you earlier."

"I do, too. I was hurt at first. Finding something like this out so late in life is hard. It's made me question everything about myself like I didn't even know myself at all. But now I know, I can heal from the hurt."

"We never meant to hurt you," Maura said. "And I'm sorry that we did. We were doing what we thought was best. Clearly, we didn't make the right choice. I wanted to tell you, but your father convinced me not to. He said it would be safer if you didn't know because kids can say things they shouldn't. And he wanted to name you heir but feared you would tell someone and the clan would renounce us."

"Did you know about Illan?" Zahir asked.

Maura shook her head. "I had no idea."

"Did he know about me?"

"Not that I know of. Unless Ryker told him, he shouldn't have known."

"Everything is so backward. The last year has been so full of change and confusion. It feels like my whole life was turned upside down. I agonized over the decision to meet Lydia; I didn't know what I wanted, and now... I must make a decision about Illan."

"You need to find Illan and get answers. You have always been the kind of person who needs answers," Maura said, pulling Zahir into a hug. "And I'm glad you got them from Lydia. I love you so much. I am so proud of you."

***

Zahir lay on his bed, his legs dangling off the edge. The silk sheets were cooling on his bare back. He covered his eyes with his left arm, shielding the moonlight streaming in through the open door to the balcony. Mari had left a note explaining that she was putting Roan to sleep; it lay beside him on the bed. The warm breeze did nothing to stop the sweat forming on the back of his neck and knees. The exhaustion from the day, coupled with the warm temperature, was terrible.

Just as Zahir sat up to slide himself backward beneath the covers, a person stood in the open doorway. Zahir flung himself out of bed and ignited his hands in flame. When the person stepped into the light, he didn't know whether to attack or pause.

"Zahir, let me explain," Illan said, raising his hands. He wore a long black cloak, much like the tattered one Morana wore. Underneath, he donned the same white shirt and black pants he'd worn during his training sessions with Zahir. It was all so familiar. Illan's red-rimmed eyes surprised Zahir—after all Illan had done, *he* was sad? "I'm not here to hurt you."

"All I want to know is why," Zahir said. After a few seconds of staring at his uncle, Zahir put his hands down and quelled his fire.

"And I will tell you," Illan said, lowering his hands. "Can we sit?"

Zahir nodded and sat on the floor, waiting for Illan to sit across from him. He wasn't sure why he was treating Illan like a guest rather than an intruder, but nonetheless, here they were.

"It was never my intention. Daria's family, well, they are descendants of the original four mages. Iowyn's grandson freed Morana after she had been slain by the titanium blade," Illan said. Zahir lurched back in disbelief that Daria's ancestors had worked with Morana for thousands of years. "She had taken so many lives at that point that she was nearly invincible. For her to stay dead, the dagger needed to stay lodged in her heart. When they removed it, she was, in a sense, resurrected. And she has been in hiding for thousands of years.

"When Daria and I married, she told me the story. She told me that Morana was alive but swore me to secrecy. It could get us both killed if the information got out, but I have known for decades." Illan paused to let Zahir absorb the onslaught of information.

"You never said anything about Morana, even after Daria passed. Why?"

"I feared for my life, as well as yours, Roan's, and Anya's. After Daria and Meg passed, Morana threatened you three because you were the closest thing I had to children."

Zahir shook his head. "A warning would have been nice but go on."

"The rebel forces... there are two. One group is a part of Morana's cause. The other originated in Brahn because they thought Ryker made a mistake choosing you as heir, as it was disrespectful to Anya. Throughout history, it has always been the first-born child who would inherit the throne."

"What did Morana have to do with the rebels?"

"The Brahn rebels were disorganized, and Morana took advantage of that. She promised them victory and glory. She promised Ryker would no longer sit on the throne. Morana told them that she would orchestrate his assassination, and those who didn't follow her were killed."

Zahir shook his head. "You *knew* she was going to kill my father. Your own brother," Zahir spat.

Illan sighed. "I... I wanted Ryker off the throne."

Bile rose in the back of his throat. "What?" he blanched. Illan had taken an active part in his father's assassination—his own brother's death. What could Ryker have done to anger Illan so? Anya was jealous of Zahir, but he didn't think she wanted him dead. And Zahir could *never* fathom treating Roan like that. Illan was more disingenuous than Zahir had ever known.

"My goal was to get him off the throne. He was going to destroy all that was good in Brahn. And after that, I was going to be done. I wanted out. You were to be king, and I *knew* you would do good by Brahn."

"What happened?"

"I never meant for it to go this far. I tried to tell Morana I wanted out once you were coronated. I told her that I wouldn't go against you. But she refused. She threatened to kill you, Anya, and Roan. She made me kill people who disobeyed her orders so I would know that I would be next if I abandoned her cause."

Illan shuddered. "I wouldn't let her hurt the people I loved. I was trapped."

"You never should have even joined in the first place," Zahir said. "He was your *brother*."

Illan stared at the ground, hunching his shoulders. "It got out of hand very quickly. I am not saying I am innocent in this, but I thought it would stop after the crown was passed to you, and she would focus her sights somewhere else. On *someone* else..." Illan took a long pause. "It was only after you took the throne did she reveal her plans not just to unite the four clans but to unite them under *her* rule. To do that, she had to oust the current leaders."

Zahir's breath was sucked from his lungs. Not only did Morana want him off the throne, but those in Lovíth, Orcian, and Yu'güe, too. Mari's parents were also at risk. As much as Zahir hated them for what they did to Mari and Hanan, he couldn't sit by while their lives were targeted. He couldn't sit by while anyone's life was targeted.

"What is her plan?" Zahir asked; his heart pounded so loudly in his chest he barely heard Illan's next words.

"She is going to hit the clans one by one. Starting with Brahn and Orcian. By then, Lovíth and Yu'güe will hear of the strife and secure their borders. She will move to Lovíth with the powers of Orcian and Brahn in her hand. And finally, she will hit Yu'güe."

"How many followers does she have?"

"Hundreds," Illan shook his head. "Some because they agree with her vision, though most out of fear."

"Are the other clans yet involved?"

"Yes, several mages from the other clans are part of her group. Most are from Brahn and Orcian, but some from Lovíth and Yu'güe."

"Why do people side with her? She is a monster."

Illan sighed. "They are tired of isolation. People want the clans reunited. News of dual mages is spreading throughout the world again. If one person could do it without ramifications, why can't everyone?"

Zahir thought about it for a minute. Why couldn't there be dual mages? His initial answer was that they were too powerful, even though the dual mages Zahir knew had never fully come into both of their magics. He struggled with fire magic, even to this day. He is not nearly as powerful as Anya or Roan. Taryn is a strong fire mage, but Zahir was unsure how much of her power came from the fact she was a twin flame. Even Lydia, his own mother, said she struggled to learn her magic. The problem lay in the notion of power. Morana was—*is*—a strong dual mage, probably the strongest to ever live. The concept of someone *possibly* having that much power was scary, which he understood. But if it isn't a common occurrence, why is there so much fear?

"Stories passed down through the years painted dual mages as evil and a crime," Zahir said, resigned. "Do I agree with Morana's views on uniting the clans? I do, actually. But she's lost me with her methods because she doesn't truly want to unite them. She wants to rule them."

"What is the difference between her ruling all four clans and having independent leaders of each?" Illan asked. "You are a king of Brahn."

Zahir shook his head. "It is different. Here, we have a council. We have many people bouncing ideas back and forth. Yu'güe has a council. Lovíth doesn't have a real form of government but doesn't need one. Instead, they rely on the traditions of their magic. Orcian is like us with their monarchy. The difference is that Morana wants to rule them all, and she does not seem like someone who would take criticism lightly."

Something flashed across Illan's face when he answered. "No, she most certainly is not."

Zahir rested his head in his hands. "You joined her cause. You orchestrated my father's death and Mari's kidnapping." All the rage Zahir had forgotten flooded back to the surface. "You hurt everyone who loved you. You broke our hearts, Uncle."

"And for that, I am truly sorry. I never meant for it to go this far."

"But it did." Zahir stood. "You must take your leave."

Illan recoiled but nodded solemnly. "I understand."

As Illan stood and walked towards the open balcony doors, Zahir turned his gaze to the ground. He couldn't watch as his uncle, the person he trusted most in this world, walked out of his home and returned to his enemy.

"I hope you can find it in your heart to forgive me one day."

And with that, Illan was gone. Once Zahir closed the doors with a loud slam and clicked the lock shut, he allowed himself to feel the hurt he had shoved so deep in his heart.

Zahir wanted to watch his enemies burn.

Chapter Twenty-Eight

Mari

Pryn had come to Mari and Zahir's bed chambers early the next morning. By the time Mari had finished putting Roan to bed, Zahir was already asleep. Roan still didn't know what had happened, and Mari wanted to keep it that way. He was nine years old; he didn't need his heart shattered for another time.

When Mari answered the door, she stepped outside with the healer and closed it softly behind her to not wake Zahir.

"Is something amiss?" Mari asked upon noting Pryn's concern. It had only been two days since they arrived in Brahn, but after just a couple of meals together, Mari knew Pryn and Markus were good allies.

"Not anything new," Pryn said, a sarcastic smile ghosting their lips. "I came to see if Zahir wanted an alignment. After yesterday, I can imagine he needs it."

"He is still asleep," Mari said, glancing at the door.

Pryn cocked their head at Mari and squinted. "You need an alignment."

Mari let out a breathy laugh. "What?"

Pryn waved their hand in front of Mari's chest. "Your energy is *really* off."

"Okay," Mari said. "Let's do it."

"Really?" Pryn laughed. "You were much easier to convince than your husband."

"He *can* be quite stubborn, can he not?"

"That is certainly one word for him."

The walk to Pryn and Markus's bedchamber was a short walk. Mari wondered if the alignment would fix the magic on her hands, as suggested in the book she'd read with Illan. Mari had started to get used to the vines of magic creeping up her arms. She no longer looked at it in fear or jumped every time she'd forgotten about it. It was simply part of her.

Pryn set Mari up supine, surrounded by several large burning candles. Between her breasts lay a large pink stone shaped like a heart. Pryn glided around the room like a phantom. They moved with such grace that Mari couldn't take her eyes off them. After spraying some perfume in the air—the scent of lavender and honey—Pryn sat beside Mari and took a deep breath. They explained what they were going to do.

"You may have a bizarre experience since it is your first time. Zahir did," Pryn said. "I won't actually touch you unless I think something is wrong. You are safe, though. I won't let anything happen to you."

"I trust you, Pryn. Before we start, I need to show you something." Mari peeled off her gloves and showed Pryn her hands and forearms.

"What is this?" they asked, gingerly touching the marks on her arms.

"It's a physical manifestation of my magic. I used it to kill fifty people when I thought my brother had been killed, and they appeared after that. I read in a book that alignment can fix this."

Pryn recoiled, pulling their arms back to their chest as they stared wide-eyed at Mari's hands. After a moment of silence, Pryn shook their head and reached back out, taking Mari's hands in theirs. "I can try, but I can't make any promises. I have never seen anything like this. I don't know how death magic flows in your body, but I'll see what I can do."

"There is one other thing, too," Mari said. "I can hear the voices of those I killed."

As Mari explained to Pryn what her head felt like, the blood drained slowly from the healer's face. It was bad. But Mari didn't realize it was *so* bad that a life mage, trained to heal all injuries, would become more panicked the longer Mari spoke.

"I don't know if I can help with that, but I can try. Close your eyes and focus on the energy you feel around your body."

Mari's eyes fluttered closed as a buzzing sensation coursed around her body. The sensation only grew stronger the longer Mari focused on it. It ebbed and flowed in different parts of her body as Pryn moved their hands along it. Whenever Pryn neared her stomach, a jolt of pain rushed through Mari, and her body twitched. Only when Pryn hovered over that spot for longer did Mari fall into a catatonic state.

She didn't know where she was. She was in a room reminding her of the bedroom she had in Yu'güe, and Mari soon realized why. It *was*. She stepped closer as she saw a younger version of herself lying on the bed, writhing in pain, surrounded by blood-soaked sheets and towels. It only meant one thing—her cycle.

A woman walked into the room, a wet towel in her hand. Mari couldn't place the face but vaguely recognized her. The woman sat beside Mari on the bed and dabbed at her face with the cloth. Younger Mari cried out suddenly until there was barely a light in her eyes. She was unconscious.

Mari was thrown into another scene where she saw herself hiking up a mountain until that all too familiar stabbing pain seized her. She grabbed onto a tree and sunk into the freezing cold snow. Horrified, Mari watched the memory play as younger Mari stood, drops of blood landing on the pristine white snow. As she trudged back down the mountain, anyone would have thought she'd been stabbed.

Then Mari was in school, her face pale and sweaty. She sat at the back of her classroom and breathed slowly to control the nausea. Her heart beat so hard it deafened her. Every time she shifted in her seat, Mari was sure she was going to throw up, and when her teacher asked her to do a demonstration, Mari fainted within five feet of her desk. She awoke in vomit, surrounded by her classmates.

Mari shot up, her eyes wide as she took a moment to remember where she was. Mari grasped at the room to ground herself. She was in Brahn. In the palace. Pryn was there. They were aligning her.

"I am safe," Mari whispered.

"Mari, I am so sorry. It's all my fault," Pryn said.

"What happened?" Mari asked, shifting her gaze to Pryn.

Pryn wrung their hands and sighed. "I tried to help, but I can't. The energy is too much. It's wound so tightly that I can't get in. It hurt you instead of healing."

"Pryn, what are you talking about?"

Pryn let out a resigned sigh. "Mari, I'm so sorry. I've only seen this a handful of times, but when I was over your stomach, I could see the part of you that carries a child. And where the energy is usually reds and pinks, all I saw was darkness. Thorns and vines wrap around you there. When I tried to remove them, they poked back."

"What does that mean? Am I sick?"

"Yes and no. Whenever I have seen this on someone, they have complained of horrible cycles and extreme pain. These people, Mari... they were never able to bear children. There is something wrong that causes it, which also causes pain during cycles. I'm so sorry, Mari, but I don't think you'll be able to have children."

"Thank you," said Mari, flooded with relief for no longer needing to tell people that she didn't *want* children but *couldn't* have them. Mari let out a breathy laugh, a slow smile spreading across her face.

"What?"

"Thank you. I am not upset. Relieved, actually." Mari smiled. The relief rushing through Mari was unlike anything she had ever felt. It was expected of her to have a child but now that she couldn't, it was like a weight was lifted off her chest. No one had ever asked her what she wanted, or if she even *wanted* to be a mother. Everyone expected she would be; now, she didn't have to be. It was one more thing she had over her father, who crushed all that was good and pure in her life. He was never going to get what he wanted—a grandchild.

"Well, then, you're welcome," Pryn said, smiling.

"Now, how is the rest of my energy?" asked Mari.

Pryn told Mari about what they had fixed for her. In the body, seven zones of energy concern different aspects of life—the Crown, Eye, Throat, Heart, Solar Plexus, Sacral, and Root. The crown was at the top of the head and signified spirituality, self-identity, and awareness. Pryn said Mari's crown was like a pane of glass that had been tapped too hard. One more hit, and it would shatter.

"I can't do anything to heal this," Pryn said. "Can you still hear the voices?"

Mari sat in silence before the buzzing in her head intensified. "Yes, but I think it's quieter than before."

Pryn shrugged. "Maybe I did something. I'm sorry I couldn't do more."

The throat is where Mari struggled. This zone controlled choice, freedom, and faith. Pryn said that it was shifted in the wrong position. Mari wondered how much of that came from the lack of choice throughout her life. Until Zahir went to Lovíth, Mari had been told what to do and who to be; she was expected to have children, an expectation placed on Zahir, too. She was a huntress. A daughter. A wife. But never in her life was she able to be *Mari*. If Mari sat back and looked at her life, she realized the thing she wanted to be was happy. Though she'd had no choice in her husband, Mari was overjoyed with the life they'd built together here in Brahn.

Pryn explained to Mari that they couldn't do anything about her hands. As Mari felt so guilty about what happened, alignment wouldn't work. They explained that maybe if Mari worked more on herself, they would be able to fix her hands. But until then, they couldn't do anything.

Where the solar plexus and root zones were solid and burned bright, the sacral zone was the worst for Mari because of the "vines" Pryn referred to. That zone would never be aligned perfectly. Even if Mari removed the organ completely, the pain and hurt would still live there. Mari would have to come to terms with it, though. There was no cure.

Mari was fascinated by life magic. Hearing Pryn describe the different areas of energy and how they functioned together was unlike anything she'd heard before. Mari asked Pryn questions about how they became a healer, and Pryn shrugged it off with a simple, "I always knew." Mari wondered what it must be like to be as self-assured as Pryn, who knew what they wanted and who they were.

Pryn's response made Mari wonder if they were inside her head. "You have your whole life ahead of you. There is time for you to figure out what you want. You have a husband and a family. A chance to start over. Zahir loves you very much, Mari. He would want you to be whatever you want to be."

Mari nodded. "Amid the insanity of not being able to choose my life, I didn't realize that my life had only just begun. I am a world away from those who hurt me, and I can start over with my new family. You are right. Thank you, Pryn. Not just for the alignment but for the wise words. Zahir has a good friend in you."

"Thank you, Mari," Pryn said, moving to stand. "I should see if Zahir is awake. He definitely needs my help."

Mari stood. "I think that's a great idea. I need to keep Roan away from this mess. I'm hoping I can distract him a little today."

Once Pryn and Mari parted ways, Mari went to Anya and Taryn's room before visiting Roan's. If she was going to keep Roan occupied all day, Taryn's bubbly personality would certainly be an asset. Taryn was just leaving the room when the pair nearly collided. Though Taryn looked exhausted, she agreed to help Mari occupy Roan for the day.

The two women grabbed Roan from his room and brought him to the kitchens. Still in his night clothes, Roan sat on the counter, and Mari stood beside him while Taryn prepared breakfast, much to the cook's discontent. He had explicitly told Taryn she didn't *need* to cook for herself, but Taryn insisted, saying it would make her happiest. In the end, the cook relented and "supervised" from the corner of the room, where he chopped vegetables in preparation for tonight's dinner. Taryn had worked in her family's restaurant for years and knew her way around the kitchen. This wasn't the first time the cook had been disgruntled with her.

"And then I whip the eggs with some milk and add a few spices for you," Taryn said, whisking the eggs in a metal bowl. She beat the eggs quickly and slowly poured in the milk. Taryn wore her hair clipped back so it didn't fall in her face.

"What is your favorite thing to make, Taryn?" Mari asked. The smell of all the spices combined was intoxicating; Mari would love for Taryn to teach her how to cook, especially if it always smelled this good.

"I actually love baking—cakes, breads, cookies, desserts. Anything sweet, especially. Baking is more precise than cooking."

Taryn served Roan his eggs and cut him a slice of warm bread. As he ate, Mari and Taryn took a minute to rest, and when their eyes met, it was clear how exhausted they both were. Trying to keep secrets from a child was not easy.

"What do you want to do after breakfast?" Mari asked.

"It's okay, you don't need to distract me. I know what's happening," Roan said, taking a sip of water.

Mari and Taryn stared at each other, their mouths agape. Mari was at a loss for words. How could Roan know what happened?

"What?"

"Morana is alive. Illan did something bad. Zahir is in a foul mood, and Anya is in a terrifying one. I'm much smarter than you all think."

Mari shook her head. "You are *brilliant*, Roan. We didn't know you knew."

Roan shrugged. "I heard the servants. They were talking right outside my door last night. They're not very quiet."

Taryn burst out laughing. "Well then, you don't need a distraction, but we can still spend time together."

Against their better judgment, Mari and Taryn agreed to play a game where Roan hides, and the two women look for him. They contained it to certain wings of the palace, so he couldn't go very far. Roan was an excellent hider, contorting his body into all kinds of strange positions to fit into obscure spots. He hid in a bookshelf in the library; he crouched into a kitchen cabinet. They found him hiding in a particularly bushy plant. And just a moment, they forgot what was happening in the world, reminded of what it was to be a child.

Chapter Twenty-Nine

Mari

Mari slammed the sixth useless book shut and shoved it across the table, grabbing the next unopened book from the stack. Zahir, off preparing a battle strategy with Ren, had asked Mari to figure out if there had ever been a recorded immunity to titanium. After the battle with Morana and Illan's subsequent betrayal, Zahir had been pouring hours into finding a way to defeat her while saving his uncle. Despite the hurt Illan had caused, the love Zahir held for his uncle outweighed the heartbreak. So, Mari did her part. She read scrolls and thumbed through books. She wrote to the Queen of Orcian and even, dare she say, to her father.

She wrote and asked if he had ever heard of such a thing. She told him about Morana, a decision she had poured over for far too long. Part of her wanted to keep it a secret, but they would not defeat Morana alone. They needed an army. As much as it made Mari sick, she needed her father's help.

Mari needed to ask another death mage about the pain in her head and the magic creeping up her arms. But she couldn't. The only other death mage who would have an idea would be Fahran, her first love, but she couldn't list her symptoms in a letter. It was too risky. She had tried writing to Fahran before crumpling up the letter and tossing it in the fire instead.

Pryn and Markus sat across from Mari, thumbing through their own piles of books. Every time Mari angrily shoved a book aside, they exchanged a glance. Mari hoped to the Gods that there was an answer somewhere in the expansive Brahn library. She hoped that Illan, at some point, regretted his choice and had put something in the library for when this day came. Yet, thus far, the trio had come up with more questions than answers.

"How could she be immune to titanium?" Mari asked Pryn and Markus for what must have been the fifteenth time. "How is that possible?"

"She has been alive for thousands of years," Pryn said for the fifteenth time.

Markus sighed and gave his normal response. "She had a titanium blade lodged in her chest for Gods know how long."

"It's not possible. How did *that* blade not kill her? It was a straight shot to the heart."

"Maybe they missed," Pryn said, straightening. "The only person alive today who was there is Morana. Maybe they missed her heart."

"How could they mistake unconscious and dead?"

Markus shrugged. "I'm sure it is possible."

"Let's operate on the assumption that they missed—just for a minute. They miss her heart, but the dagger stays in her chest," Mari said; she mimed stabbing someone in the chest. "They lay Morana to rest, but then—an unknown amount of time later—someone else comes by and takes the dagger out. What do they do with it? Why do they do it? How do they know how to do it?"

"Maybe she micro-dosed titanium," Pryn said. "Sometimes healers will ingest minute quantity of poisons so that when they treat overdoses, they know how the body feels. What if Morana was injecting herself like that, but with titanium? Ingesting poison helps build immunity against the thing you ingest. What if it works that way with titanium, too?"

"How would she have known to do that?" Markus asked. "Slaying her with the titanium blade was the first time we learned of its capabilities."

"Or so we think," Pryn said, raising a finger. "It is the first *documented* use of titanium. What if Morana knew?"

"How? She was the most feared person; no one would have trusted her," Mari said.

"Clearly someone did. She had allies."

"What if they stabbed her?" Markus said suddenly. "Her entire defeat could have been orchestrated. We had seven fucking mages trying to take her down, and we barely did any damage. One person, thousands of years ago, wouldn't have been able to land a hit when she was at her strongest."

The silence that fell over the table was deafening. Morana faking her death wasn't out of the realm of possibilities. Gods knew she was smart. She'd hid for millennia without being dis-covered or leaving behind an obvious stream of bodies in her wake. To continually increase her life span, she would have had to keep taking lives. Eventually, someone would have noticed people were disappearing. But they hadn't. She hadn't been discovered. Morana was cunning—brilliant and deceptive.

Mari put her head in her hands and closed her eyes. She thought back to her recent conversations with Illan. He had sent in the tracker. He must have known Kane was Morana's ally, and while Illan couldn't obviously lead them to Morana herself, he could drop hints. And if his words were true about not meaning to take it this far, then he would have tried to help in whatever way he could.

Over the moon cycles that Zahir was gone, Mari relied on Illan for strength, courage, and decision-making when navigating the advisors. She asked him for comfort and friendship. But what she never asked for was a history lesson. He spoke more of his wife recently than he had before Morana was revealed. Daria was the key. She was a descendant of the original fire mage, Iowyn.

"What do you know of the story of the four mages? How the child killed its father?"

Pryn and Markus exchanged a look. "The child?"

"Yes, the child of Iowyn. He killed his father and left the mother alone."

"That's not how we know it."

"What are you talking about?" Mari asked.

"When the other mages found out... they hurt Iowyn until she was no longer with child," Pryn said. "That first dual mage was never born because there was already fear in the world. After that, the four original mages begged the Gods to grant other people their magic because it was too big a responsibility, but they didn't correctly phrase their request. They wanted to be mortal yet what the Gods granted them was dozens of other mages whom they now had to train to use their magic properly."

Mari reeled and shook her head. "What?" She told Pryn and Markus the story she'd watched.

"That's the children's version of the story. It was toned down to not scare the children. The real story is so horrible," Pryn said, sighing.

"Illan's wife was a descendant of Iowyn. I was wondering if that story might have a clue in it somehow," Mari said.

Pryn sighed. "It doesn't seem likely."

Mari shoved her chair back and stood up to stretch. She had been sitting for so long that her back was beginning to cramp. Instead of sitting back down, Mari gathered the useless books and returned them to the shelves. The smell of books, which usually comforted her, only made her more stressed; she was frustrated with the lack of information. While Brahn had a massive number of books, there was very little on anything outside of Brahn's direct history. She needed access to infor-mation from the other clans. Morana was a life and death mage, yet Yu'güe kept no written records; most of their history was passed down verbally through the generations, especially after Morana. The death mages took nearly complete responsibility for her because she used death magic to wreak havoc. While Mari understood wanting to repent, she didn't understand why they hid their knowledge instead of using it to educate.

While darkness was forbidden, she'd never been told *why* except that Morana used it. When Mari used it with Fahran, she felt awful for days afterward—sometimes weeks, depending on how long they were in The After. When she met Zahir in The After, it had been so short she barely felt its effects.

Suddenly, Mari had an idea. She didn't quite know if it was brilliant or idiotic. How had it not clicked before? Once she finished putting the books back, she raced to Pryn and Markus, a smile creeping onto her face.

"I know how we can figure out what happened," Mari said, leaning her hands on the table. "I can talk to Vala and her descendants until I find someone who was alive when Morana was slain."

"Mari," Markus said, running a hand down his face. "You can't really *talk* to dead people. I know sometimes you can feel them there—my grandmother sometimes visits as a butterfly—but you can't talk to them."

Mari couldn't help the laugh that escaped. "Death mages *can*." She proceeded to tell them about her darkness. "I spoke with Vala a long time ago. It didn't click when Illan told me the story, but it did now."

"That sounds dangerous," Pryn said. "There are parts of life magic that mess with your alignment, and I am sure the same thing is true for death magic."

"I have done it before. Sometimes, I didn't feel quite right for a few days or weeks, but I eventually returned to normal."

Pryn ran a hand down their face. "But it messed with your alignment."

"So, you can just align me afterward." Mari shrugged. "Isn't that how it works?"

"Well, maybe?"

"Maybe?"

"I don't know how death magic flows through the body. Life magic is in the blood, powered by the crown chakra. Do you know which chakra your death magic sits in?"

"Well, no, but I would guess the heart chakra."

"Do you know what could happen if I can't re-align you properly? You might not be able to channel your magic."

"What if you align her while she goes into The After?" Markus asked, leaning forward on his elbows. "You will be able to see the chakras moving in real-time."

"What, and try to actively stop it? I don't know if that's even possible."

"It's a risk I'm willing to take," said Mari.

"If you lose your magic for good... you have no idea what that will do to you."

Mari was quiet for a long time. On the one hand, she was terrified of being like Illan, who hadn't been able to access his magic for nearly thirty years. But on the other, she was terrified of *using* her magic again. Mari had vowed she would never take another human life, yet in a fleeting moment of terror, she murdered fifty people. Now, she carried those souls around with her and sported permanent physical markers as reminders of her sin.

"I am willing to do it. We must try," Mari said, the blood pounding in her ears. "We have to try something."

"There has to be a way to defeat her without disturbing your alignment," Markus said.

"How do we know if Morana is attacking us?" asked Pryn. "What does it feel like when someone is trying to take your soul?"

"Like this," Mari said. She raised a hand, palm out towards Pryn. She bent her fingers slightly, giving Pryn the sensation that she would take their soul.

"Whoa," Pryn said, putting their hands up, their fingers trembling. Pryn's lips parted, and their chest heaved. "What are you doing?"

"Showing you how it feels."

Markus stepped in front of Pryn. "Mari, you could have killed them."

"No, I am completely in control of my magic," Mari said as the couple shared a look. Mari crossed her arms. "You think I'm crazy, don't you?"

"Mari, you murdered a lot of people. Your hands are still showing your magic. Your alignment is disturbed. We don't know how this affects your psyche."

"I don't feel crazy."

"We didn't say you are crazy. Just take it easy."

Mari lowered her hand. "I feel fine. I am in complete control."

"Okay," Pryn said. "Okay. Let's work with your darkness."

Mari and Markus gathered candles and lit them in a circle while Pryn took out an alignment book and a velvet bag of crystals from their bag. They cleansed the circle with an incense stick of lavender. When Mari sat down, legs crossed, Pryn moved across from her, their knees touching Mari's as they poised their hands to start the alignment.

Mari let her eyes flutter closed as she began her meditation. With every inhale, she smelled the incense that Pryn kept burning, and with each exhale, she breathed out her anxiety. The only sound she heard was Pryn and Markus's breathing. A light breeze dusted the back of her neck as Markus paced back and forth behind her.

Then everything changed.

And Mari repeated her intentions in her head.

I intend to speak with Vala, the first death mage.
I wish to speak with Vala.
Vala will meet me in The After.
I will return to this spot unharmed.
Vala will meet me in The After.

And then Mari heard the familiar crunch of snow underfoot. When she opened her eyes, she was in the valley near her home in Yu'güe, instantly eased by the familiar peaks of snow-covered mountains. But what startled her was the sight of Pryn.

"Mari," Pryn said tentatively, looking around. "You didn't say I would come with you."

"I didn't think you would. You weren't touching me."

Pryn ran a hand down their face. "Yes, I was. Get me out of here."

"I don't know how to intentionally go back. Time will run out. Come on, we only have a few minutes."

"Mari!" Pryn yelled. "I can't believe—"

"There she is," Mari said, cutting Pryn off before they could give her a tongue lashing.

Standing a few feet away, a woman in a thick coat stood staring up at the snow as it fell onto her face. Her familiar pale face and long black hair contrasted with her white coat. Vala. Mari could never forget her face.

"Vala," Mari said. "What a pleasure it is to speak with you again. I am Mari, and this is Pryn. Do you remember me?"

Vala wore a thick white coat, starkly contrasting the wispy black hair falling to her waist. Her bright blue eyes shone in the light as she peered around. Mari's heart pounded in her chest—she hadn't realized how similar Vala looked to Morana. They had the same pale skin and wispy, long hair. If Mari didn't know any better, she might have thought Vala was a young Morana.

"I do. What happened to the boy you were with last time?" Vala asked, her voice high-pitched and crackling.

"He isn't here. I must ask you, were any of your descendants alive when Morana was slain?" Mari asked.

"Yes."

"Can you tell me the name of your descendant who was alive at the time? I need to speak with them."

"Why?"

"Morana... she is alive."

"Should you be telling her that?" Pryn whispered.

"What am I going to do with the information?" Vala asked, focusing on Pryn. Vala cocked her head to the side, dragging her eyes lazily down Pryn's body. "Who do I have to tell?"

"Please," Mari cut in. "Can you tell us who to speak to?"

"His name is Benedict. You can call upon him. He was there."

The light in the sky flickered, and Mari knew her time in The After was coming to an end. "Thank you for speaking with us."

And then, Mari and Pryn were thrown back into their bodies. Mari leaned back onto her hands, struck by the force of re-entering her reality. But Markus had to catch Pryn as they fell backward.

"What the hell happened?" Markus growled. "You took them with you."

"Markus, I'm so sorry. I didn't realize," Mari apologized, her vision swimming.

"I swear to the Gods if they are hurt." Markus picked Pryn up into his arms. "We are *not* trying that again."

"I can do it alone," Mari said. Power surged through her, reminding her of when she had taken all those souls. She felt invincible like she could do anything. "Go, they will recover soon."

"When I said we are not doing it again, I meant you, too," Markus said.

"Go take care of Pryn. I need to get some answers."

"Mari, you can't. Now I *do* think something is wrong with your psyche."

"Markus, go," Mari raised a hand to him, palm outstretched. She didn't like threatening his life, but she needed to get answers. "If you try to stop me, I will not hesitate."

Mari felt more anger than guilt as Markus carried Pryn from the room. They needed answers, no matter the cost.

Mari closed her eyes one more time and began her meditation. Before she knew it, she was once again in The After, standing before a burly man with long white hair and a beard that reminded Mari of Illan. That familiar pain nestled deep in her chest, but once he began speaking, Mari focused on the task at hand.

"Who wakes me?" Benedict asked, his voice loud and deep.

"I am Mari. I am a death mage. Thank you for coming here," Mari said. "May I ask you a few questions?"

Benedict snorted. "Obviously, you are a death mage. Proceed."

"Were you alive when Morana was slain?" she asked.

"That is a trick question. She lives." Benedict rolled his eyes. "This is what you woke me for?"

Mari gritted her teeth to avoid the sarcastic response she was *dying* to say. "What happened back then? How does she live?"

"They missed."

"I see, and how is she now impervious to titanium?" Mari asked.

"She consumes small amounts. So, she cannot lose her magic."

"One last question," Mari said, thankful Benedict confirmed Pryn's theory. "How can we kill her?"

"You need all—"

Mari screamed as she was thrust back into her body. As her soul re-entered, she physically lurched and flung her arms back to catch herself, a growl escaping her lips. It was mildly painful to re-enter her body after being in The After. But she would do whatever was necessary to defeat Morana.

Benedict knew the answer. She would need to speak with him again; now she knew there was an answer on how to defeat Morana. But Mari was in no place to use her darkness again. Mari's chest heaved with every breath like she had just hiked a mountain. Her arms felt wobbly as she held herself up. She was exhausted.

Mari blew out the candles one by one and moved them out of a circular formation. She didn't need anyone coming back here and thinking she had done something horrible. After a meal and a nap, she would try again.

Mari would keep trying until she knew how to kill Morana.

CHAPTER THIRTY

ZAHIR

Zahir handed out daggers, knives, and swords to his guards while Ren instructed them where to go. Before deciding on a plan of attack, Ren needed to secure the palace, especially from Illan. Illan was the worst person to have betrayed the family; he knew every guard rotation and weak point in the palace. Morana always had the upper hand; even if Illan had only meant to oust Ryker, he hadn't done anything to stop the rebels and Morana from trying to oust him, too. Illan had helped rebels into the safe room, compromising its location and safety; he jeopardized Roan's life and allowed them into the palace *again* to kidnap Mari. Illan could do anything he wished to harm Zahir as it didn't matter if he was in danger, but he would never let him hurt the people he cared for most in the world. He would do *anything* to protect Mari and Roan. He would throw his own life on the line for them, but instead, Illan had let Mari take the punishment.

Anger boiled in Zahir's blood as betrayal nestled deep in his heart. Zahir had come to terms with his father's lies and secrets and was working through his trauma surrounding the circumstances of his birth; he forgave himself for the mistakes he made immediately after he became king, but he was so furious and hurt by Illan's actions that he didn't know how to begin processing it. Rodrick's betrayal, while hurtful, was nothing compared to this.

"Zahir?" Ren asked. "Are you all right?"

Zahir shook himself out of his trance and handed weapons to the last straggling soldiers. "Fine. We need a plan. We can't go in without one."

"I agree. Come to my office," Ren said, motioning for Zahir to follow them. "I have some maps."

Zahir put a hand to his head, where pain was beginning to sprout. "Do you have something to drink?"

"You tell me," Ren said, opening the door to their office.

Inside the dimly lit room, behind a large mahogany desk, was a liquor display that put taverns to shame. Forty bottles of various vodkas, whiskeys, and bourbons hid behind glass doors in a cabinet. Different types of glasses were stacked on a side table for each type of liquor.

"I didn't realize you were a big drinker." Zahir laughed.

"I'm not. But sometimes wine just doesn't cut it. And everyone likes a little something different. I keep it for the guards, mostly. A bad day can mean a *really* bad day down here," said Ren. "Whiskey?"

Zahir nodded. "Please. Don't be shy on the pour."

Ren handed Zahir a glass filled to the brim. "I wouldn't dare."

Ren clinked their full glass of whiskey against Zahir's and took a big sip. They motioned for Zahir to sit in a chair towards the center of the room around a long table with four unique paperweights on each corner. The two closest to Zahir were a raven atop a skull and a sun. The other two were the moon and a rose.

"Those are unique paperweights," Zahir said, taking a long drink.

"They represent each of the four clans. I found them over a few years during the solstice markets. This was the first year we didn't have one."

"What?" Zahir asked. "They didn't have it this year?"

"Well, the king usually puts it together. And you were in Lovíth. Brahn had been attacked. No one was thinking about the markets."

Zahir shook his head. "Everything is so wrong."

Ren spread a map on the table and pinned the corners with each paperweight. Zahir stood and walked around the middle of the table to see the map right side up. It was a topographical map of Brahn and its surrounding areas, where various spots were marked with a red X. Zahir remembered the last time he looked at this map. When Mari was taken by the rebels, he used this map to find potential hiding spots. Anything too low could flood, anything too high would be difficult to reach while escorting hostages, and areas too exposed wouldn't be good hiding spots. Zahir had marked each useless location with a red X so he wouldn't return. He hadn't been sleeping at the time, and his memory was foggy, at best.

The map brought back bad memories for Zahir. He had felt so helpless when Mari was taken. Even though he spent every possible second trying to find her, he'd felt so guilty, like he should have been able to protect her. But he couldn't. And now... now he knew it had been Illan's fault. Illan had *stood* there with him, offering suggestions of places to explore, which had turned up nothing; had Illan tried to lead him off course, or had he genuinely had no idea where they had taken Mari? Zahir had taken Illan's word as gospel, believing it wholeheartedly, but now Zahir didn't even know what was real or an act.

"They wouldn't go back there," said Zahir to Ren, pointing to where he had found Mari. "It would be the first place we would look."

"Or maybe they would," Ren said. "Maybe they know we would think like that, and we wouldn't go back there."

Zahir groaned. "So, we are starting with nothing."

"Not nothing," Ren said. "They had a camp in these mountains, where we faced off with them. It's where Hanan got hurt, and Mari annihilated a whole group of them. I'm unsure if they are still camping there, but it's out of the way. It's the first place we would check, and we know how to get there."

"Let's leave that one alone for now," Zahir said. He didn't want to waste time retracing their steps. Zahir picked up a black marker and circled the area Ren had pointed to in the mountains. He then made a green X where he found the rebels inside the mountains last time. "Black is areas of interest. Green is known locations of rebel camps."

"What are we trying to do, Zahir? That will change our plan of attack," Ren asked, finishing their whiskey and pouring themselves more.

Zahir thought about that for a minute. He wanted to burn every last one of them. He desired to find and kill Morana, even if it was impossible. He needed to secure his city and give his people the peace they deserved. "I want to find Illan."

"You want to rescue Illan? He betrayed us," Ren said, furrowing their eyebrows.

"What he did was unforgivable and treasonous, but he's still my uncle. If he is going to pay for his crimes, imprisonment with us is better than death by Morana's hand. I don't want him dead."

"But a prisoner in the castle is better? The last time someone betrayed you, you didn't hesitate to execute them."

Zahir flinched at Ren's words. He didn't want to act rashly again after killing one of his closest friends and simultaneously destroying his relationship with Reina. Zahir hadn't even tried to get answers from Rodrick. He acted so quickly without remorse. He didn't want to rule like his father, reacting with violence any time he was afraid. Zahir didn't want to do that to his people. And he wouldn't do it to Illan.

"No one else is my uncle," Zahir said.

He didn't quite know how to explain it to Ren, but he didn't want Illan to suffer. When they spoke last night, Zahir truly felt that Illan regretted his decisions. Zahir believed Illan didn't want anything to happen to him and that he hadn't known the whole plan initially. If that were the truth, he couldn't let Illan die. At least if Illan were here, Zahir would know he couldn't be working against him.

Ren and Zahir began narrowing down potential hideouts. Morana had Illan, but he wasn't imprisoned—at least, as of last night. Unless Morana sent Illan to speak with Zahir, he was still in her good graces, which meant he would be with her now. If they found Illan, they could capture Morana, too.

Hours and a couple of glasses of whiskey later, Ren and Zahir had narrowed it down to five locations, excluding the two the rebels had used before. By the time they were done, the two of them were quite intoxicated from the liquor. The familiar feeling buzzed through Zahir, who felt light for the first time in a long time. He had no concerns about Lydia or mastering his life magic. He wasn't worried about dying or not getting to live a full life with Mari. He was only worried about not being able to pull off a rescue.

"Ren," Zahir said. "Thank you."

"You have nothing to thank me for. This is *literally* my job," said Ren, rolling their eyes.

"Yes, that's true. But I also want to thank you for looking after Mari while I was gone."

"I do get paid to protect the royal family."

Zahir scoffed and waved a hand at Ren. "I *know*, but I mean emotionally."

"Who is coming with us to capture Illan?" Ren asked.

"Oh, no. I need you here. There are three people I trust to look after Roan. You, Anya, and Taryn. The three of you must keep him safe," said Zahir. "I refuse to put his life in danger again."

"Anya and Taryn are the strongest fire mages alive. Not to mention, Taryn is a dual mage. They would be great assets in this fight."

Zahir shook his head. "I know, but I can't let them come. Roan cannot defend himself, and I need their strength to protect him."

"There are plenty of capable guards. You need Taryn and Anya to fight," Ren insisted.

Zahir slammed a hand down on the table. He would not risk the lives of his family. "No. I am not changing my mind. The two of them will stay here."

"Okay, Zahir. Okay," Ren said, raising their hands in surrender. "What about Reina and Raf, then? Will you take them?"

"Hanan has still barely recovered, and Raf won't leave his side. I might be able to convince Reina to come with us. She is extraordinarily talented with a blade."

"Pryn and Markus? If someone gets hurt?"

"Life mages don't have an attack form to their magic," Zahir said, sighing. "I know they will be helpful for healing, and Markus is an incredible swordsman, but I don't know if I can ask them to risk their lives."

"Zahir, you need a team." Ren put their glass down and ran a hand through their hair. "War has casualties; war is dangerous. Everyone understands that. Pryn and Markus threw themselves into battle with Morana less than a day after arriving in Brahn, knowing they had no magic to attack with."

Zahir sighed and sat down in the chair behind him. "I know. I know I can't do this alone."

"Mari will not let you leave her behind," Ren said.

"I already knew she would come with me. I know better than to leave her behind. She is extraordinary."

"Reina came to find Morana the first time. I have a feeling she will come along this time, too."

"I hope she forgives me for everything.".

All this time later, Zahir still felt guilty for bringing Reina in for questioning after Rodrick was discovered to be a traitor. Of all the people, Reina would have been the next likely suspect since she was his fiancée. But after what Mari told him—how Reina found out Rodrick only 'fell in love' with her to get closer to Zahir—his guilt intensified tenfold. He hadn't yet had a chance to apologize to Reina truly, but he needed to find the time to sit her down and offer his full apology.

"I don't deserve Reina as a friend," he said. "She has *always* stood by me, and the second her fiancé betrays the crown, I treat her like a suspect. I didn't handle that as well as I should have."

"Maybe not, but I think she understands now. If she hated you for that, she would have stayed away, even from Mari," Ren said, shrugging.

Zahir nodded, unsure of what else to say. He had a battle party: a fire and life mage, a death mage, a talented swordswoman, and two life mages. Zahir wished he could take Anya and Taryn with them, but he couldn't leave Roan without the best protection. After the breach of the palace, Zahir wouldn't have trusted anyone but Anya and Taryn to protect his brother, especially as the guards couldn't even keep the queen safe.

"I need to find Mari and talk to her about this plan. Before we do anything, I want her input," said Zahir.

Much to Zahir's surprise, Ren pulled Zahir into a short hug. "It is good to have you back."

Zahir returned Ren's embrace. "It is good to be back."

The palace hallways brimmed with guards running around to secure all entries into the palace. Loud voices filled the halls and echoed off the stone walls; doors slammed loudly, and locks clicked into place as Zahir passed. Several guards stopped and offered to escort him wherever he was headed, but Zahir refused. They were needed to secure the palace, not walk him to his wife.

The chances that no other traitors existed among his staff and guards were slim, but it didn't stop him from hoping otherwise. Even after weeding out any potential dangers after Rodrick was discovered, Illan remained, and no one had ever questioned his loyalty. Even Maura never expected Illan to betray the family like this.

Zahir found Mari hunched over in bed, pouring through a book. Only when he closed the door behind him did Mari look up from it. The way her face lit up made Zahir's heart melt. He never wanted to leave her again.

"Do you have a battle plan?" asked Mari as he sat beside her in bed.

"Ren and I came up with an idea, but it's not a full plan yet. I wanted to talk with you first," Zahir said.

Zahir told Mari his idea about capturing Illan and keeping him in the palace instead. He explained his reasoning, and Mari nodded as he spoke, absorbing every word he said.

"I know it's risky..."

"Zahir, he is your *uncle*. Of course, you want him to live. But is keeping him in the palace a good idea?" she asked. "We don't know who else is working with Morana. They could easily help Illan."

"What happens to Illan then, after we thwart Morana? If she hasn't killed him by then, we are going to have to do *something*. Why don't we keep him alive while we still can?" Zahir asked. He had a point. After they defeated Morana, they wouldn't be talking about imprisoning him, but would be discussing whether they should execute him or not. Zahir knew that if it were anyone else, they would be executed.

Mari was quiet for a minute, nodding slowly. "Let's go get him. When do we leave?"

"Not now," Zahir said as he flopped back on the pillows. "Ren and I had too much whiskey."

"Zahir!" Mari chided. "You're in the middle of a war. Now is not the time to be drunk."

"I think if any time calls for alcohol, it's now."

Instead of arguing, Mari lay with Zahir and curled into his side. He wrapped her in his arms and toyed with the ends of her hair as they lay there, staring up at the ceiling, enjoying the last remnants of calm before the world ended.

CHAPTER THIRTY-ONE

ZAHIR

Zahir tied his hair back as he stalked between the trees, his sword strapped to his back. The half-moon rose in the distance, barely illuminating the ground. Draping the hood over his head, Zahir concealed his bright silver hair that reflected the little light coming from the moon. He checked the daggers at his waist to ensure they were secure and would make no noise. The chill in the evening air made the hair on the back of his neck stand on edge. The scent of smoke made Zahir's heart race.

They were getting close.

Only after checking if the clearing past the trees was empty did Zahir motion for Markus, Pryn, Reina, and Mari to follow him. They did so silently, sneaking up behind other trees near Zahir's. Before he stepped out from behind it, Zahir waited for Pryn to ready their bow and cover him if someone came out of nowhere.

Stepping around the tree, Zahir checked for thin sticks beneath his feet; the last thing he needed was to get caught. Less than a day after concocting the plan to rescue Illan, Zahir and his accomplices began their efforts and left at nightfall. The first night they went was a new moon, and since then, more light had begun illuminating the outskirts of Brahn. While leaving Brahn, Zahir had watched some of his people begin moving back into their homes from the camps outside the city. It had taken weeks, but houses were finally being rebuilt, thanks to the generous "donation" from the palace funds. After all, Zahir didn't need more fanciful clothing; he needed to help his people.

Anya and Taryn had been upset they weren't coming with them but ultimately understood why Zahir had asked them to stay with Roan. Anya had told Zahir he had nothing to worry about, and for the first time, he believed her. During the first invasion of the palace, Anya and Taryn easily held their own. As one of the only active Twin Flame pairs, few were stronger than they were.

On the other hand, Roan had been terrified that Zahir was leaving again and latched onto Zahir's waist, begging him not to leave. Zahir explained he was only leaving for a few hours to rescue Illan, but Roan didn't believe him until he *promised* to return. So Zahir did.

While they had found small rebel camps throughout their searches, they had yet to see Illan. They hadn't even engaged with the rebels during the first night, stumbling across ten people setting up tents and a campfire. Illan wouldn't have trusted them; they weren't even fire mages and used flint to start their campfire.

On the second night, the group found more people and a small cabin. Zahir went to turn around, but Mari flew past him without a second thought and demanded they show her Illan. When they didn't, she raised her hands, palms out, and slaughtered them all.

"Mari, what are you doing?" Zahir asked, his heart hammering.

"It's just like where they kept me," Mari whispered, not glancing back at Zahir.

Zahir wrapped his arms around Mari's waist and pulled her close to his chest. "You can't just kill everyone we encounter, Mari. You care about human life."

The giggle that escaped Mari's lips startled Zahir, who released her from his grasp. With a crooked grin, she said, "They aren't deserving of life."

On the third and fourth night, the party came up empty as the chosen locations showed no trace that a camp had been there. On the fifth and sixth night, they found two small camps—one with no mages and the other made up of fire mages. Mari's regard for human life was slipping; she didn't hesitate before trying to rush in, and Zahir had to physically hold her back. What was happening to her? The vines creeping up her arms were nearly to her shoulders now.

Zahir had never seen Mari act so rashly with little regard for human life. The further the vines crept up her arms, the more erratic she became. The last time Mari had killed someone, she'd been wracked with guilt for weeks. But now, it didn't even seem to bother her, and with every life she took, the unsettling smile grew on her lips.

That was the first time Zahir realized that Morana had supporters from more than just Brahn. In addition to lighting their campfire with magic, Zahir had watched them warm their drinks and food with their hands, and after putting the fire out, someone stepped up to it, pulling water from the air to snuff it completely. While the thought should have unsettled Zahir, it made him feel less like a failure. If there were mages from other clans, it meant not everyone thought his father was a bad ruler or wanted him dethroned. It meant that there were problems in other clans, too. Not every clan was perfect; he'd heard about Yu'güe and witnessed Lovíth for himself. But Orcian ran their clan very similarly to Brahn with their monarch and advisory council, and clearly, not everyone was thrilled in Orcian.

On their seventh night of hunting, Zahir hoped to find Illan. Zahir stepped into the open field and waited for a beat. Then two. On the tenth, he motioned for his party to follow. Mari snuck up to Zahir's right while Markus took Zahir's left, one hand on his sword. Zahir outstretched his hands before him, ready to ignite. Pryn kept their bow drawn as the group trudged through the field. Reina gripped a dagger in each hand, the metal glinting every so often in the moonlight. The group had decided not to wear armor as it reflected too much, but at least their thick leather vests offered some protection.

The field couldn't have been more than a quarter mile long, but it took them longer than normal to cross without a single sound. When they made it to the other side of the clearing, they all tried to keep their breathing as quiet as possible.

Zahir pointed to each person, silently asking if they were okay. After a nod from each, they continued their trek through the forest, bouncing from tree to tree. When Markus tapped his nose, Zahir knew they were getting closer to a camp. The group had come up with several signs to communicate while silent. Tapping a nose meant they smelled a camp nearby. Motioning to an ear meant they heard something. A hand up, palm out meant a break was needed, and most importantly, a point to someone was a question to check they were okay.

Since Markus was the one who smelled the fire, he took over leading the group; Zahir fell behind to assume Markus's post. Within minutes, they came upon a large camp. The remnants of fire were being snuffed and covered with dirt; smoke billowed into the air, forced by the strong winds, and rustled the leaves on the trees. Two people stood guarding rows of tents that were closed for the night. Zahir counted fifteen in total. At their size, they probably slept four each. They were severely outnumbered. But, if Illan was going to be anywhere, it would be here.

Markus motioned for Zahir to make a move. From behind the tree, Zahir drew two balls of flame and launched them at the guards. Screams filled the night air as they landed. At that moment, the group rushed forward, brandishing their weapons. Markus held his sword in both hands; Pryn dropped their bow in favor of a sword, and Reina tightened her grip on her daggers. Mari had her sword at her hip but instead chose to call on the soul of an elk to aid her. It galloped beside her, hulking and towering above everyone. She yelled for it to destroy, and it immediately began running through the tents. But, even as the group got closer, no one emerged. Mari's elk ran through them like there was no one inside.

And that was when Zahir realized their mistake.

"Fuck," Zahir bellowed. "Fuck! They knew we were coming."

As the scent of burning flesh filled Zahir's nose, the realization struck Zahir hard in the chest—no one was at the camp. They knew they were coming. And instead of challenging them, Morana and her troops had vanished.

"We made a mistake," Mari gasped.

"We will try again," Reina said, sheathing her daggers. "We *will* find Illan, Zahir. I know it."

"Let's go home," Pryn said, touching Zahir's shoulder.

"What if this is a trap?"

"It's not a trap, Zahir."

Zahir shook them off before they could calm him down, as they had done many times before. He wanted to feel his anger. Zahir kicked a rock as hard as possible to relieve some of his frustration. Lately, anger was the only emotion he was capable of feeling. It reminded him of exactly how he felt after his father died, when he discovered he was a dual mage, and that his birth mother lived across the world. The past year of his life had been painful, but amid all the pain, slivers of happiness surfaced, too. He looked at Reina, who cast him a sympathetic glance. He turned to Pryn and Markus, who shifted their gaze between each other and Zahir.

Zahir sat on the ground, legs crossed, and peered at the dark night sky. He counted the stars slowly, trying to calm his racing heart. He glanced at each of his friends in turn. Much to their credit, they tried to not look concerned, but Zahir noticed the telltale signs of their anxiety. Mari picked at her fingernails while Pryn tapped their foot, and Markus chewed on his lower lip. Reina lazily flipped a dagger over in her hand, but Zahir knew that was how she feigned calmness to disguise her worry.

Markus extended a hand to Zahir, and he took it willingly, allowing Markus to pull him to his feet. Then, they all began their trek back to Brahn. Everyone brandished their weapons again as they crossed the open field in case Morana and her rebels waited in the trees to ambush them. Zahir wouldn't put it past her; it would have been a brilliant tactical move—to set up an empty campsite just to ambush them on the way back to Brahn.

Once the group crossed the field and rested behind the tree line, Zahir glanced at his friends. Even in the moonlight, Zahir knew they were exhausted. Mari leaned her head against the tree trunk, closing her eyes while her chest heaved; Markus held Pryn in his arms as they rested together; Reina sat on the ground, drawing her knees to her chest and resting her head on her kneecaps. Zahir's exhaustion was beginning to weigh on him. He hadn't had a good night's rest in days. After tonight, they would rest and take a few days off before trying to find Morana again.

After several minutes of rest, Zahir led the group back through the forest, where no sound except their quiet footfall and the occasional woodland creature permeated the night. The breeze in the air, which Zahir usually found calming, sent a chill down his spine. It reminded him of the worst storms he used to hide from as a child, where the sky would darken and the air would still. A loud clap of thunder and a bright flash of lighting was only minutes away. A stone sunk into his stomach as he remembered all the nights he hid under his bed while the storm raged outside.

Zahir would no longer hide. He was tired of fearing his demons. He didn't have his father's disappointment to face, and the thunderstorms were easier with Mari around to talk him through it. His fear of failing lessened the more he believed in his choices, and most of all, he didn't fear Morana. He *hated* her—and all that hate turned to rage.

Zahir was ready to burn the world to defeat her.

As the group approached the edge of Brahn's city limits, that stillness turned to immovable stone. No one walked the streets; no noises sounded from the houses. Darkness flooded the cobbled paths, where light from the homes would illuminate the ground. The usually chilly wind was nowhere to be found.

"Something is wrong," said Zahir to no one in particular.

Reina nodded. "It's too quiet."

"It is quite late," said Mari. "People might just be sleeping?"

Zahir shook his head. "I've wandered these streets enough in the dead of night. Something is wrong."

As the group drew closer to the city center, that's when Zahir saw her. Morana stood at the top of the palace steps, bodies littering the ground around her.

Her men ran amuck in the streets. Flame burned in the air, and the familiar stench of charred flesh burned his nostrils as Zahir's people defended their homes. Zahir gasped as he watched the people of Brahn fighting the intruders. It broke his heart.

Zahir didn't waste a second before lighting his body in flames and racing up the palace steps, ignoring Mari and Markus, who yelled at him to stop. Zahir couldn't. His family was inside the palace, and he would rather die than let anyone hurt them.

The men who came into Zahir's path had only seconds to react before Zahir burned them where they stood, blackening their flesh to char. He didn't hear them scream as he brushed past. When titanium blades and chains swung at him, Zahir dodged them with a speed he didn't know he possessed as he knocked his assailants aside, their blades clattering onto the steps.

Taryn and Anya stood at the top of the stairs, the palace entryway protected by a wall of flames. They launched waves of fire towards Morana, who moved with the agility of a cat, dodging every flame; the ones that hit her turned parts of her clothes to embers, missing her skin entirely. It was mesmerizing to watch Taryn and Anya fight. When they realized that Morana was impossibly immune to their magic, they ran at her, trying to ignite her skin by touching her body.

Morana laughed as she fended them off. "You are weak, just like your king."

Zahir knocked several men off the sides of the stairs as Taryn jumped and wrapped her legs around Morana's torso, placing her burning hands on either side of Morana's face. Morana just laughed, a harsh, shrill sound that pierced Zahir's ears as she threw Taryn off her. Taryn's head hit the ground with a crack, and she didn't get up.

Anya screamed for Taryn as she raced to Morana, while Zahir ran up the stairs to his sister as fast as he could. Men flooded him, slowing his pace to stop him from reaching Anya, who kicked, punched, and scratched at Morana. Amazingly, Anya maneuvered around Morana's death magic several times. Just as Zahir was a few steps from the top, Morana grabbed Anya by the throat and pinned her against the wall. Much to Anya's credit, she didn't stop fighting, not until the breath was knocked from her, and she passed out. From the corner of his eye, Reina tossed a dagger end towards Morana, which lodged deep into her right shoulder; she dropped Anya's limp body to the ground.

Morana whirled with a feral grin slowly spreading across her face as she laid eyes on Zahir. Raising her hands toward him, Morana started to close her fists until a dagger lodged into her forearm, wavering her focus.

Reina rushed up the steps, and Zahir followed behind her, unsheathing his sword to face Morana. Zahir swung hard and fast, trying to land a blow; he hit her thigh, slicing through her clothing and pale flesh. Morana reached for Zahir and slashed his right cheek from eye to lip with her talon-like nails. His vision went blurry as his eyes watered from the pain. He raised a hand to his cheek, his fingers wet with blood.

Wiping his hand on his pants, Zahir picked up his sword and returned to an attack position, swinging at Morana as he and

Reina landed blow after blow. She started to slow; her hands didn't raise as quickly, and her movements were delayed. As Morana healed one wound, Reina and Zahir would land another, but when she stepped to the side and raised a hand, staring over Zahir's shoulder, he spared a glance. Mari darted up the stairs, blood streaming down the side of her face.

"Zahir, duck!" Ren called.

Zahir crouched as a titanium knife flew towards Morana, twirling in the air. It sunk deep in her right shoulder, and she let out a high-pitched screech, dropping the hand raised towards Mari. Zahir had enough time to stand and ignite his sword in flames, slamming it into Morana's side. Her clothes lit up in bright red fire, but water doused her just as quickly. Zahir turned to see one of Morana's men conjuring water to protect her.

"There's too many of them. We can't win. Get Roan out of here; you're his only hope," Zahir said to Ren.

"Zahir, the palace—"

"Let the palace fall. Get my brother. Bring him to the docks. We need to get out of here."

As Ren ran back into the building, Zahir took a breath and turned to Mari. "We can't win."

Shocked that his home was about to be destroyed, Zahir allowed Mari to lead him down the stairs, away from Morana. Somewhere along the way, Zahir had dropped his sword.

Halfway down, Mari lifted her hands and, with blood-smeared cheeks, stole the souls of fifteen people at once. They flew towards her, and she screamed as they hit her body.

Zahir tried to grab her, but his arms wouldn't move. He didn't even know how his feet were moving.

Right when Mari and Zahir got to the bottom of the steps, everything hit Zahir at once. He whipped his head towards the palace doors—Morana was no longer there. The palace doors were wide open; people screamed inside.

"Roan," Zahir said, turning from Mari to race up the stairs.

"Ren will get him out," said Markus.

"I told them to bring him to the docks if they can. We will wait for him."

Zahir and his friends ran towards the docks and commandeered a small schooner. When fifteen minutes had passed, and there was no sign of Roan and Ren, Zahir began to worry.

"We have to go, Zahir," said Pryn.

"I can't leave without Roan."

"Ren will take care of Roan. They are his best hope," Markus said.

"Hanan is in there, too, Zahir. Do you think I want to leave him? It is breaking my heart," Mari's voice cracked, "I can't save him, but we need to save ourselves. We can't help them if we're in danger."

"You're wrong. I am going back," said Zahir, stepping off the ship.

Pryn appeared in front of Zahir and pushed on his chest. "Zahir, let's go. We need a plan. We can't go in there blind."

"Pryn, move out of the way. I don't want to hurt you," he growled.

Pryn shook their head. "I can't let you do this."

"It is my decision to make."

"You can't stop her! We need a plan. If you go in there, you are going to die. Let's regroup and come up with a plan."

"I am not leaving Roan!" Zahir roared.

"He is smart. He will be fine."

"I have to go!"

As Zahir went to push past Pryn, they grabbed tightly onto his arms. "Zahir, for once in your fucking life, will you *listen* to me? If you go back there, you will *die*. And Roan will have no one. Let's get ourselves together so we can actually have a chance at saving your brother."

"Pryn, get the fuck out of my way."

"I'm sorry, Zahir," Pryn said. They slammed their hand into Zahir's neck, right next to his trachea.

Zahir's anger faded as he fainted.

CHAPTER THIRTY-TWO

REN

"Get Roan out of here; you're his only hope," Zahir told Ren.

"Zahir, the palace—"

"Let the palace fall. Get my brother out of here."

Ren ran into the palace, leaving Zahir, Reina, and Mari to ward off Morana. Ren didn't need a few minutes to get Roan out of there. If Zahir could hold Morana off long enough, they could get Roan to safety.

Blood covered the palace walls as Ren rushed through the halls, forcing themselves not to look at the bodies of their guards littering the ground. Some of their closest friends lie there, life drained from their eyes. If it were up to Ren, they would have stopped and closed the eyes of each soldier out of respect. But it was impossible. They didn't have much time.

A man approached Ren quickly, their sword raised. Ren parried the blow and struck out toward him, their swords reverberating as they collided. Their opponent stepped forward as Ren attacked. Their initial instinct was to step back, but years of training had taught them otherwise. Stepping toward their attacker, they tried again to stab him through the heart, and when he parried Ren's blow, yet again, Ren didn't waste a second before kicking at the man's kneecaps. The resounding crack echoing throughout the hallway sent a rush through Ren as the man tumbled to the ground. Looking into the man's eyes, Ren plunged the sword through his throat and out the back of his neck.

They kicked the man's body aside and took off running, praying to the Gods that Roan was in his chambers, for if he wasn't, Ren wouldn't know where to begin looking. As Ren ran and fended off opponents, they had to stop counting the rising death toll as bodies bled onto the once pristine floors of the palace. Ren's only job was to protect the royal family and the palace, yet the palace had been broken into twice and had now fallen to the enemy. If they lived through this, and Morana was defeated, they would resign. Ren should have done more.

Ren had to live through this day—they had to. They needed to know their wife was safe. They had said goodbye this morning, and she'd said the same thing: "Be safe, love." While Ren put their life on the line every day to protect Zahir and his family, they always tried to be safe and make smart decisions, only taking calculated risks. But in an emergency... they threw caution to the wind. They had to put their safety to the side if it meant protecting the royal family. Ren regretted not telling their wife to wait before trying for a baby, but now, she was six weeks pregnant, and Ren didn't know if they would see the next sunrise. Ren *needed* to see the birth of their child.

Roan's door was locked when Ren approached. Roan had to be inside. Ren yelled for Roan to open the door, pounding their fists on it. But when there was no answer, Ren took care of it themselves. They stepped back and mustered up the last bits of strength before kicking the door below the lock. The door creaked but didn't open. With several short breaths, Ren tried again. And again. And again.

On the fifth try, the door burst open, and Ren rushed in. "Roan, it's Ren. Where are you?"

The door to the armoire slowly opened, and Roan tumbled out of the closet and onto the floor. His glasses were askew, his cheeks tear-stained.

"What's happening?" Roan asked, his bottom lip quivering.

"I need to get you out of here. Come on," Ren scooped Roan up and deposited him on their back. "Hold on tight."

Roan locked his wrists around Ren's neck, and his ankles around their hips before Ren took off running. They brandished their sword in their left hand and tried to hold Roan up with their right.

"There he is!" yelled a voice down the hall.

Ren cursed as two men ran after them, their arms ignited in flames. Pushing their legs faster, Ren ran quicker than they had before. The men were faster. Before Ren knew it, Roan was ripped off their back and pushed against the wall.

"Ren!" Roan screamed.

"Close your eyes," Ren commanded.

Ren rushed forward. Within seconds, the man who held Roan to the wall had lost both his hands and screamed at the top of his lungs. Ren slid the sword across his throat and pushed him off Roan. The other man was a little too fast for Ren and put his hands on their shoulders, igniting them aflame.

Ren screamed as the flames licked their skin, but they managed to shove their assailant and stab him through the heart. As he fell to the ground, Roan swatted at their shoulders to quell the flames, and while his swatting did nothing, somehow, the flames stopped charring Ren's skin. Roan held his hands up towards Ren, flames licking his fingertips.

"Thank you, Roan. Come on." Ren grabbed Roan and dragged him down the halls.

It pained Ren to drag Roan beside them, but they couldn't carry him. Ren glanced at their charred shoulders, blackened from the flames. It took everything in them not to throw up.

Every exit was blocked. Ren couldn't walk Roan out the front door of the palace. All the back doors were flooded with assailants; Roan wouldn't be able to jump safely from the window. But... there was one place Roan could fit through.

Pulling Roan down the passageway, Ren swung the door open to the safe room tunnel and shoved Roan inside, closing it behind them. Ren didn't have time to make sure no one saw them. They needed to get Roan out of here.

"Where are we going?" asked Roan, his voice cracking.

"Out of the palace. There is a secret passage down here. Zahir uses it to sneak in at night."

"Oh, right. I didn't know it was down *this* hallway," Roan said.

"I don't have enough time to ask how you know about this, but once this is all over, you owe me an explanation."

Ren pushed Roan through the catacombs of the palace as fast as his little legs would take him. Panting, Roan asked for a break, but they couldn't afford that luxury. Ren cursed.

The tunnel was blocked. Piles of rubble blocked the hall. Ren glanced around it, searching for a gap where Roan could slip through. A small crawl space was along the left wall, but Ren would never fit through it. What if the tunnel was collapsed at the entrance? Roan would be trapped. But at least he would be safe from the attacks. He could wait it out. But... what if it collapsed on top of him? If matters couldn't get any worse, footsteps raced down the hall. Someone had seen them.

"Roan, you have to go," Ren said, gesturing to the crawl space. Roan had to get out.

"I can't leave you behind," said Roan.

"I'll be right behind you."

"Promise?"

"I promise."

This would be the first time Ren had ever broken a promise.

With some difficulty, Roan crawled through the hole. Just as he was through, Ren whirled to face the spirit of a buck and two men. If Ren was going to die, they would go down swinging.

Ren swung at their opponents, sweat beading along their neck as their shoulders screamed in pain. They connected with one of the men's shoulders, who dropped his sword. The buck raced forward and slammed into Ren, throwing them into a pile of rubble. Its horns pinned Ren to the debris, and no matter how much Ren squirmed, the buck wouldn't release them.

Ren's titanium sword passed right through the buck, and suddenly, it was gone. Ren fell to a knee and peered up at their attackers. Raising their sword, they tried to stand, but one of the men slammed their hilt into Ren's charred shoulder, who screamed, trying to catch themself as they fell to the ground.

On their side, Ren could see through the hole in the rubble and breathed a sigh of relief as Roan momentarily glanced back before pushing out of the door and letting it close behind him.

As if their wife could hear them, Ren said, "We will meet again," before a sword plunged through their chest.

Chapter Thirty-Three

Mari

The boat ride to Yu'güe was worse than Mari remembered. On the way to Brahn last year, she had fallen ill several times on the trip, but now, back on the boat, Mari wanted to die. The nausea hadn't stopped in the days they had been travelling. She couldn't believe she still had anything left in her gut, but somehow, her body continually felt ill. Much to his credit, Zahir had not left her side, holding her hair back, wiping her face with a cool cloth, and cuddling her while she rested.

After Pryn had knocked Zahir out, they dragged him below deck while Markus sailed the ship away from Brahn. Zahir had been *fuming* when he awoke, panicking about Roan. Zahir had raged for hours and tried to punch Pryn square in the face. If not for Markus, Pryn would have sported a broken nose, but instead, Markus took the blow, dislocating his jaw. The crack that filled the air as Pryn re-set it was horrifying.

Mari had tried to calm and reassure him, though she was just as worried about Hanan too. Hanan was trapped with the other hospital patients, defenseless, while he recovered from his injuries. He wouldn't be able to fight if Morana came to kill him. Mari's stomach turned to stone at the thought. She couldn't believe she'd left him there. But as much as it pained her, she knew Hanan's best chance at survival was for the group to leave and return with a plan.

The two people Mari wanted to protect were at their most vulnerable. But if they had gone into the palace, Morana would have slaughtered them all, which ultimately helped *no one*. Sometimes, you had to save yourself before saving someone else.

Pryn and Markus were right—they would have died, and then no one would be there to save Roan, Hanan, or the others. Mari hoped Roan was using his intelligence to his advantage, hiding in the smallest nooks, cloaked in the shadows as he moved around the palace for food and water.

As the days went on and Zahir calmed down a little, Mari could tell he felt guilty for his inability to save his people. On the run to the docks, they had passed the bodies of so many citizens. Blood ran through the streets like a river. Zahir's feelings were more than grief—a feeling Mari knew all too well. She wished to tell him it wasn't his fault; he was doing what he thought was best and did the right thing, but she knew he wasn't ready to hear it. Instead, she hugged him while he cried and calmed him while he raged.

Mari replayed the battle over and over in her mind, trying to see if there had been a way they could have won. Yet no matter how many times Mari killed even *more* rebels, they lost. Despite killing more people, the vibrating in Mari's skull stayed the same. Perhaps she was getting used to it. The noise no longer kept her up at night or distracted her from doing tasks. While it made for a nice change, Mari didn't want to get used to it—she wanted it gone.

Six days later, Mari, Zahir, Pryn, and Markus finally made landfall in Yu'güe. Mari taught Zahir, Pryn, and Markus how to bundle up for Yu'güe's freezing temperatures, putting their hat on first before wrapping a scarf so it covered their nose and mouth without slipping. Then, she helped them shove their hands into gloves that were way too small before showing them how to zip the coat when their fingers weren't as usable. She tightened the strings of their hoods once it covered their foreheads.

"I am starting to sweat," Zahir said, laughing. "Do we really need all this?"

Mari led her friends to the ship's deck and was immediately hit with a blast of icy wind. She glanced back at Zahir, whose eyes were wide as he surveyed the landscape. Yu'güe's shores were covered in ice and snow, which would be several feet deep at this time in the season. The Yanhua mountains were packed with snow from top to bottom, surrounding them. Back on the water, icebergs peeked out from the surface of the water all the way to the horizon.

"It's magnificent," whispered Zahir, his eyes searching the mountains.

Mari inhaled the scent of snow. "I missed this."

She led everyone down onto the shore, instructing them to tread carefully. But when she stepped onto the snow, she realized it was fresh as the ground was pliant, crunching softly under her feet. Crouching, she picked a handful of snow and formed it into a ball. As she made the snowball, she packed into it all her pain and anger before launching it at a tree, where it exploded into a cloud of powder that floated to the ground.

Mari led everyone away from the water and closer to her village. The one thing they hadn't planned for was what they would do once they made landfall. Leaving Brahn hadn't been a choice; they would either have to stay in Brahn with no support or resources, risk capture trying to rescue their family or retreat until they found a solution. And if they had been captured, there would be no one to save them. The ship to Yu'güe was the only one that hadn't been destroyed in the battle.

Returning to her parent's house was Mari's last choice. She couldn't face her father. If she was going to see him, she would need a well-thought-out plan as part of her wanted to *kill* him for what he'd done to her and Hanan, robbing them of a childhood of love and laughter, stealing years of their relationship by hurting Hanan and convincing Mari he was dead. *Nothing* her father could say or do that would make up for that heinous transgression.

Mari halted as she realized that no one was beside her; she whirled around and saw everyone standing still, their mouths agape and eyes wildly scanning the area between them. Zahir blinked twice and shook his head.

"Zahir?" she asked.

"What is this?" Markus's words came out slowly.

Mari strode over to Zahir and tried to tug him forward, but his feet were weighted to the ground. She glanced around and saw nothing except the snowy landscape that had stayed the same throughout their walk.

"The souls... They're guards," Zahir whispered.

"Who are they?" Pryn asked.

Mari stood beside Pryn; she tried to see what they were seeing but to no avail. She knew people could hallucinate from extreme heat, but could it happen from the cold? Mari had never heard of it, but that didn't mean it was impossible. Closing her eyes, Mari took some deep breaths. When she opened them, her jaw dropped.

Standing before them was an army of the dead. Thousands of souls stood shoulder to shoulder in lines formed across the flat ground and up to the mountain peaks—a wall. It was then that Mari saw the two soldiers she had killed waiting there, too, the ones who had haunted her every time she closed her eyes. Their legs were straight, their knees touching, and their hands clutched behind their backs.

"I had always heard of the guards, but I never imagined this," Mari whispered.

A story had passed through the generations about the souls of those killed at the hands of death mages and subsequently released; they were said to guard the entrance to Yu'güe, allowing in only death mages and their companions. Yet Mari had never seen them before. She wondered if they only appeared when trying to bring outsiders in.

The souls stolen by death mages remained a part of the mage until released. She knew now what happened to the two souls who had disappeared after she confessed her guilt to Hanan. They were released from her service to go and protect her homeland. As the stolen souls became part of the death mage, they would still serve them after release, returning to Yu'güe to protect its people.

"King Zahir of Brahn and life mages Markus and Pryn are my companions and will be allowed entry into Yu'güe with me," Mari said to the souls. She wasn't sure if a specific statement was required, but she hoped it was enough.

The souls stepped aside, half right and half left, forming a path for Mari and her friends to pass through. Mari tugged a wide-eyed Zahir forward through the gap, then returned for Pryn and Markus, grabbing their hands in each of her own and dragging them through the barrier. Glancing over her shoulder, Mari watched as the lines of souls closed in time as they passed. A sudden calm washed over her in the presence of the dead. She was at ease, relaxed for the first time in many moons.

Once they were through the wall, Zahir visibly returned to himself, coming out of his trance. With a violent shake of his head, he looked towards the wall that had suddenly disappeared.

"What was that?" he asked. "When did I get here?"

"The souls that guard Yu'güe needed consent for you to enter. They protect us," Mari said, smiling.

"That is incredible," Markus said. "Can Morana get in here?"

Mari shook her head. "The only people who can enter the barrier are those who have lived in Yu'güe since the clans split. The barrier was put up after Morana's 'death.' It didn't exist before that."

They walked for a few minutes; Mari pointed to the outskirts of the village and called out certain buildings as they approached. She spoke of the different council members, all of whom lived right beside each other. Mari saved her family's home for last. It was the same small house she remembered; nothing on the outside had changed, but that feeling in her heart had. Where before she viewed her home as restful after a long trek in the woods, she now only saw it as dangerous and untrusting.

As they entered the village, people began to slowly approach. Mari introduced Zahir to Laura, who made clothing for most children. She appeared older than Mari remembered, her age taking a toll on her body. Elder Myron came up and greeted Mari.

"Myron always tells the best stories," Mari told Zahir before facing Myron again. "This is my husband, Zahir, and our friends, Pryn and Markus."

"The Fire King," Myron said, nodding approvingly. "I thought you'd be taller."

Zahir glanced down at Myron. "I get that a lot."

"Do you?" Myron asked. "Are the people in Brahn short?"

"Okay, Myron. We must be going," Mari said quickly. "Please do not tell my parents we are here. I want to surprise them."

"Of course. I'll share the news but will warn others not to say anything. It's nice to see you again, Mari."

Mari pulled Zahir behind her and motioned for Pryn and Markus to follow as she went further into the town. She hadn't thought about running into everyone she knew here or that everyone knew her family, but it was a silly oversight. No one could keep a damn thing to themselves. Asking people to keep quiet would do little to keep the gossip at bay. Mari was back in Yu'güe after a year, accompanied by two friends and a handsome husband—the King of Fire, no less. The rumors would be extravagant. She was sure people would rumor she was pregnant, too, as an explanation for her return.

"Did you expect me to be taller?" Zahir asked Mari with a laugh.

Mari rolled her eyes. "I did. I thought you were going to be a hulking eight feet tall."

Zahir scoffed and nudged Mari's shoulder. She stopped and peered around her village. The houses looked the same as she remembered, and the smell of fresh snow calmed the knot in her stomach. Giggles of playing children floated around her while the cold bit at her exposed skin. It was invigorating, and only now did she realize how much she'd missed Yu'güe.

"Are you worried about being back here?" asked Zahir.

"I missed it more than anything, I think," Mari said, turning her gaze to Zahir, the man people thought her father was crazy for marrying her to—the man she had fallen hopelessly in love with. "But I am happy to be back. I get to show off my husband to the people in my homeland, the people who have known me my whole life, but don't know me a fraction as well as you do."

Zahir touched Mari's arm. "I'm happy to be here with you. I just wish it was under better circumstances."

Leaning into Zahir, Mari watched Pryn and Markus glance around the town, switching their gaze between the snow, the small homes, and the tall mountains. Mari realized she must have looked the same when she first visited Brahn. She couldn't stop staring at everything, gaping at the architecture and blue, sunny skies.

"Is it always this snowy?" Markus asked.

Mari laughed. "Yes, it is. It is always snowy, but we have slower seasons. Sometimes, by this point, we would only have a two-foot base by the shore."

"I have never seen snow before. It is beautiful," Pryn said.

"It doesn't snow in Lovíth?" Mari asked. She knew Brahn was warm but knew nothing about Lovíth's climate.

Pryn shook their head. "No. It gets cold to the point where there can be frost on the grass first thing in the morning, but it doesn't snow."

"That is so sad," Mari said. "It's my favorite part of Yu'güe."

"So, what is the plan?" Markus asked. "Where are we going?"

Mari thought about it for a minute. She couldn't go to her father's house. Returning to her father's house was another reminder that she had left her brother to fend for himself *again*.

So, Mari stopped before a familiar house she had entered throughout her youth. She took three slow breaths before walking to the door and knocking thrice. Never in her life had she expected to return to Yu'güe on the doorstep of her first love, begging him for help.

The door flung open to reveal a young man with bright blue eyes and short brown hair. With eyes wide, he said, "Mari? What are you doing here?"

"Fahran... we need your help."

Epilogue

The broken throne sat at the apex of the steps of Brahn's palace. Morana sat, her legs crossed, peering out at the thousands of people surrounded by her men at the bottom. The remaining royal family members sat to her left, chained to the palace wall. It had been easy to get the former queen and princess—Morana had forced them both unconscious. Illan had chained the princess's twin flame while she was out cold. The death mage and the mortal hid in the kitchens when Morana found them. It hadn't taken long to beat them down.

There was only one person left that Morana couldn't find—the little prince. He must have snuck out of the palace during the commotion. But if Illan was right, he couldn't have gotten far. He *was* a child, after all.

Morana stood from her throne and let her cloak billow in the fierce wind behind her as she addressed Brahn. "Your king is dead," she sneered. "I am your queen. You kneel to me."

Not a soul moved. Morana stared upon the silent crowd and raised her hands, snatching soul after soul until twenty bodies fell to the ground in heaps. Screams filled her ears, and a feral grin spread across her lips.

"I said *kneel*."

Acknowledgements

To say I wrote one book is incredible. But now, to say I wrote TWO? Unbelievable.

First, I must thank my incredible editor, Eden Northover. You agreed to take me on as a client when I was in a tight spot and I am so incredibly grateful. Thank you for pushing me through my doubts with your positivity, your love for my characters, and your brilliant ideas. I cannot express how appreciative I am of all the work you put into bringing out the best of *Life After Death*. It wouldn't be what it is today without you. Working with you was amazing and I can't thank you enough for all you did. You brought this story to its full potential and I could not be more grateful.

Thank you to Stef from Seventh Star Art for designing my stunning cover! You are absolutely incredible and deliver in a way that always shocks me. I can't wait to work with you again.

Thank you Jax and Amelia, who gave incredible feedback. I love you both so so much. Jax, our conversations where we talk writing and plot and twists helped me become the writer I am today. And I love how much you adore Markus. Amelia, your love for this story is unmatched. I appreciate how much thought you put into your feedback. And thank you for helping me with some of the psychology and trauma responses in this story.

To my husband, Dan, you have been so amazing. I can't believe you didn't think I was insane when I told you this was due to Eden the week of our wedding. Thank you for giving me so many ideas. For giving me input on everything. For encouraging me. For telling me this story wasn't crap, despite what my brain told me. For letting me read this out loud to you and offering up the title. Just thank you. I love you and couldn't have done this without you.

Thank you to all my friends and family who helped support and cheer me on as I did this! I could not have done it without your support. I love you all endlessly and you have no idea how much your support means to me.

Thank you Mom and Dad for inspiring me always to tell my truth and share my stories. You helped me become the person I am today. I would not be who I am without you.

Thank you to all the bookstagrammers and booktokers who have read, reviewed, and shared Death by Fire and now Life After Death! Your kind words fill me with such joy. I appreciate it more than you know

To you, dear reader, for picking up an indie author's book. I really hope you enjoyed the second installment of this story and are ready for the next, and final, book in The Dual Mage series.

About the Author

S. C. Muir is a queer scientist and writer from New York. She has a B.S. in Chemistry from Binghamton University and is pursuing her M.S. in Chemistry. When she can tear herself from a book, S. C. enjoys hiking, rock climbing, and watching TV shows like Schitt's Creek and Our Flag Means Death. Her current project is trying to convince her husband that they should get a cat. Currently, he is not in agreement.

You can find her on Instagram & TikTok as @scmuir.author. If you want to sign up for her newsletter to get access to deleted scenes and a first look at her upcoming books, you can sign up at https://scmuirauthor.com/subscribe